CAPWAR ECHELON

BRANDT LEGG

As always, this book is dedicated to Teakki and Ro

And to Blair Legg 1957-2017

Vinci Books

vinci-books.com

Published by Vinci Books Ltd in 2026

1

Copyright © Brandt Legg 2018

The author has asserted their moral right to be identified as the author of this work in accordance with the Copyright, Designs and Patents Act 1988. This work is a work of fiction. Names, characters, places and incidents are the product of the author's imagination or are used fictitiously. Any resemblance to actual persons, living or dead, places and incidents is entirely coincidental.
All rights reserved. No part of this publication may be copied, reproduced, distributed, stored in any retrieval system, or transmitted in any form or by any means, including photocopying, recording, or other electronic or mechanical methods, nor used as a source for any form of machine learning including AI datasets, without the prior written permission of the publisher.
The publisher and the author have made every effort to obtain permissions for any third party material used in this book and to comply with copyright law. Any queries in this respect should be brought to the attention of the publisher and any omissions will be corrected in future editions.
A CIP catalogue record for this book is available from the British Library.
Paperback ISBN: 9781036700461

The EU GPSR authorised representative is Logos Europe, 9 rue Nicolas Poussion, 17000 La Rochelle, France
contact@logoseurope.eu

By Brandt Legg

The Capstone Conspiracy Series

CapWar ECHELON
CapWar EXPERIENCE
CapWar EMPIRE

Chase Malone Thriller

Chasing Rain
Chasing Fire
Chasing Wind
Chasing Dirt
Chasing Life
Chasing Kill
Chasing Risk
Chasing Mind
Chasing Time
Chasing Lies
Chasing Fear
Chasing Lost

Chapter One

Hudson Pound sat nervously in his truck outside the local branch of Titan Capital & Trust Bank. If he didn't get the loan, the small chain of hardware stores he'd worked so hard to build would have to be liquidated. He'd lose everything.

Pound Hardware and Plumbing had eight locations in six southeastern Ohio towns. It was holding on against the big-box home centers, but in recent years, Hudson had been so busy championing his many causes that, in the weariness of juggling priorities, he'd let the stores slip. Now a cash flow crisis had to be addressed. Surely his old friends at TC&T would see him through.

Hudson checked his tie. He rarely wore anything but jeans and a casual shirt, but today called for the suit. His reputation was excellent; a real community leader, civic duties and do-gooder. However, banks were only interested in numbers, and Pound Hardware's weren't solid enough to get the loan without putting up his house, and even then . . .

But that's where years of extensive charity work might

tip the scales. Hudson hadn't done that to help get a loan. It had been out of guilt, the deep burning kind that can ruin a life. He'd been running from the pain of it for almost three decades. *When will I escape it?* he wondered while looking into the mirror. *When?*

Today, like so many times before, he had to force his past out of his mind. Take care of business. Get the loan. Otherwise, he . . . well . . . he didn't know what. Maybe he'd find a teaching job, get a cheap rental on Eighth Street.

What about my employees? Will they all find new jobs? And my reputation . . .

No. The bank would work with him. He was prepared.

"Look sharp," he whispered to himself as he got out of the truck.

Hudson took three steps and tripped over the curb, his right knee hitting a protruding piece of rebar. The twisted metal gouged his leg as he rolled onto the sidewalk. "Damn it!" he hissed, chasing papers which escaping the folder that had fallen a few feet away. The pain in his leg burned, and he saw his charcoal-grey pants were torn and bloody.

He collected his papers and limped inside. The assistant branch manager, whom he'd known for years, greeted him warmly. The two were on several local boards together, including Rotary, Chamber, Hospital, Friends of the Library, and Little League.

"Geez, Hudson, what happened?" the assistant manager asked, noticing the ripped pants.

Blood was running down Hudson's leg. The top of his sock was wet and sticky. "You should see the other guy," Hudson joked, trying to cover with a laugh, as he winced.

"No, really, let's get that cleaned up."

Hudson followed the man into a breakroom where a large first aid kit was anchored to the wall. After washing the wound, Hudson taped on a big square of sterile gauze that the assistant manager had handed him and called it good. Nothing could be done about the pants.

As they started down a long, mahogany-paneled hallway, Hudson asked his buddy about the chances of getting the funds.

"The loan committee has gone over your application and financials. Everything looks good, but we've got some questions."

Hudson stopped walking and lightly put his hand on his friend's shoulder. "Is there a problem?"

"I really don't know, Hudson. This one is *very* strange." The assistant manager started walking again.

Hudson followed, wondering what "very strange" meant. *We're talking about nuts and bolts, pipe fittings and paint.* Hudson was about to press further, but his friend was suddenly called back to the front of the bank.

With a reassuring gesture, the assistant manager left him alone in a small reception area. A few long minutes later, a woman he'd never met—although he thought he knew everyone who worked at the bank—introduced herself. With a friendly but professional smile, and no mention of his tattered attire, she asked him to follow her. The plush carpeted hallway, lined with a local artist's oil paintings of sweeping landscapes, smelled like new money. The woman opened a polished wood door, stood aside and motioned him into a spacious conference room. As the door closed, he found himself alone with a man who sat comfortably at the end of a long, glossy black table. Hudson had not met him before either, but he certainly recognized him from the media.

"Am I in the wrong room?" Hudson asked, as Arlin Vonner, famous for being one of the richest men in the world, stood and walked toward him. Hudson self-consciously tried to block his bad leg with the good, leaving him in an awkward pose.

Arlin Vonner didn't look seventy-two. Other than thick silver hair, his smooth face and dirt-brown eyes gave him the appearance of a distinguished executive, perhaps in his late fifties. He held out his hand. "You're in the right place, Hudson Pound, owner of Pound Hardware and Plumbing, school board member, US Army veteran, age forty-six, single, widower, father of two, height six-two, weight . . . hmm, I'd say about one-eighty-five."

Hudson chuckled, which is what he always did when he felt strange or uncomfortable. *Why is Arlin Vonner reciting my resume? Why does he even care?* "I'm just here about a loan for my hardware stores." He cocked his head to one side. "What am I missing?"

"What happened to your leg?"

"Old football injury," he said, trying another joke.

"You've never played football," Vonner replied.

"How do you know so much about me?"

"Hudson, I've been an admirer of yours for quite some time."

"You have?" Hudson said, bewildered, having no idea why a man worth in excess of seventy billion dollars, famous for takeovers and venture capital, would even know his name, much less "admire" him. "Do you want to buy my stores?"

This time Vonner laughed. "Are they for sale?"

"Well, I—" Hudson stammered.

"Of course they are. Everything's for sale!" Vonner boomed. "It's just a matter of negotiating the price."

"Do you *really* want my stores?"

"No, no, nothing like that," Vonner said, still smiling broadly. "But I do have a proposition for you."

"All right," Hudson said hesitantly, still wondering if he was in the right room and trying to imagine what a man like Vonner would want from him. Absently, he turned around, looking for the gag, or at least John, James, Charlie, or any of the other bank employees he'd known and worked with for more than a decade. But Vonner and Hudson were alone in the room. "You certainly have my attention."

"Good." Vonner smiled the flawless smile of a billionaire—snow-white and Hollywood-perfect. His boyish face revealed too few laugh lines for someone in his seventies with a light tan. "Then I have a very serious question for you. It may sound humorous at first, but I assure you, I never joke about politics."

"Politics?" That made a little more sense. Hudson had been approached many times about running for Mayor. After his breakthrough work on the school board, success in his business and military service, he might seem an ideal candidate, but his ambitions didn't run that deep. "I really have no interest in seeking public office."

"Who said anything about *seeking*?" Vonner asked, still smiling. "I want to know if you'd like to be the next President of the United States?"

Chapter Two

Hudson stared at the billionaire as if he'd just told a joke that had the wrong punch line. "Excuse me?" he said, laughing nervously.

Vonner held the hardware store owner's gaze, wearing a friendly but serious expression, silently allowing the weight of his question to sink in.

Hudson filled the silence. "Me, running for the *presidency*? That's impossible."

"I assure you, Hudson, it's *very* possible," Vonner said evenly. "And more than just running . . . you'll win."

"Why me? Why do you want *me*? Why would *anyone* want me? I have no experience, I—"

"Don't be so modest, Hudson. I've put together a list—the criteria, if you will—for the perfect candidate."

"There must be hundreds, or thousands."

"Yes."

"How did I get to the top of the list?"

"Did I say you were?"

"What exactly are my qualifications?"

"You're a seasoned executive running a successful business, your leadership on the school board turned the district around and has been a model for the entire state—and even other states."

Hudson had received a lot of attention in Ohio after that success. He'd been appointed to chair the Governor's Blue-Ribbon Commission on Education Reform, and the Ohio Chamber of Commerce had made him Citizen of the Year.

"That's not enough to be president," Hudson said.

"Don't forget, you bravely served our country, and you're a native son of a key swing state."

"I've never held elective office."

"That's the best part."

"I don't see how."

"Come on, Hudson, you're smarter than that. I've seen your university transcripts."

"Because the electorate is desperate for an outsider?"

"I knew you'd catch on. The recent elections taught us many things, but the biggest was that the voters don't trust, don't like, and don't want career politicians."

"Even if I was interested, which I'm not, what makes you think America would want a nobody like me?"

"You're exactly what they want," Vonner replied. "They may not know it yet, but they will. I'll make damn sure they will."

"How? I don't understand."

"Hudson, I'm a powerful man. I have more money than most people can comprehend, but all of that only matters if I can *do* something with it. Something monumental."

"Then why don't *you* run?"

"No, you're missing the point. The country wants—and, more importantly, *needs*—a regular guy. One of *them*. That's where we've come to. First Catholic president, first black president, first woman president—well, almost, anyway. Now it's time for the first average joe American president."

"Okay, but I still don't get it," Hudson said, finally sitting down, his leg throbbing. "You've got thousands of possibilities, why me?"

"Do you think the country is on the right track?"

"Well, no, but—"

"Don't you think we need to get government spending under control? Isn't it time for *real* tax reform? Education? How about term limits for Congress? Aren't there a hundred things you'd like to change about the world?"

"Sure, but every voter on the planet has a wish list like that."

"But the difference is that *you* can do something about it. We need fresh ideas like you brought to the school board. Look how you've run your hardware stores, thriving against the onslaught of Home Depot and Lowe's. *They* send *you* customers! You distinguished yourself in the military. Single dad, community involvement like nobody's business—I mean when do you *sleep*? You're a fantastic speaker. I've seen videos of you in front of the school board, hospital fundraisers, and the veteran's memorial dedication. You're a natural. And, torn pants aside, your Robert Redford looks are no small thing," Vonner concluded, flashing his big smile.

They continued talking for another forty minutes. It became increasingly clear to Hudson that Vonner had more than a plan for his candidacy. He had a vision.

"We've got to return the Republican Party to its roots, the party of Lincoln. We need to get the country back on track, and really make it happen this time," Vonner proclaimed. He spoke of change and reform in a way that not only captured Hudson's imagination, but also mirrored his own beliefs. "There is so much to do!"

The hardware store owner watched, mesmerized, as Vonner ran through a presentation that included a campaign commercial, incredibly well-researched material, and obscure polling data. For a few moments, while listening to the billionaire pontificate, Hudson could actually imagine it all happening. Maybe it wasn't so crazy,

"President Pound" does this, signed that, vetoed a detrimental bill, ordered troops . . .

In the early days, Hudson's favorite part of the hardware business had been fixing things. All day long he'd solve problems—a missing screw, a broken bolt, a stuck lock, a broken window pane, a leaky faucet. He loved to help people, but what Vonner was offering went way beyond just helping a handful of individuals . . .

Just as he was having those fleeting thoughts, Vonner clicked for the next slide—a bright blue campaign sign that read: "Hudson Pound the Problem Solver."

Hudson couldn't help but smile. "That's the motto for our stores. We're the problem solvers."

"I know," Vonner said, grinning. "Makes a perfect campaign slogan for you, don't you think?"

Hudson nodded and wondered if Vonner knew *everything*. How could he not, with his fortune and resources? How could he make such a proposition, stake so much on Hudson, without having investigated every aspect of his life?

Still, there was something that only Hudson and two other people knew—and one of them was in prison, something Vonner could have no way of knowing.

Hudson suddenly felt self-conscious. He'd been silent too long. "How do you know I'm not a closet alcoholic, or that I'm not a deranged arsonist, or something worse?"

"Don't be silly," Vonner said. "You've been fully vetted. I know more about you than you do."

Hudson managed a weak laugh and looked back at the screen. The slide shifted to a photo of him that must have been taken at a school board meeting, but it had been Photoshopped so that Hudson appeared to be speaking to thousands of supporters with a "Pound for President" sign affixed to the podium and a large American Flag behind him. Hudson had to admit he looked presidential, in a Kennedy-esque kind of way. His good looks had helped him throughout his life, no denying that. Six-foot-two, blond hair worn in a shaggy version of JFK's style, slate-blue eyes, and a runner's build. Yeah, he was telegenic, photogenic, some might even say magnetic, and on top of that, public speaking and debating had always been passions of his. Maybe he *could* do this . . .

No, that's insane, he thought. *This doesn't make even a little sense.*

The screen switched to images of his grown children, Florence and Schueller.

"They don't exactly share my politics," Hudson said.

"Yes, I know," Vonner said, amused that Hudson thought this might be news to him. "But they love their dad. They'll be good, loyal kids . . . and they'll play well with the youth vote."

Hudson nodded, half proud, half confused, and the rest just made him dizzy.

The conversation ended fifteen minutes later when Vonner seemed to instinctively realize that Hudson had reached his limit. "Here's how to contact me," Vonner said, handing him a small, cell phone-looking device. "It will reach me directly. Securely."

Hudson, still dazed, stood and headed toward the door.

In the hall, he suddenly turned back, and through the doorway asked, "Hey, one last question. Did I get the loan?"

"Don't worry, kid. You'll get the loan."

"Even if I don't run?" Hudson asked.

Vonner raised an eyebrow. "Yeah, don't worry. Either way, we'll take care of you."

"Thank you," Hudson said, making eye contact before turning and limping away.

Once the door closed behind him, Vonner pushed a button on his phone, waited for the voice on the other end, then said, "He's in."

Chapter Three

The five individuals—two women and three men—seated at a large, round, mahogany table had arrived in secret. If their attendance were to be discovered, prison might be their best hope.

"Thank you for coming," their host, a man codenamed AKA Washington, began. "We all know the dangers of proceeding, but the time is now. After years of work, North-Bridge is ready." Each of them had adopted an alias inspired by the original American revolutionaries.

"We have eleven billion dollars, with more coming in every day," AKA Jefferson, one of the women, announced. "As you know, Franklin, has created digiGOLD, a cryptocurrency which will ensure our funding continues even if the US economy collapses."

"It's time for the final vote, AKA Hancock said. "Our point of no return."

"Then let's be clear," Jefferson said, looking at Adams, the other woman. "We're talking about more than protesting the government. This may well lead to civil war, revolution . . . overthrowing the United States government."

"Let us hope it doesn't get to that," Adams solemnly added.

"We have access to advanced weapons, and a backdoor into the NSA's surveillance apparatus, the CIA's computer systems, and the key to destroy the US military's networks," Washington said, as a monitor displayed their plans. "So when it does 'get to that,' we'll be prepared."

"But it can't be that easy," Jefferson said in a questioning tone, putting on her glasses for a closer look, as if not quite believing what she was seeing.

Washington shook his head. "Phase One will take at least two years. Hopefully we'll get our person into the White House." He looked at Adams. "By whatever means necessary."

"Even if we don't," Hancock said, pointing to a multi-colored bar graph on the screen. "There are millions of Americans who will side with us, if we manage the media right," he paused and made eye contact with Jefferson. "We're counting on you."

She nodded. "Thomas Paine once wrote, '*We have it in our power to begin the world over again.*'"

Washington surveyed their faces one last time, then announced, "It's time to vote."

"To quote my namesake, Benjamin Franklin, '*We must all hang together, or assuredly we shall all hang separately.*'"

The five leaders of NorthBridge then agreed, one-by-one, to commit treason, launch the most well-funded and technologically advanced revolution ever, and change the world.

Hudson, back in his pickup truck, sat trying to figure out what had just happened. For a second, he thought it might all be part of one of those elaborate reality TV show hoaxes. Cameras would record him making a fool of himself, actually believing that one of the richest men in the world, or *anyone* for that matter, would want him to be the leader of the free world. But then he remembered Trump. A reality TV star *had* become president. *Surely I can do a better job than Trump did. After all, I might have been born poor, but I've never bankrupted a business—not yet, anyway.* He still needed that loan.

After a few moments of attempting to dissect the unfathomable event, he dialed the number to the most grounded person he knew: his girlfriend, Melissa, an efficiency expert who worked from home when she wasn't visiting a client in some other Midwestern city. He pulled out of the bank parking lot and steered his truck toward Melissa's house, even while waiting for her to answer.

Melissa Atwater, a forty-year-old CPA with a law degree from Georgetown, wasn't just grounded and efficient. The attractive and athletic blonde was also the most driven woman he'd ever met. Unable to have kids, early in their relationship she'd managed to befriend both of Hudson's adult children—Schueller, his twenty-two-year-old drifting musician son, and Florence, his twenty-five-year-old daughter, an RN, who also ran a popular health blog. Hudson and Melissa had been dating seriously for two years, and enjoyed the kind of easy relationship he'd thought he'd never find again after losing his wife to cancer twelve years earlier.

"How'd it go at the bank?" Melissa asked, as she took his call.

"You won't believe it," Hudson replied.

"You did get it, didn't you?" she asked almost defensively, since she'd done most of the work on the loan package.

"Yes. No," he stammered. "I mean, I don't know. It turned out to not be about that." Hudson swerved to miss striking a mailman, realizing he'd not come to a complete stop at the last intersection. "I really shouldn't talk about this now, on the phone. I mean, while I'm driving." He chuckled at the absurdity of it all. "I'll be there in ten minutes."

Chapter Four

Melissa greeted him as he pulled into the driveway of her ivy-covered brick house, a home easily worth three times what his would bring. Two guys dressed in green shirts and khakis worked in the yard. The dogwood trees would soon bloom, along with a sweeping array of perennials. He told her the incredible story of meeting Vonner while they sipped coffee in the sunroom.

"President of the United States," she repeated several times. "No offence, but what kind of sense does that make?"

"None taken. And I have no idea."

"Vonner isn't crazy . . . or maybe he's crazy like a fox." She paused. "I actually met him once. He gave the commencement address when I graduated from law school. He's a Georgetown alumni, and, well, I can't really say I *met him* met him. It was a meet and greet at the post-grad ceremony reception, and I had maybe three minutes with him, but I've followed his career ever since. He's influential. They say it's nearly impossible to win the Republican nomination without his support."

"Good, then I'm a shoo-in," Hudson said sarcastically, musing at the same moment that she'd make a perfect president's wife. Then, instantly, he was shocked that his mind had so easily produced such a thought.

"This is the wildest thing I've ever heard," she said. "I mean how did you even get on his radar? Did you ask?" She looked at him, caught his smile, and raised her eyebrows.

"He's got people. Sometime after the last election he developed criteria, and his staff has been looking at computers, databases . . . I was a match."

She touched his hand. "The only match?"

"I guess. I don't know."

"What did you tell him?"

"That I needed to think about it."

"And are you?"

"One of the world's richest men, a known political kingmaker, has asked me to run for president, *and* pledged his support. How could I *not* think about it?"

Melissa laughed. "Hudson Pound, President of the United States."

"It's nuts."

"It sure is strange . . . " She hesitated, then got up and plucked dry leaves off a few plants. "But we're missing something. Don't get me wrong, I think you could be a good president, better than most of the jokers running, but this is so far out there. I think we might need to do some investigating."

"Then we'd better get busy. If I run, Vonner wants me to announce in three weeks, and he said I needed to do one thing first."

"What?"

"Get married."

A family meeting was arranged, but it would be several days before the schedules could be matched. Florence, who now lived in Charlottesville, Virginia, found someone to take her Thursday shift at the UVA Medical Center, because it was the first day that Schueller, who at least for the moment resided in Cleveland, didn't have a gig. Melissa postponed a client visit to Indianapolis. In the forty-eight hours while Hudson was waiting for his "top-advisers" to convene, he studied the other candidates who had already announced.

The crowded field didn't seem to leave much room for a Pound candidacy. Each party already had an impressive array of seasoned politicians; well-funded, experienced in campaigning, and knowledgeable on the issues. Both sides also had a couple of outsiders who'd announced, and although they appeared to be long shots, the novices seemed to have more going for them than Hudson did.

For the Democrats, there was "Newsman" Dan Neuman, a former news anchor who'd already stunned the establishment by winning the Oregon governorship two years earlier. Neuman had decent name recognition nationally from his news days, but little else.

A bigger threat, with pockets not as deep as Vonner, but deep enough, was Tim Zerkel, a tech billionaire who actually believed he could change the world by using money and technology to tackle all the biggest problems—hunger, poverty, war, etc.—as if they were startup businesses. Vonner had called him "a socialist in bad disguise."

The Republicans had their own pair of newcomers. Thorne, a "shock-jock" who claimed to be a "thorne" in the side of the status quo, had been getting tons of media attention in the post-Trump era. With twenty-seven million listeners to his popular show—that skewed young but otherwise crossed the demographic spectrum—some considered the dark horse a legitimate threat. Often claiming to dislike the GOP as much as he did Democrats, he had decided to run as a Republican because he thought elephants were "cooler" than donkeys. Announcing his intentions on his radio show, he elicited the first controversy when addressing LGBTQ rights: "Gay people don't bother me except when they tell me who they like to screw. Do I go 'round telling you I prefer doing Asian women? Shut up already!" His next stir came when he argued that soldiers who'd seen combat should be charged with crimes against humanity because war was the ultimate sin. No one thought he'd make it through the first primaries, but the media loved his constant controversies.

There was also Pete Wiseman, a Yale professor who had written a bestselling book about a new form of government, but few believed he'd scrape together enough funding to even make it to the Iowa caucus.

Hudson reviewed the complete list to date.

Republicans

- Bill Cash, Texas Governor
- Brian Uncer, Arizona Senator
- Chuck Brickman, Former Pennsylvania Governor
- Dan Stein, Florida Congressman
- Paul Jones, Oklahoma Governor
- Thorne, shock jock
- Professor Pete Wiseman
- Celia Brown, Illinois Senator
- General Hightower

Democrats

- Hap Morningstar, California Governor
- Andrew Kelleher, New York Governor
- Cindy Packard, New Hampshire Senator
- Henry Beck, New York Congressman
- Hart Sweeney, California Senator
- Newsman Dan Neuman, Oregon Governor
- Tim Zerkel, tech billionaire

By the morning of the family meeting, he'd learned all he could about the sixteen candidates, who, if he accepted Vonner's offer, would become not only his colleagues, but also his most fierce competitors. They all seemed formidable, he considered several of them absolutely unbeatable—such as Senator Uncer and Governor Cash—but Vonner had reminded him that politics, and presidential campaigns in general, were totally unpredictable, a fact that was hammered home as he and Melissa were waiting for his children to arrive. A news flash lit up the TV screen.

"Presidential candidate and Arizona Senator, Brian Uncer, is believed to be dead."

Chapter Five

Hudson and Melissa stared at the screen in horror—the fiery shell of an automobile still being extinguished, replays of Brian Uncer, the US Senator from Arizona, getting into that same car after a campaign event in Tucson.

"Uncer had been considered by many pundits to be the frontrunner for the Republican nomination," the newscaster said somberly. "The Senator, his driver, and an aide have just died, and there seems little doubt that this was not an accident. This was an assassination."

The graphic images were difficult to watch as the Senator was seen waving and smiling moments before his car exploded, engulfing him and two other occupants in an immense fireball. The third-world-style hit immediately drew comparisons to many similar attacks in Europe, Asia, and the Middle East carried out by Islamic extremists. During the initial aftermath, with the media already rushing to judgment and assuming it to be the act of Middle Eastern terrorists, shocking news surfaced that a mysterious domestic group was claiming responsibility.

"Uncer was one of the people you had to beat," Melissa said. "The Republican nomination was his to lose."

"I know, I know," Hudson said, unable to take his eyes from the screen.

"The previously unknown group signed their statement simply as NorthBridge," the newscaster reported. "In their release, the 'NorthBridgers' said they represented a large number of Americans who were tired of waiting for 'change.' Instead, they have decided to begin what they are calling 'a second American Revolution'," he said in a monotone.

"Oh my God," Melissa whispered.

The newscaster read from the group's website: "We honor the actions taken on the North Bridge of Concord, Massachusetts, in 1775 by Minutemen against the English King's troops, to open the American War of Independence. Ralph Waldo Emerson rightfully referred to that exchange as 'the shot heard around the world.' We declare that the politicians and elites who have corrupted the freedoms our forebears fought and died for are far worse than a distant monarch inflicting his whims and wrath on a good people."

In the days since the bank meeting with Vonner, Melissa and Hudson had talked of nothing else. Hudson was leaning heavily toward running, but still wanted to talk with his children first. Now, however, this attack made him reconsider everything.

That could have been him, and it certainly demonstrated the mood of the country, or at least a part of it. Hudson wasn't sure if it was because of his time in the service, his own frustration with the state of the world, or even events from his past, but seeing a US Senator murdered like that made him even more interested in being president. Things had to change, there was no question, but such change had to come about peacefully.

Hudson pulled his laptop across the coffee table and went to the NorthBridge website. He found the home page text familiar.

We hold these truths to be self-evident, that all men are created equal, that they are endowed by their Creator with certain unalienable Rights, that among these are Life, Liberty and the pursuit of Happiness.

That to secure these rights, Governments are instituted among Men, deriving their just powers from the consent of the governed, That whenever any Form of Government becomes destructive of these ends, it is the Right of the People to alter or to abolish it, and to institute new Government . . . when a long train of abuses and usurpations reduce them under absolute Despotism, it is their right, it is their duty, to throw off such Government . . .

Hudson then heard the newscaster repeating the line.

"*'Whenever any Form of Government becomes destructive of these ends, it is the Right of the People to alter or to abolish it,'* Thomas Jefferson."

For the next two hours, a parade of prominent politicians appeared on every news channel to condemn the horrible act as terrorism. Celia Brown, an African-American Senator from Illinois, and also a Republican candidate for the White House, said, "For these cowards to hide behind the bravery of the Founding Fathers is an insult to their memory. The Founders established the Constitution and our great democracy in such a way that grievances can be addressed in a public and civilized manner. The NorthBridgers are nothing more than murderous thugs, and we must use every resource to hunt them down."

Only Thorne broke from the unanimous condemnation when he said, "People are sick and tired of the rigged system, and the NorthBridgers have a point. Now, I'm not condoning murder, but perhaps some of these corrupt politicians *should* be arrested and charged." When asked if he had specifics on crimes committed by Members of Congress, he declined to answer, but offered, "More than ninety percent of US Senators, and eighty percent of House members, should be put on trial."

"That guy's crazy," Melissa said, pointing to Thorne on the screen. "He's inciting them."

"Do you know what this means?" Hudson asked, seemingly not hearing her last remark.

"What? That a bunch of crazies are intent on making our country into the next Iraq?"

"No," Hudson said, his gaze still far away. "I could actually win the presidency."

Chapter Six

Schueller arrived first. Hudson took a deep breath. He didn't approve of his son's bohemian lifestyle, nor his anti-everything attitude. But he tried, he always tried.

As he hugged him, he recalled the young boy who had lost his mother at age ten. Hudson thought his son looked too skinny, and he could smell the aroma of tobacco—at least he *hoped* it was only tobacco. His shaggy brown hair hadn't seen a comb in months, the stubble on his face meant days without a razor. Thrift store clothes and his mother's eyes; the combination always left him wondering what his late wife would have thought.

She probably would have reminded me to relax and support him. "The more you fight it, the more he'll fight back."

It just bothered Hudson that his son, who'd tested off-the-charts smart, was seemingly wasting his brains, and his life.

Melissa hugged Schueller, too. He liked her. He could talk to her, and, oddly, they had the same taste in music. "How'd the gig go last night?" she asked.

"It was just a coffee shop thing," Schueller said, obviously pleased she'd remembered. "Kota posted a couple videos already." He glanced at his father, knowing he didn't much care for his girlfriend, Dakota.

"Oh, good. I'll watch later," Melissa said.

Schueller nodded and smiled, knowing she really would, knowing he'd get a text that night saying what she liked most. The venue had been small, but he'd packed the place and sold a good handful of CDs. "So, what's the emergency?" he asked.

"Let's wait until Florence gets here so I only have to say everything once," Hudson replied in a serious tone.

"You're not sick, are you?" Schueller asked, suddenly sounding younger. They all knew he was thinking about his mother's cancer battle.

"No, I'm in great shape."

"Schueller, did you hear about Senator Uncer?" Melissa asked.

"The sinister senator from Arizona?" Schueller replied. "What'd he do now? Put out a plan to outlaw solar power?"

"No," Hudson said. "He was assassinated."

"Really?" Schueller almost smiled. "Well, no loss there."

"Schueller!" Melissa admonished. "He had a family."

Hudson shook his head.

"I'm sorry, but the guy was a bastard."

Florence came through the door. Blonde, like her father, but with her mother's face; high cheekbones, thin nose, and a playful sprinkle of freckles. She hugged her brother first.

"Good drive?" Schueller asked sarcastically.

"Well I made it in five hours," she said, moving to hug her father and then Melissa. "No cops on the road. I think they've all been pulled to the cities. Everyone's freaking out about these NorthBridgers. The radio's full of it. Have you heard?"

"We were just telling Schueller. He missed it since his car is a music-only zone," Hudson said, leading them into the living room. The TV was repeating the profile of the NorthBridge terrorists. They watched for a few moments.

"How awful," Florence said, seeing the images for the first time.

"No one knows much about this group," Melissa said. "Hopefully it's a couple of fanatics trying to make themselves sound bigger than they are."

"Your brother thinks the Senator deserved it," Hudson said.

"You do not," Florence said, giving Schueller a little shove.

"It gives Thorne a better shot," Schueller said. "And Thorne is the best chance we have for real change. For truth."

"You're not serious about supporting that clown," Florence said. "He's not fit to be president."

"Oh, he's serious, all right," Hudson said. "Although, I always thought you were a liberal, Schueller. You do know Thorne is running as a Republican, don't you?"

"Maybe we shouldn't talk politics right now," Melissa said, motioning to the TV.

Hudson gave her a quizzical look. "Actually, this all relates to why I called you here today."

"Are you getting married?" Florence asked.

"They could have told us *that* over the phone," Schueller said, resisting the urge to delve into a full political debate with his father.

"Yes, we are," Hudson said, glancing at Melissa in time

to see her surprised expression. "But there's more to it than that."

"Congratulations," Florence said, hugging first her father, and then Melissa.

"I'd say welcome to the family," Schueller said to Melissa, "but you've been family for a while now."

Melissa gave him a peck on the cheek. "Thank you, Schueller."

"You said there was more," Florence said. "A baby?"

"Oh my goodness, no!" Melissa said.

Hudson laughed at the thought. "No, it's much crazier than that. I've been approached to run for political office."

Neither of his children were surprised. They knew people had tried to get their father to run for mayor, but surely that wouldn't have required them to drive home on such short notice.

"Governor?" Florence asked.

Schueller raised his eyebrows.

"President," Hudson said, holding his breath.

"Of what?" Schueller asked.

"The United States."

"Dad!" Florence said. "Come on."

"Seriously," Hudson said.

"Who approached you?" Schueller asked.

"Arlin Vonner."

"Arlin Vonner? Why?" Florence asked. "I mean, I think you can do anything, but you're my father. Why does he think anyone other than me and Schueller would vote for you?"

"And Melissa," Melissa added.

Florence nodded, smiling. "Okay, he's got three votes, maybe a few hundred more from friends and relatives, but hardly a landslide victory."

"Vonner is a pig," Schueller snapped. "The guy buys politicians. He's part of the problem. He spreads corruption like the flu."

"Do you know him?" Hudson asked.

"Of course I don't *know* him. He doesn't associate with regular riffraff like me. So why does he want you?"

"He thinks the American people are ready for some 'riffraff'," Hudson said.

"And you're the best he could come up with?"

"You may not believe your old man is very cool, but a lot of people think I'm a pretty good guy."

"Dad, seriously. I love you. I do. And I'm proud to be your son. We may not see eye-to-eye on many things, but I know you're smart and honest and into helping others. You'd be great, but don't you see the only way you can win is if Vonner *buys* it for you?"

"We don't live in some Third World country. Contrary to your radical views, you can't actually buy an election in America. Vonner may help with funds to pay for the tons of advertising we'll need, and his media connections can get my name out there, but I'll have to convince everyone that I'm the guy. *I'd* have to get the votes."

"And what about this?" Schueller asked, pointing to the image of Senator Uncer's burning car on the TV.

"What about it?" Hudson asked.

"Is Vonner just going to have all your opponents killed?"

Hudson recoiled as if someone had taken a jab at his face. "Vonner had nothing to do with that."

"How do you know?"

"I know."

"*How*? Like you *know* that some angry Muslim on dialysis orchestrated the 9/11 attacks from a cave? That a collection of misfits and losers managed to hijack four commercial airliners at the same time, on the same day, and kill three thousand people on American soil?" Schueller was pacing, his arms punctuating his points. "And let's not forget they crashed into the Pentagon, *the Pentagon*, and of course somehow brought down the two World Trade towers *and* Building Seven—a building not even *hit* by a plane, and yet it collapses at free fall speed in a perfect controlled-demolition for no apparent reason. Have you ever read about Building Seven and the other crazy-unusual stuff that happened that day?"

"Look, I know you believe 9/11 was some wild conspiracy, but—"

"If you don't believe *me*, read about it yourself. Just search the internet for '9/11 conspiracy' or check one of the video sites. People have researched this in incredible detail, and if you would just watch some of it you'd know—"

"Know what?" Hudson said, rising from his seat.

"That Vonner is *using* you."

"Why?"

"That's the question you should be asking yourself, Dad." Schueller stopped right next to his father—the two were the same height—and looked him in the eye. "Why did one of the richest men in the world pick *you*? Why?"

Chapter Seven

Arlin Vonner, sitting in the three-thousand-square-foot "Pacific room" of Sun Wave, his massive Carmel, California estate, secretly listened live to every word of the Pound family meeting. A butler handed him a scotch as he mounted his custom exercise bike. Vonner liked to "drink and ride."

Joining Vonner in the magnificent room, enjoying a stunning view of the Pacific, was Rex Lestat, a sturdy-looking man with a wide face and curly brown hair that appeared impossible to tame. A man Vonner called "the fixer." Rex had been with Vonner's organization for more than twenty years, but few knew of his existence. His power lurked in the shadows, a master of both the DarkNet and the deep web, places that could not be accessed from the regular internet; places where criminals and conspirators lived.

"Schueller could surprise us," Vonner said as they listened to his conspiratorial rant.

"I don't think so," Rex said in his deep baritone voice, making each statement like an announcement. "He's a twenty-two-year-old musician. He doesn't know what the hell he knows. He's a punk."

"It sounds like he knows exactly what he thinks he knows," Vonner said. "What about his footprints online?"

"Done," Rex said firmly.

Vonner smiled, knowing Rex had erased all traces of Schueller's internet browsing history—one filled with conspiracy, left-wing radical, anti-war, anti-Federal Reserve, and similar assorted sites going back years. The fixer had replaced it with more standard American teens' preferences. He knew the media would start digging as soon as Pound announced, and wanted to be sure they didn't find anything too exciting. "And the daughter?"

"Nothing I could do to make her any more perfect. Excellent grades all the way through her academic career, a top nursing student, lots of charity work, and she's already earned distinction at work. She doesn't drink or smoke and has a steady boyfriend—a lawyer. And, although Florence is a Democrat, she's far more to the center than her brother."

Vonner smiled again. He knew all this, but liked to be reassured. There was so much riding on his choice. "Each election demands more finesse, more excitement."

"Like telling a bigger lie to cover the last," Rex added, rolling a pair of green dice in his hand.

"It's really more like making each successive action movie bigger than the one before."

"Where does it end?"

"I don't ever want to know the answer to that question," Vonner said, an uncharacteristically worried expression appearing on the youthful face of the seventy-two-year-old tycoon. He covered it quickly with a phony smile, but both men had the same concern. Would this be the year that things spun out of control? Each cycle had gotten bigger, the battles more brutal, the players more than willing to do anything it took.

The voice of Melissa Atwater broke the tension. Vonner had read the latest on Hudson's girlfriend—now fiancée—and still believed she would be an excellent First Lady. Beauty, business, and brains meant she would be an asset on every campaign stop with both men and women. Melissa was explaining to Schueller that she, too, had been suspicious of Vonner.

Vonner raised his eyebrow.

"Not to worry," Rex said.

Vonner knew she wouldn't be a problem, but these were the times to be most careful. They listened as Melissa explained that she'd followed Vonner's career for years, and had, ever since learning of Hudson's meeting with him, added to her knowledge of the man with extensive research. The specifics didn't exactly sway Schueller, but they could tell that Hudson's son respected his soon-to-be stepmother, as he definitely softened his stance. What seemed to make the biggest impact was her point about how much good his father could do.

"And, Schueller, what if you're right about everything?" Melissa asked. "What if the Federal Reserve *is* manipulating and controlling the economy? What if 9/11 wasn't the work of Al Qaida? How do you propose to expose and change all that? Couldn't having an honest man like your father in the White House be our best chance at getting to the truth?"

Schueller's reply wasn't audible, but they assumed he nodded, based on the brief pause before Melissa pushed on.

"He can make the world a better place."

"Sounds a little corny," Hudson said, "but that's just what I want to do."

"They won't let you," Schueller said.

"Who is 'they'?" Hudson asked, exasperated.

"Whoever is really running things—Vonner, the Fed, the Rockefellers, the Rothschilds. If I knew for sure who *they* were, I would probably be dead."

"Are you serious?" Hudson asked, more concerned than angry.

"I just know the world isn't as it appears."

"Why? Because some website claims to know the truth? Some guy in New Jersey or wherever makes a video about the Illuminati and suddenly his version of the world becomes fact?"

"You don't have to believe it."

"I'm all for the truth. Show me some real facts and I'm right behind you, but if you don't have any, then you sound kind of ignorant, and I know you're not."

Schueller nodded. "Don't worry, Dad. I won't mess up your campaign. I'll keep my views to myself, because if I'm right, maybe you can fix it, and if I'm wrong, then maybe you'll prove it and then fix it anyway."

"Either way, Schueller, I want to make you proud of your dad. If I win—and that's a long, long, looooong shot anyway—but if I do, I'm going to try to do as much right as I can. And I promise I'll look for any secret government cover-ups for you. UFOs, Kennedy's assassination, Elvis hiding out somewhere—"

Schueller laughed. "Okay, Dad."

"Fake moon landing," Hudson continued. "Paul McCartney is dead—"

"Very funny, Dad," Schueller said, laughing harder, but

adding, "We'll see, though. Keep an open mind and we'll see."

"My mind is totally open," Hudson promised. "Now, what about you, Florence?"

"Careful, Florence, they're listening to every word we say," Schueller said in a sinister voice.

Vonner knew Hudson's son was joking, but still got an adrenaline jolt.

"A real wise-ass, that one," Rex said. "He couldn't know."

"But he may be smarter than he looks," Vonner said.

"He will not be a problem," Rex said emphatically. "But if he ever becomes one, we'll handle it."

Vonner nodded. He knew the plan. Rex had handled hundreds of "situations" before. He'd hired the former Marine out of the CIA after Vonner had been tapped to covertly help fund a coup in Central America. Rex had been one of the lead operatives, and Vonner's go-between reported back to his boss, "If you want a 'fixer,' this Rex Lestat guy is the real deal." Vonner threw the right amount of money at Rex, and he'd been his number one lieutenant in charge of starting or containing trouble, depending on what the situation called for, ever since.

"Dad, I'm so excited for you," Florence said. "But are you ready for all the attention? It seems every year the political campaigns get nastier."

Vonner winked at Rex.

Hudson smiled at his daughter. She'd always been the worrier in the family. "Vonner thinks the media is going to love me. He believes I'm just what everyone's been waiting for—a real person running for president, an honest guy with common sense."

"I think it's awesome, Dad. You've got my vote. Just stay

safe, okay?" Vonner couldn't see it, but Florence nodded toward the TV, still replaying Senator Uncer's fiery death.

"Looks like you've got yourself a candidate," Rex said.

"Candidate nothing. Hudson Pound will be the next president of the United States."

Chapter Eight

After lunch, Hudson and Melissa went for a drive to Lake Hope State Park. It had long been a favorite destination of Hudson's. He rowed the rented boat out into the 120-acre lake and found a picturesque cove. The sun sparkled on the water, and a fragrant spring breeze teased Melissa's hair. Hudson smiled as he fumbled in his pocket and produced a stunning engagement ring.

"When did you get this?" Melissa asked in surprise.

"I'm a resourceful fellow," Hudson said quietly. "I want to do this right. This shouldn't be about political expediency, or the timing of my announcing, it should be about us . . . Melissa, I love you, and I couldn't imagine going on this journey, or anywhere into the future, without you. What I'm trying to say is, will you marry me?"

Melissa beamed, but remained silent for nearly a minute. Hudson believed she loved him, and knew she'd been thinking about their potential marriage ever since Vonner suggested it. They'd been happy and serious enough that she must have had thoughts even before Vonner entered their lives.

So why is she taking so long? he wondered.

There was a lot to consider, the rigors of the primaries and then, if luck was on his side, the general election, and, incredibly, she could become First Lady of the United States. That sent a jolt through him. *Could this all really happen?*

But Melissa was no lightweight. In many ways, she was more suited for all that lay ahead than Hudson. After graduating Georgetown, she got a gig with the National Governor's Association, which exposed her to political contacts in all fifty states and Capitol Hill.

Her expression softened, then tightened. Melissa had a classic beauty. Expensive looks, Hudson had always thought, but out on the lake, or during hikes in the woods, a natural, rustic side came out that he found especially irresistible.

He took her hand and slipped the ring on her finger. "What do you say?"

Melissa smiled. "Are we ready to do this?" she asked. "Our lives will never be the same. Not like this." She motioned out to the isolation of the lake. "Do you really want to be President of the United States?"

He nodded. "I really do." Pausing, Hudson looked into her eyes. "But the question on the table right now is do *you* want to be First Lady?"

"Yes, I'd love to be your first lady." She hugged him.

"You already are, baby," he whispered. "You always will be."

Back on land, they took a walk along the pebbled shore and enjoyed an early dinner at the Hope Lake Lodge. Ohio marriage law only required a license from the county clerk. They decided to have a quick courthouse ceremony in the morning before Florence and Schueller left town. Every other moment of their "romantic" afternoon was spent discussing the upcoming announcement and campaign.

Meanwhile, at Hudson's house, his children were still debating their father's strange opportunity.

"What do you *really* think?" Schueller asked his sister as they munched snacks in the living room. "And save the cheerleader stuff for Dad."

"It's incredible. Dad will get to travel the country talking about all his great ideas for education reform. He'll get his name known. Probably write a book. Maybe he can even get out of the hardware business."

"What are you talking about? Dad's going to be the president."

"What are *you* talking about? He's never going to win. He won't even get the nomination. I think he could win the Ohio primary, but how could he ever last that long?"

"Vonner," Schueller said. "Do you know who he is?"

"I've heard of him. Everyone has. He's like a zillionaire."

"Yeah, and he picked Dad. That means Dad is going to win."

"You can have billions and still lose. Remember Ross Perot? I mean, I think a lot of voters will like Dad, but how many will *really* get a chance to get to know him, and is anyone going to trust someone with zero experience?" She dipped another carrot stick into a bowl of hummus. "I looked at the polling data Vonner sent them. I get that people are tired of career politicians and billionaires, that they want an ordinary person like themselves, and that Dad fits that, but—"

"And remember," Schueller said scornfully, "once Vonner decided they wanted someone like Dad, they had to pick someone. It just turns out Dad is most like Dad. He's a veteran from Ohio, a former teacher big on education, honest, small town, no politics, no skeletons in his closet, blah, blah, blah."

"And he looks like a movie star," Florence added.

"Oh yeah, you're right. Let's not forget Dad *does* look like a movie star."

"You really think he can win?"

"He's going to win," Schueller said. "Vonner is a robber baron."

"A phrase only the son of a history teacher would use in this century," Florence said, laughing.

"You want to talk history?" Schueller snapped, pointing to his father's collection of antique textbooks as if they contained the answer. "I'm telling you, it's a historical fact that whoever holds the purse strings of a country ultimately rules the country, and in our case, that's the Federal Reserve. They manipulate and control the economy."

"I may not be up on history and government as much as you, little brother, but isn't it the Fed's *job* to manipulate and control the economy?"

"They shouldn't even exist, but their official role is to provide the nation with a safe, stable financial system, which includes combatting inflation. But it's all a scam to consolidate and maintain power and wealth for the greedy elite." Schueller had paced to the other side of the room and stopped to stare at another of his father's collections, this one a group of about forty vintage tools. "Why does Dad keep this rusty old junk?"

"How is Vonner connected to the Federal Reserve?"

"All the super-rich are in on it. Do you really think you can make billions of dollars being honest? Vonner is a criminal just like the rest."

"Dad's a smart guy, Schueller. He knows what he's doing. All your conspiracy theories are just that . . . *theories*."

"I'm not the only one who believes this stuff."

"Yeah, the internet is full of nutcases," Florence said. "But tell me this, why *Dad*? He's not in on it. Why not just put in a puppet who would do exactly what he's told?"

"I don't know." Schueller sat back down next to his sister on the big leather couch while grabbing a carrot. "That's what worries me the most . . . why Dad?"

Chapter Nine

The wedding ceremony was very quick, or, as Hudson put it, "It takes longer to get checked out at the grocery store than it does to get married." Florence and Schueller acted as witnesses and Hudson's sister, Trixie, who was the general manager of Pound Hardware and Plumbing, brought flowers. Twelve minutes later, Mr. and Mrs. Hudson Pound stepped out of the courthouse into the cold, sunny Ohio morning, taking the first steps of a journey at least one of them hoped would eventually lead them to the White House.

"It's a long road," Hudson said to his sister, who only that morning had been told of both the marriage, which didn't surprise her, and the plan to seek the presidency, which shocked her to the point of humor. Trixie was tall and blonde like her younger brother, but her hair color, like her tan, was manufactured.

She'd actually been with the Pound Hardware company longer than he had. An old army buddy of Hudson's owned the first store and gave Trixie a job as a favor. A few years later, when Hudson, a young untenured teacher, lost his job to budget cuts, he hired him, too. Within weeks of Hudson coming on board, they were offered the chance to buy out a competitor. Hudson's meager savings, together with some money his wife had inherited, made the deal possible, and suddenly Hudson owned half of a mini-chain of stores. By the time they had four more locations, his buddy had met a woman while on vacation in Mexico and wanted to sell out his share. That's when Hudson's relationship with Titan Capital & Trust Bank began.

In the years since, he'd doubled the number of locations and tripled revenues, until a major factory in the area closed and weakened the local economy. Now everything he'd built was at risk.

Less than four weeks after he married Melissa, Hudson stood behind the curtains of a sturdy platform in Columbus Commons, a six-acre park in the middle of Ohio's capital city. The surprisingly large crowd included hundreds of representatives from the national media. Word had "leaked" forty-eight hours earlier that the Super PAC, Real Americans for Real Change, which had already raised a record $290 million, was going to support an unknown candidate, "a real American," with no political experience. Every major cable news channel and all the network morning shows had booked the mystery person. Even before anyone knew his identity, he was already famous. And now, only moments remained before the unveiling, before Hudson Pound instantly became a household name.

He stood thinking, repeatedly twisting his wedding ring and trying not to panic. For a month, he'd been subjected to seemingly endless sessions with "handlers." Vonner had sent media consultants, foreign policy and economic teams, strategists of all types, and experts on everything in order to prepare the former history teacher. Once, he had complained about all the efforts to "mold" him.

"I'm supposed to be running as an 'everyman' and ought to be allowed to be myself."

"As a former teacher, Hudson, you should know that one must never stop learning," Vonner had responded.

Hudson was, in fact, a natural. His love of history, debating, and public speaking, combined with an impressive military background, running a small business, and amazing school board achievements, made easy work for his "tutors." And his daughter was right on both counts; Hudson *was* smart, and he *did* look like a movie star.

"Any second thoughts?" Melissa asked, squeezing his hand.

"Hundreds of them!" Hudson laughed. "I wonder if Vonner has any?"

The billionaire had decided to stay away, knowing his presence would only invite controversy. "Hudson needs to shine on his own," he'd said.

Florence and Schueller were on hand, both nervous for different reasons. His son still believed his father had fallen into a web of corruption that none of them understood, and his daughter worried that the NorthBridgers, who wanted a second American Revolution and who'd yet to be captured, might decide to take out another presidential candidate. Hudson hugged them both. Now wasn't the time for further family debate, but Hudson reminded both his children that Vonner had provided a large security detail.

He strode confidently onto the stage and surveyed the large gathering. Minutes before, Emmitt "Fitz" Fitzgerald, his recently installed campaign manager, whispered in his ear that there were more than ten thousand people in attendance.

"Where did they come from? What are they doing here?" Hudson had asked disbelievingly.

Fitz, a wiry, nerdy-looking man sporting big square eyeglasses and an infectious smile, which he seemed to use as a weapon, gave a vague response. "They're here for you, the man who promises to take back their house!"

He stepped onto the stage. "Thanks for coming out today. My name is Hudson Pound. It's safe to say that not many of you know me, although a few of you might have traveled to the southeastern part of the state and shopped in one of my hardware stores. Maybe one of you served with me in the United States Army, or perhaps a former student of mine is in the audience. Because, although I did serve in the army, taught history in the public school system, served on the school board, and grew a small business here in Ohio, there is one thing that I have never done. I have not held public office."

A raucous smattering of applause interrupted him.

"I'm just a regular guy, a true American willing to serve this great country and then, as soon as possible, return to my normal life. Being a politician should never be a career."

More applause.

"Being a politician should be a very short and unpleasant route to showing which person is best qualified to serve the public at a given time. And right now, it's the right time for one of us—one of the commoners—to bring back some basic common sense to Washington."

Someone in the crowd began the chant, "Pound, Pound, Pound!"

"I am running as a Republican, but I do not exclusively

hold every traditionally Republican idea as sacred." His voice escalated. "Lincoln was a Republican, and I believe our country is more divided now than it has been at any time since the American Civil War. So please don't think of me as a Republican, think of me as a regular American, a veteran, a teacher, a small businessman, a citizen involved in his community, and concerned, like all of you, about our great country. It is time to return to our Founders' vision and bring regular Americans back into government. Of the people, by the people, *FOR* the *PEOPLE!*"

The crowd erupted.

Chapter Ten

The days after his announcement were an awful grind during which Hudson relied on Fitz or other staff members to keep him informed on who, what, and where throughout constant TV appearances, interviews, and travel, with little food and even less sleep.

"How did we get such a big staff already?" Hudson asked his campaign manager, who always seemed to have a phone to his ear and a Coke in his hand.

"Money talks, my friend," Fitz said. "But don't get the wrong idea, everyone loves you, loves the idea of an average joe running for president." Fitz sucked down the last of his soda and immediately grabbed another can. "They can trust you. Imagine that . . . trusting our leader."

Hudson gave a half-hearted laugh, trying to decide if he actually liked Fitz.

"We'll be doing a major, *major* media blitz to get your numbers up fast," Fitz said with a wink. "Got to make sure you qualify for the debates."

Hudson got through the media storm because he'd been

well prepared and, along the way, discovered that he had actually enjoyed it. Talking about issues, recounting history, and meeting new people excited and invigorated him. The media did truly seem to love Hudson, and he'd become such an overnight sensation that a few of the other candidates were already taking swipes at him. Even Thorne, the Republican shock-jock, tried unsuccessfully to engage Hudson in a Twitter battle.

When Hudson finally returned home for a quick two-day break, he found himself sitting alone in his hardware store office, hardly knowing what to do. It felt as if a warped reality had taken over his life. During the brief respite, he and Melissa hoped to get out to the lake. Otherwise, sleep and normal food had been prescribed to recharge his batteries. Already what he wanted most was as much isolation time as possible.

He'd gone into the store only because he felt so comfortable and grounded there. Plus, even though Trixie could handle everything, there were still the TC&T loan proceeds to manage and a few other matters she wished to discuss. Hudson had to keep the stores going. He knew there was no way he'd actually become president, and after Governor Cash or Governor Morningstar won the election, he'd have to go back to selling nuts and bolts.

When Trixie knocked on his office door, Hudson said he was ready to review the accounts, but his sister had a distressed look on her face.

"Trixie, what's wrong?"

"There's a reporter out there."

"Another one?" Hudson asked. They'd quickly become a nuisance at all the hardware stores. "Get rid of him, like you've done with all the others."

"This one is different," Trixie said. "This one is Fonda Raton."

"*The* Fonda Raton?" Hudson swallowed hard and looked at the phone. He considered calling Vonner, but remembered the billionaire was unreachable for the afternoon—some big meeting in Zurich. He could have probably reached Fitz, and knew that's really what he should have done, but fresh off the success of his whirlwind media tour, he felt confident. "Send her back," he said. "Might as well get her over with."

Fonda Raton wasn't blonde-bombshell-gorgeous like so many women in the media, but the thirty-something brunette definitely had a kind of beauty, which she wore like a faded pair of jeans, because when anyone described Fonda, looks were several notches down on the list. First came her cleverness, then the strategic mind, next her political instincts, followed by a powerhouse of intelligence, computer skills, networking, the ability to "win friends and influence people," and, last on the list, was her pretty face. Fonda Raton had built a mini media empire on the internet that brought in millions, but it wasn't the money, it was the power. The Raton Report had scooped every other news organization on hundreds of important stories, including a dozen major ones. She specialized in corruption of the fat cats and justice for the underdogs. Her unofficial motto was "It's raining cats and dogs."

The fact that she showed up at his office unannounced shouldn't have been a surprise. It was her style, and it worked, as Hudson had already second-guessed his decision to see her. It unnerved him that she *knew* he was there, at the store. Hudson was, after all, running for president of the United States. He could have been anywhere, but she *knew*. A woman like Fonda didn't waste time on wild goose chases.

Maybe she'll go easy on me if I face her fire now, like I have nothing to hide, like I'm not afraid, he thought. *And I* don't *have anything to hide.* But he knew he did have something to hide. *She may know how to find me, but she can't know about that.*

No one could know his greatest secret.

"Hudson," she said sweetly as she walked into his office, taking in the room like a Commando checking a strike zone. While they shook hands, her left hand came up and casually lingered on his shoulder. "Thanks for seeing me with no notice. I'm sure you're getting barraged with requests."

"You took a chance I'd be here."

"Oh, I was in the neighborhood."

Hudson smiled. "Of course you were." Fonda was thinner than he'd expected from the few photos he'd seen online. She had a lean, athletic build. Her long, safari-brown hair seemed sunny, and was styled in one of those cuts that looked like each hair had been cut individually.

"I love the trucks," she said, pointing to his collection of toy old-fashioned hardware vehicles. "You really are a hardware man."

"Did you think we made it up for the election?"

Fonda laughed. "It wouldn't be the first time. Ol' Vonner is a wily devil."

"Devil is a strong word, Ms. Raton."

"It is, it is," she said distractedly, pulling her hair back in a ponytail. "And, Hudson, please call me *Fonda*. You and I are going to be good friends before this is over."

He was pretty sure she winked at him, but Fonda was a whirlwind, so it was impossible to be certain.

"What exactly *is* your relationship with Arlin Vonner?" she asked.

"He's a supporter," Hudson said carefully.

"Yes, the whole world knows he's backing your

campaign. If you pardon my bluntness, that's the only reason anyone has heard of you, the only reason you're even showing up on the most recent CompuPoll."

"I appreciate his support, along with thousands of other Americans who have been sending in twenty, fifty, a hundred dollars at a time."

"That's so generous of the commoners to help you buy bumper stickers," she said. "But Vonner is paying for everything else. Why?"

"I'm sorry, Ms. Raton, I don't think you have your facts right."

She looked at him, a crooked smile growing on her face. "Really?" She stepped closer to him. It was then that he realized they still hadn't sat down. Fonda came in close, too close, too personal, as if they were on their fifth date. "I understood you were an honest Midwestern boy, Hudson. I must have been misinformed." She looked him up and down. He could feel her warm breath, smell a floral scent. "Is this how you want to play it? Really?" She waved a finger close to his lips in what could only be taken as an admonishment.

Hudson was knocked off his game. Even before the campaign, he'd always thought he was good with the press, but that false sense only came from the fact that he was a kind of folk hero in southern Ohio, and also an advertiser. The local press had been easy on him about school board issues, hospital events, Little League, and all his other community work. But compared to Fonda Raton, the local press were two-bit amateurs. The morning shows had been easy for Vonner's people to control, but Fonda was a surprise, not settling for his prepared statements and catching him without his handlers.

What the hell, she came uninvited and unannounced.

Her charmingly hostile manner left Hudson suddenly feeling attacked, ambushed, vulnerable. His instincts told him to be truthful, but she scared him, and in that instant stir of emotions, he realized for the first time that he was willing to fight to become president. Without any further calculations, he decided to lie.

"My campaign is original in the modern era. The Founding Fathers envisioned a country governed by its people in the true sense of the word—farmers and merchants, common folk who would take time from their regular lives and give service to their country, then return home to resume that ordinary life."

"Ah, yes, the history teacher."

"It may sound corny to a sophisticated media mogul like you, but Vonner and many others see it as the authentic return to our roots, to a time before big money and special interests had overtaken the system."

Fonda laughed indignantly. "Hudson, do you not see the hypocrisy in your statement? 'Before big money and special interests?' Vonner, your largest supporter, is the ninth richest man in the world. He *is* big money and special interests. He could buy you the presidency." She allowed a dramatic pause, squinted her eyes, and shot her next question as if it were a revelation. "Is that what he's doing, Hudson? Is Arlin Vonner buying you the presidency?"

Hudson stared at Fonda coldly. "You've insulted me, Ms. Raton."

"Oh no, have I? I'm sorry, and remember, we're friends, it's Fonda." She forced a smile.

"We are *not* friends, Ms. Raton. And I am not for sale. I am an honest, honorable man. My life speaks for itself. Now, I'd like you to please leave."

"Is that really what you want Hudson?" Her gaze was at

once pleading and threatening. "We're not talking about raising test scores in county schools or why your brand of paint covers better than Home Depot's anymore. This is about leading the free world, about the nuclear codes . . . This is the big leagues, the very biggest. Are you ready to take that on?"

"I like to think so."

"Do you? And you can't even handle sweet little me."

"With all due respect, Ms. Raton, you are not the American people. You are a reporter."

"I am a voter, Hudson."

"Something tells me that you won't be voting Republican."

"Stranger things have happened." She smiled. "But I could never vote for a liar."

"Then that eliminates most of my opponents. Maybe you'll vote for me after all."

"Are you going to talk to me?"

"Not today."

Chapter Eleven

Hudson had already made two big mistakes that day: first, agreeing to see Fonda Raton, and then deciding to tell her to leave. So, when Trixie chased him down, just as he was reaching his car to head for home, he should have known more trouble was coming.

"Guess who's on the phone," his sister said.

"I'm in no mood," he replied, opening the car door.

"You'd never guess anyway. This one goes back to when we were kids."

Hudson felt the adrenaline rush and tasted the acidic memory that had begun one horrific night when he was seventeen. For nearly three decades, he'd tried to forget, tried to pretend, but it would not let him go. He looked at his sister. Even without knowing the secret, she could tell something was wrong.

"Are you okay? Don't worry about Fonda Raton, she can dig all day and won't find anything in your boring life other than all the good you've done," Trixie said, misreading the cause of his anxiety.

"Thanks," he said, feeling as if his mouth was full of cotton. "Who's on the phone?"

"It's the Wizard," she sang, as if this might cheer him. "Can you believe it? How long has it been?"

Hudson sank into the driver's seat and closed his eyes. This was the last call he wanted. He'd been expecting it, or rather *dreading* it, since the announcement, but part of him had hoped it might not come. Hudson had even convinced himself that maybe the Wizard wasn't even alive anymore.

"Okay, I'll be there in a minute."

She nodded and jogged back inside.

Hudson took a deep breath and tried to think. What was the Wizard going to say? Was this going to be the end of the shortest run for president in history? He thought back to his teen years when the Wizard had been his best friend. They'd known each other since seventh grade, when Hudson stupidly started a fight with Gouge, a tougher kid who quickly shoved him head first into a porcelain water fountain. The Wizard, new that year from South Korea, who had already earned the nickname for his ability to take apart and rebuild any electronic device, witnessed the event. Gouge and the Wizard helped get Hudson to the school nurse. Gouge, not interested in fighting, had only meant to push Hudson away, but the principal suspended him for three days. When Hudson found out about the unjust punishment, he confessed to being the one who'd started the fight and took the suspension instead. Somehow, out of the mess, the three kids became best friends, and no one could recall what had prompted the fight in the first place. For the rest of junior high, and all through high school, the trio remained inseparable.

By the time Hudson reached his office in the back of the hardware store, his trip down memory lane had fast-forwarded six years to the night that destroyed their friendship while simultaneously ensuring they'd be bound together forever. With those dark and grainy images swirling in his head, he picked up the receiver.

"Man, is this true?" the Wizard asked as soon as Hudson said hello, as if it hadn't been nearly a quarter of a century since they last spoke.

"Is what true?"

"Are you joking? How about the part about you running for President?"

"Yeah. Crazy, isn't it?"

"My best friend from the old neighborhood running for effin' president of the effin' United States of America. Whoa."

"I know. I still don't believe it. How've you been, Wizard?"

"Dude, how did this *happen*? I mean, I know it's been like three decades since we hung out, but president of the United States!" The Wizard sounded the same as when they'd last seen each other. Hudson had forgotten how much he liked him, how much he'd missed him. "The enormity of the universe! Big cosmic flips happening, man."

"It's kind of a long story."

"It would sure as hell have to be." The Wizard's voice filled with enthusiasm. Hudson remembered his old friend always sounded like he was delivering a joke, even when he wasn't, as if the world constantly amused him. "I guess probably all kinds of long lost pals from back in the day have been calling you out of the blue."

"There have been a few," Hudson admitted. "Including relatives I never knew I had."

"Have you heard from Gouge?"

No, thank God, Hudson thought. The Wizard was at least

somewhat stable and predictable, but Gouge was a complete wild card. "Isn't he still in prison?"

"No, he got out seven or eight months ago. I lent him some money. I mean, I don't *have* any money, but I found him some."

"You know you'll probably never see that cash again."

"Old times, you know? He's a good guy, just got on a bad road."

"Have you heard from him since?"

"Nah."

"Right."

A long silence left Hudson wondering if the connection had been dropped.

"So, you've done pretty well for yourself, Hudson. Hardware stores, big shot on the school board, and now . . . " He laughed like he was stoned. "And now running for Supreme Commander. Aye yi yi."

Hudson braced for the blackmail. Only two people on earth could derail his campaign—his two oldest friends. They had both been there that night. Before then, the three of them would have done anything for each other, and after that night, they did, but it destroyed them.

"Where you living these days?" Hudson asked, trying to keep it neutral.

"San Francisco."

"Expensive city," Hudson said, recalling the Wizard had just told him he didn't have any money.

"Tell me something I don't know. I live in an eight-by-ten storage shed in someone's backyard."

"Are you serious?"

"Yeah. Well, as a kid, back in Korea, I lived in far worse places before moving to the States. And it's temporary." He paused as if remembering something bleak, and then his voice perked up again. "Anyway, I'm working on something big."

"Such as?"

"I'm a computer guy. Programmer, hacker, designer, write code, you name it."

"Still the Wizard, huh?" Hudson said, remembering how the Wizard always defended his perfect grades by saying it was expected because he was Asian. "Let me guess, you're with some hot new start-up?"

"Nah, I'm working on an extraordinary secret, unifying thing, but it's waaay too much to go into now."

"Sure," Hudson said, definitely not wanting to lengthen the call.

"So anyway," the Wizard continued, "what's with this Super PAC funding you? Why *you*?"

"I've asked myself the same thing a thousand times," Hudson said, still uneasy with that question, which had churned in his gut since that first meeting with Vonner a month earlier. "But basically I'm the quintessential outsider. Seems they don't think a career politician can get elected anymore."

"So you're gonna be their puppet."

"No."

"No?"

"That's what I said."

"Then why would someone pour millions into you? Come on, Dawg, you know they expect something." Hearing his old nickname, a derivative of "Dog Pound," which only Gouge and the Wizard ever called him, took him back to where he didn't want to go, a time and place where frustration and rage were waiting, as always, to smother him again.

"All they expect from me is that I beat whoever gets the

Democratic nomination. And if I do . . . " He hesitated. "Sure, they'll have access. I can't deny that. That's just the way the system works."

"System works? There's an oxymoron if I've ever heard one," the Wizard said.

"I'm sure you're one of those guys who thinks the system is rigged."

"Nah, it's not rigged, Dawg. The system isn't even real."

"We haven't talked in twenty-five years, you call as I'm just starting the biggest undertaking of my life . . . and all you have to say is a bunch of cynical garbage? Nice." The anger grew in him from deep in the past, anger that had nothing to do with the call.

"Dude, take it easy. I just called to wish you luck, but after talking to you, I do have a little warning for you."

Here it comes.

"There's an old saying that politicians should never believe their own press, and an even older saying. Never believe your own lies."

Chapter Twelve

After the call with the Wizard, Hudson took a couple of ibuprofens and headed to Melissa's, where they'd been living since the wedding. His place was already on the market.

The conversation with his childhood friend had left a nagging dread, but it wasn't something he felt comfortable talking to his new wife about. He didn't know how to tell her about the Wizard and Gouge without discussing what happened that horrible night twenty-nine years earlier.

But he knew that the Wizard would want something, and sooner or later, Gouge would, too. He knew them. There'd be others, too, if he made it to the presidency, or even the nomination. Power like that would attract all kinds of characters with bluffs and scams, looking for a piece of it. But Gouge and the Wizard wouldn't need a scheme if they wanted to make trouble. His old friends knew the truth—the hard, dark truth.

Melissa saw it on his face.

"You look awful," she said, hugging him. "What happened? Did Oprah decide to get in the race?"

He couldn't help but chuckle. "No, Fonda Raton ambushed me today."

"Oh, damn!" Her irritation surprised him. "What did she write?"

"Nothing yet. I only spoke with her a couple of hours ago."

"You *talked* to her?"

"Yeah, she just showed up at my office."

"*In person*? Fonda Raton is *in town*? She got in to see you?"

"It's not that bad. I didn't give her much, but I did manage to tick her off pretty good."

"Maybe you better call Vonner," Melissa suggested.

"Why? I know he owns a lot of the media, but isn't part of Fonda's claim to fame the fact that no one influences her?"

"How should I know? And we certainly don't know what Vonner can and cannot do."

"I think it would make things worse. She was looking for something, some Vonner angle that made us look like co-conspirators. Why is it so hard for everyone to believe that a wealthy businessman and a down-to-earth school ex-board member might see eye-to-eye on a vision to get the country back on track? It's certainly no secret that the voters are sick of politicians. Am I the only one who sees how much sense my candidacy makes?"

"I'm glad you're finally starting to believe in yourself." She glanced outside as a member of the security detail, provided by Vonner, passed the window. "Let's at least check the Raton Report and see if that barracuda has posted anything about you yet," she said, reaching for her laptop.

"I'm afraid to look," Hudson said, grabbing a beer.

"Oh my God," Melissa breathed as the Raton Report website opened.

"What did she write?" Hudson growled as he raced over.

"No, not you. It's the NorthBridgers. They've struck again."

"What's happened?"

In the weeks since the revolutionary group had first burst into the national consciousness with the brutal assassination of Senator Uncer, they'd abstained from further violence. However, almost daily they leaked all kinds of hacked materials and data dumps which had been covertly accessed from a variety of government servers. NorthBridge seemed to be able to reach anywhere.

"They've bombed the Federal Reserve Bank building in Kansas City."

"How bad?"

"It's demolished," she said, reading the screen. "Quick, turn on the TV."

Moments later, a news anchor relayed the facts. The bomb was detonated at five-forty p.m. local time. Most employees were already gone for the day. At five-fifteen, NorthBridge had apparently notified the local media, police, and fire department, as well as the Federal Reserve, of the planned attack. An immediate evacuation took place. It was believed that only members of the bomb squad were still inside at the time of the blast. The NorthBridgers released a statement that officials were warned not to send anyone in to attempt to defuse the bomb. A NorthBridge leader called AKA Jefferson released a statement simply saying, "Banks are the conduit for oppression." The anchor noted the similarity in the real Thomas Jefferson's words: "I believe that banking institutions are more dangerous to our liberties than standing armies."

"Cowards," Hudson said. "Using the names of the Founders and twisting their words to justify violence. This is not the way to bring about change."

"The country figured that out in the sixties," Melissa said.

"You really think we learned?" Hudson asked.

"You're sounding like Schueller," Melissa said, and kissed him.

Hudson's special "phone" buzzed. It had to be Vonner, since it connected only to him. Vonner had tried to explain the encryption and untraceable technology, but Hudson still thought of it as an exclusive cell phone, and dubbed it "the communicator."

"You've seen the news?" his benefactor asked.

"We have it on right now," Hudson responded.

"A damned mess . . . I've sent your statement to your campaign email account." Hudson did understand that about being on a secure server. Fitz had reminded him about the email scandal that had plagued Hillary Clinton in the 2016 election.

"What statement?"

"About the NorthBridge attack. You didn't have to make a statement when they killed Uncer because you weren't a candidate yet. As we speak, three of your rivals are live on various cable news channels discussing the bombing and calling for more funding for the FBI and all kinds of exotic anti-terrorism measures. And, incredibly, that idiot Thorne is off on some inappropriate anti-Fed tirade."

"Okay, let me look."

"Fine, yes. Review it. I've already sent a copy to Fitz.

Assuming you're good with it, we'll get it to all the outlets right away."

Not surprisingly, Hudson agreed with every word. Vonner employed several good speechwriters who made the rookie candidate sound like a polished pro, yet still very much himself. He pushed the button on the communicator and instantly heard Vonner's voice again.

"The statement looks great," Hudson said. "But these damned NorthBridgers are changing the dynamic of this election in more ways than just killing the frontrunner."

"Don't worry about the NorthBridgers," Vonner said gruffly. "They may think they can dictate the agenda with these kinds of tactics, but in the end, people don't like bullies, and they don't listen to them. Thorne needs to learn that, but it doesn't matter; you'll be one of the few voices of reason, and one good thing is the NorthBridgers are making sure everyone is paying attention."

Hudson looked back at the screen. The former Fed building had been reduced to rubble, part of it still burning. *Why Kansas City?* he wondered. *And why can't they track these NorthBridgers down?* He was about to ask if Vonner had a theory, when Melissa whispered, "Tell him about Fonda Raton."

Vonner listened silently while Hudson recounted the incident with the journalist, then in a stern, grandfatherly voice delivered a lecture about getting off-message. "Hear me on this, Hudson. You will be the next president only if you let us manage. I chose you because I believe you have all the right ingredients, but *we* have the recipe. Understand?"

"Don't talk to Fonda Raton," Hudson answered.

"There are very few places our influence doesn't reach with the media, but Fonda Raton is one of those dark corners. So, yes, please stick to the script. In the meantime, we'll have to see if we can clean up whatever mess she makes of your little talk."

"Sorry. I was tired."

"Don't worry about it. It's early, and now NorthBridge has stolen the headlines again. I think we'll survive. Now remember, this weekend is our first big fundraiser, your debut with the folks who have the real money in the party."

"I know. We'll be there." Melissa was excited about the new gown she'd be wearing. In fact, the campaign had provided an extensive new wardrobe for both of them.

Hudson glanced at the screen as "Newsman" Dan Neuman spoke about resisting the urge to politicize the NorthBridge attacks.

"The Republicans seem to want to make these tragedies into partisan issues," Neuman said from a television studio. "But we all need to remember they are thugs, nothing more."

"Who's he calling 'thugs'?" Melissa asked, laughing. "The NorthBridgers, or the Republicans?"

Hudson didn't answer, because in spite of the attack, the flurry of comments from his competitors, Fonda's ambush, Vonner's lecture, and the upcoming fundraiser, all he could think about was the Wizard.

Chapter Thirteen

The two hundred guests wearing tuxedos and formal gowns had paid $50,000 each to the Super PAC hosting, instantly generating $10 million for the first in a long series of fundraisers. Those in attendance were expected to make additional donations, which would add considerably to the evening's take. Quite a few A-list celebrities mingled with the nation's elite business titans.

The exclusive Venus Resort in Santa Barbara had been carefully selected for the event; fabulous ocean views and a banquet hall, straight out of Gatsby, leading out to a pool and "patio" which could only have been dreamed up in Hollywood. The weather and sunset seemed specially ordered for the evening. Hudson wondered if there were any limits to what Vonner's wealth could arrange.

Melissa was swept away with one of Vonner's people to work one part of the room while Fitz, Coke "cocktail" in hand, guided Hudson to all the right people. As he made his way through the guests, Fitz came and went with practiced ease, always there at just the right time to introduce the candidate to another well-heeled donor. However, it was during one of Fitz's longer absences that a refined African-American gentleman wearing a dark linen suit approached.

"I was on my way out," the man began as he extended his hand to Hudson, "and I thought I should take a moment to speak with the person I paid fifty grand to meet."

"Yes, I'm glad you did," Hudson replied, searching his mind for the identity of the man. He'd seen photos of every guest and had tried to commit as many as possible to memory, and, although he looked familiar, at that moment he couldn't recall his name.

As they shook hands, the man squinted at Hudson and seemed to grasp the candidate's predicament. He smiled. "I was a last-minute addition to the party. Allow me to introduce myself. I'm Booker Lipton."

"I'm sorry, of course you are," Hudson responded. How could he not have recognized the wealthiest man in the world? "Thank you for coming. I can't tell you how much your support means to me."

Booker laughed. "Oh, I'm not supporting you."

"I'm sorry?" Hudson stammered, not understanding.

"I just wanted to stop by and take a look at Vonner's latest entry." Booker stared into Hudson's eyes. "You have no idea, do you?"

"What?"

Just then, a beautiful young woman with a slight Asian appearance walked up. "I've been looking for you," she said to Booker.

Hudson's gaze met hers and he gasped. The woman's eyes were lit up as if starlight had been captured, stored, and projected back at that very moment. Hudson was surprised at his thoughts. There was something about this woman that changed something in him. And her eyes held something else, too; a wisdom which belied her age by decades. Hudson felt certain that in a single look, she knew everything about him. *Everything*.

As he stared in a slow-motion pause, she nodded slightly. He took that almost imperceptible action as an answer to his silent question. She *did* know everything.

Surely, he was just being paranoid. Ever since the Wizard's call, he hadn't been able to stop thinking about that long-ago night and what would happen if Gouge or the Wizard decided to talk. But for now, that was all gone, as he couldn't take his eyes off the woman.

Is she some kind of mind reader? Does she really know the secret? How could she?

Hudson tried to stop staring at her. He'd forgotten about Booker until Fitz returned.

"Booker Lipton, what a nice surprise," Fitz said.

"Yes, you probably thought the guest list had the right quota of black folks already, but I thought one more couldn't hurt," Booker said smiling.

"Oh, come on, Booker, you're welcome anytime."

Hudson suddenly realized the woman had slipped away.

"Fitz, you look good in a tux," Booker said, his tone more sarcastic than charming. "But isn't it a tad warm for wool?"

"It's not wool."

"My mistake. I assumed you always wore wool." Booker offered an obviously phony smile. "Take care of yourself, Hudson. I'm sure when we next meet, you'll be in the White House."

"From your lips to God's ears," Fitz said.

"Oh, Fitz, you know that God has absolutely nothing to do with it," Booker said, smiling for real now.

"Either way," Hudson said, "you've got a pretty good

track record at predicting the future, Mr. Lipton, so I hope you turn out to be right in this case."

"Prediction?" Booker asked rhetorically. "In order for it to be a prediction, there has to be a chance it might not happen."

"Where did your companion go?" Hudson asked, ignoring Booker's "double-talk."

"You mean Linh? Oh, she's probably gone looking for fresh air. She's allergic to wool." He smiled at Fitz again. "Remember, Hudson, people who want to change the world usually end up getting changed by the world instead." Booker turned and walked away. Hudson lost sight of him in the crowd as he continued searching for the woman named Linh.

"Do you know the woman he was with?" Hudson asked Fitz. "He said her name was Linh."

"No, I'm afraid that's one person I don't know." He laughed. "So that must mean she isn't very important."

But Hudson thought she might actually be *very* important. He felt a little like the prince in Cinderella. Not because he wanted a princess, but rather because he thought she knew his secret, and that she might also have one of her own. One that he *needed* to know.

Chapter Fourteen

Back on the campaign trail in Iowa, Hudson tried to forget about the Wizard and Gouge, the NorthBridgers, and Linh, the woman with the magical eyes. His request to Fitz for help in locating Linh was met with a sharp rebuke.

"Look, we don't need another Gary Hart, or Bill Clinton," Fitz said, slamming down his soda. "Damn it, man, just because you look like a Kennedy doesn't mean you have to act like one."

"It's nothing like that," Hudson shot back. "I just need to talk with her."

Fitz rolled his eyes. "Talk to Melissa."

A staffer burst in. "Brickman just proposed a special task force to go after NorthBridge."

"Damn!" Fitz shouted. "Great idea. We should have been on that first." Brickman, the former governor of Pennsylvania, also a Republican candidate for president, had been rising steadily in the polls and threatened to take the late Senator Uncer's place as the front runner. "Put out a statement that denounces Brickman for second-guessing the brave men and women of the FBI, and push again that the governor is trying to get to the top by standing on the bodies of the victims of terrorists."

The staffer glanced at Hudson. The candidate nodded his approval, happy that *some* saw him as the one in charge.

In the hotel lobby, Hudson and his entourage collided with Democratic hopeful, tech billionaire Tim Zerkel. A reporter caught the two close enough and shouted for the two men to shake hands. Several photographers caught the moment which, an hour later, was the banner on the leading political website with the headline: "A Preview of the General Election?" The piece was mostly click-bait, since both were still considered long shots, but it was the first time anyone in the media mentioned Hudson with a serious chance at getting the Republican nomination.

Fonda Raton still hadn't run anything on Hudson. It had been ten days since their meeting. Hudson wondered if Vonner had found a way to get to her after all. Or, maybe, as Melissa suggested, "The barracuda is just waiting until she has enough to bury you." The Raton Report was anything but a fluff factory, and the stories that Fonda wrote herself were always irrefutable and packed full of verifiable facts. Whenever Hudson dwelled on it, he felt instantly sick, thinking about her finding Gouge or the Wizard.

The next two months were a blur of fundraisers, stump speeches, minor endorsements, sound bites, and events that kept the Star-Spangled Banner ringing in his ears. There were also no less than five trips to New Hampshire, six more to Iowa, and two to South Carolina, plus stops in several other early primary states. He'd quickly grown accustomed to Vonner's private planes and luxury hotels, and wondered if every campaign had it so good. Even though there were regular fundraisers, he never worried about money. The Super PAC brought in cash faster than they could spend it.

"Don't worry," Fitz said. "We'll need all of it, and more, for the general."

"Everyone seems so sure that I'm going to be the nominee," Hudson told Melissa on one of the rare nights they spent together, since she was doing her share of campaigning across other states, having referred all her clients to other consultants.

"Aren't you?"

"Not yet," Hudson admitted.

"Well, Schueller sure is," Melissa said. "I had lunch with him today."

"I thought you were in Pennsylvania earlier."

"I was. He's got a gig in Erie."

"How is he?"

"Still convinced you're being manipulated by Vonner."

"On many days, I could agree with him."

"I know, but you're still making the decisions. It's like you're the quarterback and Vonner's the head coach."

"And you?"

"The cheerleader!" she shouted triumphantly.

Hudson's cell phone played "Bang the Drum All Day," by Todd Rundgren. They both knew the ringtone meant Fitz.

"Listen, Hudson," the campaign manager said. "There's been a threat."

"What?" Melissa said before Hudson could get it out.

"The FBI is trying to run it down, but someone claiming to represent NorthBridge said they're going to kill you in the next three days."

"Good God!" Hudson exclaimed.

"No, listen," Fitz said. "We don't know if this is really NorthBridge, or just some quack."

"As if NorthBridge aren't quacks," Hudson said.

"Well, either way . . . " Melissa began, "this is terrifying."

"You're getting Secret Service protection, you and Brickman," Fitz said. "It seems the former governor's continued calls for a special task force to go after NorthBridge has angered them."

"When is the Secret Service coming?" Melissa quickly asked.

"They're on their way," Fitz answered. "And there'll be no way to keep this a secret. The media will see the Secret Service presence and ask why you've gotten protection so early, so we'll just refer to threats and offer no comment beyond that. No specifics, no mention of NorthBridge. Got it?"

"Yeah," Hudson said. "What about my kids?"

"No Secret Service, but Vonner will assign a team to both of them."

"Schueller's going to hate that," Melissa said.

"Too bad," Hudson said. "Risking my life is one thing, but my children must be kept safe. Fitz, I'll call you back. I need to talk to the kids right away."

His son took the news better than he expected, and agreed to the security detail. Florence thought her dad should drop out, but knew he wouldn't. Hudson always said he learned one thing in the army, and that was never to back down from a fight.

Before he called Fitz back, the Secret Service arrived.

"Mr. Pound," the lead agent said, after presenting his credentials, "we have to get you out of here now. This instant!"

"Why?" Hudson demanded.
"Governor Brickman has just been assassinated."

Chapter Fifteen

Vonner Security, the billionaire's control and protection division, coordinated with the Secret Service, and almost immediately a convoy of four vehicles—two of them black SUVs—was speeding toward the Interstate. Seated next to Melissa in the back seat, Hudson took calls from the FBI, Fitz, and Vonner.

A sniper had caught Governor Brickman leaving a campaign stop in New Hampshire. A single shot ended his life, and not one of the hundreds of people on hand had seen the gunman. In an audacious move, NorthBridge, through a statement signed by AKA Hancock, claimed responsibility almost a full minute *before* the trigger had even been pulled. The terrorists had timed the calls so that the FBI and five media outlets were all notified simultaneously.

The Secret Service's plan to protect Hudson was to keep moving until a better plan could be developed. All appearances for the next three days were cancelled, and in yet another surprising development, two candidates who had only been in the race for five and seven weeks, respectively, dropped out.

"NorthBridge has capabilities far beyond anything we've ever seen before," the FBI director said in a press conference that followed a brief statement from the president. "Today we are announcing something that has been in the works for several weeks; a joint task force led by the FBI, comprising agents and representatives of the National Counterterrorism Center, the National Security Agency, CIA, Secret Service, Homeland Security, Department of Defense, and involved state and local law enforcement. The collaborative operation will be known as the "Brickman Effort."

The Brickman Effort's first official action was to increase security around the remaining presidential candidates. There were not enough Secret Service details to give each of the remaining twelve Republicans and eight Democrats in the race round-the-clock protection, so a patchwork was utilized—private contractors and a pool of military and law enforcement personnel with protective services. The two top-polling candidates from each party got the full Secret Service treatment. Hudson qualified additionally only because of the direct threat.

A few hours later, Hudson, Melissa, and their Secret Service detachment boarded one of Vonner's private jets in Cincinnati. Once at cruising altitude, Hudson asked his wife the unspoken question that had been tearing at him.

"Should I quit?"

To him the idea wasn't only rooted in the threat, Brickman and Uncer's assassinations, and the other two rivals dropping out. He knew a time bomb sat ticking in his past, waiting to destroy his dreams of the future. But Melissa knew only of the current events.

"Are you serious?" She could see that he was, but it surprised her. The man she knew had never been afraid of a fight. The man she believed would become the Commander in Chief was a determined tough guy, undaunted by any challenge, an optimist who believed he could solve any problem. "Is it because of the kids?"

"The kids?"

"Are you afraid to leave Schueller and Florence without a parent? Or are you trying to protect them?"

Hudson certainly carried the terror that the North-Bridgers, or even some other monster, could go after his children, but he believed it unlikely, and he had confidence in Vonner's security people. "No, but I just don't want to be crazy."

"Then don't let the bastards win," Melissa said, squeezing his hand and looking into his eyes. "They threatened you because they're afraid of you. They're afraid because you're different."

"But it doesn't make sense. Have you read their manifesto? I'm the exact type of candidate they want."

"They may share some of your views, but they don't want to use the system to change. They're like drunk, spoiled children with guns. You want a peaceful return to our roots, real American values. They want a revolution, a bloody war, and then what? This isn't 1776. No one will ever be able to put the pieces back together again."

"You're right."

"And don't forget, NorthBridge sees the Super PAC backing you, and probably thinks you're just another typical politician who will say and do anything to get elected, and once in office will morph into the same old leaders we've had for decades. But you're not like that. You're different.

You're the one who's going to fix this whole mess. You're the problem solver!"

His phone started playing "Bang On the Drum All Day."

"I guess Fitz can reach me anywhere," he said, looking out the window as the jet soared above a storm. He answered on speaker.

"You hanging in there, Hudson?" Fitz asked.

"I'm alive."

"Glad to hear it. Listen, we released that statement condemning the attacks and offering condolences to Brickman's family, blah, blah, blah, and we've been flooded with media requests. *'Were specific threats made against Hudson Pound? Is Mr. Pound in hiding? Is Pound staying in the race?'* Even a few *'Is Pound alive?'* You've just answered that one, but I think we're going to need to do a presser."

"But I'm in hiding," Hudson said.

"Right, right, but no one needs to know that. Still, the Secret Service prefers you don't go in front of cameras at your final destination. Better no one knows where you'll be for a few days. So, we're going to have you land in Vegas. Some military convention is going on there, so enough reporters can be brought in for a quick Q&A right at the airport. You up for it?"

Hudson looked questioningly at Melissa. She shrugged.

"Do I have a choice?" he asked Fitz.

"This is a good day to look courageous and hit back at NorthBridge," Fitz said. "Even before Brickman, safety had blown past the economy as the number one issue voters care about. Safety and security even beat jobs."

"Fine."

"They're almost done with your speech. I'll zip it over as

soon as it's ready, and Hudson, this one's important. Please stick to the prepared remarks."

The next time his phone rang, the music "If I Had a Hammer" signaled that his sister, Trixie, was calling from one of the hardware stores. She wanted to make sure he was okay. "It's a five-Pound day," she said.

"Really?" Hudson said, knowing the expression had been used by their mother whenever she talked to all five of her adult children, and it meant Trixie had enjoyed the somewhat rare experience of speaking to all four siblings in a single day. Hudson had had a five-Pound day when he'd announced he was running for president. Prior to that, he'd only had two in the past seven years—one when his father died, the other when they lost their mother. The Pounds cared about each other, but just weren't a very close family. "What about?"

"You, of course. Everyone thinks you might be North-Bridge's next victim."

"Did you reassure them?"

"I did my best, but I'm a bit frazzled myself. There've been hundreds of calls, and so many people have come in wanting news. A lot of them did end up buying stuff, so you'll notice quite a sales increase on the weekly report."

"At last, some good news."

"I just emailed you a list of the calls you might want to know about, but in case you don't get to look at it until next month, there's one in particular you'll probably want to return."

Hudson knew before she said his name.

"Tommy Gouge. And did you know he's out of prison?"

Chapter Sixteen

Hudson found a private seat at the back of the plane, put in earbuds, and punched the information into his computer. Gouge had specifically requested a video-call. Hudson couldn't wait anymore. It had been eating at him. He wanted to know how Gouge was going to play it. As always, Hudson liked to have all the pieces before he could solve the problem—and Gouge *was* a problem.

"How you doing, Dawg?" Gouge said, smiling. "I wasn't sure you'd call back."

"Why'd you insist on Skype?" Hudson asked, perhaps a little too formally.

"I wanted to look into your eyes," Gouge said, his expression turning serious.

Hudson looked up the aisle to see if anyone could hear him. Gouge looked the same as when he last saw him twenty-five years earlier—except for the gray hair, the etched and hardened face, and the stockier, more muscular build. But underneath all the age and batterings of a hard-drinking, tough-fighting life—a substantial part of it spent behind bars—Hudson could see the familiar guy he'd grown up with. Gouge could still light a room with his smile, still had the mischievous look in his dark eyes that gave the impression he knew things others did not, and although that old piercing stare seemed a bit more vacant, it could still inspire followers with a passionate plea for action.

"So Daaaaawg," Gouge began, "how in the world did you get here?"

"Beats me. It's a long way from Tampers Land," Hudson said, referring to the old dirt drive that led into the endless woods of their childhood.

"Yeah, I've spent as much time in those woods in my mind as we did when we were kids. Prison is only prison if you *live* behind those walls," Gouge said, his voice rising with some secret and a trace of excitement. "But *I* never did. My mind explored and wandered the world. Did you ever read Jack London's *Star Rover*? Pretty wild book. The Wizard gave it to me the first time I got locked up."

"No," Hudson said, "I'm not familiar with it. And, Gouge, I'm sorry I never visited you back then. You know I had two young kids. I just couldn't seem to . . . "

"Back then? Dawg, you never visited me once. I've spent fifteen of the last twenty-five years inside, and you *never* came. Not. One. Single. Time."

"I know."

"We were more than friends, Dawg. We were brothers, and the tire shop gang. Don't Tread on Me."

"I know," Hudson said again, thinking back to the tire shop, all the good times and then that awful time.

"You ever think about it?" Gouge asked.

"I try not to."

"But you're thinking about it now, aren't you? And Rochelle, do you think about her?"

Hudson nodded.

"Rochelle didn't deserve none of what she got, and all these years later we ain't ever fixed that nightmare."

"We were *kids*," Hudson protested.

"We ain't kids now. Neither is Rochelle. And damn, look at this. Now you're gonna be President of the United States."

"I have to win first."

"Oh, you're gonna win. The Wizard said it's a sure thing. I hear you have Arlin Vonner backing you. *Arlin Vonner*. How did *that* happen?"

"I really don't know myself."

Gouge laughed. "Did you hear what you just said? Well, I know you, Dawg. I damn sure know you. Nothing can take what I know; not twenty-five years, not Arlin Vonner, not nothing."

"Have you talked to Vonner?" Hudson asked, suddenly panicked.

"He'll buy the thing for you."

"Have you *talked* to him?" Hudson repeated.

Gouge laughed again. "Damn, relax, Dawg. I ain't talked to your sugar daddy, but maybe I should. Maybe he'll pay me something on his way to buying the election for you."

"Incredible. Am I the last guy left who believes that you can't buy the presidency?"

Gouge looked at his old friend as if he'd just said something funny. "Yeah, and Elvis is running a restaurant in Akron."

"Anyway, there's a lot of votes still to be cast."

"Sure," Gouge said, shooting him a stare, this one saying I'll play along. "But are you gonna make things right?"

"What do you mean?"

"Rochelle."

"What can I do?"

"You'll be president. You can do a lot."

"I hadn't thought about it. Like I said, I have to *win* first."

"Haven't thought about it? Shoot, you're a piece of work, Dawg. What happened to you? I *never* stop thinking about it, and Rochelle. How can you let that go? Maybe it's 'cause I had so much time to think. Maybe it's that I got what she got. But I'll tell you this, if the truth ever got out, you can bet that even all Vonner's money couldn't put you in the White House."

"How would they find out?" Hudson asked slowly. "Only you, me, and the Wizard know."

"Old secrets have a way of eroding what holds them," Gouge said, eyeing Hudson intently. "And when they do leak out, it's messier than if they'd just been told in the first place."

"Is that supposed to be a threat? Gouge, are you *threatening* me?"

"I'm just telling you the truth," Gouge said, clenching his right fist and slow-motion pushing it in front of the computer's camera like a punch. Hudson saw for the first time the tattooed gothic letters, one on each finger and thumb: T R U T H.

Gouge, after seeing the recognition in his eyes, nodded. "Truth shall set me free."

Chapter Seventeen

Hudson still hadn't shaken the call with Gouge when he walked to the podium in the small airport hospitality room, already jammed with a dozen journalists and even more police and security agents. Everyone had been searched, cleared, and rechecked.

Scanning the unfamiliar faces, he spotted a woman he knew sitting in the back row. He sucked in a breath as he made eye contact with Fonda Raton. She smiled at the recognition; not the friendly kind he so desperately needed, rather the know-you-didn't-expect-to-see-me kind of self-satisfied smirk that screamed "You're in trouble now!" Instinctively, Hudson looked around for Fitz, but then recalled he was on his own.

How the hell did she get here? It's an unscheduled press conference. Did she just happen to be in Vegas? Coincidence? That's a mighty big one. Damn it, damn it!

Several members of the media noticed her at the same time, puzzled expressions on their faces. This wasn't Fonda's thing. She didn't show up to events like this, she sent somebody. The reporters, like sharks, smelled blood. Hudson felt the tension in the room ratchet up as if an electrical current had moved across the floor.

"No time to panic," Hudson told himself, taking a deep breath. He banished all thoughts of Gouge as he calmly began his prepared remarks, hitting a sympathetic tone when speaking of Brickman's family and successfully switching to a tougher we're-coming-for-you edge when calling for swift action to stop NorthBridge. He even pulled off criticizing the current administration for being unable to prevent the terrorist attacks, while at the same time thanking the president for ordering the Secret Service protection, which he now appreciated.

It went well. Picture-perfect, in fact. He hadn't strayed, and he knew Fitz was watching somewhere with an approving smile on his face.

"Thank you," he said, turning toward the exit fifteen feet away.

Someone shouted a question. A staff member responded with the standard, "Mr. Pound will not be taking any questions at this time."

Then, with only eight feet to the door, he heard Fonda's voice above all the others. "Isn't it time you came clean about your relationship with billionaires Arlin Vonner and Booker Lipton? You're running as a so-called average joe, and yet how many average Joes are close friends with billionaires?"

Hudson took two more steps.

"Mr. Pound, both men, two of your largest donors, are currently under federal investigation," Fonda continued. "Can you explain your connection to Titan Capital & Trust Bank?"

He took another step, but it was too late. The room had

erupted in follow-up questions as the others tried to compete with another Raton Report scoop.

Hudson had only seconds to make a decision that could easily destroy his chances at getting to the White House. He knew Vonner and Fitz were watching, probably screaming at their televisions, telling him to take those final few steps, telling him to *run*!

"Ms. Raton," he said, stopping midstride and turning back toward the vultures, deciding this was not the time to look like a coward. "I'll be happy to set the record straight," he said, speaking without a mic above the din. The room quickly fell silent. "I have met Booker Lipton exactly once. Our 'relationship' lasted for approximately five minutes. This occurred at a large fundraiser in California. As far as I know, that evening was the only time he gave anything to my campaign since it was a per-plate event. However, Mr. Lipton stated, unequivocally, that he would not be voting for me."

Fonda laughed. "Perfect. And can you explain Vonner away as easily?"

"I'm not interested in explaining him away. Arlin Vonner is more than a great businessman, he's a great American, and I'm proud to say he has said he *will* be voting for me."

"I'm sure he will," Fonda said. "But did you know he's under investigation by the Department of Justice?"

"I am not aware of that."

"Well, I'm happy to enlighten you. It seems the government is alleging that your friend, Mr. Vonner, 'the great American,' has illegally packaged mortgage-backed securities and other derivatives."

"Ah. I'm going to take a guess here that whatever 'investigation' you're referring to is actually involving the bank holding company Stronet, and not Arlin Vonner personally."

"Yes, that's correct, but it's no secret that Stronet is controlled by Vonner."

"That may or may not be so, but I believe that, worldwide, Stronet employs more than 180,000 people."

"Are you denying any wrongdoing by Vonner?"

"That is not for me to say. I suggest you ask Vonner. But I stand by the man that I know. Now, I have a plane waiting."

"You didn't speak to Titan Bank."

"I've banked with them for years. They're my local bank back in Ohio. Titan Bank has been instrumental in the growth of my hardware stores. I'm grateful for my relationship with a great community bank."

"And who owns Titan, Mr. Pound?"

"Shareholders."

"Would it surprise you to know Arlin Vonner is the bank's largest shareholder?"

"Not if you say so." But it did surprise him.

"Of course, it's done through a series of shell corporations, and may or may not be legal."

"I'm curious, Ms. Raton. You seem to be making a lot of legal claims here today. Are you a lawyer, because—"

"Yes, Mr. Pound, I *am* an attorney."

Her answer caught him off-guard, but he recovered quickly. "Excellent. Then I'll look forward to your opinion being issued. I'm sure you'll let us know when you complete your investigation." He took the final steps. "Thank you everyone."

Hudson slipped out the door, his communicator already buzzing.

Chapter Eighteen

Vonner praised Hudson for not backing down with Fonda. The billionaire also assured the candidate that although Stronet might have crossed a few technical lines—still to be determined—it was nothing that all the other big banks had not also done.

"A billion-dollar fine is the worst-case scenario, nothing to worry about," Vonner said, as if talking about a ten-dollar parking ticket. "As for me, personally, I've done nothing wrong, and my attorneys are already drafting a letter to Fonda Raton warning her to tread lightly if she doesn't want to get bombarded with libel, slander, and defamation suits."

Even before he got off with Vonner, "Bang On the Drum All Day" began playing on Hudson's cell phone. He ignored the first two calls from Fitz, but once he was back in the air, he took the third.

"You should have left the room," Fitz whined. "Never mind how it looked, we had a stellar excuse! You were under threat, and you went down to assure the press how brave you were, and instead you get ambushed by that low-life Raton witch. You should have left the damned room," he repeated.

"Vonner thinks I handled it well."

"I don't care what Vonner thinks. *I'm* the one who has to get you elected. We were on the high ground, and engaging with Raton like that took us right back into the mud. Thorne is already questioning your all-American image, saying you're nothing more than another politician owned by Wall Street."

"Thorne is a nutcase."

"A nutcase with twenty-seven million listeners and a growing base of supporters who love his candor. He's the second coming of Trump."

"I think Fonda appreciates straight answers instead of 'duck and run,' and that she'll treat me more fairly because I faced her."

"Oh, do you?" Fitz snorted. "Well, why don't you take a visit to her website right now?"

Melissa, sitting next to Hudson, already online reading more details about the Brickman killing, clicked on a hot button and was instantly at the Raton Report.

"Damn that woman," Melissa said. "Listen to this: 'Hudson Pound today denied any wrongdoing by Stronet Banking Chairman, Arlin Vonner, and claimed he'd only met Booker Lipton once, although the reclusive billionaire, and the world's wealthiest man, paid $50,000 to attend a fundraiser with Candidate Pound.'" Melissa pointed to a photo showing Hudson and Booker standing next to each other and smiling. "It goes on to question your readiness to be president." Melissa scanned the article. "Although she gives you high marks for your time in the military and innovations in public education, she concludes that those are not enough qualifications, and even though the idea of an average American as president is quaint, it isn't very realistic."

"It's a hatchet job," Fitz, still on speakerphone, said.

"How did she get this up so fast?" Hudson asked. "I talked to her forty-five minutes ago."

"Raton obviously had it all ready to go after your first ill-advised meeting with her, and she just inserted your quotes from the airport," Fitz said. "Clearly this woman doesn't like you, and that's going to make my job tougher. She's not just an ordinary reporter."

"I know," Hudson said, frustrated.

"This is just the beginning. She wants to cook you, and every day she'll turn up the heat a little more. I've seen her do it a million times."

Melissa put her hand on his and mouthed, *Don't worry*.

Hudson nodded at her and tried to smile. "How do we change Fonda's mind?" he asked Fitz.

"You don't. All you can do is convince everyone else. If you're perfect, she can't hurt you too much."

"Oh, good. Then I'll just be perfect from now on," Hudson said sarcastically.

"That's the plan, and the way you get there is by doing everything I tell you to do," Fitz said. "I'm the best there is, Hudson. We can win this."

Melissa rolled her eyes. Hudson smiled.

"All right, I'll see you at debate prep."

"Stay safe," Fitz said. "You've got bigger things to worry about than hostile journalists."

As the call ended, Hudson thought again about Uncer and Brickman.

"He's right," Melissa said. "This won't be the last, and

press attacks are a lot easier to recover from than the kind with bombs and bullets."

"Sticks and stones," Hudson agreed solemnly.

By the time they arrived at Sun Wave, Vonner's Carmel estate, Hudson and Melissa were exhausted. The billionaire was attending a late meeting and did not greet them; they only cared about sleep.

The following morning, the newlyweds ate breakfast on a cliffside patio overlooking the ocean. They then joined Vonner in his "command room," a very large office which accommodated a staff of four. Giant monitor-wrapped walls brought in live news and data from around the globe. It felt like being inside electronic superstores. The media churned with details of NorthBridge and Brickman. However, the big story belonged to Fonda Raton—the Raton Report had broken another one.

It seemed that a company with strong ties to Booker Lipton's organization—and possibly indirectly owned by Booker—had manufactured the top-secret military grade explosive used on the Kansas City Federal Reserve building.

"This stuff, known as 'Gruell-75,' is extremely expensive, and only made by one company," the commentator declared. "That company, SkyNok, a stealthy defense contractor based in Nevada, has a murky ownership trail which appears ultimately to end with Lipton."

Images showed the Nevada plant and photos of Booker, including the recent shot of him with Hudson at the fundraiser.

"Now I guess we know why Fonda happened to be in Nevada," Melissa said.

The commentator continued: "This is not the first time that the often-radical billionaire has been linked with terrorism. Several years ago, Booker Lipton faced allegations that he'd funded Inner Force, an extremist offshoot of the allegedly peaceful Inner Movement, a controversial organization attempting to bring about change by raising consciousness and embracing one's soul."

A photo of the woman Hudson had met with Booker at the fundraiser flashed on the screen. Hudson let out a quick gasp.

She's the leader of the Inner Movement . . . whatever that is.

The commentator wrapped up coverage by citing yesterday's Raton Report tying Hudson to Lipton. "The Pound campaign declined to comment for this story."

On another screen, a roundtable of political talking heads discussed the implications of NorthBridge on the presidential campaign and what repercussions the Booker Lipton revelations would have on Pound's chances.

"You need to distance yourself from Booker immediately," Vonner said.

"Distance? I'm not even remotely *close* to him. What I told Fonda is true."

"Guilt by association," Vonner said. "You need to condemn him, call for congressional investigation into his secretive businesses. And we need to release a plan for how you would stop NorthBridge."

"The election is more than a year away. Don't you think any plan would be premature?"

"It doesn't matter. It sure looks like NorthBridge isn't going anywhere, and imagine if the accusations that they're backed by the world's richest man are true. We really could be in for a second American revolution."

Chapter Nineteen

Within a few days of the Brickman assassination, NorthBridge released documents showing that both Senator Uncer and Governor Brickman had been in the pockets of the big banks, Wall Street, and large multinational corporations. The terror organization not only had emails and recorded phone conversations proving their allegations, but they had developed a sophisticated algorithm which, after analyzing voting records, proposals, and speeches of the dead men, clearly showed their bias and corruption. Like most of the other materials NorthBridge had linked, this material was signed by AKA Franklin.

"What the hell?" Vonner ranted as he paced in front of the windows of the Pacific room. "Do these maggots have an NSA key? Where are they getting all this?"

Fitz, who had flown out for the debate prep, looked up from his laptop. "I'd like to get my hands on the algorithm they're using. It might help us in the campaign."

"I thought you said I didn't need any help," Hudson said, sitting across from his campaign manager.

"He killed it," Melissa said, entering the room.

"Please, honey, don't use the word 'killed' in this campaign," Hudson said, only half joking. "It could get us all indicted as co-conspirators with NorthBridge."

"I just wanted to remind Fitz that everyone agreed you had the best performance in a mock-debate anyone could remember. You're a natural."

"Plus, I'm super smart," Hudson said, smiling.

"And he looks like a damned movie star," Fitz added, laughing.

"Yes, he does," Melissa said, dropping on the sofa next to her husband, swinging her legs over his lap, and giving him a long kiss.

The whole campaign staff had been giddy with Hudson's debate abilities and command of topics. His knowledge of world events, rooted in his love of history, coupled with his comfort and confidence on stage made for a can't-lose combination. The excitement had been tempered by the need to completely realign the campaign, create strict security protocols, and change schedules. The threat from NorthBridge meant that everyone running for office from now on would have to campaign differently. There'd be no more walking around the Iowa State Fair or dropping by a New Hampshire diner. The new reality in American politics meant bulletproof stage shields, TSA-style searches for attendees, and substantially less personal interaction between candidate and voter.

Not a single NorthBridge operative had been caught. It was as if the government was chasing ghosts. The members used aliases based on historic figures to sign the statements regularly sent to media outlets. Their "also known as" names offended Hudson and his reverence for the Founding Fathers. So far, they'd used AKA Jefferson, Adams, Washington, Hancock, Franklin, Paine, and there was even an AKA Ross, presumably a woman taking her moniker from Betsy Ross. The organization's imagery evoked the spirit of '76 and historically patriotic themes from the days of the American War of Independence such as the Liberty Bell, the Declaration of Independence, the Yankee Doodle drum and fife painting, and Patrick Henry's "Give me liberty or give me death." Hudson also was appalled by NorthBridge's use of the "Don't Tread On Me" flag, the very same one adopted by the Wizard, Gouge, and Hudson for their teenage tire shop gang.

Making matters worse was the fact that a not insignificant portion of the population seemed to be sympathetic, and even *agreed* with NorthBridge on the drastic need for change. For the first time since the American Civil War, the country faced the real threat of being ripped apart by a violent revolution. Thorne fanned that sentiment on his daily radio show. Without actually condoning the violence, he highlighted the crimes and corruption of lawmakers in recent decades and made salacious allegations against many currently in power. The government denied the validity of NorthBridge's claims against Uncer and Brickman, instead calling the charges terrorist propaganda. But unlike many of Thorne's unprovable accusations, NorthBridge provided proof.

Proof that the media mostly ignored.

Hudson issued several statements denouncing Thorne, called for an immediate special investigation of Booker Lipton, and demanded increased funding for the Brickman Effort and law enforcement in general, but he was still just a candidate. Most of his opponents from both parties had positions in government and were actually able to introduce bills, or, at the very least, produce symbolic results.

"We've got to get him back out there," Fitz said to Vonner as if Hudson wasn't in the room.

"No question about it. Your face needs to be all over the news," Vonner said, turning to Hudson.

"Like Uncer and Brickman's faces?" Melissa asked, never missing a beat, especially someone else's beat.

"He's right, honey. Everyone else is laying low. I need to show them I'm not scared."

"Obviously, there's some risk," Vonner cautioned.

"I'm not afraid of risk," Hudson said.

"Geez, it's not like he'll be out there naked," Fitz said. "We've got the Secret Service and the best private security force money can buy."

"Second only to Booker's," Vonner corrected, as if the fact bothered him greatly.

"Whatever," Fitz said. "He'll look brave, but there'll be a hundred people protecting his every move." Fitz turned to Hudson. "Not to mention million-dollar advance work. You'll be fine."

Fine? Hudson thought. *My freedom and privacy are already restricted, but now they'll be eliminated altogether.* Part of the new plan included increasing the size of the press pool who traveled with him, which, combined with the extremely heightened security that would surround his every move, made Hudson feel as if cold, clammy hands were squeezing around his neck.

He had to face more than just NorthBridge. Only a small envelope of time remained to try to bury his past for good, but it would require a far greater risk than going back out onto the trail. Hudson had to confront the terror and guilt of that night twenty-nine years earlier, and the consequences of what came after.

Chapter Twenty

Melissa flew back to the Midwest to continue efforts for winning endorsements from key political figures. Fitz had tapped Melissa because of her relationship with many of the region's biggest business leaders. Along the way, she'd pick up Florence and Schueller and they'd all join Hudson on the trail.

Hudson took advantage of his final free afternoon before resuming the campaign to work on keeping the past in the past. During the two-hour drive to San Francisco, he arranged to meet the Wizard in Golden Gate Park. His Secret Service detail was outraged at the idea, but he'd been insistent. Hudson agreed to wear a bulletproof vest and a disguise. It wouldn't fool anyone up close, but a shaggy brown wig, shorts, and a t-shirt, along with a beat-up pair of running shoes, did not scream presidential candidate, or even anyone important. Only because Vonner and Fitz had also left for New York and Washington, respectively, was he able to, at least temporarily, keep his trip a secret.

Four agents in casual attire canvassed the area. Hudson

found his old friend waiting atop the antique Drum Bridge in the Japanese Tea Garden.

"Nice wig, Dawg," the Wizard said, amused. "None of us are really who we are, are we?"

"Dangerous times to be running for president," Hudson replied.

"Yeah, the key word is 'running.' Man, I'd hug you, but I'm afraid one of your ear-piece-adorned attack dogs would shoot me."

Hudson extended his hand. "This is probably safer."

The Wizard's long black hair, blue jeans, white linen shirt, and leather sandals added to Hudson's camouflage. No respectable presidential candidate would meet an old hippie like this in Golden Gate Park.

The Wizard shook his hand warmly. "So, Dawg, you've come a long way, risked your life." He motioned to the nervous Secret Service agents. "What's so important?"

"You know what."

"Rochelle?"

"Of course, Rochelle."

"So, are you going to help her? Finally correct our tragic mistake?"

"That's what Gouge asked," Hudson said, looking down at the water's reflection of them on the bridge. The high, arching design made a complete circle in the still water below. "I can't help her."

"Not yet, maybe, but once you're the president, you can fix it, Dawg. And you *gotta* fix it."

"It's not that simple."

"Nothing about that night is simple, but we screwed up." He turned and stared into Hudson's sunglasses. "We're *all* at fault for what happened; each of us owns a piece of the endless chain of damage. You know a lot of lives got twisted up. It's time to fix it."

Hudson took off his glasses, his eyes tearing. "Damn it, Wizard, I can't undo all that! The past is over."

"Yeah? Is that why you came, to make sure I wasn't going to talk, to make sure your secret's safe? There's a dark place in the president's past—"

"I'm not the president yet."

"That's right, *yet*. But that's only because the election hasn't happened *yet*." The Wizard slapped the smooth wooden railing of the bridge and the closest Secret Service agent flinched.

"Why is everyone but me so sure I'm going to win?"

"Because you're a history teacher. You believe it happens like in the history books, but it doesn't. It never did. Who do you think writes those history books you love so much?"

"There is something that could prevent my victory." His gaze held the Wizard's eyes.

The Wizard shook his head. "Damn, Dawg. And I thought you might have come to ask me to help you figure out how to do it."

"Do what?"

"Make it right."

"Come on, there's no way to make it right," Hudson hissed, then, through gritted teeth, added, "Two people are dead, and nothing we do can bring them back to life."

"Two people have died in the presidential race, too. Don't you find that ironic? Do you believe in karma?"

"There's no connection."

"*Everything* is connected," the Wizard said. "People forget that, but cause and effect plays us every moment. It's all like this enormous, complex web inside a maze with moving corridors and reversing gravity . . . know what I mean?"

Hudson's phone chimed "Bang On the Drum All Day."

"Rundgren," the Wizard said, recognizing the ringtone and nodding his head approvingly.

Hudson ignored the call from his campaign manager.

"Look, I can't do anything to help her unless I get into office, and I'll never get there if you or Gouge go public."

"Oh, man, when did you become such an idiot?" the Wizard asked. "I always thought it was Gouge who took the worst of what happened that night, and I know it seriously screwed *me* up, but I kinda believed you were okay, that you somehow shook it off."

"No," Hudson replied mournfully. "No, I didn't. How do you ever let something like that go?"

"You don't, but you swallowed it, dude. You let it eat you from the inside." The Wizard looked at Hudson as if trying to see back through the decades to the person he knew. "I can't speak for Gouge, but don't you realize you're still my best friend? Man, our bond, even before that night . . . that's part of our DNA. We came from that, you know?"

"I know," Hudson said, suddenly more relieved that his old friend was still there than the realization that he wasn't going to go public. Without thought, he turned and hugged the Wizard. "I'm sorry, man. I'm so *damned* sorry."

"That's all we are," the Wizard said, slowly pulling out of the embrace. "It's time we're more than that."

Hudson nodded. "It's a lot."

"Yeah. And you need to talk to Gouge."

"I have."

"I mean in person."

"That might not be so easy. NorthBridge has made moving around difficult." Just then, the Communicator buzzed. Hudson muted it and shoved it back in his pocket, glancing at the Secret Service agents. One of them was speaking into his wrist. "I'm going to need to head out."

"Listen, Dawg, you need to imagine . . . imagine reality *isn't* what you think it is. Gouge and I are the least of your worries. Even NorthBridge isn't your biggest problem," the Wizard whispered. "It's Vonner and his people that you need to fear."

"Vonner and 'his people' are the ones giving me the chance to get to the White House."

The Wizard stared at Hudson for a long moment. "That's true, Dawg, but just remember who you're playing with, and where *you* came from."

Fitz rang again, and Hudson ignored it. Even before "Bang on the Drum" ended, he felt the vibration of the communicator. "I really got to go."

"One last thing," the Wizard began. "Why do you think I wanted to meet here?"

"I don't know. Because you live in a storage shed?"

The Wizard smiled. "I thought you'd think that, but I don't care about you seeing my pad. We go too far back for that. We needed to do it here because I don't want *them* to see it, to know where I live. These spooks have no doubt already ID'd me with facial recognition software and are running down everything they can find on me, but they're in for a surprise. There is *nothing* to find. I've erased myself from the grid. I mean *all the way*. The kid you grew up with is long dead. I don't exist. I'm gone."

"You're a freak, Wizard," Hudson said with only a partial smile, slipping a hundred-dollar bill into his hand. "A paranoid freak."

"One day, when all else fails, my paranoia will save you."

Chapter Twenty-One

Back in the SUV, the communicator and phone were both still going off. Hudson decided to take the biggest hit first and opened the connection to Vonner.

"Walking around Golden Gate Park? What were you thinking!?" Vonner blasted.

"I needed some time to myself."

"Do you *want* to die?"

"No one knows I'm here."

"Really? Hasn't NorthBridge proven they know everything? They can find *everyone*. Do I need to remind you that it's NorthBridge no one can find?"

"Well, congratulations to me, I survived a walk in the park."

"Who did you meet?"

"It was a personal thing."

"Personal?" Vonner scoffed. "You don't *have* personal anymore!"

"Apparently not."

"Hudson, you knew damned well what you signed up for."

"I guess so."

"Tell me then, do I have anything to worry about?"

"No."

"Good. Back on the trail in the morning, debates, Iowa—one, two, three. We're just getting started."

After he finished with Vonner, Hudson directed the driver to an address on Mission Street and then took a call from Fitz.

"You had us scared," the campaign manager began. "How about letting me know when you're going AWOL so I can get ready for the media circus after NorthBridge kills you."

Hudson took the lecture that followed good-naturedly, then reviewed the plan for the coming days, including the first Republican debate. Afterwards, he checked in with Melissa, and by the time that call ended, the driver told him they'd arrived at the destination.

Hudson, who had ditched his wig and changed into jeans, stepped out onto the street and briskly entered the building. Two agents escorted him inside while two others remained out on the sidewalk.

A large curved teakwood reception desk occupied the center of the lobby. Five-inch white letters spelling out "THE INNER MOVEMENT" seemed to float in the air above, the "magic" momentarily distracting him, but then he saw the fishing line that held them. Hudson strode across the polished marble floor. An attractive woman sat typing rapidly into a transparent keyboard, but stopped as he approached.

"Good afternoon, Mr. Pound." She smiled. He guessed

she might be his daughter's age. Her big brown eyes made him feel comfortable. "How may I help?"

Hudson, still not used to being recognized by strangers, felt startled, but he'd received almost nonstop media attention for weeks, and even more since the NorthBridge threat, plus the obvious Secret Service presence. Still, the woman didn't seem the least bit surprised by his presence, almost as though she'd been expecting him.

"I don't have an appointment, but I wonder if it would be possible to see Linh."

The woman eyed him carefully, as if waiting for something more. "I'm not sure she's here today. Please have a seat and I'll see if I can find her." She pointed to a strange array of what looked like stretched sheets of linen off to one side. It turned out that they were hemp. A little sign announced they were also organic, and although the crisscrossing fabrics looked rigid, they contoured nicely to his frame. He found them quite relaxing.

For the next six minutes, he waited, during which time the Secret Service agents seemed to grow increasingly agitated. Finally, she called him back over.

"I'm so sorry to have kept you waiting needlessly, but Linh is not here."

"Okay," he said, disappointed. He took out a card and scribbled his private cell phone number along with the note "Please call" and handed it to her.

She smiled. "I'll see that she gets this."

He thanked her and left.

On the top floor, watching him exit the building on security monitors, Linh closed her eyes and offered a mental wish for Hudson's well-being.

"Are you sure you shouldn't have seen him?" another woman asked. "He's in a very difficult situation. He may not survive until the election."

"I know," Linh said quietly.

"He came here today. He must want our help."

"Yes, he does," Linh said introspectively. She walked to the window, looked down to the busy street far below, and watched his SUV drive away.

"Are you sure there will be another chance?" the woman asked.

"No, I am not," Linh said. "But today . . . this was not the time."

"Then let's hope he makes it to whenever the time is right."

Linh nodded, then picked up a phone and dialed the number of the one person who could help make that happen.

Chapter Twenty-Two

The debate stage at the Ronald Reagan Presidential Library in California had that made-for-TV glow—all red, white, and blue shine. Each of the twelve Republican candidates stood behind a clear lectern. The politicians, stretched in a wide semi-circle, looked the part; modern day gunslingers ready to spew endless promises and double-talk. The two women, including Senator Celia Brown of Illinois, the only African-American in a sea of white, seemed to be doing their best to fit in with their male counterparts—dark suits with scarves to match the men's red or blue ties. All except Thorne, who, wearing black jeans, a dark gray shirt, long black trench coat, and a black leather tie, could have passed for a cowboy.

As the frontrunner, Texas Governor Bill Cash took center stage, flanked by Hudson, Thorne, and Brown.

The audience, crew, and staff had been subjected to vigorous background checks, searches, and scans. Along with the Secret Service, state and local police, the California Governor, himself a candidate for the Democratic nomination, had assigned dozens of National Guard troops to secure the building. In a national sigh of relief, it turned out that all the action was among the candidates.

After the first few questions, the moderator had difficulty maintaining control. The Congressman from Florida made fun of Thorne's attire, who in turn ripped the others for bowing to outdated conventions.

"I prefer to be comfortable. I'm not here to fit some image. The voters need to see who I am and hear my ideas."

It continued like that, bickering back and forth, personal attacks, exceeding time limits. The banter grew particularly heated after it became obvious to everyone that Hudson was running away with the debate. The others stumbled over at least a few questions, or gave answers that were nothing more than fluff or didn't relate to the original question. Hudson's responses, heavy on substance and fact, continuously received loud applause. Several of his opponents were clearly impressed, but not Thorne. He went on the offensive.

"You're supposed to be some kind of 'regular Joe' who's somehow going to save the country from itself," Thorne sneered. "But Pound, you're nothing more than Arlin Vonner's latest lap dog."

"That's ironic coming from somebody who can only reach the voters through a radio show, since your campaign hasn't raised enough money to compete in the larger markets," Hudson responded. "Instead, you incite your listeners and the media with attention-grabbing remarks with no substance."

"Gentleman, please," the moderator said.

"Are they really gentlemen?" General Hightower asked, to light laughter.

"I built my following one listener at a time," Thorne continued, "by covering issues with truth instead of political correctness."

"Like you're covering the NorthBridgers?" Hudson shot back. "You're encouraging the terrorists."

"Gentleman, you must yield," the moderator said, raising his voice.

"NorthBridge may be going about it the wrong way, but they're right on a lot of the issues," Thorne said.

"See, there you go again. You should be brought up on charges for aiding and abetting. "

"What about you, Pound? You keep saying we need to return to the values and systems the Founding Fathers envisioned. That's code for NorthBridge's agenda."

"No. It is not," Hudson snapped.

As Thorne began a tirade of additional accusations about Hudson, Vonner, Booker Lipton, and large banks, the producers interrupted the debate, and both candidates were warned that they would be ejected from the remainder of the event should they ignore the rules again. The moderator managed to rein things in, and several rounds occurred with no major trouble.

Hudson received another raucous ovation when he answered a question about one of his favorite subjects, specifically what role the federal government should play in education.

"Why are the best teachers confined to teaching a relative handful of children each year?" Hudson asked rhetorically. "Why not use technology and have those teachers, who breathe excitement and relevance into subjects, teach more, so that the drive and imagination of students is ignited? The best we have could teach tens of thousands every day. Their lectures and Q&A sessions can be broadcast over the internet around the nation to as many homes as needed. And yes, I said homes."

Fitz, watching with another staff member, cursed and then muttered under his breath, "I guess Hudson doesn't care about the teachers' union endorsement that was all but a lock for us."

"The students would receive the instruction and multimedia presentations at home or at central learning centers, manned by quality counselors," Hudson continued. "And then the next day, they'd go to school where educators would work with them on assignments based on what they'd seen. It will save money, broaden the subjects they will learn, and, most importantly, it will work."

The audience was clapping as he finished. "Just because we've always done something a certain way doesn't mean we should keep doing it. In response to Gandhi's advice about being the change you wish to see in the world, I say this: We *are* the Change!"

Chapter Twenty-Three

Vonner watched the debate from his Washington, DC, hotel suite as if it were an NFL playoff game—his team's quarterback on an unstoppable march to the end zone with a Super Bowl appearance imminent. A knock at the door caused him to check the time. He smiled. As usual, Rex was never late.

"Have you been listening to our boy?" the billionaire asked.

Rex, who looked like a former football player himself, strolled inside, bringing the presence of a bull. "I caught most of it," he said, pulling a digital tablet out and handing it to his boss. The fixer eyed the door to the balcony. He wanted to smoke, even though he'd just finished a cigarette in the car. Instead, he fidgeted with a pair of black dice in his pocket.

"Is this it?" Vonner asked.

The big man nodded, then turned toward the TV. Thorne was blasting Hudson again. Rex wanted to comment, but knew Vonner wouldn't want to be interrupted while he was reading the report.

"This is nothing," Vonner finally said, obviously disgusted.

Rex shrugged, mindlessly moving his thumb as if flicking a lighter. "Should we invent something?"

"Not yet, too risky."

Rex wasn't surprised at his boss's answer. Fonda Raton was not a normal target. She was not only clean, as the report Vonner had just read showed, but she was also very powerful. That alone had never stopped them before. Beyond being a media mogul in her own right, Fonda was also protected. The problem that had befuddled them for weeks was that they didn't know *who* was protecting her. Once upon a time, they would have guessed Booker Lipton, but she'd been on a warpath against him of late.

They couldn't actually verify she was protected, but they knew. Everything about her screamed it. Rex had said, on earlier occasions, that it was as if the woman had been invented out of thin air. They had addresses, known associates, employment history, school records going back to kindergarten, even childhood photos, but it was all "too perfect."

Rex repeated his frustrated claim. "I've never seen anything like it. Something's there."

"Then we've got to find it."

"I've had people watching her house," Rex said. "She's never there."

"She travels a lot."

"No. I mean she is *never* there."

"She has to sleep somewhere."

"With someone," Rex added.

"Don't let up," Vonner ordered. "Put more people on it, but make sure we don't show."

"Right," Rex said. He knew at some point his boss might well order Fonda Raton eliminated altogether, and should that day come, there could be no prior links to Vonner's organization. "What about Thorne?"

"There's an aptly named s.o.b. if I've ever known one," Vonner said, switching to the shock-jock's file on the tablet. "This clod thinks he's going to win the nomination."

"Maybe he did *before* the debate. Hudson's mopping the floor with him."

"With everyone," Vonner corrected.

"Brown is holding her own, and last I checked, Professor Wiseman is giving a nice performance." Rex tinkered with tech gear assembled on a glass table in a corner of the suite. Vonner typically travelled with enough equipment to launch a satellite into orbit.

"The Professor is going nowhere, and Brown is anti-war. Who ever heard of an anti-war Republican getting the Republican nomination?" Vonner said. "Why, that's unpatriotic, that's what it is."

"These are strange times," Rex said, nodding to the tablet. "Thorne's popularity is growing faster than Hudson's."

"Before tonight, maybe."

"Before tonight, *definitely*. And the youth vote may think he won the debate."

"Hudson's kids are going on the trail with him starting tomorrow," Vonner said confidently. "They'll help." He stood, and walked over to several fruit platters on a large dining table, grabbing some grapes. "Want some melon?"

Rex shook his head. "No thanks, you know my stomach can't handle fruit."

"Right," Vonner said. "Not good for your joints, either."

"Don't bring up my knees," Rex said, moving back to the three laptops he'd left earlier. "Even Schueller is going out with them? Do you think that's wise?"

"The kid will fall into line," Vonner said, noticing Rex's limp and thinking it had gotten worse in the past year.

"I'm not so sure about Schueller anymore."

Vonner nodded, suddenly lost in a fog of thought. "If not, then we get to play the sympathy card. The campaign trail can be a dangerous place."

"Especially this year."

Chapter Twenty-Four

Until the final minutes of the debate, Thorne had remained on his best behavior, which meant he pushed the producers to the line several times, but managed to stop just short of crossing it. Then, prior to closing statements, Thorne raged again.

"Just *look* at him, folks." He motioned across to Hudson. "He looks exactly like a presidential candidate is supposed to look. He was *chosen* for the part. The banksters knew the voters wanted a non-career politician, someone we could all identify with, so they groomed this momma's boy and pushed him out here like a big, fluffy piece of cake that we all want to eat. Speaking of which, have you noticed his wife? Even she's picture perfect, another piece of . . . something!"

The producers cut to commercial, and when they came back, Thorne had been removed. After watching the downward spiral of American politics in recent years, Hudson suspected that Thorne's becoming the first candidate ever removed from a presidential debate stage would make him a hero in many circles. No doubt the shock-jock had planned the whole thing.

It didn't matter; Hudson knew he'd won the night. He confidently began his closing remarks. "I've never held political office, and many have called this a liability, but I believe it is an asset. This is how it was meant to be—how it *used* to be—but let me assure you of this." He stared straight into the camera. "I have served my country in other ways. I have seen combat, and I will not allow aggression against our nation to stand, be it foreign or domestic. A Pound administration will act swiftly and resolutely to see that order is maintained."

He had originally intended to end with the line from his stump speech: *I have the audacity to think I can be a good president because I am a student of history. I have studied the great leaders who came before us, and by understanding the past, we can recognize the future. THE FUTURE IS NOW!* But Vonner had specifically requested he come out strong against NorthBridge and foreign terrorists.

"Trouble's brewing in the world," Vonner had told him. "NorthBridge is getting all the attention, but the United States is facing increasingly complex dangers around the globe."

During the many hours of debate prep, Hudson had noticed a heavy emphasis on obscure foreign policy issues which might entangle the country into another war. If he won, he prayed it wouldn't happen on his watch, but Vonner and his advisers repeatedly stressed, "We must be ready for war."

The following morning, Hudson ate breakfast with Melissa and his children in their hotel suite. It was the first time they'd all been together since the family meeting, and the wedding, when he told them he intended to run. The television in the background echoed the near unanimous opinion that Hudson had easily won the debate.

"What's with all the talk of war, Dad?" Schueller asked after a former member of the Joint Chiefs of Staff told a morning show host that he believed a Pound administration would be strong against our enemies.

"To win a war requires more than military supremacy," the Admiral said in an interview. "It takes smarts, a strong sense of history, and a cool head, and Hudson Pound has all three."

Hudson wondered if it was an unsolicited endorsement, or if Fitz had arranged it. Either way, he knew it would help.

"Schueller, there are those who believe NorthBridge is being funded and even directed by rogue states hostile to us. If that's true, then we must be prepared to take action."

"Come on, Dad, it's all part of the ruse. There's always an excuse for war. Bush taking us into Iraq for weapons of mass destruction, oil, or some other business interest of the big corporations."

Hudson's face tensed.

"Careful, Schueller," Florence said. She knew what was coming.

"I suppose my buddies and I wasted our time in Desert Storm?" Hudson said, speaking of the first Persian Gulf War where he had served. "I saw friends die."

"I'm sorry about that, truly," Schueller said in a gentle voice. "But what did they die for?"

"We stopped an incredible act of aggression by a

country that threatened an entire region. If we'd done the same with Nazi Germany in 1939—"

"The corporations got their war."

"Over forty nations joined the coalition against Iraq!" Hudson said defensively.

"The multinational corporations have unlimited influence. *They're* running things now, not representatives elected by the *people*."

Hudson shook his head.

"Dad, I've been researching this stuff, and it's worse than ever. And Vonner is as dirty as the rest of them."

"The rest of who?" Florence asked.

"Schueller, I love you, but you're a twenty-two-year-old college dropout. Your research isn't valid. It's the *internet*. Nothing is real." Hudson looked at his son, wondering how he'd drifted so far. "Half the stories online are lies, and the other half are incomplete, taken out of context, or selectively biased. Fake news, fake history—"

"Just read this stuff, Dad," Schueller said, pulling a worn file folder stuffed with fifty or sixty pages. "I printed it for you, so you could read it without leaving a trail online."

"That was considerate of you," Hudson said sarcastically, taking the folder.

"Promise you'll look at it?" Schueller asked. Suddenly, Hudson saw his little boy, trying to prove he was a big boy. As usual, he softened.

"Okay, okay. I'll take it on the campaign bus. I'm sure it'll be more interesting than the policy papers they're always giving me."

Melissa was about to say something when an image on the television stopped her. "Oh, *no!*" she screamed.

Everyone turned to see live footage of Hudson's house in flames.

Chapter Twenty-Five

Just as he was forcing his brain to accept the fiery images on the screen, Hudson's phone played "Bang on the Drum."

"Did you see!?" Hudson shouted to Fitz as he answered.

"That's why I'm calling," his campaign manager said. "You're not in that inferno, are you?"

"No, we're still in California."

"I know, but I mean you finished moving out of that house and into Melissa's, right?"

"Yeah, but—"

"Apparently, someone didn't like the fact that you won the debate."

Hudson looked at the sad and stunned faces of his children. It was the home they'd shared with their late mother. They'd pleaded with him not to put it on the market, but he couldn't afford to keep it. Now, seeing it destroyed, the pain rekindled the loss of her, twelve years earlier; devastation amplified by a longing for their mother.

"Do we know?" Hudson asked bitterly. "Was this NorthBridge?"

"No claims yet," Fitz said. "But it's gotta be."

"Why are they doing this? What do they gain by . . . this is my family. It's the memories in that place." He looked at his kids again. Florence had tears welling in her eyes. Schueller glared like he wanted to hit somebody.

"They want to rattle you, to terrorize you. I'm sorry, Hudson, but we're gonna find these monsters, and with any luck, you'll be president when they get the death penalty."

Another channel played a clip from Thorne's morning talk show. The shock-jock continued where he left off during the debate, calling the firebombing of Hudson's home justified because, "The candidate is just another lying politician, except worse since Pound has no experience."

"Screw him!" Hudson said.

"Who?" Fitz asked, alarmed.

"Let's go after Thorne with everything!"

"What? Did he say something? What network are you watching?" Once Fitz caught up, he tried to calm Hudson. "You whipped him last night. He's just baiting you. Don't fall for it. This guy is going nowhere. Do *not* talk to the media."

As the day went on, Fitz appeared to be right. The initial CompuPolls showed Hudson had pulled ahead of even Texas Governor Cash by four points, and Thorne had collapsed into tenth place, a full thirty-two points behind Hudson.

However, some pundits speculated that Hudson's bounce was more than a great debate performance, saying there's no denying the candidate was also benefiting from sympathy and publicity generated by the firebombing of his house and the threats from NorthBridge. By the next day, polls showed him even beating the top three Democrats in a head-to-head matchup.

NorthBridge, through AKA Adams, claimed responsibility for the fire, but released no other statement. The FBI added it to their NorthBridge investigation, and the Brickman Effort had agents at the scene within hours. But NorthBridge proved as elusive as ever.

Hudson rode the wave of attention into a heavy schedule of campaigning at one highly secured rally after another. His average crowd had grown to over ten thousand, and several stops drew three times that. In order to take advantage of the momentum and swelling support, he took Florence with him while Melissa and Schueller covered other states.

A reporter asked if he thought it was risky bringing his children on the trail in light of the NorthBridge threat. "I want them where I can best protect them," Hudson shot back, but in truth, he didn't know where they'd be safest.

Hudson had learned on that awful night, twenty-nine years earlier, that no one is safe. And again, in the army, while fighting in Iraq, the lesson was amplified—we are not safe. Finally, when his wife died, it became ingrained. Life can turn on us anytime. The helplessness of that feeling had tortured him for decades. Could being President of the United States finally give him the control he so desperately wanted? Could it really make him feel safe? Keep his children safe?

At a rally in Georgia, the Secret Service had cleared a large crowd that had waited hours to see him. Hudson, knowing of all the precautions, was happy to spend time mingling with the voters. Like so many recently, they wished him well and hoped he could do something about NorthBridge. Cameras caught every second, as his frontrunner status meant a larger press pool traveling with him. He'd become accustomed to the cameras and microphones everywhere, so when a woman shook his hand and whispered, "The Wizard sends his regards," he didn't flinch when she unexpectedly palmed him a flash drive memory stick.

"Thank you for your support," he said, nodding, smiling, while carefully slipping the drive in his pocket. The woman was swept into the mass of supporters before she could say another word.

That evening, alone for a rare moment in his hotel room while headlines announced that "Real Americans for Real Change," the Super PAC supporting Pound for President, had raised another $124 million, he slid the drive into his laptop.

Chapter Twenty-Six

Hudson's laptop screen burst to life with a seemingly random matrix of numbers and letters showering across so rapidly he feared he'd just installed a virus that would destroy not just his data, but the computer as well. Finally, a chat window opened.

Hey, Dawg!

Only two people called him "Dawg" but that meant nothing. Anyone could be typing the words on his screen.

Who is this? Hudson, surprised and suspicious, asked.

The Wizard.

How do I know?

What? Do you think it's Gouge?

I don't like talking this way.

Fully encrypted, my friend. NSA-proof and synch-evaporative.

What does that mean?

Look at our conversation.

Hudson realized that as soon as he replied, the Wizard's words disappeared, and when the Wizard responded,

Hudson's words were also erased. Still, he needed to be sure. He typed: *Where did you always sit?*

With the Pirellis, of course.

Hudson smiled and let out a breath. No one else could have answered that question other than the Wizard, Gouge, or Hudson. Back in the day, when the three of them hung out in the storage loft of the old tire shop owned by Gouge's father, the Wizard always sat next to the Pirelli Girls calendar. Hudson laughed, recalling all the jokes, the fun and . . . and then he caught himself. It was impossible to separate the good from the bad, the beauties from the ugly truth.

Hudson typed: *What do you want?*

You're in danger, Dawg.

Hudson shook his head. *Like I don't know that.*

Not just from NorthBridge.

He squinted at the screen. Not this again. *Who?*

A group of powerful people that you don't know.

He typed again. *Who!?*

They don't have a name, but I can tell you this – NorthBridge isn't always NorthBridge.

Meaning?

Meaning, sometimes people with other interests may use NorthBridge's m.o., but it's not them.

Who? Prove it.

NorthBridge didn't do your house.

They said they did.

They didn't.

So, someone claimed it for them? Then why didn't NorthBridge deny it? They certainly know how to get to the media and anyone else.

Maybe they saw no harm in taking the credit. No one was hurt. Maybe they want to play with who did take credit. Remember, it's all about connectivity . . . consciousness.

Last time – who?
Ask Vonner.

The screen went all digital again. After about three minutes of the matrix pattern, his screen returned, and a popup window told him to remove the drive and keep it in a safe place. For the first time, he questioned whether maybe Schueller might be right about something.

How did the Wizard get a hold of this information? Who the hell does he work for? Can I believe it?

A knock at his door startled him. He stuffed the flash drive into his pocket and went to the peephole, then quickly opened the door for Florence.

"Did you get the text from Schueller?" she asked as she flopped on the bed.

"Oh, yeah, right." He checked his watch. "Is it now?"

"In a few minutes." Schueller had played a couple of songs at a rally in Florida earlier in the day, and it was supposed to be on the national news. He wanted them to watch. Hudson found the right channel and asked if Florence wanted to order some dinner.

"Too late, I ate already, but are you hungry? I could get you something."

"No, I'm good."

The news came on with a special report banner, one of those news graphics which had become all too familiar.

NORTHBRIDGE – Homegrown Terrorists – A REVOLUTION

"Oh no, now what? Florence asked.

The reporter told of a document release detailing improprieties and, in one case, several crimes which had taken place in the past of two presidential candidates—a

Republican and a Democrat. Nothing too horrible, but enough that both had immediately withdrawn from the race. "Apparently, AKA Franklin from NorthBridge notified the campaigns hours ago in order to time the release with the candidate's dropping out," the announcer said.

"Nice," Florence said sarcastically. "It's like they want to show how powerful they are, how they can just knock people off without even resorting to violence."

Hudson had remained silent. He stared at the screen, his stomach tightening. The report said the material had been hacked and assembled from numerous sources. A reporter in front of one of the fallen candidate's campaign headquarters said, "NorthBridge seems to know where all the skeletons are hiding, and their influence over this election may be far from over."

Hudson pulled the flash drive from his pocket and thought about what the Wizard had said. Wondering if this was the real NorthBridge or the other one, he wanted to talk to the Wizard again. He wanted to call Vonner, but the reporter's word about the skeletons had momentarily paralyzed him.

Chapter Twenty-Seven

Later, Hudson and Florence watched Schueller's ninety-second segment, which the cable news channel intro'ed as: "The Republican front-runner's son singing songs about peace and social justice." The commentator called his music protest songs, but Florence reminded her father that Schueller had been tempering his lyrics while on the trail. Hudson sent a text to his son saying he enjoyed it. Afterwards, room service delivered the candidate's favorite—bacon cheeseburger, extra bacon, extra cheese, fries, and a ginger ale. Florence headed off to her own room, but not before warning her father of the heart-attack food he was eating. Hudson, who'd heard her nutrition lectures many times, blew his daughter a kiss and picked up the communicator.

"How's the next president?" Vonner said cheerfully.

"Wondering," he replied. "The next president is wondering who firebombed his house."

"What? Again?"

"No, not another one, just the original. Just the place

where I lived with my late wife, where we raised our kids . . . my goddamned *home*!"

"Oh, I thought they'd hit you again."

"Did *they* hit me the first time?"

"Sorry, Hudson, I'm not following you."

"Was it NorthBridge who burned my home, or was it someone else?"

"That's a rather strange question seeing how North-Bridge admitted to doing it," Vonner said. "What's going on?"

"I was hoping you could tell me, because my house burning down sure seems to have helped me in the polls."

"Oh, come on, don't believe the garbage your detractors are peddling. You're up in the polls for the same reasons I picked you. You're smart, you're a hell of a debater, and people want someone fresh. You're it, Hudson. You're doing it."

"It's just this hasn't been a typical race."

"That's for damned sure, but there's really no such thing as 'typical' anymore. I told you that on the first day."

"Then it *was* NorthBridge?"

"How should I know who it was? NorthBridge claims they did it. Why would they lie? In order to protect their good name?" he asked sarcastically. "Who do *you* think did it? The Democrats? Or, wait, you think it might have been the Republican National Committee wanting to boost your visibility? Maybe the Watergate guys came out of retirement. Damn, Hudson, I don't know where you're getting this junk, or where your head's at, but get a grip, and get some sleep."

"You're probably right."

"I think you know enough history to understand that

when a terrorist group claims they blew something up, they're generally the bastards that blew it up."

"Yeah. Sorry. It's nerve-racking out here with all the security and news every other day of some new North-Bridge attack, digital or physical, or . . . I just . . . I think I should try to find a day off. Maybe two."

"Good idea. I'll tell Fitz. We'll have to come up with a line. Maybe Melissa gets a cold, or we could do a quick trip overseas to meet a world leader or two. You're the front-runner now. It's time to flex that muscle, put more distance between you and Governor Cash."

"Can't we just tell the truth? That the 'front-runner' needs a few days off?"

"The truth in politics? I love your sense of humor. Seriously, nobody wants a president that can't take the pressure."

"I can take it. I'm just . . . "

"I know. It's hell out there. This is the craziest election ever. Don't worry, we'll get you a couple of days."

"Thanks, Arlin."

"None necessary. Now, go to sleep, and Fitz will have a new plan by lunchtime tomorrow."

After the call, Vonner picked up another phone and waited until Rex came on the line. "We have a problem," the billionaire said. "Pound knows."

Chapter Twenty-Eight

Although it hardly seemed like a break, Melissa, Florence, Schueller, and Hudson were whisked off to Europe to meet the British Prime Minister and the Chancellor of Germany. Still surrounded by press and security, at least they weren't campaigning, and the change of pace did him good. Things seemed calmer when they returned to the States.

Based on the pages Schueller had printed from the internet about Vonner, Hudson could see why his son disliked the billionaire. Half of it detailed how the Illuminati—of which Vonner supposedly was part—secretly controlled global events. The rest contained countless allegations over the years of price fixing, bribery, money laundering, and a long list of other apparent wrongdoing by Hudson's backer. But Vonner always had an answer; price fixing only looked that way because he had built near-monopolies in several industries.

"Can I help it if people love my products?" he'd say. "Bribery? Don't be silly, that's legal lobbying."

Money laundering was legitimate transfers among his

many multinational corporations and their subsidiaries. Nothing ever seemed to stick. Hudson knew that could be taken two ways: either Vonner was innocent, or he's so corrupt that he's untouchable. For a practical man like Hudson, it came down to one thing. He thought he knew Vonner, he respected him, and most important, he liked him.

Considering Fonda's stories, the Wizard's charges, and Schueller's conspiracy clippings, Hudson did wonder deep within himself. But, in the end, he attributed the chorus of "Vonner is a bad man" to the fact that it takes a lot to make and manage a fortune that large, and even more to win the White House. So, in the absence of *anything* from the Wizard, Hudson accepted Vonner's convincing denials and tried to concentrate on preparing for the next debate. Fitz had warned that the nine remaining Republicans would all be gunning for him.

"You'll be getting it from all sides," the campaign manager had told him. "You're a great debater—best I've ever seen—but the competition aren't amateurs, and, all together, they could take you."

By October, with the second debate just days away, and Hudson still riding high in almost every poll, he scored several important endorsements—a well-known Republican senator, a congresswoman, and a few local police unions. But the big one came from the governor of Iowa. They received word of the nod from the governor's aide while campaigning in Colorado.

"We've got to get back to Iowa," Fitz said as Hudson came off stage from a rally.

"He's endorsing us?" Hudson asked excitedly.

"Hell yes!" Fitz had been working on it for months. "He wants to announce it tomorrow. He's giving some big education speech and wants you there. We may even be able to use this to get the Teachers Union back on board."

Hudson nodded. As a former teacher with golden school board credentials, he was set to become one of the first Republicans ever endorsed by the Teachers Union, but ever since he'd suggested a hybrid of home/internet and teacher-based alternative education, the big union had soured on him. Iowa's governor, also a friend of the union, meant the huge impact of his endorsement could also help them get back into the good graces of the union's executive board.

"We're going to let the campaign bus go on ahead. It's too slow on these mountain roads; we'll never make it in time," Fitz said. "You, Florence, and I will take a car. Vonner's sending a plane, which should be at the airport before us."

"Okay," Hudson said. "Hope I can sleep on the plane." He'd never been good at sleeping in the air, but exhaustion and necessity had taught him several new tricks.

Hudson, Florence, and Fitz sat in the back of a large SUV along with a Secret Service agent. Another two agents sat in the front seat, one of them driving. Security was tight. They also had lead and follow cars, each with two additional agents, plus drivers.

"Hey, who's the new Secret Service agent?" Florence asked.

The agent turned and smiled at them. "I'm agent Bond."

"Agent *Bond*? Are you kidding me?" Hudson asked.

"No, I'm not a kidder."

Florence laughed. "We have an Agent Bond protecting us."

"What's your first name?" Hudson asked.

"James."

"Incredible." Hudson laughed, too. "Your name is James Bond?"

"No. I was joking about the James part. My name's actually Trent."

Florence laughed again. "He really *is* funny."

"No, seriously, I'm not."

"Ha! He did it again," Florence said. "'Seriously not funny.' Trent Bond, you've just become my favorite Secret Service Agent."

Bond gave a slight nod and just the hint of a smile. "Honored."

Florence had received a text from Schueller earlier that day with highlights from his most recent college appearance. He'd been enlisted by the campaign to get out the youth vote. His charisma, authenticity, singer/songwriter persona, and social media presence had made him quite effective in bringing young people into his father's cause.

"I have to admit," Hudson said, "I'm very surprised and impressed with your brother's work on my behalf."

"He's even shelved the conspiracy theories," Florence added.

"At least publicly."

"Damn, I can't get a signal," Fitz interrupted. "Mountains do nothing but get in the way. I'm looking forward to getting back to Iowa where at least my phone works."

Hudson smiled at Florence, who was about to laugh at

the campaign manager. At that moment, she'd been admiring the view. A river snaked through a canyon five hundred feet below them. The golden leaves of aspens and cottonwood trees fluttered in the sunlight.

BOOOOM! BOOM!

The car right in front of them suddenly exploded. The driver of their SUV swerved to void the flaming debris, but it was too late. The inferno swallowed them, as if they had driven into a burning barn.

"Dad!" Florence screamed as they careened off the road.

Chapter Twenty-Nine

Hudson saw the panic in his daughter's eyes, and wondered if it would be the last time he'd ever see her. Blinded by black smoke and engulfed by expanding flames, their driver lost control of the vehicle. Suddenly, the toxic storm which had trapped them cleared. For that split second, Hudson thought they might be okay. Then he heard Fitz scream, and realized the reprieve had occurred only because their SUV was flying through the air.

His whole world swirled as he tried to reach for his daughter. The accelerated G-force of their flight made it incredibly difficult. At the same time, Fitz was yelling something, but it all blended into a slow-motion kaleidoscope of fear and agony. The crunch and grind of trees gouged the vehicle and smashed windows as a rapid descent pushed them down, down.

My God, how far down can we go?

Hudson recalled seeing the seemingly bottomless canyon as they were heading up the pass.

We're going to die.

The sounds of crunching, twisting metal grew louder than the snapping wood as giant trees caught the airborne vehicle and forced it to stop. A hard, violent stop. Airbags inflated all over the place. Grunts and screams. Oomph. Hudson flew into something, or something hit him. Glass had come in on them like a hurricane. Everything moved fast, scraping, grinding, spinning, another *snap*, and then eerie stillness. Total, loud, deafening silence.

Hudson felt as if he had lost consciousness, but he hadn't. A catastrophe so horrific could not be real. He reached up instinctively, but that went backwards, or rather upside down. Maybe both. His hand found flesh. He thought it was Florence's ankle, but nothing was sure. The vehicle interior was shrouded in a strange darkness. Twisted in the lower trunks of trees, deep under a thick canopy of evergreen, the canyon was smothered in shadows. His brain was not working quite right. Every move brought more pain. And the glass, as if they were in a pool of it—diamond-like chunks.

"Daddy . . ."

The sound of his daughter's voice pulled him from his despair.

"Are you okay?" he asked, desperately celebrating that she was alive, his tone begging that she was not seriously hurt.

"I think I am. You?"

He realized he was sprawled over the back of one of the seats. Nothing fit. The vehicle had been so mangled that half of it lay upside down while the rest of it tilted sideways, suspended, the driver's compartment above them. Hudson tugged and tore, straining with all his strength, and somehow got himself turned around. He saw Florence, blood on her face, pain in her eyes, then smelled the smoke.

"Smoke!" It quickly filled the area. Choking, blinding. "We've got to get out."

"Where?" she cried.

It seemed impossible in such a small space, but there was no clear escape. With fading visibility, and the disorientated way they'd landed, they were trapped. He coughed and rolled onto the inverted ceiling. Florence was coughing, too, and then he heard Fitz cough, and maybe another. What was the agent's name? Jim? Phil? He couldn't remember.

"Fitz!"

"Yeah, I'm alive. Unless this is hell."

"Me too," Agent Bond said in a strained voice. "I'm at the window, but it's partially blocked."

"Where's the smoke coming from?" Hudson asked.

"Fuel," Fitz said urgently. "This thing could blow any minute."

They scrambled and contorted themselves until Florence found a way out through the opening that used to be the back window. One by one, they dropped through thick brambles. The SUV, dangling four feet above the ground, had rammed in between two massive trunks, as if the trees had grown through the painted steel. Agent Bond was the last to pull himself out, mostly falling to the ground, where he screamed and collapsed.

Florence, her nursing instinct taking over, jumped over to him.

"My leg," Bond moaned, but it was the blood that worried her.

"Hang in there, 007," Florence said, while checking his

injuries. His condition was serious. "You're going to be okay," she lied.

The smoke increased. The smell of gas grew more intense.

"It's gonna blow!" Fitz warned again. "We've got to get away!"

Chapter Thirty

It was the Wizard's first trip back to Ohio in many years. He hated the place because of the memories, but he loved it, too, because of different memories. His escape from the Buckeye State hadn't been easy for a poor kid with brown skin and no college, but finally, in the early 90s, he hitch-hiked west with nothing but what fit in his backpack—mostly books, a few clothes, and a computer he'd built from parts he'd scrounged. Even with his brains, work was tough to get, but by the turn of the century, Silicon Valley was so high-throttle that even an oddball without an engineering degree could get a job writing code. It wasn't enough to afford housing, but the Wizard honed his skills and made lots of contacts. Now, he was back in the town where he grew up because things that happened there decades earlier had forced him to return.

He and Gouge sat in the cheap motel room, pizza boxes and empty Chinese food containers strewn about. The Wizard looked at the monitor of his laptop and shook his head.

"What is it?" Gouge asked.

"Proof."

Gouge nodded, but didn't bother to check the Wizard's screen. He never did understand computers all that well, and even if he did, the kind of codes the Wizard dealt with gave him a headache. "Is it enough to convince Dawg?"

"It ought to be," the Wizard replied, not looking up. "But I'm not sure he wants to know."

"Remember that movie with Nicholson and Cruise?" His voice got lower and louder. "You can't handle the truth!"

"Yeah." The Wizard leaned back and rubbed his eyes. "It's like that. And in this case, not many people *can* handle the truth."

"But the truth is the truth," Gouge said, shaking his fist as if to empower the word tattooed below his knuckles.

The Wizard's eyes followed the movement of Gouge's hand. He'd seen the tattoo before, and knew why he'd gotten it. The Wizard had the same tattoo, only his was permanently burned onto his brain where no one could see it, but he felt its sting every day.

"Dawg wants to be president," the Wizard said, turning back to the screen. "And when someone wants to be president of the United States, the truth just gets in the way."

Gouge lit a cigarette. "That's good, though. We want him to be president. It's the only way we can make things right for Rochelle."

The Wizard looked at his old friend, eyes squinting, as if seeing the past in the gray-blue exhale of smoke from Gouge's Marlboro. Two ashtrays already overflowed with butts. The motel room, Gouge's temporary home, was bigger than the Wizard's storage shed, but it felt much smaller. "It's not exactly going to make it right."

"I know, but damn if it's the closest we're ever gonna get."

"At what price?" the Wizard asked. "Dawg's life?"

"Come on," Gouge said, flicking ash onto his jeans, then rubbing it into the dirty faded denim.

"What do you think's going to happen when Dawg doesn't do what they want?"

Gouge looked puzzled.

"Sure, they'll manipulate him for a while into following their agenda," the Wizard said. "They may even let him think he's making his own decisions, but you know Dawg. One day he's going to decide something's wrong, he's going to want to do something they don't, and that's when the trouble will start."

"You think they'll kill him?"

"I do. Either that, or they'll drum up some kind of scandal to remove him from office, but that can be long, messy, and unpredictable. *They* don't like that kind of thing. My guess is a quick assassination or a sudden heart attack. Maybe a brain aneurism."

"Nice," Gouge said sarcastically. "But what if he plays along with them?"

"Dawg, play along? Are you joking? Nah, man, Dawg's a patriot. He believes in right and wrong. Dude treats history as a religion. He'll fight them . . . and he'll think he can win."

"Maybe he can."

The Wizard looked back at his screen and shook his head. "No. It's too big. No way Hudson Pound walks out of this alive."

"Then what do we do?"

"I'm still workin' on that one," the Wizard said. "It's

profound, though. It's warping my holographic mind and stressing my interactive consciousness."

"What if he wins, deals with Rochelle and a few other things, and then shocks everyone by resigning before they can stop him? Claims a health issue or maybe—"

"I've been thinking about something similar, but it'll only work if Dawg believes the proof."

"Why wouldn't he? Proof is proof, right?" Gouge said, shaking his fist again.

"You're confusing proof with truth. Maybe in the movies that works out, but in the real-world, proof and truth only have one thing in common. They're both moving targets, and the more you look at one, the blurrier it gets."

"What *is* the proof, then?"

"That we're at the final CapWar."

"What's a CapWar?"

"A CapWar is everything that's choking the material world." The Wizard stared hard through bloodshot eyes into the screen. "And this one is out of control."

Chapter Thirty-One

Hudson looked up through the heavy smoke. "What about the other agents that were in the front seat?"

Fitz stared at the mangled mess of steel above them. "They can't be alive."

"We've got to find out," Hudson said, already climbing up through a tangle of splintered tree limbs.

"Damn it, you're going to get us killed," Fitz said, reluctantly following him.

Florence, ignoring the blood running down her own cheek, tore strips from Bond's shirt to staunch his bleeding.

"My leg?" he asked.

"Broken," Florence replied flatly, "but that won't matter if we don't get this wound closed soon." The major gash in his left side continued to pump blood.

At the same time, Hudson and Fitz, both bleeding and dazed, reached the guys in the front seat. The agent in the passenger seat was mashed into what used to be the windshield. A folded part of the hood pinned him in. Neither answered when Hudson shouted to them.

"Let's get out of here!" Fitz yelled, coughing.

They both knew the smoke meant fire. Any second the fuel would ignite and engulf the whole vehicle. Images of Senator Uncer's firebombed car flashed through Hudson's mind.

"This one's breathing," Hudson said about the passenger. Looking at the other man, the driver, Hudson grimaced. The driver's skull had been split open. He could not have survived, but Hudson, reached across to check his pulse anyway.

Fitz looked past Hudson to the driver. "Oooh God, forrr-get him. He's dead."

No pulse.

They worked frantically to pull the passenger free.

"It's the damned seat belt," Hudson said. "I can't reach the buckle."

"We're going to have to leave him," Fitz wheezed.

"No. Do you have a knife?"

"Why the hell would I have a knife?"

Hudson stretched and grappled. "Got it!" He'd miraculously found the button and released the buckle. The agent's body came down on top of Hudson, who, in turn, slid into Fitz. The three tumbled back to the ground, with Fitz taking the worst of it.

"Florence," Hudson called, climbing out of the pile-on, "can you do anything for him?"

"Hold this," she said, pushing the saturated cloth into Bond's hand, briefly meeting his eyes to be sure he understood if he let it go, he would bleed out.

He tried to nod.

"Save your energy, 007." She moved toward her father. "Dad, your arm."

"It's nothing." Badly cut in the crash, his struggle to get

the belt undone had resulted in a fresh gash.

"Come on," Fitz shouted, dragging the agent they'd rescued. "We've got to get away from this vehicle *now*!"

"Okay." Hudson looked at agent Bond, and then back to Florence.

She shook her head—007 wasn't going to make it. "He shouldn't be moved until paramedics get here."

Hudson shot her a look with his eyes as if to say, *When will that be?*

"I can do it," Bond said.

Florence wasn't going to argue, Bond was dead either way, but she went back to assist his efforts while Hudson helped Fitz move the unconscious agent they'd rescued from the front seat.

"What about the other cars?" Hudson asked breathlessly as they struggled through the underbrush.

"There can't be anything left of the lead car," Fitz said. "We're damned lucky the follow car didn't land on top of us."

Amid the blood, smoke, and death, Hudson had a hard time considering being lucky, except that Florence had survived. But for that grateful miracle, he gave credit to something more powerful than luck.

"We've got to get to the road," Hudson barked.

"We're safer in the cover of the trees," Fitz said. "We need to protect you. NorthBridge may want to finish the job."

For the first time, Hudson realized that this had been an attempt on *his* life. *I'm the cause of all this.* "Let's find the agents from those other vehicles! In the army, we don't abandon the fallen in order to save ourselves."

"We're not *in* the army," Fitz argued.

"You could have fooled me."

Somehow, Bond had gotten to his feet. It was slow going as he limped and sometimes crawled, but Florence was mostly dragging him. "No further," she yelled to her dad. "He's losing too much blood, and—"

She dropped and covered her head instinctively as an explosion ripped through the air behind her. Their SUV, forty or fifty feet below them, burst into flames.

They crawled to a semi-flat area and Bond crumpled to the ground.

"Are we far enough?" Hudson asked, wiping blood and sweat from his face.

"It'll have to be," Florence said.

Thirty feet above, they spotted part of what had to be the follow vehicle.

"Let's go!" Hudson said.

Judging the distance from their burning SUV one more time, Hudson left Florence to tend to the two injured agents. As he and Fitz scrambled up the steep bank, Fitz slipped on some loose rocks. His rolling slide ended more than forty feet later, when he somehow stopped himself from plunging over a cliff and falling hundreds of more feet down into the river.

"Hang on, Fitz!" Hudson called. "I'm coming!"

At that same moment, a cry of help came from above.

"Someone's alive up there. Are you all right, Fitz?" Hudson asked.

"Hell no, I'm not all right!"

"What happened?"

"I slid down a big friggin' cliff!"

"Can you climb back up?" Hudson was already moving up toward the follow vehicle. "I've got to get up there."

"Go!"

Hudson reluctantly left Fitz down on the cliff and

continued to claw his way up to the follow car. He was only a few feet from the mangled vehicle when he heard a helicopter. Relieved that help had arrived, he paused to catch his breath. That's when the first round of machine gunfire tore through the trees all around him.

Chapter Thirty-Two

Hudson's army training kicked in. He dove for the ground and rolled back down into the thicker trees. *Keep away from the vehicle.* He knelt and surveyed the area. For a moment, he considered going back to try to protect Florence, but his presence could only make matters worse. Everyone had heard the shots and would be seeking cover. No doubt this was the real NorthBridge.

These bastards really want me dead!

"Help!" The cry came again from the follow car.

"What's your condition?" Hudson yelled as the chopper circled around, obviously readying for another attack.

"Two of us are alive, but I'm the only one conscious . . . I can't seem to move my arms."

"Okay. As soon as they make the next pass, I'll come and get you." Hudson shouted, while estimating the time it took the chopper to make the return arc—ten or fifteen seconds. Hudson wedged himself behind two thick trees.

The helicopter returned with guns blazing. Chunks of wood, dirt, and rocks blasted through the air. The shooters seemed to know where he was, as most of the shots tore up the area closest to his hiding place. The instant the gunfire stopped, Hudson began counting.

One-one thousand, two-one thousand.

He bolted toward the car. The sight that greeted Hudson rivaled anything he'd seen in the army. The driver had been decapitated by a huge tree limb, which had come in through the windshield.

Seven-one thousand, eight-one thousand.

The agent he'd talked to had just been hit from the last wave of aerial attack, his face and chest opened by the high caliber bullets.

Nine-one thousand, ten-one thousand.

Hudson heard the chopper coming back and quickly opened the door, grabbing the unconscious lone survivor.

Eleven-one thousand, twelve-one thousand.

The man was heavier than he looked and Hudson weaker than he thought.

Thirteen-one—

Another round of gunfire rained in on the area as Hudson pulled, carried, and pushed the man behind a sturdy tree. Then he started counting again.

Hudson saw the growing column of smoke from the SUV just below where Florence and the injured agents were. It was burning out of control, but still hadn't exploded. Still counting, he called down to Florence, hoping she could take a look at the guy he'd just pulled from the follow car.

"If he's stable, I'd rather not leave Bond right now," she shouted back. "When the chopper last fired on us, the bullets came pretty close. We had to move him again."

"I don't know if he's stable," Hudson yelled back. "He's

breathing, and only seems to have cuts and bruises." He continued counting.

"Sounds stable!"

"Okay. What's the fire like down there?"

"It's starting to spread."

Hudson knew the forest was so dry that it could go up in flames any minute and they'd be trapped.

Seven-one thousand.

"Is Fitz back?" he shouted.

"Just," Florence answered. "Catching his breath."

"I'm coming to get you," he yelled, his voice hoarse. "We've got to get to the road."

Ten-one thousand.

The chopper swooped in and sent a missile into the follow car. The force of the explosion knocked Hudson off his feet. The flames instantly ignited nearby trees. Fire spread so fast that Hudson feared the unconscious agent would be burned alive if he left him.

"Fitz, I've got to move this guy," Hudson yelled while dragging the agent farther from the fire. "Bring my daughter up here!"

Three-one thousand.

"Dad, I can't leave my patients!"

"Yes, you can! If *that* fire doesn't get you, then *this* fire will."

"Hudson, I don't know if I can drag this guy up that hill," Fitz shouted. He and Hudson both knew it was much more than a "hill".

"I'm coming!" Hudson yelled, pulling the agent as far away as he dared.

Eight-one thousand.

Whoosh-boom! Another missile hit their SUV. Flames spread everywhere. The fire moved rapidly, closing in from three sides. By the time Hudson reached Fitz and Florence, the other agent had regained consciousness.

"Can you walk?" Hudson asked, counting silently, knowing they were low on luck and out of options.

"Yes, sir," the agent said unconvincingly.

Against Florence's protests, Hudson and Fitz picked Bond up. Florence tried to keep a hand on his wound to slow his bleeding, but the climb made it almost impossible. The newly conscious agent straggled behind, weak and foggy. The fire, picking up fuel and speed, chased them. A wall of flames raged less than twenty feet from them. Hudson kept counting.

They finally reached the unconscious agent from the follow car. If they didn't take him, the fire would. Florence dragged him up the grade with some help from the weak agent, who had somehow caught up to her.

Nine-one thousand, ten one-thousand.

They were almost to the road when they heard a second helicopter . . . then a third. Hudson caught a glimpse of them through the trees.

"Finally, the cavalry has arrived," he said, squeezing his daughter's shoulder as she bent over Bond's body. Hudson looked down at the ashen-faced agent. The man, no longer conscious, couldn't possibly live long enough to make it to a hospital. Hudson wasn't sure if Bond was even still alive at that moment.

"That looks like a State Police bird, and maybe even the Forest Service, here for the fire," Fitz offered. "That North-Bridge gunship will just blow them out of the sky."

"Let's hope not," Hudson said.

"They'll know that the police have already radioed for backup," the other agent said, panting. "I bet they run."

He was right. The chopper, pursued by the police,

disappeared over a ridge. The Forest Service helicopter dropped water on the fire, and then it, too, went away.

"It sure as hell would be nice if someone dropped down to help us," Fitz said, motioning to the two unconscious agents.

All of them looked like refugees from a war zone. Hudson was covered in sweat, dirt, and blood—his and that of several agents. Florence had even more blood on her, but most of it belonged to Bond. Hudson, Fitz, and the agent felt safe enough to climb onto the road, leaving Florence in the trees with Bond and the other critically wounded agent. Half a dozen cars had stopped for the fire. People spotted them on the narrow shoulder and ran to offer help.

Fifteen or twenty minutes later, the first medevac landed and airlifted Bond. About the same time, police arrived. Soon the area was teaming with activity. Several ambulances, a reporter, and a film crew showed up. Hudson refused to be interviewed, but Fitz was only too happy to give a full account.

Medics attended to the almost unrecognizable Hudson and loaded him in the back of a rescue squad, but not before the media got plenty of footage. The candidate had insisted on leaving the scene last.

"I want to make sure everyone is safely out of here," he said. "I'm not hurt that bad."

Hudson's departure hit another delay after the FBI got there. He gave a statement at the scene. By the time he'd been examined and placed in a private hospital room where they'd keep him overnight for observation, the story was monopolizing the worldwide news. He and Florence sat in his heavily guarded room watching the footage while waiting for Melissa and Schueller to arrive.

"The worst day in Secret Service history," the commentator announced. "Six agents dead. Their burned bodies likely won't be recovered until tomorrow. Three more injured, with one still in critical condition."

Hudson squeezed his daughter's hand. They didn't know if Bond would make it through the night.

"NorthBridge, in a statement signed by AKA Washington, has claimed responsibility for the attack, which was clearly an attempt on the life of Hudson Pound, the frontrunner for the Republican nomination."

Hudson thought of the Wizard angrily. *This wasn't Vonner. These people did everything they could to kill me, to kill everyone around me.*

"The attacking helicopter, which had been pursued for a time by a much slower State Police helicopter, was discovered a short while ago burning near an onramp to the Interstate. The passengers are believed to have escaped in a waiting car. There are no immediate leads, but the FBI is asking anyone with information, or who may have seen anything, to contact the number on your screen."

There was a knock at the door. Fitz peaked his head in. "It took me fifteen minutes to get through all your security," he said, exasperated. "They took my Coke. What do they think? How could I hurt you with a soda?"

"I hope NorthBridge doesn't try to bomb the whole building," Hudson responded with a worried look. "My being here is putting everyone at this hospital in danger. I tried to get the doctor to discharge me."

"They've got fighter jets in the air," Fitz said. "The feds are treating you as if you really are the next president."

Hudson nodded. "You know what really bothers me? How did NorthBridge know where I'd be? Our route, the whole trip to Iowa, was unplanned."

"They must have been watching us," Fitz said. "Probably planning to hit the bus today . . . that would explain the missile . . . when we ditched the bus and went solo, I bet they just improvised the rest."

"Six agents," Hudson said, shaking his head. "I want to call all their families."

"Of course," Fitz said.

"And we've got to suspend the campaign for a few weeks, at least."

"Not a good idea," Fitz said. "A few days sure, but we've still got the Iowa endorsement and the debate, and you're the frontrunner, you can't —"

"I'm not sure I want to be the frontrunner anymore."

"Daddy," Florence said quietly, "maybe you don't want to be president anymore."

And then she just looked sadly into his eyes.

Chapter Thirty-Three

Hudson woke in the middle of the night to find Melissa sitting next to his hospital bed, and Schueller asleep in the chair next to his sister. They'd arrived while he was sleeping.

Melissa took Hudson's hand amid the glow of the vital signs monitors and a sliver of light from the hallway. "I thought I'd lost you," she whispered.

"No way," he replied softly. "We're just getting started."

She leaned in to kiss his cheek. "I hope so."

The next morning, they left the hospital under heavy security. The media, kept half a block away, had not been told of the candidate's departure until thirty minutes afterwards. A hospital statement released to the press simply stated that the candidate and his family had been moved to an undisclosed location. The campaign also announced that Hudson would skip the next debate and do very little in-person campaigning for the next ten days. The Secret Service and FBI wanted to move them to a military base, but, after a call with Vonner, Hudson changed the plan.

"You can't hide," Vonner told him over the communicator as the motorcade raced toward the airport. "NorthBridge wins if you cower."

"How have we come to this?" Hudson mused. "I can't believe this can happen in America!"

"We're in a war," Vonner said. "These guys are serious about their revolution, but this time it isn't going to be muskets fired in open fields. NorthBridge's revolution could go on for years depending on how many there are, how much money they have, and, most importantly, what kind of technological infrastructure they control. Thus far, their tech seems to be superior to the government's!"

"The country has been growing more rigidly divided with each election cycle, but open warfare? Do they not recall the first American Civil War?"

Suddenly, the sound of a helicopter above their vehicle sent fear through Hudson. Florence, sitting behind him, grabbed his shoulder.

The agent in the front seat heard it too, and sensed their apprehension. "Not to worry, Mr. Pound, that's our escort. They'll be with us until we make destination."

"Why do they think tearing the country apart with terrorism and war will do anything?" Hudson asked, resuming the conversation with Vonner.

"You've seen their propaganda," Vonner said. "They don't think there's any other way to bring about change, and they might be right—except for you."

"That's a lot to put on my campaign. Saving the country from civil war. Surely the government can stop these terrorists before the election?"

"NorthBridge has more supporters than you would think. The media is downplaying that right now, but reality will eventually catch up. A significant portion of the population is fed up with the government, and attempts to change it haven't worked. For decades, more and more people have grown impatient. They've hoped and waited and tried and hoped again, but now they're done with all of that. Now they're taking matters into their own hands, and they're willing to use force."

"We can't let a civil war happen."

"You are the last best hope, Hudson. The people might give a non-politician one more chance to change things peacefully. They believe you. You're the one. But you can't hide. Lincoln didn't hide."

"Okay," Hudson said, "but you know how Lincoln ended."

"We've got to stop this war, Hudson," Vonner added before the call ended. "And you want a truly sobering thought? Think about this: we're the most armed nation on earth. Neither side will ever run out of weapons."

Another revolutionary war. Another civil war. Hudson could see it now, see that his outsider status put him in a unique position to stop it, to hold the country together and finally get real change accomplished.

He explained the stakes to his family. "I can't back down."

Reluctantly, his children agreed. Melissa's support was unwavering. "We can't allow these anarchists to take over," she said as if addressing a large crowd.

The Secret Service and FBI were informed of the decision to resume actively campaigning. Fitz told him that an international firm, which handled protection and security for Vonner's organization and many heads of state, would be brought in to work with the Secret Service for a coordinated and "smart" plan to minimize the risk to Hudson and his family, "Twenty-four-seven."

They flew immediately to Iowa. The press pool traveling

with them had been heavily screened and included the top correspondents covering the election. Hudson had spoken with them briefly after takeoff, and noticed a difference in how they treated him. They were softer, more respectful. It felt good. His sound bites were relayed on media around the world.

"I will not be deterred. I am not afraid. Terror and fear will not win!"

About an hour into the flight, Schueller came over and sat by his father in the private suite occupied by the family.

"I thought you might want to use this in Iowa," Schueller said, handing him a legal pad.

Hudson read the page-and-a-half of handwritten lines and then turned back to his son, smiling. "You wrote this?"

"Yeah."

"I had no idea."

"I'm a songwriter, Dad. I just thought of the speech as a song."

"I knew you could write, I just wasn't sure you believed in me."

"Of course I do. It's the system I don't believe in, and Vonner I don't trust. But I know *you're* the real deal. My dad is our best chance to change things for good."

Hudson realized that even Schueller sounded like the people Vonner had described. He shuddered. How had the greatest country in history let so many of its people become disenfranchised to the point that they no longer trusted their own government? How had it gotten to a point where patriots could support a group like NorthBridge? He felt a renewed weight of the responsibility of his candidacy.

"I wish I could tell you what your support means to me," Hudson said.

Schueller patted his dad's knee. "You just did."

Hudson nodded, smiling mostly to himself. His unwashed son, scruffy brown hair, unshaven, wiry thin, the constant debater, a firm contrarian, and still the coolest guy he knew.

"So, you'll use the speech?" Schueller asked.

"Of course I will, about a hundred times. I hope you'll keep them coming."

The crowd was enormous when the governor of Iowa endorsed and then introduced Hudson in Des Moines. Bomb sniffing dogs and more than a hundred law enforcement officers and Secret Service agents patrolled. Hudson stepped out onto a stage rimmed by clear, bulletproof panels, thanked the governor, and delivered Schueller's speech.

"In the sixties, we were promised 'a change is gonna come,' that 'the times, they are a changing,' and during the turmoil of those times, for an instant, it did seem like the truth. Then, something terrible happened. Our hope was stolen, and the dream murdered. A crumbling chaos of despair and near constant war followed. In my lifetime, I have seen politician after politician claim they were going to reform, improve, repair, transform, correct, or fix. They swore to give us change to believe in again, but things only got worse. The truth slipped away in the smoke-filled backrooms of Washington, and, in the glare of the television screen, the dream faded from our memory.

"You know I'm not a politician, yet still I hesitate to utter the words; to look into your tired, skeptical faces and plead for your faith; to promise that it *is* different this time; to ask for your help. But I must. For the most important thing history has taught me is it cannot be done alone. I do *need* your help. We can find that change, we can push and pull and build it into something real, but first we must bring ourselves together. We need to be strong. We have to believe it. Just. One. More. Time. Because this time . . . WE ARE THE CHANGE!"

Chants of "We are the change" swept the crowd and built to a deafening roar for three full minutes. WE. ARE. THE. CHANGE!

Chapter Thirty-Four

Vonner reviewed the data Rex had just presented him. "This can't happen."

"Bastendorff is supporting Newsman Dan," Rex said. "That changes—"

"I know what it means!" Vonner barked. Bastendorff, perhaps the most secretive billionaire in the world, richer even than Vonner, had managed to stay so far out of the public view that few people had ever heard of him.

"We can't stop it."

"Like hell, we can't." Vonner smacked a fist into his other hand. "A *bullet* will stop it!"

Rex raised an eyebrow and studied his boss's face.

"Bastendorff is abandoning Governor Kelleher because he knows Hudson has it locked up," Vonner said, pacing the plush carpet of his five-room, $80 million jet in flight to London for a meeting which would decide matters even more important than who the next American president would be. Bastendorff would be in attendance.

"Then why bother with Neuman?" Rex asked. "Bastendorff should know he can't win."

"Maybe he thinks he can."

"How?" Rex rolled six small yellow dice on the polished walnut table next to him. "We have AEIO." Accounting Election Information Operations was the leading company which manufactured and sold touch screen voting machines and election management systems. Its products and services were currently in widespread use—1,700 jurisdictions in thirty-six states, serving forty-eight million people, nearly one-third of all registered voters.

"You and I know," Vonner said. His eyes cut into Rex so sharply that he stopped fidgeting with the dice. "Money, my boy. It really just takes money. Obviously AEIO is an advantage, but not the ball game."

"Hudson's an American hero," Rex said. "Newsman Dan is a former TV anchorman."

"And governor of Oregon."

"Not exactly a power state."

"No, but Bastendorff must have something."

"Something bad on Hudson?" Rex asked. "Or something good on Neuman?"

"Isn't that what I pay you to find out?"

"*That's* why you're dragging me to London? I could have gotten more done at my desk in California."

"I need you in England because it's closer to Paris."

"What's in Paris?"

"AKA Thomas Paine."

Rex stared disbelievingly at Vonner. "NorthBridge? They've contacted you?"

Vonner nodded slowly.

"Why?"

"I don't know."

"It's about Hudson."

"That's my guess."

"What is AKA Paine doing in Paris? I thought this was an *American* revolution."

"The French helped out with the first one," Vonner said. "Perhaps . . . why do you always roll those damned dice?"

"It helps me think," Rex said, carefully checking the last numbers he rolled before scooping them up.

"Well they're giving me a headache," Vonner said.

"Is that really what's giving you a headache?"

Vonner ignored the question. "I'll get off at Heathrow and meet with Bastendorff. You go on to Paris and find out what AKA Paine wants."

Rex nodded. "I can't wait to hear what one of the most wanted persons in the world has to say."

"Me neither," Vonner said. "Now excuse me, I have a meeting." He walked two doors away where fourteen staff members, accustomed to meetings at thirty-eight thousand feet, were waiting.

Alone, Rex pulled out his dice again, but these were orange. He watched almost hypnotically as they landed over and over again. Then he opened his laptop and entered the dark web. "Changing the world is a tricky business," Vonner had often said. Rex believed this, and knew that it would all come down to two people—Hudson Pound and Dan Neuman. Bastendorff had something, and Rex needed to find it. He considered that piece of information infinitely more important than his pending meeting with NorthBridge.

It suddenly occurred to him that the two assignments might be connected.

Chapter Thirty-Five

The day after Iowa, Hudson walked onto the debate stage in Houston, Texas, to wild cheers and a standing ovation. The adoring reception happened before the start of the televised portion, but everyone in attendance knew who the most popular candidate was. Even the hometown favorite, Texas Governor Cash, could feel it.

It quickly became evident that several of the candidates, including Celia Brown, the African-American Senator from Illinois, Professor Pete Wiseman, and the Governor of Oklahoma, had decided not to go after Hudson directly. They knew it would be awkward to be seen attacking a man who had just survived such a brutal assault, particularly when he had simultaneously risked his life to save three downed Secret Service agents. Just prior to the debate, hospital officials in Colorado had announced that all three, including Agent Bond, were expected to make a full recovery. Florence had already received a thank you note from Bond's wife, and crayon-colored pictures from his two kids, aged five and seven. She was elated.

Governor Cash, General Hightower, a Florida Congressman, and especially Thorne, were not going with the gentle strategy of the other candidates. Cash had too much at stake. He'd have few chances before the Iowa caucus and the New Hampshire primary to go after Hudson one-on-one. Due to the threat from NorthBridge, there would be far fewer debates this year than usual. For Thorne, however, it was personal. He'd never stopped hitting Hudson. Even the morning after the Colorado attack, Thorne's syndicated radio show went all out on criticizing the novice front runner.

The debate moderator chose that radio harassment as her first question to Thorne, citing his specific comments from that morning saying that NorthBridge is no different from the Founding Fathers, who, faced with no other way to throw off the chains of a tyrannical government, chose force.

"They showed us the way," Thorne had said. "Is trying to assassinate yet another puppet of the same elites who have controlled the government for decades such a bad idea, when voting hasn't worked? I don't know. What would you have them do?"

"Are you saying it's okay to assassinate presidential candidates, the president, senators? Is there anyone it's not okay to murder, if you decide they are unworthy in some way?"

"Thank you for that question and allowing me to set the record straight," Thorne said, smiling at the moderator before turning to the camera. "The American people know that something is wrong when they keep voting for hope and change, desperate for something new, and yet nothing happens. In fact, it continues to get worse, and worse, and wooooorse!"

The moderator tried to speak, but Thorne talked over her.

"And here we go again," the shock-jock continued, motioning to Hudson. "Now it's Pretty Boy Pound, a hardware store owner, who claims to be the agent for change this time, yet he's anything but. He's an agent for the banksters and corporations who control the government."

"Please answer the question, Mr. Thorne," the moderator said. "Do you believe it is okay to assassinate Mr. Pound and others, even yourself?"

"First, it's just Thorne, no 'mister' necessary." He smiled as if he'd just given her a gift. "Second, I'd prefer to see people like Pound, the current president, most members of congress, and a long list of other politicians, arrested and tried for crimes against the people. You can see the list of those who should be investigated, arrested, and convicted at ThorneInTheirSide.com, by the way."

"I still don't believe you have answered the question. Would you like me to repeat it?"

"No, thank you. Let me see if I can help you out. If there is no other way to rid the henhouse of the fox than to shoot the fox, then sometimes that's what you have to do."

A murmur went through the crowd.

"So that's a yes, then?" she asked, exasperated. "It's okay to kill political opponents, people you disagree with?"

"Look, the system is so corrupt that it may be impossible to arrest them and have a trial. In that case, our Founders made it clear, by their words and their example, that a revolution would be necessary. And in a revolution, people are killed." Thorne looked straight into the camera and said, "Ramener la guillotine."

"If I remember my high school French correctly, you just said, 'Bring back the guillotine,'" the moderator said.

The audience gasped.

"Mr. Thorne, are you now, or have you ever been, a supporter or member of NorthBridge?"

"Is your last name McCarthy?" Thorne asked, squinting at the moderator and then turning back to the camera. "Is our country still free? Is the First Amendment still in place? I will not remain silent while our once great nation is returned to the descendants of the very monarchs our forefathers fought to free us from."

Hudson closed his eyes briefly, stunned that a presidential candidate would be so reckless as to align himself with a terrorist organization.

I've got to win, or this might end up being our nation's last election.

Chapter Thirty-Six

Once again, after Thorne's controversial opening, Hudson dominated the debate, easily winning. Combined with the governor's endorsement, he now led in Iowa by more than twenty points. A surprising result of the debate came when Thorne vaulted to number three in the polls in Iowa and New Hampshire. Although the Secret Service briefly detained the shock-jock for his "threatening" statements, ultimately, he was released, and continued daily rants on his radio show.

A few days later, Fonda Raton created another stir by posting a story alleging that Arlin Vonner, through a series of shell companies, actually owned United Days Network, "UDN," the nation's largest radio syndication company. UDN aired the "Tangled Vine," Thorne's wildly popular daily show.

"Is this report for real?" an outraged Hudson asked Vonner once the billionaire answered the communicator. "Thorne works for *you*?"

Vonner, on his jet, finally returning from London—a

trip that had gone on days longer than expected—was not in the mood "to hold his rookie candidate's hand." The "quick London meeting" had turned into a marathon of negotiations with Bastendorff, or, as Vonner would characterize it to Rex, a chess match to determine the next half-century of world affairs.

"Fonda Raton can make *anything* into *a* thing," Vonner shot back. "Don't worry about it."

"Then it's true?"

"I own *a lot* of things," Vonner said, trying unsuccessfully to not sound as annoyed as he felt.

"*You* should've been the politician," Hudson said. "You're so good at evading questions."

"Last time I checked, I owned UDN," Vonner finally admitted. "But it's not a big deal."

"Really? This is the guy who's made it his mission to destroy my campaign, the snake that suggested killing me is probably a pretty good idea, and 'it's not a big deal' that he's on *your* payroll?"

"Calm down, Hudson. As I said, a lot of people are on my payroll—hundreds of thousands. Democrats, Republicans, Christians, atheists, Muslims, black, white, brown, yellow, I really don't know or care."

"Well, *I* do."

"What do you want me to do? Talk to him? Ask him to go easy on you?"

"Fire him."

"I can't fire him."

"Why not?"

"For one, he's under contract, and for another, his ratings have never been higher. He's making us a fortune."

"Don't you already *have* a fortune?"

"You have no idea how much it costs to run the world," Vonner said reflectively.

Hudson couldn't tell if Vonner was being serious or sarcastic, and he wasn't sure he *wanted* to know.

"You're playing in the big leagues," Vonner said. "I'm sorry if all the meanies are hurting your feelings, but get used to it. Even when you win the election, half the country will hate you." The billionaire went on to assure Hudson he'd have people talk to Thorne, but cautioned that he didn't want to do anything that would give Thorne—or Fonda Raton for that matter—anything they could use to further embarrass Hudson.

After the call ended, Vonner turned to Rex. "Raton is a menace. This is dammed lousy timing."

"Yes, extremely," Rex agreed. "Making Thorne more important at the same time that NorthBridge has made their offer—"

"It boggles my mind that they actually think we'd withdraw Hudson from the race," Vonner interrupted. "Any indication as to why they fear Hudson so much?"

"None," Rex answered, while calculating how long until he could smoke. "But, these aren't stupid people who are running NorthBridge."

"Obviously not." Suddenly the plane lurched and dropped. *Turbulence*, Vonner thought, *unless NorthBridge is making a very big mistake.*

"Right," Rex said, as if he hadn't noticed the turbulence. "My guess is they want Pound out for the same reason you want him in."

Vonner scoffed. Nothing upset the billionaire more than knowing there was something he didn't know . . . something he knew he *needed* to know.

"I did manage to discover something very interesting

this morning," Rex said, absently pulling out two clear dice, but after catching Vonner eyeing them, put them back in his pocket. "I probed AKA Paine for the source of their funding. I thought perhaps Bastendorff or Booker."

Vonner nodded. The subject and Paine's responses were of extreme interest to him. He double-checked to make sure the door to the rest of the plane was still shut.

"Of course, Paine denied it was either of them, and I've been digging ever since."

Vonner leaned forward. He knew Rex could find things, even transactions meant to leave no trace, even deleted, erased, rerouted, encrypted things. "What did you discover?"

"They *are* getting their funds from Bastendorff—"

"I knew it!"

"—*and* Booker, *and* . . . " Rex hesitated.

"And?" Vonner pressed, leaning closer.

"And NorthBridge is getting funds from you."

"What are you talking about?" Vonner asked angrily.

"I've still got lots of work to do in order to flesh it all out, but I've found enough to know that NorthBridge could not only bring down the US government. They could bring the entire world to its knees." He fidgeted with the dice again. "It's incredible. Pure brilliance. They've found a way to shave a few fractions of a cent off every major financial transaction."

"*Every*?" Vonner asked, his eyes widening.

"Every. Single. One," Rex replied. "At least the ones over one hundred thousand dollars."

"But even fractions would be missed. Any instant audit built into the programs would catch it the moment it happened."

"You said the key word: 'program.' They created a

program that does it and covers it up. At the same time, it moves the money into a digital currency."

"Like Bitcoin?" Vonner asked, referring to the leading form of encrypted digital currency, meaning it operated independently of central banks or government control. Bitcoin was controversial, but had grown incredibly popular, and many other forms of digital currency were trying to establish themselves.

"Similar," Rex responded. "As you are aware, Bitcoin is the best known, but several others, including digiGOLD, have been gaining traction. Not only does NorthBridge's little shaving scam convert the stolen funds to untraceable digiGOLD, making it impossible to know how much they've taken—no doubt billions—but it also appears that NorthBridge may actually be the ones *behind* digiGOLD."

"But digiGOLD started up four or five years ago. Now it's about to overtake Bitcoin. Are you telling me that NorthBridge has been planning all this for four or five years?"

"Almost six years," Rex said. "They haven't even begun to show the world their power."

"What do they want?"

"In the long run, that's hard to say, but any answer you can come up with is damn scary. Right now, they want Hudson out of the race and Thorne to win. Even before Fonda's piece connecting you and Thorne, they knew that you could make it happen."

Vonner looked at Rex. The fixer knew many of his secrets—a great many of them—but not all. "You know," Vonner began, "Thorne was always an option, but near the bottom of my list. He's too hard to control, impossible to predict, and way too polarizing."

"Too much like NorthBridge."

"I guess that's why they want him."

"They didn't say. But remember, through their shaving scam and digiGOLD, they could bring down the world's economy anytime. What would that do to you?"

"I'm not going to do it." Vonner pounded the glossy wood table. "Hudson already has this thing won. Thorne would be a disaster." He looked out the round window at clouds tinged gold with sunlight. "Don't worry about me. If NorthBridge wants an economic war, they're in over their heads."

"NorthBridge has people running wild on DarkNet. People I can't keep up with, doing things I can't even understand yet," Rex said, as if admitting this caused him physical pain. "They're self-funding, heavily armed, and seem intent on not just having a revolution, but winning it."

Chapter Thirty-Seven

During the next six weeks, the multiple investigations into Vonner's Stronet bank holding company and Booker's corporate structure stalled. The two powerful men employed armies of attorneys and lobbyists. They'd made enough contributions to the campaigns of those in authority so that without a "smoking gun," not much appetite existed to pursue them. Even SkyNok, the maker of Gruell-75—the military grade explosive used in the Kansas City Federal Reserve bombing—managed to get "closed-door" Congressional hearings.

Since the attack, SkyNok, a company allegedly owned by Booker, had become the target of five separate government investigations. However, citing national security issues —as SkyNok's largest customer of top-secret high-tech weaponry and explosive devices happened to be the US military and seventeen intelligence agencies—the inquiries were combined into a single probe under the jurisdiction of the US Senate Select Committee on Intelligence. Even

Fonda Raton failed to get any progress after posting several follow up pieces. One commentator noted that "Those issues seem to have fallen into the bureaucratic morass of Washington, and subsequently disappeared from the public's consciousness."

Thorne's relentless harassment of Hudson continued, resulting in a slight dip in the frontrunner's numbers. Surprisingly, even Thorne's constant attempts to raise the issue of Vonner's and Booker's questionable dealings fell flat when no other media outlets picked up the ball. Still, beyond those issues, across the rest of the political field, the rhetoric heated up. Heading into the holiday season, it seemed to be a three-way race for the Republican nomination among Hudson, Cash, and Thorne, while the Democrats were divided among Governor Kelleher of New York, Governor Morningstar of California, and Senator Packard from New Hampshire. Newsman Dan Neuman remained in fourth, but had been steadily edging higher in the polls.

After the Colorado attack, NorthBridge had gone eerily silent. The loss of so many Secret Service agents had so stunned the nation that security had been drastically increased everywhere. NorthBridge's wake of violence and the lack of leads had everyone on edge. Major shopping malls installed metal detectors, security companies went on hiring sprees, as did nearly every law enforcement agency in the country. Billions of dollars of emergency funding spilled into local police departments and the National Guard. Citizen groups formed to monitor areas wherever governmental presence was thin.

But the biggest casualty of NorthBridge's reign of terror was the absolute destruction of what remained of American's privacy.

Within days of the Colorado attack, Congress passed the Deter and Detect Domestic Terrorism Act, which became known simply as "3D". On the day the president signed the bill into law, cameras were installed *everywhere*. The idea was to create grids of cameras so that virtually all population centers could be monitored in real time by artificial intelligence algorithms. The ACLU and other privacy advocates screamed about the middle of the night passage and the president's quick signing, but the public was scared, and the 3D system was welcomed by the majority of citizens as the best way to keep safe and find the North-Bridgers.

Fonda Raton posted that a highly placed source had claimed yet another Booker Lipton company had received the contract to install and operate 3D. She went after the story hard, but couldn't find enough evidence to actually verify the allegation.

"There's another war coming," she told her best three reporters as she assigned them the 3D story, "but this one is going to be against the American people . . . and they don't even seem to notice that it's already begun."

"What are we supposed to do?" one of the reporters asked her.

"Same as always," she said wearily. "Expose the truth, before it's too late."

The secret backing of Newsman Dan Neuman by Bastendorff, the mysterious billionaire, had thus far gone undetected, but some political insiders were starting to notice that the two small political action committees supporting the Oregon Governor seemed to have a steady and never-ending stream of donors. Fonda had people checking out those PACs as well, but in her twenty-three years of investigative reporting, she'd never been so frustrated.

"Something's different about this one, something very wrong," she said to an assistant, trying not to sound as fearful as she'd become. "There's no doubt this election is going to change everything."

Chapter Thirty-Eight

Hudson and his family arrived back in Ohio to celebrate Thanksgiving. They'd moved into Melissa's home not long before Hudson's old house had been firebombed. It had since been turned into an armed camp. Only weeks before, Vonner had acquired the two adjacent properties to create a buffer zone. The additional space also housed Vonner's security team, campaign staff, and Secret Service agents whenever the candidate was in town.

The last time Hudson, his four siblings, and their extended families had been together was their mother's funeral years earlier. This time it was a festive gathering with lively conversation, laughter, and reminiscing. The Pounds had a lot to be thankful for; Hudson was the frontrunner for the Republican nomination, people had started to believe he could be the next president, but most of all because Florence and Hudson had survived the Colorado attacks. The drama had drawn his extended family closer than they'd been since Hudson's parents had died.

His top position in nearly every poll made his friends

and family giddy. The country was scared. NorthBridge's reputation as "phantom terrorists" seemed able to strike anyone, anywhere, anytime. People had stopped believing that the government could protect them, but Hudson had personally beaten back a major attack from NorthBridge. His outsider status and "everyman" persona offered fresh hope to a weary electorate. Many voters believed he might really be *the* one, that his words 'We are the change,' might really be true.

Trixie, who ran Hudson's hardware stores, was everyone's favorite, even though she was the only liberal in the Pound clan.

Jenna, the oldest Pound sister, had followed the family tradition and served in the military, where she met her husband, a Special Ops soldier who had been killed on a covert mission in the Middle East. She'd returned home after her husband's death and started an army surplus store in a neighboring county, which had grown to two locations and made her a comfortable living. She had encouraged Hudson to join up after he became reckless and withdrawn for a period following high school. She didn't know what had caused the change in her younger brother, but she had believed a stint in the military could straighten him up.

Adam "Ace" Pound was perhaps the greatest success in the family. He had also done time in the military, learning to fly in the Air Force and later becoming a commercial airline pilot for United. He'd flown all over the globe, never married, but seemed to have no shortage of girlfriends in many cities. Although aloof and somewhat self-centered, Ace's sense of humor and world travels made him hard to dislike. Ace was also even better looking than Hudson. Jenna called them her movie star brothers.

Then there was Dwayne, who showed up for the free

meal and some laughs, but didn't have much to say. Dwayne was essentially homeless, but with the Pound's deep roots in the area, he often landed on someone's couch or spare room for a few days at a time—at least until his drug and alcohol problems flared and he found himself back on the streets. Dwayne called himself "the lost Pound."

They were a proud family. Their father and both grandfathers had served in the military, and their tough, hardworking mother had cleaned houses when she had time. Respect for their parents and country was a common trait, but with their parents gone, the siblings, other than Trixie and Hudson, saw each other less and less.

Hudson finished a toast by raising a Samuel Adams beer. "I look forward to the Pounds' spending more time together."

"At the White House," Ace added, to cheers.

After the big meal, everyone lounged around in small groups talking and finishing up the family favorite dessert—a triple layer German chocolate cake with extra pecans on top. Schueller, who'd been skimming his email, called across to Hudson, "Dad, do you know what this means? I just got an email from someone called 'Athens28.' All it says is, 'Tell your father to follow the yellow brick road.'"

Hudson nodded. "Uh, yeah . . . thanks. Go ahead and delete that."

Schueller gave his dad a puzzled look, but caught the "don't ask questions" expression on his face before shooting one back meaning "tell me later," then did as he was told.

Hudson, with the song "I'm off to see the wizard" irritatingly playing in his head, grabbed his laptop and slipped into an upstairs bathroom. After locking the door, he took the flash drive out of his pocket and pushed it into the USB port. The screen went into "matrix-mode" and, after a painfully slow minute, a chat windowed opened.

Hey, Dawg!

New test – Who was Smedley?

Ha! I have missed you, old friend . . . Smedley wasn't a who, rather a what. It was our code name for those deadly and dangerous things called cigarettes.

Good, Hudson replied, unable to suppress a smile as he typed. *I can't be gone long, so why don't you tell me what's so important that you needed to interrupt my Thanksgiving.*

First, on a quantum level, I'm glad you survived the trip to Colorado. Do you know they don't know where the seat of memory is held? And that time is dependent on memory—at least linear time? It's how it's embedded on space.

What are you talking about? As before, as soon as Hudson typed a reply, the Wizard's words disappeared.

What you went through, Dawg, it's all part of spacetime now, somewhere between here and the Pleiades. The agony of your screams is part of the infinite signal. So you survived, but it's never over, you know? And part of that circle is this possibility. Have you ever heard of a man named Karl Bastendorff?

No. Hudson shook his head, knowing the Wizard didn't do drugs, but wondering if he felt as stoned as he sounded all the time.

Any guess who you'll be facing in the general election?

Probably Governor Kelleher of New York.

How about the governor of Oregon?

No way. But very possibly the governor of California.

No, not Morningstar, not Kelleher. It'll be Governor Neuman from Oregon.

Newsman Dan may be stirring a bit, but he'll never go the distance. He'll drop out after New Hampshire. It'll be Kelleher, maybe Morningstar.

Do you believe me about Vonner? Have you looked into it?

Why would I? Vonner believes in me. And I believe in him.

The man is bad news. You don't get it. In an esoteric sense, this can't be resolved, but you've got to see the connection in the quantum trajectory.

I'm done here. Bye.

No, Dawg, wait. I'll make you a deal. If Newsman Dan Neuman drops out after New Hampshire, I'll never say another bad thing about Vonner again.

Nice of you.

But if Newsman Dan wins New Hampshire, then you agree to make me Secretary of State.

Joking. All I really want is to be Ambassador to South Korea.

I have to go. Hudson couldn't believe he was wasting time with his old spaced-out ex-best friend, who had obviously read too many books on physics, or quantum physics, or metaphysics, or something.

Okay, seriously, when did you lose your sense of humor?

You know when.

Hudson felt bad, knowing his comment would hit the Wizard like a blow to his gut. ***When Newsman Dan wins New Hampshire, you agree to open up that great big mind of yours and listen to me.***

He's never going to win.

Then you agree?

Sure, Hudson typed. The bet intrigued him. Sure, anything could happen in the ten weeks before New Hampshire, but there were three political superstars ahead of Newsman Dan Neuman, including New York's powerhouse Governor Andrew Kelleher, California's popular and charismatic governor Hap Morningstar, and Cindy Packard, the senior senator from New Hampshire. Even in this wild year, he could never imagine Packard losing her home state and either Kelleher or Morningstar not coming in a close second.

Cool. One last thing. Find a way to see Gouge while you're home.

I can't.

You have to.

Why?

You know why.

Does he want something?

He wants to see his oldest friend. Understand the wavelength.

It's impossible. I could never get away. And I can't be seen with him.

Find a way.

Or what?

Find. A. Way.

Chapter Thirty-Nine

Vonner was in the Washington area for a rare personal meeting with a secret, high-level government contact. Vonner's holdings meant that he had offices in more than a hundred cities around the world, but he did most of his work from either his Carmel or Miami estates, and occasionally the Manhattan penthouse atop his tower in the financial district. But there was something about this Rosslyn, Virginia skyscraper with its panoramic view of the nation's capital that he especially liked, as if seeing the power made it more in his control.

His appointment was at nine, but Vonner had been in the office since four a.m. The seventy-two-year-old usually had the stamina of a fifty-year-old; however, this campaign had already taken a lot out of him, and he was tired. The billionaire had been born into money; his father had paved his way and taught him how to manipulate the strings of power. He'd spent his life behind the scenes in a dozen presidential contests and hundreds of senate races, but he knew this one was different. Not just because of NorthBridge and the stakes, which increased every year.

This one meant everything because it would be the last one.

Vonner read reports on all the regular staff who were close to Hudson. A large percentage of them were Vonner's own operatives, planted at all levels of the campaign. These moles, and more just like them in the organizations of every other candidate in the race, answered to one of Vonner's lieutenants.

The excitement around Hudson had grown to the point where he attracted plenty of organic and enthusiastic supporters. One such person was Hamilton, a "kid" fresh out of college. He'd impressed enough top people in Hudson's Iowa headquarters that he got some face time with the candidate on a recent swing through the important caucus state. Hudson liked Hamilton, and invited him to join the national team.

Hamilton, who coincidently worked at a hardware store in Ames, Iowa, had to give two-weeks' notice, and it would likely be another week until Hudson rolled back through when Hamilton could jump on. In the meantime, Vonner had to decide whether they should try to convert the "kid" or let him go.

"What do you think of this kid?" Vonner asked a severe looking woman dressed in a dark suit who ran his covert political personnel operation.

"He's one of those idealistic youths. Republican family, but his girlfriend is a screaming liberal. He seems to think Pound is going to change the world."

"Then you don't think he'll play ball with us?" Vonner asked while looking out the window, across the wide and gentle Potomac River, at the Washington monument.

"Too risky. My bet is that if we approach him, he goes to Pound with it. Why do you care? He's a kid. A nobody."

"I don't want anyone even running errands for Hudson that we don't control." Hudson Pound's national headquarters occupied three floors of the very building they were in. Vonner had left nothing to chance. Every day, trusted staff reviewed transcripts of every word said in every campaign office, emails, phone calls, all of it.

"You don't know if Pound is going to give this kid the time of day. They've moved plenty of other people to national, and he hardly notices. Every campaign does it with good and enthusiastic people. We're *trying* to win, right?"

"Those others were different," Vonner said, ignoring the woman's quip. "Pound is going to see himself in this kid."

"Because of the hardware store connection?"

"Not just that. Military family. Five kids. Raised poor in the Midwest—"

"Damn!" the woman said, jumping to her feet and moving to a large touch screen. "We've got bigger problems than your dumb Iowa kid."

"What?"

"NorthBridge just went insane."

Vonner clicked a few buttons and what appeared to be a ten-foot wide seascape oil painting transformed into a high definition screen showing cable news. The scene of smoke, ash-covered cars, mangled steel, and the burnt-out lobby of a skyscraper could have been footage of the September 11, 2001 World Trade Center attacks, but the images were being broadcast live. They showed 200 West Street in lower Manhattan, a building Vonner knew well—the forty-four-story Goldman Sachs Tower.

"Now they've done it," Vonner sneered.

"It's one thing to go after presidential candidates," the woman added, "even the Federal Reserve, but Goldman Sachs? I'd say NorthBridge has taken things nuclear."

Vonner pushed a button on his communicator. Rex answered a few seconds later.

"Have you seen the latest handiwork from those idiots?" Vonner asked.

"I assume you mean NorthBridge," Rex answered. "Gutsy, bringing the battle to Wall Street."

"They've miscalculated."

"Depends on who they're working for," Rex replied with a barely audible laugh.

"This isn't funny."

"NorthBridge is courting the populists. Everyone on Main Street hates Wall Street. It was a safe bet. And they did it at sunrise, minimizing casualties. In fact, there's already a statement on NorthBridge's website from AKA Jefferson," Rex said. "They issued a warning to NYPD, the fire department, and even hacked into Goldman's internal security to force an evacuation of the building twenty-five minutes before detonation. See, they didn't want casualties."

"How nice of them," Vonner said sarcastically. "Can you reach AKA Paine?"

"I can try."

"With all your magic, you still can't get into the shadows of the *world-wide web*," he said the words as if they were poison in his mouth, "and find out who and where these menaces are?"

"Not yet." Rex laughed.

"Now what's funny?"

"Just how you can characterize a deadly terror organization that just blew up a building, has murdered a couple of presidential candidates, multiple Secret Service agents, attacked the Federal Reserve, and generally brought American intelligence and law enforcement agencies to their knees, simply as a bunch of 'menaces'."

"These are dangerous times. People fear the wrong things. They always have. It isn't the threat of World War III, or gangs rising in the street, or Islamic terrorists, it's the people and institutions they revere, whom they should not trust . . . whom they'd be wise to fear."

Chapter Forty

Rex was right. In the weeks that followed the Goldman Sachs attack, WebSkeer, a company that used algorithms to detect far more data than traditional polling could, showed support for NorthBridge had increased. WebSkeer also claimed to be able to predict, or even sway, future events by tracking keywords and other behavior across the internet. Rex, a fan of the company, had befriended one of the developers and paid him handsomely for a back door. That access allowed him to show Vonner that the billionaire was also right; the masses were indeed fearing the wrong thing.

"Everything is mixed up," Rex told his boss as the two sat sipping cocktails in the expansive Pacific Room back at Sun Wave, Vonner's Carmel estate.

"That's how we like it," Vonner replied, but Rex knew he was worried.

Dangerous times, indeed, the fixer thought as he continued his efforts in tracking NorthBridge, a dozen projects meant to derail Bastendorff, and even more things aimed at pushing Hudson Pound closer to the presidency. Rex oversaw a team who made sure the media reported what Vonner wanted, and another that monitored every aspect and conversation Hudson had—at least the ones they could. Rex obsessively rolled translucent purple dice while listening to summaries. He didn't have the time he needed to stay involved in everything, and bothered only with the bits flagged by the head of each department.

Vonner had his own private intelligence agency—a cross between the NSA and CIA—and sixty-eight people were assigned to Hudson. They analyzed everything, looking through every thread of his life, so Vonner could be sure it all went according to plan. It frustrated Rex that he couldn't know everything. It gave him headaches, but he continued to multi-task while multi-tasking and believed artificial intelligence would one day make it possible for him to fill every void in his knowledge. He worked for Vonner, not so much because he believed in what the billionaire was trying to do, but rather because by mixing his brain with Vonner's incredible wealth, it was his best chance at obtaining what he craved most: unlimited knowledge.

Hudson spent December exhaustively campaigning and preaching both the need for law and order, and the desire for change. Other candidates tried similar tactics as polling consistently showed the two biggest issues for voters were terrorism and corruption. Most people felt the politicians were merely giving lip service to those topics, while Hudson was viewed as believable. Voters thought the hardware store owner would deliver on his promises. Thus, his numbers continued to rise, along with the mudslinging from Thorne and the threats from NorthBridge.

Vonner had pushed Hudson to spend Christmas in Florida, but the frontrunner needed a break and wanted to get back to Ohio. He'd hardly seen Melissa since Thanksgiving, and required a good dose of her grounding. Another reason called him back to the Buckeye State, and on Christmas Eve, he was finally able to tend to a pressing matter from his past.

A chopper with armed agents patrolled the sky over Lake Hope State Park. The 120-acre body of water had three vessels patrolling, and there were six two-member units of Vonner's special security in the woods. All of that, plus a three-person Secret Service detail for each of them. Hudson and Melissa strolled along the shore until they saw a man walking up ahead.

"Is that him?" Melissa asked.

Hudson stared hard at his past. "Yeah." He then called one of the Secret Service agents over. "Listen, I just spotted an old friend of mine. I'm going to talk to him, but I don't want to scare him."

"Sir, we really need to screen him."

"No. That's not necessary."

"Sir, with all due respect, that is not your call."

"Actually, it is," Hudson said. "You can follow us, but do *not* bother us."

The agent looked at Melissa, as if she might join his protest, but she did not. Instead, she nodded, signaling her approval.

"Okay." He went back to the other agents. They all looked over at Hudson. The senior one spoke into his wrist.

Hudson turned to Melissa. "Thanks for helping with this."

She smiled.

"So you'll be good here?"

"Sure. I'll just be skipping rocks. But remember, you agreed. Don't go too far."

Hudson nodded and gave her a quick kiss. He'd told her as much as he could without telling her *everything*. Still, it felt like he was lying to her, probably because he mostly was. The story he'd told her was that Tommy Gouge, a childhood friend who'd been down on his luck and in and out of jail for most of the past few decades, had asked Hudson for help.

"Obviously, it's better if I'm not seen with him, but I have to speak with him," he'd said. Melissa had tried to talk him out of it, even offering to send someone with an envelope of cash if that's what Hudson wanted to do, but he'd insisted. "I don't want to insult him. He's a good man. We grew up tough and poor. If I hadn't joined the Army, I could have wound up just like him." Melissa argued that point, but knew Hudson would never turn his back on a friend, and finally agreed to help facilitate the meeting.

Hudson had cleared the encounter with one very reluctant Secret Service agent on the detail who would reassure the others. As previously planned, Gouge and Hudson crossed paths just before the trail wound into the trees. Melissa stayed back so that only three agents would follow him, but she felt safe knowing Vonner's people in the woods would also pick them up.

"There's the only politician who's survived a tangle with NorthBridge," Gouge said, opening his arms. "You look good, Dawg."

"Sorry, Gouge," Hudson said. "No contact. The Secret Service crew is already nervous they didn't get a chance to—"

"To shake me down?" Gouge looked back at them.

"Hell, I ain't afraid of any spooks. I knew this guy on the inside, came out of CIA special division, he told—"

"We don't have much time." Hudson started walking.

"Yeah, yeah," Gouge said, moving next to him, matching his stride. "Okay, so thanks for coming. I know you don't want to be here, that it wasn't easy."

"I'm glad to see you again." Hudson remembered the "TRUTH" tattoo across Gouge's fingers and thought of the lie he was telling Melissa by not telling her. *Damn the past that chokes the present and terrifies our future.*

"Last time we talked you looked scared. Said you thought I was threatening you." Gouge coughed. "Freaked out that I might tell and take all this away from you?"

"The Wizard tells me you're still my friend." Hudson stopped walking and looked Gouge in the eye. "Are you?"

"I don't understand you, Dawg. How do you think we could be anything else? It's you that should be answering that . . . Are you still *my* friend?"

Hudson nodded and started walking again. Thirty paces behind them, the Secret Service detail shadowed him.

"Anyway, a lot more than just friendship binds us together," Gouge said, lighting a Marlboro. "But we finally have a chance to fix what happened that night."

"That night can't be fixed any more than the nightmare that happened five years after it."

Gouge took a long drag, then slowly exhaled the smoke, watching as the bluish haze dissipated into the organic air of the woods. "You're right, Dawg. We can't fix it all, but that doesn't mean we can't try to fix what we can."

"Have you ever thought . . . I mean, what happened that night . . . it was beyond horrible, but Rochelle didn't have to do what she did. There were consequences and victims of her act that went beyond what—"

Gouge glared at him. "I swear if the Secret Service wouldn't shoot me dead, I'd knock you to the ground right now and beat the hell out of you."

"I can get them to stand down," Hudson said, tensing. "I don't need them to protect me from you."

"You did when we were kids."

"As you're so fond of pointing out, we ain't kids no more."

Gouge held a mean stare. "Rochelle was entitled to do whatever she needed. They made her into what she became."

"No," Hudson said, looking off into the trees, catching a glimpse of one of Vonner's people watching them. "She made it worse."

Gouge scowled. "So you aren't going to help her?"

"I didn't say that."

Gouge looked at him with a crooked smile, then nodded.

"But first I have to win."

"Looks to me like no one can stop you."

"Really? How about NorthBridge, a handful of governors, Fonda Raton, the voters, a skeleton from a dark closet . . ."

Gouge shook his head. "I don't think so."

"Fine, assuming I win, then . . . I'll only have one option."

"A presidential pardon?"

"Yeah, but that's political suicide, at least until the end of my second term."

"Second term?" Gouge raised an eyebrow. "Look at you, Dawg. Saying you might not win, but already figurin' on the *RE*-election." Then he turned serious. "She can't wait that long."

"Have you talked to her?"

"No, but I've spent eight years in prison," Gouge said, taking another long drag. "And she's already done two dimes."

"Twenty years?" Hudson said.

"And then some."

"She killed a man."

"She never admitted to it."

"We both know she did it."

"I don't know nothing 'cept if Rochelle did it, she had a right to do it."

"So you want my first act as President of the United States to be to pardon a murderer?"

"It's the right thing to do."

"How am I ever going to explain it?" Hudson looked back at the Secret Service agents and lowered his voice to a whisper. "What will I say when they ask me why I pardoned the woman who assassinated the governor of Ohio?"

Chapter Forty-One

The day after Christmas, Hudson spent a few hours in one of his hardware stores. Melissa thought it was a bad idea, but he told her it would help to clear his mind before they hit the campaign trail again the next morning. Schueller and Florence were back catching up on their lives, with full Secret Service protection. Fitz and Hudson had agreed the "kids" could sit out December and rejoin the campaign in January.

The Secret Service and Vonner's people had doubled protection around the store, and yet somehow, they didn't bother the customers too much. Most of the locals were respectful of Hudson's privacy, although quite a few of them couldn't resist wishing him well when they found him on the retail floor.

"Can you tell me where to find a plunger?" a woman asked him from behind. "There's a big clog of . . . *stuff* that I'm trying to clear up."

The familiar voice filled him with dread and despair.

Hudson turned slowly. "I have nothing to say to you, Ms. Raton."

She smiled big and pulled her head back as if surprised. "Oh, come on, Hudson. After all we've been through and you're *still* not calling me Fonda."

"I could call you all kinds of things, but 'Fonda' isn't the first thing that comes to mind."

She laughed. "I'll bet."

"I'm serious," he said, moving past her. "I have nothing to say to you."

"Oh, I think you do."

"Well, you're wrong."

"Really? You don't want to talk about Rochelle Rogers?"

Hudson froze.

She walked around to face him. "See, I thought you'd—" His expression, much more panicked than she'd expected, surprised her. It looked like genuine fear, but then she decided it was more like terror. Fonda moved in for the kill. "What about Thomas Gouge? Or Cabot Schifflet? Wade Allen, Mooney Moore, Louis Rich, Michael Plummer, Richard Hirsh—"

"Wait."

"Oh, I've got more," she said. "Seems Vonner and Booker Lipton aren't the only criminals you associate with. In fact, you have twenty-one people with criminal records working for your hardware stores—ex-cons, felons, all kinds of *baaad* people. Even two of your army buddies went on to serve time. And this Gouge character, he's got an ugly record. It's three pages long. I have it right here. Do you want to take a look?"

Hudson shook his head.

"Apparently, you two were good friends back in the day. Were you also friends with Rochelle Rogers? Did you know she killed the governor of Ohio?" She smiled as if she'd just given him a cupcake. "Yes, of course you knew."

Hudson noticed several customers listening. "Gouge and Rochelle went to the same school as I did. She was a few grades back." His mouth was clumsy and dry. The words stuck in the back of his throat, seemingly trying to push through dust and cobwebs, as if he were forcing them through time. "The others are good people. I've always believed in giving folks a second chance. We have a program to help them get back on their feet." Hudson stared off to a display of hinges and locksets, suddenly feeling dizzy. "Can we go back to my office?"

"Oh . . . " Fonda smiled and mock fanned herself. "My, my, now I'm invited back to the king's chambers?"

He looked from her to the customers.

Fonda winked at a chubby man holding a gallon of paint and a couple of brushes. "He wants to have a chat . . . *in private*," she whispered loudly to the customer. "What do you think? Should I risk it?"

The man looked at her, confused.

"Could be an escaped convict back there," Fonda added, laughing. "If I'm not back in an hour, send help."

"Fonda, please," Hudson implored, seeing the man with the paint was also uncomfortable, and others were gathering. A Secret Service agent moved closer.

"Oh, it's 'Fonda' now?" She smiled coyly. "Why yes, Hudson, I'd be delighted." She bent her arm in his direction, waiting to be escorted.

"It's okay, Sammy," Hudson said to the man with the paint. "She's a reporter trying to get a story."

Sammy nodded, as if that answered everything.

"Remember, Sammy," Fonda yelled as she followed Hudson to the back. "If you don't hear from me, call the law."

The man, as if trying to distance himself from the reporter, backed into a cardboard bin of paint roller covers and nearly knocked it over. Fonda could hardly suppress a smile as she and Hudson vanished behind the swinging doors.

Once in his office, Fonda lounged back in a chair across from his desk as if she were a frequent visitor. "Nice touch," she noted, pointing to a large POUND FOR PRESIDENT poster hanging on one of the walls. "That wasn't here last time."

"Fonda, please, you can't post this story."

"What story?" She studied him closely during a long pause. "Oh, you mean the one about your crime syndicate?"

"Crime syndicate!?"

"What would *you* call it when a man has close ties to more than two dozen criminals, embezzlers, thieves, and murderers?"

"Rochelle is the only murderer on that list."

"Not true."

Hudson looked surprised.

"Cabot Schifflet."

"Oh, come on, that was involuntary manslaughter. It was an *accident*."

"Have fun explaining *that* to the voters." She smiled. "And then there's Vonner and Booker."

"Really? Who did they murder?"

"Do you want a list? It's a long one."

"What are you talking about?"

"They haven't been convicted because they *also* kill the witnesses."

"Do you have any proof?"

"If I had enough, don't you think I would have already posted a story?"

"That's what I thought."

"I've got enough proof about *your* gang of criminals. Care to comment?"

"Don't run it."

"Why not?"

"You just can't."

Fonda laughed easily. "Do you know who I am? We're not *really* old friends. Maybe if I'd robbed a liquor store, we'd be friends, but I didn't, and we're not, so you don't get to ask me to trust you. I'm not interested in doing you a favor."

"Just what do you have against me?"

"Vonner."

"You don't like Vonner, so you're going to ruin me?"

"Ruin you? Is this story going to ruin you?" Fonda cocked her head for a moment and then squinted her eyes. "Talk to me, Hudson. I may not be able to trust you, but you can trust me."

Hudson scoffed. She stared back in silence. He could see her calculating.

I never should have said 'ruined me', he thought. *She shouldn't be here. I shouldn't be talking to her. She's going to run the damn story no matter what I say.*

"Hudson, this story, the one I'm going to run, is going to cost you six or seven points in the polls. That's nothing. You're an American hero. Fitz and Vonner's spin-doctors will explain all this away. I believe you. You have a long history of helping ex-cons."

He nodded, and knew her words should be a relief, but he felt even more uncomfortable.

"But . . . if there *is* something else. Something I haven't found yet . . . and there is, isn't there?" She licked her lips slowly.

"No," Hudson said a bit too eagerly while trying to maintain a poker face.

"Oh, Hudson. Why do you insist on doing this the hard way?"

"You're the one looking for a story that isn't there."

"And when I find it," Fonda said, standing up, "I'm going to bury you." She stared into his eyes. "Because even though I think you're a good man, or at least once were, the thing I like least in the world is liars."

She held his stare. He could not speak. He could almost see the calculations and possible scenarios whirling in Fonda's mind. She'd find it. After all these years, someone was going to dig up the secret, and it would be her.

In an attempt to end her probing and the uncomfortable silence, he finally asked her why she hated Vonner so much.

"I don't hate anyone," she said. "But if I did, he would definitely be on the list."

"That's not an answer."

She shook her head as if disappointed in him. Hudson knew her thoughts were still back on what secret he was hiding among the group of criminals who clouded his life.

"Even though your office is bugged," Fonda began, "and even though I don't think you're ready—"

"My office is bugged?" he asked, surprised, looking around expecting to see hidden cameras and dime-store-novel PIs.

Fonda raised her eyebrows. "Your naïveté is amazing." She laughed to herself. "Normally I wouldn't do this," she said, rubbing her hands together, "but since you insist on continuing to lie to me, I'm going to send you straight into the hornet's nest. But when you get stung, don't come crying to me. You asked for this."

"What? I didn't ask for anything."

"You want to know why I don't like Vonner? When you have a little time, do an internet search of his name and the word 'conspiracy' and that will give you some idea. I'm surprised you haven't done it already, but obviously . . . " She paused and stared at him, like a cat about to pounce on a mouse. "Obviously, you haven't."

"The internet is filled with crazy conspiracy theories, especially about the super-rich."

"Let me give you two more pieces of advice. First, some of those conspiracy theories online are actually *true*. And, second, just remember they will know *everything* you search for."

"Who is 'they'?"

Fonda shook her head and sighed, then spoke into the desk lamp as if it were a microphone. "Vonner, you sure found a Boy Scout here . . . incredible." Then, turning back to Hudson, added, "I truly hope they don't kill you."

"Who is '*they*'?" he repeated.

Fonda rolled her eyes impatiently. "Don't worry, I can see my way out," she said while walking into the hall.

It took him a few seconds to shake her words, then he scrambled to the hallway. "Hey, Fonda," he called after her. "Plungers are on aisle seven."

"No thanks, you don't have one that's big enough."

Hudson couldn't help but laugh, but the enormity of what had just happened quickly snuffed out the humor. He had things to do—prepare Fitz, warn Gouge—and then he needed to take a quick drive to Cleveland.

But first he had to do something he'd never tried before.

Hudson reached in his pocket, pulled out the flash drive, and shoved it into his computer.

Chapter Forty-Two

Suddenly paranoid by Fonda's claim that his office was bugged, Hudson grabbed his laptop and snuck back into the warehouse. He set the computer on a pallet of furnace filters, grabbed a roll of electrical tape, and used a piece to cover the in-screen camera.

The monitor filled with the rapidly scrolling characters of matrix mode, and a few seconds later the Wizard's typed greeting came through. **Dawg, is something wrong?**

Everything.

Good, you're finally catching on. This is no accidental universe we live in.

Fonda Raton knows about Rochelle.

There was a noticeable pause on the screen before the next typed line appeared.

What does she know?

Hudson, realizing in his panic that he hadn't tested the Wizard to proof his identity, typed, *How many cases of beer did we take on that trip after graduation?*

Eight. Eight cases of Molson, came back the immediate response. **What does she know?**

So far all she knows is that I knew Rochelle and Gouge. She's doing a story about my criminal associates.

She can't find out about that night.

She can if she gets to Gouge.

Gouge is a rock. Don't worry about Gouge.

I do *worry about Gouge.*

Some people worry too much, some don't worry enough, and others worry about the wrong things. You, Dawg, are deep in the latter category—you've always worried about the wrong things.

Maybe, but how do you know?

You were in the army. Wasn't there a guy, maybe a couple of them, that everyone knew would fall on a grenade to save the others?

Sure, Hudson replied, thinking back on several soldiers he knew in the service who fit the Wizard's description.

Gouge is that guy. He'll do anything for you. But you've got other friends to worry about.

Who?

Vonner.

Not this again.

But as Hudson typed, Fonda's warnings replayed in his head. He'd convinced himself that Vonner chose him because research showed voters wanted a non-politician; that Hudson's record in the Army, on the school board, and as a small business owner made him a perfect fit.

But what if there's more to it? he thought. *What if I'm being set up?*

His doubts were seeded now, yet he had no idea what it meant. Vonner could have chosen anyone. Schueller's question echoed: "Why you?" He still couldn't answer, but one thing Hudson did know was that he was expendable. *Everyone* is expendable. And in the age of NorthBridge, with presidential candidates dying all around, that terrified him.

Do you think Vonner has my office bugged?

Are you kidding? Yes, of course he does . . . and your car(s), home, phones, shower, toilets, everything! Why do you think I go to so much trouble to talk to you encrypted this way?

Hudson read the screen. The words had the effect of food poisoning. *Wait a minute*, he typed in, then got up and bought a ginger ale from the soda machine next to the double doors that led to the restrooms—where he figured he might be headed next—took a slow sip, and then responded by typing a question he didn't expect the Wizard to be able to answer. *What's Vonner's game?*

He's trying to win a war.

The response surprised him. *With who?* Hudson pounded the keys as if his fingers were hammers.

I'm not sure, but my guess is it's against Bastendorff.

This is the second time you've mentioned Bastendorff. Who is he?

One of the richest men in the world.

Then why haven't I heard of him?

That's how you know he's super rich; he's got the power to make sure people don't know about him. But in order to even understand what that means, what's at stake, you need to first look at something that you do think you know about, something that is very different from what you believe.

Which is?

History.

Hudson looked at the word, trying to figure out what his

old friend was talking about. He'd loved history his whole life, and would still be teaching it if circumstances hadn't taken him in another direction. *Wow, how far away from the classroom have I gotten?* he wondered.

How can this help me deal with Fonda Raton?

Just listen, you need to know this. The Wizard's words began filling the screen again. ***It goes way back, but it's primarily the events of the past hundred years or so that have brought us to this point. Many of the highlights of the history of the last century didn't happen the way you think, and the people that created it are using you to make a huge power play. Dawg, it's the endgame, and they're on the final move.***

A Secret Service agent poked his head into the warehouse. "Sir, are you okay?" he asked, scanning the innocuous massive space, checking the bay door to the loading dock.

"Yeah, thanks, Jason. I'm just working on a speech. Needed a little privacy."

The agent spoke into his wrist. "Teacher secure," he said, using Hudson's code name, and then ordered another agent to move outside to the loading dock. With a long look up into the rafters, he nodded, then motioned over his shoulder. "I'll be right over there if you need anything."

Hudson thanked him again and turned back to the screen. Even though all the text had erased, he was still glad he'd kept the computer facing the wall.

I don't have much time, Hudson typed.

Let's hope you're wrong about that. In the meantime, I'll get you a digital file with the true history of the 'American century', and how it relates to the CapWars.

CapWars?

You'll understand when you read it. Too much to get into now.

Is it going to just be more of your conspiracy theories?

There is no 'theory' about it. The CapWars are real, and so is the danger to our country . . . and to you.

What should I do?

Win the election!

The answer surprised Hudson. *But if I'm part of some outrageous scheme . . .*

You are. And that's precisely why you must win . . . because you're the only hope to stop it.

Hudson shut his laptop, bent his head, and broke down.

Chapter Forty-Three

During the drive to Cleveland, Hudson thought about what the Wizard had said, and about Fonda's visit. He missed Florence and Schueller, but even with their dad running for president, they had their own lives to lead. Schueller and his girlfriend had gone to her parents' house for the holiday, and Florence had taken a shift for a friend.

Hudson had alerted Vonner and Fitz of the upcoming Raton Report detailing his association with felons. Fitz had cussed up a storm and generally acted as if he'd been a victim of each name on the list, but the campaign manager quickly came around to what he did best—building a narrative that neutralized the story. By the end, even Hudson had to admit it might make him more appealing to voters.

"Hudson Pound, struck by the sad paths taken by two of his classmates and two members of his army unit, instituted a plan within his company to give those who had paid their debts to society a second chance. Just another way Pound has repeatedly given back to the community. Forgiveness and redemption. We are the change."

Vonner didn't seem fazed in the least by the bombshell.

"Raton can't stop you. Have you seen the latest CompuPoll?" Vonner laughed. "I'm just sorry we have to waste any more time with these damned primaries."

"Well, that's the process," Hudson said. "And we haven't even gotten past the first one yet."

"Don't worry about that. Once the dominoes start falling . . . "

"I wish I shared your confidence."

"Spend your time thinking about the general election and knocking out Neuman."

"Neuman?" Hudson echoed, quite surprised. "You think the Democrats are going to nominate Newsman Dan?"

"Uh . . . well, shoot. I mean, I can hope, can't I? Clearly he'd be the easiest to beat. Don't you agree?"

"I don't know," Hudson said, remembering the Wizard's prediction about Neuman winning New Hampshire. A sick feeling came over him. "I kind of figured it would be Kelleher or Morningstar, maybe Packard."

"You can't always believe the polls," Vonner said.

"Except when they say I'm winning?"

Vonner laughed. "Damn right! Oh, hey, I've got to jump, been waiting for this call."

After Vonner was gone, Hudson stared at the communicator for a long time, thinking about everything his billionaire backer had said, and what he *hadn't* said.

Damn it, Vonner knows it's going to be Newsman Dan and me in the general! How in hell can he know that?

Schueller had been surprised when his dad emailed saying he'd be there in a few hours, but when Hudson insisted on taking a cold walk along the shore of Lake Erie, the younger Pound became worried. Edgewater Cleveland Lakefront State Park was one of Schueller's favorite places—sandy beaches, a wilderness of trees, scenic vistas, and the distant skyline of a beautiful city. Hudson liked the park's privacy, and although Secret Service and Vonner's security agents tailed them, he believed their conversation could not be overheard.

"Listen closely," he whispered to his son as they stared out into the massive body of water that seemed more ocean than lake. "I need you to do some *real* research. Get a new laptop, make sure it can't be traced to you."

"On Vonner?"

"Yeah," Hudson said, almost sadly.

"Something happened? Something that made you believe me?"

Hudson nodded. "I think so. I don't know what to think. How could I have been so naïve?" He thought of Fonda Raton. "How did I let myself believe it was so simple?"

"Simple?"

"That I'd led the perfect life and had all the right attributes to become the first common man to become president."

"Dad, you'll be a great president. The campaign has proven that, your actions in Colorado, the fact that North-Bridge is so threatened by you."

"But who do I believe?"

"Me," Schueller said, turning to his father. "You can believe me."

Hudson nodded. "I know." His words had many meanings.

"Now tell me what you need me to do."

"Find every conspiracy theory, every controversy, every

anything that you can, not just on Vonner, but also Booker Lipton, and some billionaire named Karl Bastendorff. Especially anything that connects the three of them."

"I've never heard of Bastendorff, but there's plenty on Vonner and Booker. I've already accumulated a ton of stuff on them."

"I read those papers you gave me a while back. That stuff was way too general, and not enough facts. Forget the global conspiracy stuff, just concentrate on those three names: Vonner, Booker, and Bastendorff."

"Vonner and Booker are at the center of the storm."

Hudson glanced back at the agents, and then at his son. "What storm?"

"The Illuminati, or whatever you want to call it."

"I remember back in college a few friends really got into that Illuminati stuff and the whole alternative history track. I looked into it, researched, read, dug. Part of me wanted to believe it, but nothing . . . The Illuminati is a myth."

"Yeah, maybe the whacky cult stuff. Maybe the Masonic rituals and secret societies don't add up to a true conspiracy, but someone is pulling strings. It may not be organized, or it may have another name, a dozen names, no name, I don't know. It just seems obvious that this isn't all happening by accident. Look at you. Rich dude decides you'd be a good president, and you go from complete unknown to frontrunner in six months. Is that a coincidence?" He threw a flat stone, skimming the water's rippled surface several times.

Hudson shook his head, leaned down, chose a rock, and skipped it, even more than Schueller. They scrambled for flat stones, competing with each other for several minutes. They both laughed openly, and then looked at each other.

"If the Illuminati don't exist, then why are you telling

me to get a new untraceable computer?" Schueller handed his dad a perfectly flat stone.

"You know why." Hudson threw the stone, then stared at his son, his expression conveying sorrow, a plea for forgiveness, fear, and most of all a desperate demand for caution. "Promise me you'll not just be careful, you'll be perfect."

"I will."

"I can't stand putting you at risk, but there isn't anyone I trust more than you."

"We're already in it."

Hudson shook his head, dismayed.

"What about Florence and Melissa?" Schueller asked.

"Keep them out of it. Melissa will never believe it. I don't even believe it, but when I get some facts, I'll talk to her." Hudson looked back out over the lake. "And Florence has already been through too much," he said, thinking of the horrors of the Colorado attack. "You I can keep close."

"We take care of each other." Schueller held his father's stare. "And what will you do with whatever we find?"

"It depends on what we discover. I just want the truth, but we'll have to sort that out of the rumors and lies that clog the internet."

"Dad, you won't believe how much more is out there than when you looked into this twenty-five years ago."

"Facts, remember. Stick to the facts. If there's enough, then I'll take it to the next level, maybe even withdraw."

"Dad, please, whatever we find, whatever you do, don't quit. Even if we find out Vonner is the worst guy in the world."

Hudson nodded. He knew what Schueller was going to say. His son reminded him of the Wizard and Gouge, and how he himself used to be. Schueller's idealistic nature both warmed and worried him. Hudson had shared that idealism, too, until the night his innocence and trust had been stolen. What would the Wizard, Gouge, and he be doing now if it had never happened? The Wizard lived in a storage shed chasing conspiracies, ghosts, and who knew what else; Gouge, an eternal wrecked ex-con, was a shadow of who he once was.

And what about me? Hudson thought. *I've spent my life trying to help people, trying to fix everything, desperately hoping it would all make up for the mistake we made so long ago. I've been trying to erase something written in blood, trying to forget and simultaneously never forget, until I atoned for it. How long to cleanse that? And there's only one thing left to do, the only way to get close to being back to good. One final gesture. Free Rochelle. And I can only do that if I'm President. Schueller wants me to win so I can somehow defeat a global conspiracy I don't even know exists, but I have to do it to get her out of prison. Saving her is the only way to save Gouge and the Wizard and . . . and the only way to save myself.*

"Dad, are you okay?" Schueller asked, hugging his dad.

Hudson realized there were tears in his eyes and quickly rubbed them away. "I won't quit," he said, grasping both of Schueller's shoulders and staring into his son's eyes, seeing himself at that age. "I won't back down."

"Good."

Hudson hugged his son harder and whispered urgently into his ear instructions for getting hold of the Wizard. "If you have nowhere else to go, and I'm dead, he'll help you."

Schueller pulled back, a little shaken. "Okay, but I won't ever need him. You're gonna live forever." He looked past his father at the agents in the distance, not sure he believed his own words.

Chapter Forty-Four

Vonner stared at the report on his computer. "What the hell is Hudson doing in Cleveland?"

"Visiting Schueller," Rex answered, not bothering to look up from his own computer.

"Just like that? No warning?"

"It's nothing."

"How do you know?"

"I know *everything* about Pound. His entire life, personality profile, every move he makes is filtered through my systems. I eat and sleep this guy. *I know*."

"Okay, so what are they talking about?"

"I don't know."

"Are you serious?"

"It isn't possible to record every conversation, but we have film. I'll review it, body language, facial movements, if we're lucky some lipreading, etcetera. Don't worry, everything will be dissected. He's not meeting with a head of state, another politician, or God forbid a lawyer. It's his pot-smoking kid."

Vonner kind of grunted and flipped to the next report—Bastendorff. It had come in from one of Rex's teams. Rex hadn't even had a chance to look at it, too distracted by NorthBridge. He'd become consumed by tracking them on the DarkNet, amazed by their skills at acquiring data and funds while at the same time avoiding detection. Rex had admitted that even with all his experience and limitless resources, he felt lost in the woods. But bit by bit, millisecond by millisecond, Rex was getting closer.

"Bastendorff thinks he can beat us again," Vonner said, grabbing his scotch and heading to his exercise bike.

"He might," Rex replied absently.

Vonner, ready for a fight, looked over at his most trusted fixer, but quickly saw Rex was wrapped up in three massive screens filled with moving code. Bastendorff had beat them before, but they both lost in 2016. Vonner, knowing Bastendorff wanted the Democrats to win the White House in 2016, had readied himself for the general election. However, he hadn't realized the secretive billionaire was also manipulating the Republican primary until it was too late. This time, Vonner had played both sides by backing multiple presidential candidates from each party. Hudson had always been his first choice, but too much was at stake to let it rest with one novice.

Even Vonner couldn't have predicted just how popular the hardware store owner would become. Vonner worried though that Hudson might be peaking too soon. He appeared to be running away with the election. In politics, one never wanted to be on top too long. Given enough time, anyone could be knocked off.

Melissa greeted Hudson warmly, as usual, when he returned home. She'd done a quick trip to Vegas to give a speech to a convention of top women executives.

"I thought you weren't getting in until tomorrow," Hudson said as she met him in the driveway.

"I thought I'd surprise you," Melissa said, kissing him quickly. "But as it turned out, you surprised me. Where were you?"

"I made a mad dash to Cleveland."

"Cleveland? Is Schueller okay?"

"He's fine," Hudson said as they walked inside. "I, uh, needed to see him. I miss them both so much."

"You're still getting over Colorado," Melissa said, squeezing his hand.

"Yeah . . . I'm kind of a mess." He reached into the fridge and grabbed a Coke.

"And you've been spending too much time with Fitz. You have enough bad diet habits of your own without borrowing any of his."

Hudson didn't laugh at her good-humored dig. He stared at the wall-mounted cordless phone as if it was a gun pointed at him.

Noticing what had his attention, Melissa asked, "Expecting a call?"

"No," he replied absently.

"Are you okay?"

Hudson hugged her and whispered in her ear, "Let's talk out back." Then he held a finger to his lips.

She gave him a strange look, grabbed a coat, and followed him out the sliding glass door to the back yard. Dark, cold, and expansive, the backyard was fenced. He knew the Secret Service had two agents patrolling the other side, but he didn't know where they were. Hudson led his wife to the center of the lawn where two large oak trees grew. He stopped just past where the floodlight's glow faded to shadow and stood inches from her.

"I think our house is bugged," he said, so quietly that she barely heard him.

"Who would do that?"

"Vonner."

"What? Why?" she asked, stepping back as if to give the idea space to find validity.

"I don't know. Why did he choose me? Why does a guy like Vonner do anything?"

"But our home?" She looked back toward the house.

"I know it sounds crazy at first, but when you stop and think about it, Vonner has a lot riding on me."

"Yeah, like the future of the free world."

"Exactly."

"So are you saying we shouldn't be offended? Because I am. It's creepy, Hudson. What have we said in there? I mean . . . does he listen to us having sex?" Her voice raised. "Does he *watch*? Are there cameras?"

Cameras hadn't occurred to Hudson. "I guess that's possible, I don't—"

"How did you discover this?"

"I had a hunch after Vonner seemed to know about some things I only discussed here."

"So you don't know for sure?"

"I'm sure." Hudson didn't know how to tell her about what the Wizard had told him without getting into the whole Rochelle situation, and he knew she would think Fonda was just messing with him.

"But maybe you're just being paranoid."

"No."

Seeing Hudson get defensive, Melissa said, "I believe you, I really do, but let's find out and get them removed."

He looked at her blankly. It had never occurred to him that this problem could be solved so easily.

"Do you remember last year," Melissa began, "when I did some work for Conner Moore, just before he was indicted for that fraud case?"

"Yeah."

"The FBI was monitoring everything he did, and he had a guy find all their stuff and clean it up."

"But he still got indicted."

"That's only because he found it too late. I can get the guy he used. It's not just a guy. It's a big security firm."

"Yes. Definitely. I want them to do the house, my office, my phones . . . *your* car."

"I'll call him first thing in the morning."

"But not from here."

"No, not from here. Just because I'm beautiful doesn't mean I'm an airhead," she said, giving him a friendly shove.

"Oh, I know that," he said, pulling her to him.

"Hey, none of that. I'm not having sex in that house again until we know it's clean."

Hudson laughed, something he hadn't been able to do in a while. "How about out here then?"

"Have you forgotten who's on the other side of the fence?" Melissa said, smiling. She always made him feel better. He knew at that moment that soon he'd have to tell her about that night so long ago, which now threatened everything.

Chapter Forty-Five

The next morning, his last day off before getting back on the trail, Hudson, surrounded by his large security team, headed to one of his hardware stores. He'd been planning to work on a speech and catch up on position papers at home, but couldn't bring himself to stay around until Melissa's contact "took care" of the place. Fonda's warning about his office also being bugged kept him out of there.

Why am I even here? he asked himself as a campaign aide met him in the parking lot.

"Looking for a little normal?" the man said, almost reading his mind.

"I don't know what that is anymore," Hudson replied, motioning to all the Secret Service and Vonner agents. However, he realized his aide was right. He needed a dose of reality, a few hours of his old "normal" life, in spite of the Secret Service's trying to discourage the idea. "Hell, if I listened to all the security people, I'd be living in a bunker."

The aide nodded and gave him the news of the day: Thorne had predicted that NorthBridge would take over a major American city if Pound won the nomination; an oil tanker hijacked off the east African coast; an earthquake in Mexico, significant death toll expected; numerous demonstrations against the 3D system in a dozen states . . .

Hudson lost the rest as he wondered, *How did they get 3D up so quickly?* Schueller had voiced his suspicions that the government had been waiting for an excuse to put 3D in place for years. Hudson realized much more clearly now that little by little, privacy had been traded for security.

Fitz had called. They'd all be back on the trail in the morning; latest poll numbers; a few more endorsements had rolled in; they'd lost a couple of others they had been courting; three fundraisers on the schedule. Vonner's backing gave Hudson the luxury not to feel pressured about bringing in funds, but, at the same time, it was vital that no one be able to say that Vonner was paying the bills. Hudson's popularity had taken care of that. In spite of Fonda Raton's assertions, Hudson was raising more cash, even without Vonner, than any other candidate.

Fitz had also said something in passing which was deeply troubling to Hudson. "Each cycle, the elections get crazier. Each month, the news gets wilder. It's clear that even after you win, this will always be known as the year of the political assassinations." The call had ended before Hudson realized the implications of the statement and how much it bothered him. And his campaign manager's next statement was even stranger. "What can top this for grabbing the public's interest? I guess revolution is next."

Trixie appeared holding a phone. "It's Gouge."

Hudson didn't want to take it, but he had to. "Hey," he said, and as always happened whenever he spoke with Gouge or the Wizard, he was, for a moment, instantly taken back to their good times and teenage adventures.

Then the memories inevitably turned dark as they flashed to that terrible night which had ended his carefree youth.

"Fonda Raton is all over me," Gouge said.

"Not on the phone," Hudson said, annoyed. "Can you get to our friend?"

"You mean in person?" Gouge asked.

"No, I mean can you *talk* to him? *Safely*?"

"I think so."

"Gouge, you can't *think so*, you have to know."

"Okay, okay. I can."

"Good. Do it. And don't talk to *anyone* else for any reason."

"Got it."

Hudson turned back to his aide, still hovering fifteen feet behind him, and resumed the morning briefing. He then made a series of campaign-related calls, but the whole time he felt himself sliding back through the decades to Rochelle.

Later, Melissa phoned and told him that the team of "sweepers," as she called them, had found bugs in the phones and one in the living room, but nowhere else in the house, and no cameras. He felt relieved, even though the feeling of being violated remained and his distrust of Vonner had grown. Melissa pointed out that they couldn't be sure Vonner had done it, and they debated whether they should confront him about it. She voted yes, but Hudson was still undecided. He didn't tell her why, but he wanted to see what the Wizard thought. A part of him also wished he could ask Fonda Raton for advice, but that would be suicide.

The sweepers also said neither of their cars had been bugged, which he assumed was for the simple reason that they'd only used them a handful of times since he'd announced his candidacy. By the end of the day, the sweepers did find listening devices in the SUV he'd been using since he'd been back in Ohio, and another one in his office.

That was too much. Hudson called Vonner.

"Did you bug my home and my office?" Hudson asked angrily as soon as Vonner answered the communicator.

"Of course I did," Vonner said charmingly, as if he'd been doing Hudson a favor. "You're running for President of the United States. Too much at stake, not the least of which is your life. It helps our security."

"Who do you think you are?"

"The man who is going to make sure you become king."

"By any means necessary?"

"Hey, Hudson, this is life in the big city. The *biggest* city."

Hudson wasn't ready to give Vonner another pass, but he also wasn't ready to quit. He had started to truly believe he could win—that he was *going* to win. Not just the nomination, but the whole thing. "You should have told me, dammit."

"How do you think you got this far?" Vonner asked, a smile still in his voice. "You think your Captain America routine has done all the magic? It's nice, but I've done the heavy lifting. This only *looks* easy. Don't start thinking it actually *is*."

Hudson could hear the ice cubes clinking in Vonner's glass as he spoke. "You want to do something like that again, try asking me first."

"Really? Do you want me to ask you every time we do anything gray? I know you prefer things black and white, but anything important happens in the gray areas."

"I guess everything is gray in the shadows."

"Except in the darkest corners."

"I'm sure." Hudson had to remind himself that Vonner was not the enemy. They'd all been paranoid about North-Bridge, and Vonner had taken him from a guy looking for a bank loan to the frontrunner for the Republican nomination. "Do it again, or anything like that, without my consent and I'm out."

Vonner suppressed a laugh. "You have my word."

Chapter Forty-Six

Snow flurries filled the night sky as Schueller and Florence sat at a concrete picnic table in the dimly lit interstate rest area. Florence stared at her brother while she zipped up her down vest against the cold. "You look like hell."

"That's better than I feel," he said, taking off a knit cap and rubbing his head. She saw the reddish-purple circles around his eyes, the strain in his expression.

"Is Dad okay?"

"Kind of."

"What does that mean?" Florence had already been through too much in the campaign and seen dangers too close, too graphic, to take that kind of response lightly.

"He gave me a name to contact in case he dies."

Florence wasn't sure how to react. The risk of his being killed during the campaign was not news. It kept her up nights. But she knew her brother, and had never seen him this stressed. "What is it, Schueller? You've got me here at some freezing rest stop after driving half the day because the phones aren't safe, Skype, email, text—nothing. What's going on?"

They'd both shaken their Secret Service details. It was easier than most people would think because the Secret Service assumed you *wanted* their protection. Schueller felt oddly safer without them as the darkness enveloped the area. The light snow was still visible in the pool of yellowish light cast from the nearby restrooms and streetlights, part of a series of pale lights which illuminated the parking area.

"Vonner. I was right about Vonner."

Florence searched her brain for all the warnings and dire predictions Schueller had made about their father's sponsor.

"Vonner is part of the Illuminati," he added.

She almost laughed at the words, but it was too serious. "You've finally convinced Dad of your whacky beliefs?"

"It's not just me."

"I know. But Schueller, supposedly a group of wealthy families have controlled global events for centuries? Come on. The Illuminati isn't real."

"Maybe not. But what if, like most myths, this one is rooted in fact? I'm not saying they're some secret sect with candles and rituals and all that nonsense. It's not even close to that simple."

"Whatever."

"You may still think I'm crazy, but Dad doesn't." He stood up and fished the last cigarette from a pack in his coat pocket, lit it, and inhaled deeply. The first drag was always his favorite. All the while, he watched silently as Florence took it in.

"Dad *believes* you?"

Schueller nodded, exhaling the smoke away from his sister. She'd long given up trying to get him to quit, but if even the smell of it got anywhere near her, she would go ballistic. Schueller glanced back over to the parking lot as a black van pulled into a nearby space. A guy in a dark suit got out and headed toward the restrooms. Schueller's eyes didn't leave him until the man disappeared inside.

"Vonner is part of a group that's using Dad?"

"It looks that way."

"Is Dad going to quit?" she asked.

"He can't."

"Why not?"

Just before inhaling the mellow smoke from his hand-rolled cigarette, he lowered it, looking sharply into his sister's eyes. "Because he's Dad."

She knew what her brother meant. Hudson Pound was a patriot and a brave man, but more than anything, he was an obsessive problem solver. If he saw something wrong, he couldn't rest until he righted it. "He can't fix that kind of corruption."

"He thinks he can," Schueller said, staring back at the restrooms as a husky man in jeans and a flannel shirt came out, straightening his belt.

"Because he's smarter than they are?"

"No, he just assumes he understands the game better." His eyes followed the man in jeans until he got into a battered F150 pickup truck.

She rolled her eyes, thinking of her father's arrogance about his knowledge of history, as if everything going on now was rooted in something from the past. "The world isn't some old book filled with maps and dates. It's too complex now. Doesn't he get that?"

"I told him that very thing," Schueller said, watching the man in the suit exit the restroom and head back to his van. "I said, 'Dad, the stuff that's going down today isn't based on history, it's about things that haven't even happened yet. Current events are more affected by the future than the past.'"

"What did he say?"

"That I was wrong. So then I asked him what happened to the last guy who thought he could change things, thought he could challenge the puppet masters. I told him I didn't want my father to be the next JFK."

Florence shivered.

"Dad didn't want me to tell you any of this." The F150 pickup finally pulled away, heading back out onto the Interstate.

"Why not? Does he think I'm not already crazy worried? After Colorado, what—"

"It's not that. He doesn't want you to try to talk him out of it." Schueller took another drag from his cigarette and tried not to be too obvious while watching the suit now just sitting in his van, talking on a phone.

"What is it?" Florence asked, following Schueller's eyes to the van. "Did the Secret Service find us?"

"That's not Secret Service."

Chapter Forty-Seven

Schueller looked over his shoulder, wondering if there were more people watching them, more coming for them. "I think it's one of Vonner's goons," he said, taking a quick drag.

"As long as it's not NorthBridge."

"I'm not sure there's a difference," Schueller muttered, crushing out the butt.

"You think Vonner's connected to NorthBridge?" she said, her anger flaring as she remembered what North-Bridge did to them in Colorado.

"He's connected to *everything*. And it's not cool that he's gonna find out about this."

"What?"

"Us sitting here together. It looks pretty suspicious."

"You're my brother."

"Yeah, but why are we meeting at a rest stop at night?"

"Then why did we risk it? Did you just want to scare me?"

"No, I need your help." Schueller leaned into his sister and whispered, "Let's go for a walk."

They moved briskly to the other side of the lot where three semis were parked. Schueller nervously kept an eye on the van from underneath one of the big rigs.

"Do you keep in touch with Zackers?" he asked.

"Zackers?" she echoed, surprised. "Not really. His ex-girlfriend, Sabrina, and I are Facebook friends, but—"

"Can she get in touch with him?"

"Maybe. Why?"

"I need someone who can find stuff I can't."

"Like what?"

"I don't think we have time to get into that right now," Schueller said, noticing a 3D-system camera on the light pole above them. "Man, those things are everywhere."

Florence glanced up.

"And those are the ones we can see," Schueller added. "Bet Vonner has access to them."

Florence shook her head. "Everything isn't a conspiracy."

"Find me Zackers," Schueller said. "Please. And don't even mention his name on Facebook."

"Why? Is Facebook part of the Illuminati, too?"

Schueller reached for a cigarette to avoid screaming *yes*. He found the pack empty, but knew a sealed one waited in his car. "Let's get out of here," he said. "Three-D has facial recognition, and the Secret Service is probably already on the way."

The man in the van watched as Hudson Pound's children left the rest area in the same two cars in which they'd arrived. There was no need to follow; both vehicles were tracked and bugged. He phoned in his report.

Florence didn't believe in a global conspiracy—not because it didn't seem possible. She didn't believe in it because she was afraid it might be true and couldn't bear the thought. Still, after Colorado and knowing her dad's life was at stake, she would do anything to help. She stopped for gas, messaged her old college friend on Facebook, and got lucky. The woman lived in Hancock, Maryland, a tiny town on the route home to Charlottesville. Once Florence explained she'd be passing through, the two agreed to meet for a drink at the Shotgun Tavern.

The bar, decorated with the heads of various animals and neon beer signs, was busy. Florence couldn't help but wonder what else people in the sleepy town did at night. Even there in the nowheresville bar, 3D cameras were present. She caught a glimpse of two men better dressed than the crowd, and silently cursed Schueller for making her paranoid. Sabrina showed up just as a waitress handed Florence a sparkling water and slip of paper.

"That'll get you entered to win a gun." The waitress smiled as if she'd just given a sure-thing stock pick.

Sabrina and Florence hugged, quickly calculating it had been three years since they'd seen each other. Sabrina rambled about the excitement of knowing a presidential candidate's daughter, and how worried she'd been when news of the Colorado attack broke. Florence was tired and wanted to get back on the road, so she quickly steered the conversation to Zackers.

"My dad is looking for computer geniuses to work on the campaign, and I thought of Zackers."

"He's definitely a genius," Sabrina said. "Kind of dark and crazy, too, you'll remember."

"A lot of geniuses are. Do you know where he is?"

"Landed in Manhattan with some start-up doing crazy nano-medical stuff. I should have stayed with him. He'll probably make a zillion dollars when the company goes public."

Florence smiled.

"Of course, no one can stay with a freak like that—"

"But you've got a number for him," Florence pressed, stealing a glance at the two well-dressed guys across the room.

"Yeah, here." Sabrina pulled a number up on her phone. "I'll send you the contact."

"No," Florence stopped her. "Let me just write it down."

"O-Kay."

Florence fumbled in her purse for a pen and scribbled the number on a napkin.

"Hey, are those guys your Secret Service escort?" Sabrina asked after catching Florence looking at the well-dressed men.

"No, they're waiting outside," she lied. "In fact, apologies, but I should go."

"Already? Come on, catch me up quick. I'm a physical therapist, still single, but I am seeing a great guy. Now you!"

"Nurse at UVA, and I run a health blog. I'm married to a very patient man—a lawyer."

"And your dad is running for president. Life is good," Sabrina said genuinely.

"It is," Florence said, smiling as she got up. "Sorry, I

have to run, but next time we'll do a proper visit. I promise!" She opened her purse.

Sabrina waved her off. "I got this."

Florence thanked her and moved to the door, suddenly worried she'd put Sabrina in danger, afraid of the men in the corner, terrified of the 3D cameras, of Vonner's "goons," of everything.

Chapter Forty-Eight

By the next day, Florence managed to put Schueller in touch with Zackers, as well as get word to her father that she wanted to join him in New Hampshire on the weekend.

Schueller caught a last-minute flight to New York in order to meet with Zackers in person. The 3D cameras' facial recognition system at the Cleveland Hopkins International Airport ID'd Schueller before he'd even gotten out of the parking area, but the system had already predicted his destination based on his movements. A woman whose mission meant finding out why Pound's son was going to New York, and also to record everything he did there, quickly reviewed the data. She had just enough time to board a private jet which would arrive at LaGuardia Airport ahead of Schueller.

As the campaign bus rumbled along a snow-packed side street, Hamilton, the young staffer from Iowa who'd distinguished himself by working eighteen hours a day for weeks and always asking for more, sorted lunch orders. He hustled to the private room in the back and handed Hudson a turkey-cheddar club sandwich, fries, and a ginger-ale, then gave Fitz two Cokes, two bags of chips, and a Philly cheese steak.

The candidate read a carefully worded text from Schueller, which might not have made sense to anyone else, but Hudson got the meaning and worried about his son going to New York. Fitz interrupted with the latest poll numbers and a revision to Hudson's stump speech to give more attention to the tax-reform wing of the party.

The snowy streets outside of Keen, New Hampshire, were starting to ice over as the clouds closed over the sun thirty minutes before it was due to disappear below the horizon. The *Pound for President* bus, already ten minutes late for a speech, cruised along as fast as conditions allowed. Hudson stared out the window as the rural countryside, awash in blue shadows, rolled by. His thoughts were far from New Hampshire as the scenery he'd grown so used to in recent months became hypnotic. Hudson stood, stretched, and walked toward the front of the bus where he knew he'd find Hamilton.

Suddenly, the bus slowed as it eased around a car pulled off on the side of the road, hood open. A woman stood staring at the engine.

"Stop the bus!" Hudson yelled.

Fitz came bursting from the back room as if they were under attack by NorthBridge. "Why?"

Hudson pointed back out the window. "That woman is stranded."

Fitz looked out the window, and then toward the section of the bus where the press corps rode. Hearing the candidate's outburst, the reporters were already craning to get a view of the woman.

"Look, Hudson, we'll call someone. We're late."

"No!" Hudson said, a little too loud, as he moved toward the driver. "Stop the bus!"

The driver pulled over. Hudson put on a jacket.

"What are you doing?" Fitz asked.

"I'm going to see if she needs help."

"Wait a minute," Fitz said, moving to block Hudson's path to the door. "She could be a NorthBridge suicide bomber. There could be NorthBridge snipers waiting for you."

Two reporters from major news outlets were now standing next to them.

"I don't think so," Hudson said.

"Colorado!" Fitz barked through gritted teeth. "Let's just call someone for her." He snapped his fingers, pointing to Hamilton. "Get Triple-A on the phone."

"Okay," Hudson said. "But we're waiting here until a tow truck arrives."

Fitz pulled Hudson a few feet away from the reporters and spoke in hushed tones. "That could be half an hour, and we're already behind schedule. What the hell is this about?"

"She's in trouble." Hudson was shaking.

Fitz noticed the candidate's agitated state and saw that the reporters hadn't missed it either. "She's *fine*," the campaign manager assured him. "Nothing is going to happen to her. This isn't Afghanistan."

"Really? A minute ago she was a suicide bomber and snipers were waiting."

"We'll leave Hamilton to wait with her," Fitz said. "Will that be alright?"

"I'm on it," Hamilton said, moving past them and jumping out of the bus.

Hudson nodded.

"Let's go," Fitz called up to the driver.

Hudson watched as Hamilton jogged back to the woman, wondering what he would do if she suddenly turned and shot him. He saw her grateful smile as the bus resumed its journey and thought back nearly three decades, wondering if Rochelle had smiled like that.

Chapter Forty-Nine

For the next few weeks, Hudson endured a whirlwind schedule of stump speeches, luncheons, town hall meetings, and debate prep. There had been some cynics in the media who thought his dramatic plea to help a stranded motorist was more image-building than sincerity, yet many of the reporters present at the scene reported on Hudson's sincere rage at not being able to do it himself. Polls showed his base and a growing number of swing voters believed him to be trustworthy, honorable, even heroic.

During the blur of his pre-primary sweeps across key states, Hudson read the CapWar history file the Wizard had given him again and again. The contents so crushed his world view and shook his faith in history that he hardly knew what to do, but slowly, it sank in. If the CapWars had really happened, if the mysterious author of the file was right, then Hudson had to stay in the race and win. As crazy as it seemed, he repeatedly uttered a phrase to himself that would have sounded comical before he'd seen the CapWars file.

"I have to save the world."

On the eve of the final debate before the Iowa caucus, Melissa and Hudson found themselves alone in a hotel room—alone for the first time since forever. Although they spoke daily on the phone, Hudson had not been able to tell her about Schueller's search for information on Vonner and his ties to an Illuminati-like group, or the CapStone conspiracies that the Wizard had presented. There seemed to be so many secrets.

"Are you okay?" Melissa asked while taking off her shoes. "You're too stressed."

"I know."

She walked over and pushed him down on the bed. "You can't forget to relax." Melissa straddled him and playfully pinned him down.

"I wish I knew *how* to relax."

"Are you worried about the debate?"

"No, that may be the one thing I'm not concerned about," he said as she stripped off his necktie. "I just don't trust Vonner."

"Of course you don't," she said, leaning back as she helped him get his sport coat off. "Why do you have a problem with that?"

"Why? Why did he choose *me*?"

"Because . . . you . . . are . . . the . . . change."

He raised his eyebrows.

Melissa stood up and pulled off Hudson's shoes. "Remember, people elected Trump for the same reason they're voting for you. They knew something wasn't working, and realized only an outsider could fix it. Trump failed because he didn't understand there was only one way to take on the establishment."

"Which is?"

"The coastal elites, with all their money and power, have one weakness: there are so few of them, and that's no small thing. Even though the masses forget they have the advantage of numbers, the ruling class has never forgotten that fact. That's why, for so long, they've pitted us against each other. Divided we fall, united we stand."

"Clearly Trump missed that point."

"Yes," she said, kissing him. "Half the people despised him. Fueled by his own faults, the media, being the elites' propaganda machine, fanned those flames and portrayed him as the devil. Remember all the comparisons to Hitler?"

"Why won't the media do that to me?"

"Because they can't. You're not a billionaire, you're one of the people. The people love you." She undid the button on his shirt, opened his belt. "If the media tries to vilify you, it will only expose their corruption even more."

"It won't be that easy."

"You're a former teacher, an army vet, a hardware store owner, a small-town hero, an all-American every-man, and that's the reason Vonner picked you. You're exactly what the masses want; a man without scandal who will do what he says."

Hudson felt his stomach tighten when she mentioned scandal. "The media will invent something."

"Nothing anyone can prove." Melissa pulled him on top of her.

"That hasn't stopped them in the past."

Getting updates from Schueller was difficult since virtually no means of communication could be trusted other than face-to-face, and with 3D, even *that* couldn't be counted on any longer. However, in a few days, they would see each other in New Hampshire, and Schueller had promised answers.

Was Vonner connected to the CapStone conspiracy, and was there any truth to the CapWars history? From what Schueller had told him about Zackers and the information Zackers had come up with thus far, Hudson was impressed, but also concerned.

He went into the final debate before the Iowa caucus distracted and uneasy about the prospect of an incredible decades-old conspiracy swirling around him.

Fitz had insisted that Hudson go after Thorne as much as possible, and so he did.

"Don't you see? NorthBridge isn't releasing anything bad about Thorne," Hudson said at the end of an answer about the many disclosures and intercepted communications from politicians and government agencies coming out of NorthBridge. "They're targeting me, and others, but they want Thorne to win. Why is that?"

"Maybe because they know a true leader when they see one," Thorne broke in.

"Are you supporting NorthBridge?" the moderator asked the shock-jock.

"I can't help it if they like me," Thorne replied, smirking. "But Pound is the one who speaks their language—constantly talking about what the Founders wanted, returning the country to its eighteenth-century grandeur."

"Not by blowing people up," Pound protested.

"Ha! You gave them the idea! You started their revolution with your empty rhetoric," Thorne said. "Even if you don't believe the BS you spew, those patriots do."

"Are you suggesting Mr. Pound is somehow supporting NorthBridge?" the moderator asked. "Need I remind you they have on more than one occasion attempted to assassinate him?"

"*Allegedly*," Thorne replied tersely. "For all I know, the media made it all up."

"Are you serious?" Pound asked.

"You may pretend to be anti-establishment," Thorne said, raising his voice, "and maybe you even think you are, but Vonner *is* the establishment, and you're his boy. He *owns* you. *That's* why the mainstream media loves you. *That's* why I don't have a chance. They're using you to fool the voters into thinking it's going to be different this time, but it won't be, because there is only one *true* anti-establishment candidate in the race, and that's *me*."

"Yet isn't it true that *you* work for Arlin Vonner?" the moderator asked Thorne.

"I'm on the radio, part of the media," Thorne said. "The elites control the media just like they do everything else. I've never met Vonner, and he's not involved in my show in any way."

"He just owns it," Hudson said.

"He may own my show," Thorne shot back, "but he doesn't own *me*, which we've already determined is something you damn sure can't say."

"I want to return to the subject of NorthBridge," the moderator said.

"Vonner does not own me," Hudson interrupted, with less conviction than he would have liked.

"We're moving on," the moderator said.

"That's what you think, Pound!" Thorne shouted. "I just hope you find out the truth before you're sitting in the Oval Office."

"The truth?" Hudson asked.

"That you should have voted for me. I'm real. Pound is fake news!"

"*Gentlemen . . .* " the moderator said firmly. "NorthBridge has become the number one issue voters are concerned about in this election. The country has never experienced anything close to this level of domestic terrorism. And Thorne, I have to ask you this because throughout the campaign you have refused to condemn the terrorist organization. Would you explain that position? And are you prepared to denounce NorthBridge and their violent methods here today?"

"One, I think it is unfair to brand them as terrorists," Thorne began.

"Unbelievable," Hudson muttered, still reeling from Thorne's "fake news" statement, feeling a little too much truth in it.

"Two," Thorne continued. "NorthBridge may be no different from our own Founding Fathers. Would you call George Washington a terrorist?"

"They're murdering innocent people," the moderator said incredulously.

"So did George Washington—"

The moderator cut him off. "Washington's army killed other *soldiers*."

"Not exclusively," Thorne said. "Check your history. Civilians were killed."

"We were at *war*," the moderator said, incensed.

"So is NorthBridge," Thorne replied. "I suggest that

NorthBridge sees their cause as no less important than the signers of the Declaration. They're fighting a revolution against a corrupt government which benefits only the elite ruling class while the majority of the population suffers . . . sounds like 1776 to me."

"Just to be clear then," the moderator said. "You are refusing to condemn NorthBridge?"

"I do not condemn them. I am fighting a similar revolution. However, I prefer peaceful means, but I certainly understand NorthBridge's frustration."

Hudson shook his head. "He is not fit to serve."

Thorne stuck out his tongue at Hudson, then laughed raucously. He smoothed his shiny, clean-shaven head as if looking in a mirror, then eyed the moderator while rubbing his nose with his middle finger. "Got any donuts in craft services?"

Chapter Fifty

Only one person seemed surprised when Hudson won Iowa—the candidate himself. The victory suddenly made it real. All the polls and pundits had been predicting it for weeks, but until the voters actually spoke . . . now it was history.

The results hadn't even been close. Hudson won the Iowa caucus by the widest margin ever. Before Hudson could begin his victory speech, it took seven full minutes for the crowd to stop chanting "WE. ARE. THE. CHANGE." The media had expected a win, but nothing like the trouncing he'd given his rivals.

General Hightower, who'd been hoping to do well with his "law and order" message and tough talk against North-Bridge, came in last, and formally withdrew his candidacy for the Republican presidential nomination. Fitz had already been talking to the general about endorsing Pound, dangling but not promising the position of Secretary of Defense.

"Your boy sure is confident," Hightower had said

gruffly, but that was just posturing. The endorsement would come a few days later.

The Democrats had their own Iowa surprise when Dan Neuman edged out the three frontrunners—the governors of New York and California and Senator Packard—in a tight, four-way race. Hudson recalled the Wizard's then-insane prediction that Neuman would win New Hampshire. Suddenly the impossible looked possible, and the consequences meant that not just the past was a lie, but also the future.

"Hudson Pound, you're on your way," Melissa told him between kisses as he sat dazed in their hotel room. "Do you believe it now?"

"Barely," he said, almost giddy.

"Get used to it, baby. You're going to be the next president."

"Plenty of people have won Iowa and gone on to not even be their party's nominee," Hudson cautioned.

"You're all optimistic and rosy when you're out there giving speeches, but in private—"

Hudson cut her off. "My speeches are about the country's future, not mine."

"Silly man, when will you realize that the country's future and your future are the same thing?"

Three days later in New Hampshire, Schueller acknowledged the Secret Service agent posted at Hudson's hotel room door.

"He's expecting you at this hour?" the agent asked. "It's four-thirty a.m."

Schueller nodded, and the agent reluctantly knocked.

Hudson answered, hugged his son, and ushered him inside. Hudson had just finished breakfast—doughnuts and a banana. Schueller had not been asleep yet.

"You look like hell," Hudson said, concerned.

"Don't worry, I feel much worse than I look," Schueller replied with only a quick half-smile. "How much time do we have?"

"Thirty minutes, unless Fitz gets up early, and since that's never happened, we might be safe."

"Good. We should go outside."

Hudson looked apprehensive.

"We *have* to," Schueller said impatiently.

"I know, but it's minus eight degrees out there."

"Better get coffee."

"Better get a campfire," Hudson said as he bundled up and pointed to a donut he'd saved for his son. Schueller nodded.

A couple of minutes later, the two, trailed by a couple of tired Secret Service agents, were trudging through a few inches of crunchy snow as they walked down an alley and into an open area between a gas station and a diner. Neither one was open, although the early shift inside the diner could be seen starting their jobs.

Schueller lit a cigarette. "It's not good, Dad. Like I told you before, all I found was theories and circumstantial stuff that showed Vonner might be a jerk, might be affiliated with the corrupt corporations, banksters, defense contractors, criminal cartels, dictators—lots of unpleasant characters."

"*Might* be," Hudson repeated.

"Yeah, but there's lots of stuff, *reams* of it, connecting the dots," Schueller said, exhaling a line of smoke, exaggerated in size as it mixed with his warm breath in the frigid air. "But it would take a full-time staff weeks and weeks to sift through, and it wouldn't be worth it because it doesn't really prove anything except, like you said, rich men are always the targets of conspiracy theory nuts."

"But?" Hudson asked, knowing his son had more.

"Zackers," Schueller said, bouncing on his feet, trying to stay warm. "Zackers doesn't drive the same roads on the information superhighway."

"Tell me more about him."

"His name is Zack, and you know he went to school with Florence," Schueller began. "Back in college, he hacked into the school's servers, but not for why'd you think; not to give himself a four-point-oh GPA, or to rearrange his class schedule, not even to see what his professors were earning. Instead, he went for donors, the endowment—"

"Wait, he embezzled funds?" Hudson asked, alarmed.

"No, nothing like that. He wanted to know where the money came from and where it was going. Investments, connections, research grants, corporate ties, the whole shooting match. Remember when the university financial scandal broke?"

"Of course. It was huge. And you're telling me this guy, Zackers, was *the* source?"

"Yeah. Seventeen schools implicated."

"But no one ever knew where the media got their information."

"No, but now *you* know. 'Zack the hacker,' also known as 'Zackers'."

"So what did he find on Vonner?"

"A lot," Schueller said. "So much, in fact, that he's scared to death."

Hudson went through the day on muscle memory—the speech he'd given hundreds of times, the smile, handshakes—all of it choreographed and led by Fitz. No one could have noticed that with each breath, he heard his heart beating, and felt as if he were trying to run uphill through an avalanche. Doubts stabbed at him as he uttered mantras on policy and made promises he was no longer even sure he could deliver.

Questions choked him: *Are the CapWars real? Is Vonner involved? Why did he choose me? Who is behind NorthBridge? Why haven't they been caught?*

The last two mysteries also echoed across the Internet and cable news. Many Americans wanted answers about the greatest terrorist threat in the nation's history. With each passing day, more conspiracy theories surfaced—the most popular being that someone in the government, most likely the NSA, was behind the attacks in order to advance an agenda meant to seriously restrict civil liberties. Others believed it was a CIA plot to swing the election so the current president could declare martial law and remain in power.

Several websites claimed to have evidence that the Chinese were funding and controlling NorthBridge, which fueled still more sites to suggest *that* was part of a greater conspiracy attempting to bring about war, or at least the cause for a massive military build-up. Underlying all the fear-mongering and far-out ideas was a simple truth that could not be denied: the government had not made a single arrest, or even identified one suspect. In eight months, there had been dozens of leaks and attacks attributed to North-Bridge, yet the authorities appeared no closer to stopping them.

With all of that, and the added pressure of trying to get

the nomination, it was the CapWars that robbed Hudson of desperately needed sleep. The possibility that the precious history which held his world together was wrong, terrified him. It would mean that if truth is the first casualty of war, then the last century of civilization had existed as a lie.

Yet even the CapWars and those NorthBridge monsters paled next to the demon that tormented him most—Rochelle, and the thought that Fonda Raton would somehow put the pieces together.

Chapter Fifty-One

The New Hampshire primary wasn't the blowout that Iowa had been, but Hudson still won by eight points. Professor Wiseman was a surprise second place finisher. Cash came in third. Thorne impressed with a solid fourth place showing.

However, the real stunner, at least to everyone other than the Wizard, had been on the Democrat's side. Newsman Dan—the Oregon governor—not only defeated Governor Kelleher again, but also beat New Hampshire's own senator, Cindy Packard. His win had been by less than eleven thousand votes, but it was enough to end Packard's once-promising campaign.

The Oklahoma governor and two others dropped out of the Republican race, leaving Hudson with five challengers: Cash, Wiseman, Thorne, Brown, and the Congressman from Florida. The results meant Hudson Pound was for real, and some pundits even mentioned the possibility of the race being decided on Super Tuesday, the day when twelve states would vote and approximately twenty-five percent of the Republican delegates would be awarded.

Hudson didn't care what the political talking heads had to say about his victory. It was Newsman Dan's New Hampshire win that mattered. It meant the Wizard knew things, *dangerous* things, and that Hudson had to talk to his old friend immediately.

As urgent as he considered the need to reach the Wizard, Hudson couldn't make it happen right away. *A candidate's life is not his own*, Hudson thought, not when he had just won Iowa and New Hampshire.

It took two days before he could be alone long enough to initiate contact. Hudson was finally able to lock himself in a Las Vegas hotel suite just after two a.m. A full day of rallies loomed after what would already be not enough sleep. Fitz had just left. Melissa was in South Carolina (they'd talked earlier, but likely wouldn't be together again until Super Tuesday). While eating crackers and guzzling a ginger ale, Hudson glanced at the schedule. In five hours, he'd be at a morning prayer breakfast. He needed to get to bed, but this might be his last chance for several more days. He'd sleep on the plane tomorrow night.

Hudson shoved the flash drive into his laptop as if he were pushing a knife into an attacker and wondered if the Wizard was awake. Less than a minute later he had his answer when the matrix cleared from the screen and his childhood friend's words typed across a small window.

New Hampshire, new problem, huh?

More like a new nightmare. Hudson typed back first their code question, and then what he really wanted to know. *What year was the "rustang" we never finished? And How did you know about Neuman?*

Nineteen sixty-seven primer gray Ford Mustang, the Wizard typed. ***Because Bastendorff is backing Neuman.***

With the help of Schueller and Zackers, Hudson had learned a little more about Bastendorff, but the guy was still like a ghost. His wealth, referenced in only non-official fringe sites, was estimated to be in the hundreds of billions, making him the world's wealthiest man, depending on what one believed about Booker Lipton.

Who is Bastendorff? How come he's not listed on Forbes Four Hundred Wealthiest list? How come Bloomberg has nothing on him? How does someone hide a couple of hundred billion?

Have you been looking into this?

Of course I have!

Don't do that, Dawg! It's too dangerous.

More dangerous than Colorado? This is all dangerous! I need to know what's going on.

I'm serious. They'll know you've been looking.

Who? Vonner? Bastendorff? Who cares? Hudson rubbed his eyes.

They do. They care about everything. These guys are into control.

I get that, at least if all that stuff in the CapWar file is for real. Where'd you get your information?

They can't do what they do without leaving a trail, even if it's a small one. Over the decades, little shreds of evidence get dropped, leaked, mislaid, stolen, whatever. It's a war, Dawg. Wars are messy. And in this one, there are many, many sides.

How many?

It fluctuates.

How many currently?

Six? Maybe more. We don't know for sure.

Who is 'we' Wizard? Who do YOU work for?

Look, man. I'm trying to help you. I'm in a

thousand things, quantifying the edge aspect of protons, gravity control, infinite energy, artificial intelligence, infinite vibration . . . are you aware that every point contains the whole? Do you get that? What I'm saying is that what's going on can be corrected, or not, in many different ways. This is huge. You have no idea.

No idea? They have me on track to become the next President of the United States. I'd say I have some idea of the scale of what's going on.

No, you don't. This is much bigger than the presidency. And with Bastendorff backing Neuman, your road to the White House just got a lot tougher.

Again . . . who do you work for?

That's a lot to type, the Wizard replied. ***Richard Feynman points out that, "It does no harm to the mystery to know a little about it." Particles are not isolated, Dawg, the particles are related. See?***

How hard could it be to type a name? Or just initials? CIA? A foreign government? Exxon? Who? WHO?

Dawg, you think I'm out there? Man, you're waaay out there. Look, when this all began for me, I had not the least interest in politics. I was looking for the unifying theory of everything. You know, physics, metaphysics, quantum physics, space time, life, death, everything. I got deep and heavy into it, and eventually found UQP, Booker Lipton's scientific foundation. He's into the same stuff I was trying to link together.

So, you're working for Booker Lipton. That makes sense.

No, it doesn't, Dawg. I'm not working for Booker, but that's when I began to find out more about Booker and why such a rich dude would be

into all the wild esoteric stuff I am. **THAT** *made no sense. And the more I looked into him, the more I found. And it wasn't just his interest in quantum. I came across conspiracies within conspiracies. About that same time, I first discovered Bastendorff, and that's when it all got really weird. That's when I went down the rabbit hole.*

You haven't answered my question.

What do you want me to say? That I work for the anti-CapStone league? That there's some group out there trying to right the wrongs and take back the world from these freakin' parasites? I can't say that, Dawg. I wish I could, but the truth is that no organization like that exists. I'm afraid the sad fact is that I just work for you.

Me?

You. As soon as I found out you were running on Vonner's dime, I knew you were in trouble. So, I dove deeper than ever into CapStone. Before that, it had just been a frightening hobby, like a drug habit. Like, I knew I shouldn't shoot up, shouldn't do another line, but I couldn't resist the danger, the overwhelming weight of it. Their power is like . . . these guys are like **GODS.** *Do you get that?*

Hudson had trouble sleeping after the chat with the Wizard. At one point he paced to the window and stared out at the Vegas strip, still glittering with brightly lit neon. The surreal, futuristic backdrop juxtaposed against the reality that for more than a century a secret group—or several groups—

had been fighting for control of the United States and, ultimately, the world.

No one knew exactly when the CapStone conspiracy had begun or how many CapWars there had been, but Hudson could see the origins of the Illuminati and Free Mason legends in the CapStone story. The people vying for total control over a world were referred to as REMies, the origin of the name as murky as that of the groups they represented. Their efforts to manipulate the masses were seen as the symbolic building of a pyramid—each level built upon the one beneath it, always trying to reach the top: the CapStone. The competing groups struggling to get to the top first turned on each other, and the CapWars ignited. Yet even while fighting among themselves, they continued to use and deceive the unsuspecting populations.

Hudson reviewed the list of CapWars in his head; events he knew well from history, but now believed had been artificially created by the CapStone conspirators or REMies.

• 1913 – US Federal Income Tax begins and Federal Reserve Bank System established, creating the authority of the private bankers to issue Federal Reserve notes (known as US Dollars today).

• 1929-1935 – US Stock market crash and worldwide depression. After which, the pyramid with the all-seeing eye in the capstone first appeared on the back of the US dollar bill.

• 1939 – World War II begins.

• 1963 – US president John F. Kennedy assassinated for refusing to cooperate with the REMies.

• 1976 – US president Jimmy Carter elected – REMies involvement unclear.

• 1987 – US and world stock markets crash.

• 2001 – Terrorist attacks of September 11th.

• 2008 – Financial crisis and great recession which followed.

• Today – Current presidential election allegedly caught up in the CapWars.

Those were the events that the Wizard and others had thus far linked to the CapStone conspiracies and thought to be CapWars, but many others—including most wars and US presidential elections—were suspected. Hudson couldn't shake the sick feeling that it was too big to take on. Even if, by some miracle, he became president, he knew he wasn't as smart or brave as JFK. How could he hope to bring down the richest and most powerful people in the world? These people that had been working together for decades, and generations before that, in the greatest conspiracy the world had ever known?

The Wizard's words pounded in his head, like the glare of the blinking lights from the casinos below.

"They control **EVERYTHING** and *EVERYONE*!"

Somewhere in the hours before dawn, Hudson managed a few hours of sleep. He snuck in a quick call to Melissa while shaving. Grateful for her grounding, he wished they could be together more.

Fitz greeted him early with two cold Cokes. "No thanks," Hudson said. "I'll get coffee downstairs."

"Suit yourself," Fitz said. "I wanted to drink them both anyway."

Later, after two quick appearances and three cups of coffee, Hudson excused himself on the way to his motorcade. Two Secret Service agents accompanied him to the men's room. One of the agents swept the restroom.

"All clear, sir," he said to Hudson, joining the other agent guarding the door outside.

While Hudson washed his hands, a man exited one of the stalls. The room was supposed to have been empty. Hudson's first instinct was to yell, but then he recognized the man. Booker Lipton stepped up to the sink next to him and rinsed his hands.

"Hudson, good to see you again."

"How did the Secret Service agent miss you?" Hudson looked around, alarmed, but the polished black marble and gold didn't seem to be hiding anyone else.

"He didn't."

"He didn't miss you? He let you stay?"

"Agent Pearce works for me . . . on the side."

"I don't think that's allowed."

Booker raised an eyebrow. "Since when do the rules matter?"

"Okay, whatever," Hudson said, still thinking about yelling for his security detail. "You've gone to a lot of trouble. You must have something to say to me."

"I do," Booker said, drying his hands and then tossing the paper towel in the trash can. "You need to be careful of Bastendorff."

"I don't know who you're talking about."

Booker frowned. "Let's not waste each other's time. You know *exactly* who I'm talking about."

Hudson nodded apologetically, angry at the same time. "You mean your fellow REMie?"

"Bastendorff doesn't want you to win under any circumstances," Booker began, ignoring Hudson's comment. "He's backing Governor Cash and Governor Neuman—"

"Wait, Newsman Dan *and* Cash?"

Booker nodded.

"Why would he support a Democrat *and* a Republican?"

Booker smiled and cocked his head. "You don't really still believe there's a difference, do you?"

"I'm different," Hudson said.

Booker smiled. "Bastendorff will do anything. This is the first time a presidential candidate has been assassinated since Bobby Kennedy, and they've killed two already." Booker paused and stared at Hudson, making sure he had his attention. "There will be more."

"But that's NorthBridge, not Bastendorff."

Booker gave Hudson an incredulous look. "Let's say I wanted to meet you for a private conversation and I ask a Secret Service agent to arrange it. Now, *I'm* the one who wanted the meeting to happen, but the Secret Service agent is the one who *made* it happen. Do you understand what I'm saying?"

"NorthBridge works for Bastendorff?"

"We live on a round planet spinning through space. Sometimes up is really down and vice versa, we have no way to ever be sure. Bastendorff and NorthBridge may want the same thing today. Tomorrow, they may not. You're a history teacher. Remember, Stalin and the Soviets were our allies during World War II, then we spent the next forty-five years fighting them in a so-called Cold War. We trained and funded Osama Bin Laden, used to be pals with Saddam Hussein—get my meaning?"

"Okay, so you're supporting me now?"

"Let's just say that you're no good to me dead, and no good to me if you lose."

Hudson smiled uneasily. "I definitely also prefer to live through this."

"There is no guarantee, and even less of a sure thing is your victory. Bastendorff is a formidable foe, and a bastard.

Now, I'm sure you'll get the nomination. Vonner, who's another type of bastard altogether, ought to be able to pull that off. But the presidency is a different matter. Rigging the general election may sound easy, but believe me, it's not."

"Does Vonner know you're helping us?"

"No. Vonner doesn't like me much."

"It's mutual, isn't it?"

"Oh, I don't know about that. Suffice it to say, we need Vonner for the time being."

"Donations from you could cause trouble. Fonda Raton, Thorne, others think—"

"You don't need my money," Booker said. "I'll be assisting behind the scenes."

"There's a lot going on behind the scenes already."

"You have no idea," Booker said, looking toward the door. "Just remember that no matter what cable news says, what Fitz and Vonner claim, your rise is not a foregone conclusion . . . But it *has* to happen. Bastendorff must be stopped."

"I need to know more."

"You will. I'll be in touch," Booker said, shaking Hudson's hand. "Now, you'd better go."

Hudson turned back when he reached the door. "Hey, Booker, how'd you know I'd come in here?"

"I didn't."

"What if I hadn't?"

"That doesn't matter."

"Why not?"

"Because you did."

Hudson just shook his head.

"And, Hudson? Let's keep Agent Pearce's moonlighting just between us. Never know when you'll need to reach me."

Hudson didn't trust Booker, he didn't trust Vonner, and now he didn't trust the Secret Service. *I'm running out of people to trust*, he thought as he caught up with Fitz, who always seemed to be in midsentence about their next event. *Why would I ever need to contact Booker?* Hudson wondered, glancing at Agent Pearce before getting into the vehicle.

Chapter Fifty-Two

Schueller didn't want to tell his girlfriend about the call he'd just had. He didn't want to tell *anyone*.

It had been his dream since he'd first picked up the guitar at age twelve to get a record deal, and now it had happened. Or, at least, the *offer* had happened. And not just some small-time indie deal. No, this was *Warner Music*—the big time! But Schueller had become jaded by all he'd learned in the past few months. He knew that Vonner's reach was everywhere, that the music industry was just another tool for the billionaire to use to get what he wanted. He couldn't tell his girlfriend because he'd have to tell her why he wasn't going to take the deal, and then she'd want to know *why*, and he'd have to tell her everything. No way. Too dangerous for her and everyone else.

Instead, he called his sister. At Zackers' insistence, they used burner phones now—disposable and cheap from big box retailers, and much more secure. Schueller knew enough now to understand it was all but impossible to beat the NSA. The government spy agency would still intercept and store the call, but if they were careful about what they discussed, it would be a long time before the NSA knew who was talking. Burner phones also meant Vonner couldn't monitor them. At least they *thought* he couldn't.

"How do you know it's Vonner behind the offer?" Florence asked. "You're a talented guy—videos on YouTube, great tracks on iTunes, Pandora, Spotify—maybe someone finally noticed."

"I'd like to think so," Schueller replied, "but the deal is too good. And they want me out in Los Angeles right away. No, it's Vonner. He wants to shut me up."

"Couldn't he do that another way?" Florence asked, almost whispering.

"You mean like *permanently* shutting me up? I think that would be too messy, too risky given Dad's situation."

"I guess so. I *hope* so," Florence said, thinking about Colorado. "Have you told Dad about this?"

"No, and I'm not going to. I don't want Dad thinking he's messing up my life. He doesn't need one more distraction, one more stress."

"Won't Vonner get even more crazy when you turn it down? I mean, he'll know that the only way you'd say no to a record deal is if you're onto him."

"Yeah, I thought of that." He was quiet for a long time.

"So what are you going to do?"

"I don't know."

On the eve of Super Tuesday, Hudson was on fire. Wins in Nevada and South Carolina had given him a perfect four-state winning streak going into the big day. However, Governor Cash was expected to win his home state of

Texas, as well as Arkansas and Georgia. Thorne even had a chance in Vermont and Tennessee. The Democrats were more competitive, with Morningstar acing Nevada and Governor Kelleher taking South Carolina.

"They don't call it Super Tuesday for nothing," Fitz said. "Come Wednesday morning, we'll have a damn good idea who's going to get the nomination."

As it turned out, they knew by the end of Tuesday night. Hudson won seven of the states, and came in a close second on four more. It would be very difficult for any of his rivals to catch him now. Senator Celia Brown, the Florida congressman, and the Oklahoma governor withdrew from the race, and just like that, the Republicans were whittled down to three—Hudson, Cash, and Thorne. For the Democrats, a similar house cleaning occurred, leaving only the three governors—Morningstar, Kelleher, and Newsman Dan. During the next two weeks, a smattering of ten more primaries and caucuses were held with mixed results.

The first debate featuring the three remaining Republican candidates would be held in Miami two days before what Fitz called "the real Super Tuesday", when Florida, Illinois, Ohio, and a couple of other states would vote.

The day before the debate, fresh off almost meaningless losses in the Guam, Washington, DC, and Wyoming caucuses, Hudson was in Florida readying for the face-off with Cash and Thorne. Staying at Vonner's $70 million oceanfront estate, Hudson had much more on his mind than prepping for a debate he was sure to win.

Taking advantage of the rare chance for some outdoor privacy, Hudson joined Schueller and Florence for a walk on the beach. Melissa, flying in from North Carolina, would join them for dinner. Checking to see that the Secret Service agents were far enough away that they couldn't be overheard, they talked about Zackers' progress. Hudson had asked for space, said he wanted to relax with his kids, but after the agent Pearce/Booker restroom meeting, he was being extra cautious.

"It's insane, Dad," Schueller said. "Zackers uncovered this old post from a person using the screenname 'Augusta30.' I have no idea if that's a man or woman, but I'm going to just assume it's a guy." Schueller, wearing rolled up jeans and a black tee-shirt, steered the group a little farther from the surf as the waves lapped his calves. "Anyway, Augusta30 must have been an insider working for one of the wealthy families."

"The Wizard calls them REMies," Hudson said, looking again at the four Secret Service agents, the closest about fifty feet away. Hudson, wearing shorts and a linen shirt, with a warm salty breeze blowing through his golden hair, would like to have relaxed, but looking the part was the best he could do.

Florence, in shorts and a tank top, stopped to examine a shell. "REMie?" she asked.

"Rising Emperors, or Empresses," Hudson said. "The folks who are building an empire and fighting over the empire at the same time." He was about to list some of the other theories for the strange name, but Schueller beat him to it.

"This guy, Augusta30, also refers to them as REMies. In his post he lists several possible reasons, but his favorite was that the elites have put us all in a sleep state, like REM sleep."

"Brain activity as if we're awake," Florence said, "but we're asleep."

"Yeah," Schueller added. "He said the REMies manipulate us all the time so that it's almost impossible to know what's true."

"Like who's the best presidential candidate," Hudson said.

"Wait until you see what he wrote," Schueller said, bending down to pick up a shell and showing it to Hudson to conceal him slipping a small flash drive into his father's hand.

"Thanks," Hudson said, making an overly obvious motion to drop the shell back on the sand. "I collect these things."

"Zackers has been able to verify a few of the things Augusta30 wrote about, but it'll take time to confirm the rest."

"Do we have any idea who or where Augusta30 is?" Florence asked.

"No," Schueller said. "Apparently, the post was made about three years ago, and remained up for less than eighteen hours. No word of Augusta30 since, but he provided lots of details and painted an incredible conspiracy by the elites, the REMies, to covertly rule the world. Everything we see in the media, that governments tell us, that multinational corporations do, it's all lies directed by the REMies."

"The CapStone conspiracy," Hudson said, glancing over his shoulder.

"Right," Schueller said. "How'd you know?"

"An old friend told me."

"Do Augusta30 or Zackers name any of the REMies?" Florence asked.

"Yeah . . . " Schueller hesitated.

"Vonner?" Hudson asked.

Schueller stopped walking. "Yeah. Vonner is definitely a REMie."

"Now we have corroboration," Hudson said, his voice strained. "I can't deny it any longer."

"What are you going to do?" Florence asked.

"Expose him. Have him arrested," Hudson said through gritted teeth.

"You're joking," Florence said.

Hudson stared out over the ocean, silent for a few moments. "No, I'm not joking."

"He'll kill you," Schueller said, grabbing his father's arm.

"I know," Hudson said. "I'm dead if I do it *now*. I need real proof anyway."

Obviously the fragments of a three-year-old internet post by some anonymous whistleblower combined with the testimony of a basically homeless guy called "the Wizard" isn't going to get an indictment, Hudson thought as he stared into the frightened eyes of the two people he loved most in the world.

"That's why I'll have to wait until I'm president. *Then*, I'll get Vonner. Him *and* all the others."

Chapter Fifty-Three

Hudson told Schueller to ask Zackers to keep going. "Get it all. Find everything he can on Vonner, Bastendorff, Booker Lipton, the Rothschilds, the Rockefellers, and any other REMies he discovers."

That evening before dinner, Hudson asked Melissa to join him for a walk on the beach.

"You know how we've always been a little suspicious about Vonner?" Hudson asked as they stepped from the perfectly manicured grass of the billionaire's estate onto the still-warm sand.

"Yes," Melissa said hesitantly, as he helped her put a light wrap around her shoulders.

"We were right. Apparently, Vonner has done this before. He and several other billionaires are locked in a battle over who's going to be the next president."

"Politics is expensive. It's a rich man's game. We knew that."

"No, this is more than that," Hudson said, trying to control his bitterness. "One way or another, just about every

US President in the last seventy-five years has been owned by these people. They aren't just trying to buy influence, they're trying to take over the world. They want to run it like emperors, but the people won't stand for emperors anymore, so they let us think we elected someone—"

"Take over the world? Isn't that a little dramatic? It's not even possible."

"Yes, I think it is. If they control the money, and they do, the media, and they do, the politicians, and they do—"

"You mean a puppet?"

"Yeah, and, obviously, it's not just the president. It's congress, governors, probably every US senator."

"You mean these politicians knowingly agree to just work for these people?"

"Yes, mostly."

"But Vonner hasn't made that deal with you."

"Maybe not overtly, but it won't be easy to say no to him if I get elected. This election is my first. Our past presidents were all previously something else—congressman, senator, governor, vice president. By the time they went for the presidency, they already knew the score."

"Not Trump," she countered.

"Yeah, but don't you remember how much he changed after only a matter of weeks in office?"

She nodded. "Where did you get this?"

"I've had people looking into it."

"You have?" Melissa's tone and expression filled with indignation. "When were you going to tell me?"

"Right now."

"Oh, thanks," she said sarcastically. "Damn it, Hudson, we're a *team*. I believe in you, and I believe we're going to be in the White House nine months from now, but you need to be honest with me, and that means keeping me in the loop."

Melissa's voice was firm, her eyes hard, yet teared. "I'll fight Vonner with you, or anyone else that crosses us, but I can't do that unless I know what's going on."

"I know, I'm sorry," Hudson said. She was an efficiency expert, after all; a woman who could turn around a company or solve a major public relations crisis facing a business. Melissa, also an attorney and CPA, knew how to get to the core of any situation. His wife could find a way out—a way to lose Vonner, but win the presidency.

"I have to know who our enemies are!"

"You're right." Hudson felt guilty, and knew this was probably his last chance to tell her about Rochelle and what happened that night three decades earlier, but as soon as he tried, the first words of the story fell back down into the pit of his stomach.

A short while later, as his children joined them for dinner outside on the patio, Schueller added to the anti-Vonner discussion by telling them about the record deal.

"Oh, Schueller," Melissa began. "That's awful, getting your hopes up like that. I know how badly you want a deal like that."

Schueller nodded.

"Why don't you take the deal?" Hudson asked his son while he sliced into a tuna steak.

"It's not real," Schueller said, surprised he needed to explain.

"I know," Hudson said, his words heavy. A strong silence hung for a moment as everyone caught the irony. "But you all think I should take Vonner's deal. Cheat to get what I want."

"That's different," Florence said, pointing her fork.

"How?" Hudson asked, glancing at the Secret Service agents, always wondering if they were far enough away so they could not hear, suspecting there were listening devices in the table somewhere, trying to decide how many of them worked for Booker Lipton, or if any of them were on Bastendorff's payroll.

"You have a chance to get the power you need to fight them," Florence said.

"She's right," Melissa said. "As much as I love you, without Vonner, you will not become president. But Schueller doesn't *need* Vonner. He'll eventually get a record deal anyway."

"I'm sure he will," Hudson said, smiling to his son.

Schueller's burner cell phone rang. He checked the number, then quickly excused himself, jogging out to the beach. When he returned a few minutes later, he stared at his father for a moment.

"Everything okay?" Melissa asked.

Schueller motioned for them to join him on the beach. They followed him twenty feet out on the sand. The Secret Service moved around them in a perimeter, but still allowed for some privacy.

"That was our friend," Schueller said in a whisper. "He's found more . . . *big* stuff."

"What?" Hudson asked.

"He didn't want to say too much over the phone, but it's about Vonner. Zackers is flying down here tomorrow. I'll meet him at the airport. His plane gets in at four."

"You'll have to shake the Secret Service," Florence reminded him.

"I don't like that at all," Melissa said sharply.

"And get back in time for the debate," Hudson said.

"Why does he have to shake Secret Service?" Melissa persisted. "They don't work for Vonner."

"We don't know that," Hudson said. "Everyone works for one of the REMies."

"Zackers did say something crazy, though," Schueller interrupted.

"What?" Hudson asked.

"He uncovered something that seems to show Vonner isn't the dirt bag we think he is. He didn't say what it was, but Zackers believes Vonner might actually be on our side."

"What does that even mean?" Florence asked.

"I don't know," Schueller replied. "Zackers said he'd fill me in tomorrow, but his final words were, 'If I'm right, and Vonner *is* one of the good guys, then that means this is far worse than we imagined.'"

Chapter Fifty-Four

Hudson spent the following day crisscrossing Florida, attending one rally after another, while his opponents were hunkered down preparing for the debate. Since he was undefeated, he had already put in enough time polishing for this one.

When he reached the University of Miami shortly before the event, he checked his phone again. Still no word from Schueller. They'd all been hopeful that perhaps Vonner could be trusted after all, even though Hudson couldn't imagine how that could be possible. But he did enjoy thinking about telling the Wizard that he'd been wrong about the billionaire.

Just after they told Hudson it would be ten minutes to airtime, Schueller's call finally came.

"How did it go?" Hudson asked, relieved to hear from his son.

"Zackers is dead."

"What?"

"Oh, God . . . he's dead."

"Take a deep breath and tell me," Hudson said, looking around, trying to figure out how he could get to his son.

"His flight was late," Schueller stammered. "We met for like ten minutes, then he said he didn't feel well, needed to use the restroom. I waited maybe eight minutes, figured he was in there sick or whatever. He hadn't looked very good. Finally, I went in to check—" Schueller's voice broke. "Damn it, Dad, I should have gone sooner."

Hudson closed his eyes, struggling to remain calm, then opened them staring directly at Florence. Melissa and Florence, sensing trouble, were trying to coax information from him with their expressions. Hudson shook his head and spoke to Schueller in a deliberate, parental voice. "Keep calm. Now, how did it happen? Start when you went in."

"Zackers was locked in the stall. His arm was tied off, needle on the floor."

"He'd shot up?" Hudson asked.

"Yeah, but I don't believe it. He wasn't like that. Zackers' drug of choice was the internet, maybe Mountain Dew and M&Ms. They . . . I ran out and got someone. Medics were there in a few minutes. We were still in the airport. Dad, someone did this to him."

"Did you see anyone go in or out?"

"I wasn't watching." Schueller's voice trembled, fell, and rose. Hudson thought his son might cry. "Damn, damn, *dammit*, I should have been watching!"

"It's not your fault."

"Dad, the police came. They know who I am. It'll probably make the news."

Hudson's eyes closed again, envisioning the headline. *Republican frontrunner's son caught in the company of a drug addict at the Miami Airport. Addict dies in men's room overdose.*

Florence and Melissa tried again to get Hudson to tell them what Schueller was saying, but Hudson was overwhelmed.

I might even get asked about it during the debate, but what does that even matter? Because what if Zackers' death wasn't accidental? What if he was killed—murder made to look like a suicide or overdose? What if whoever did that is now going after my son?

"Where are you now, Schueller?" Hudson asked, suddenly urgent.

"I'm still at the airport. The police just finished questioning me and taking my statement."

"Stay there, I'm coming for you," Hudson said, pacing.

"Dad, no. The debate."

"To hell with the debate."

"What's going on?" Melissa demanded.

"Zackers is dead," Hudson finally blurted. The taste of the words coming out of his mouth made his knees soften, and he backed into a chair.

Florence grabbed the phone. "Schueller, Zackers is dead?"

"Yeah."

"How?"

"They killed him, Florence. As sure as I know anything, I know that the REMies killed Zackers."

"We need to go get Schueller," Hudson said.

"I'll go," Melissa volunteered.

"The candidate's wife needs to be at the debate," Florence said.

"To hell with the debate," Hudson repeated.

"No, I'm fine!" Schueller shouted after hearing the argument.

"He says he can get here himself," Florence relayed.

Hudson grabbed the phone back from his daughter. "You may not be safe."

"Send the Secret Service," Florence said.

"Can we trust *them*?" Hudson asked, thinking of agent Pearce.

"So far, they've kept us all alive," Melissa said. "Although his usual agent must be furious right now."

Hudson thought for a few seconds. "Okay. Schueller, stay there until the Secret Service gets there. It'll be agent Croft. Ask him for ID."

Schueller, still shaken, but knowing there was no point in arguing, agreed and told his father his exact location. By the time Hudson explained the situation to Agent Croft and had a brief, hushed conference with Melissa and Florence, he was late to take the stage. He walked into the glare of lights, the probe of cameras, and the roar of applause, shakier than he'd been since Colorado.

Twenty minutes in, Thorne, instead of responding to a question about legalizing marijuana, turned to Hudson. "Pound, are you aware that your son was with a drug addict at the time of his death just a couple of hours ago?"

Hudson stared blankly into the camera for a few startled moments.

"From a drug overdose," the shock-jock emphasized. "In a dirty bathroom stall."

"I am," Hudson finally replied. "I appreciate your concern. My son is safe, and has cooperated fully with Miami-Dade police."

"Was your son wasted at the time—err, rather, under the influence of a controlled substance?"

"This is hardly relevant," Hudson said. "But I'm sure the police will confirm that he was not."

"I beg to differ," Thorne shot back. "You want to lead

the country, but you have no real experience in leadership other than maybe being a father. So how did you do with your kids, huh, Pound?"

"My daughter is a nurse. My son is a musician. He submitted to a drug test. He was clean. My children are exceptional. Beyond that, my children are off-limits."

Hudson had won the moment, and even with a few stumbles due to his shock over Zackers and concern for his son, he would go on to win the night, as expected.

Schueller sat in the busy North Terminal of Miami International Airport suspiciously eyeing anyone who looked his way. From his seat, he could see dozens of eating places and shops, but hunger never crossed his crowded mind. All Schueller could think of was Zackers' lifeless body slumped in the men's room stall, and of what the brilliant hacker had told him in the minutes before his death.

As a man in a suit approached, Schueller fidgeted with the flash drive Zackers had given him, and one horrifying thought suddenly replaced all the others.

They killed him for this. What dangerous secrets must it contain?

Chapter Fifty-Five

Vonner watched the debate from Sun Wave, his Carmel, California estate, far less attentively than usual. Rex had just given him a disturbing report.

"This kid, Zackers, what did he know?"

"A lot," Rex replied.

"I know what you told me yesterday, but beyond the Augusta30 post, what did he find this morning? Before his flight? And how much time did he have to tell Schueller whatever the hell he *did* find?"

"He was a sharp one," Rex said, still reading data. "I'd have liked to hire the kid. But he didn't get as far as he could have. A few more days, and he might have had it all."

"Incredible," Vonner said, while skiing down his artificial treadmill ski slope, complete with blowing snow flurries. "How the hell is that stuff still accessible?"

"It's not."

Vonner shot him an angry, confused look.

"Not really. I mean, he's parsing, or *was* parsing," Rex continued, correcting the tense with which he referred to the now-dead Zackers. "He was parsing the data from many layers, many historic digital tombs. Brilliant, nothing less than brilliant."

"I'm glad the kid impressed you, but who else is going to get where he got?"

"Hard to say. But they can't get there without our knowing about it."

"Really?" Vonner barked. "Then what happened with this Zackers kid?"

Rex pointed to the data on one of the screens. "We knew."

"Not before it was too late."

Rex nodded. "Depends on how you look at it."

Vonner shook his head, in no mood to continue the argument. "You realize the problem we have now? That *we're* going to get blamed?"

"No, the police can't touch us on this," Rex said, puzzled by his boss's statement.

An ocean breeze blew in, ruffling a few papers on his desk. "I don't give a damn about the police, I mean Hudson! Hudson is going to throw this on his bonfire of 'Vonner is Satan' pile and toss the match."

"Depends on what Zackers said before he died." Rex tossed five red dice on the table, made a mental note of the numbers, then scooped them up before Vonner could protest.

"We need to get Schueller before he gets to Pound," Vonner said, turning to the screen showing the continuing Republican debate.

"On it," Rex replied, rolling the red dice over and over in his hands. "One of our security guys is riding along with Secret Service heading to pick up Schueller."

"What's he going to ask him?" Vonner asked, putting down his ski poles as a butler brought him a scotch.

"Nothing," Rex said. "Whatever Zackers told Schueller has been said. As long as Schueller is alive, he's going to pass it on to his father."

Vonner stared at Rex, letting the statement register.

"I'm not suggesting we kill Schueller right now," Rex said. "Way too close to the Zackers mess. My point is that whatever he tells his old man is without proof unless Zackers *gave* him proof."

"You mean on a flash drive or something?"

"Exactly. You can bet Zackers didn't fly from New York to Miami to have a chat with Schueller he could just as easily have had on one of their burner phones. No, he was delivering something, and Schueller has it, which means it will be in Pound's possession within the hour unless we get it first."

"How do you propose we accomplish that? He isn't going to just hand it over."

Rex shot a look as if he were insulted.

"I have no doubt our man can overpower the kid," Vonner continued, "but the Secret Service agent might take issue with our manhandling a presidential candidate's son."

"We'll get the drive."

As soon as Schueller noticed the tough-looking man breaking from the crowd, he knew the thug was coming for him. Quickly scanning the area for more enemies, Schueller started moving. He already had a planned escape route, having chosen this spot precisely because there were so many exit options available. He headed toward his first choice—the escalator.

The big man saw his target bolt and ran to cut him off. Schueller descended fast, weaving through startled travelers. By the time his pursuer made it to the top, Schueller was at the bottom. The man, trying to avoid causing a scene, couldn't be as aggressive as he wanted, but managed to get down quickly enough to keep Schueller in his sights.

A cop, I just need a cop, Schueller thought while racing onto a moving walkway. It was a mistake. The crowd ahead compressed. There was no way through.

The man chasing knew he had to reach Schueller before the Secret Service did, and as long as he didn't lose him, the farther they got from the rendezvous spot, the better.

Schueller looked back, saw how close his pursuer was, and scrambled over the black rubber railing. Several of the harried travelers gave him annoyed looks, one person even shouted at him, but most people just assumed he was late for a flight.

The man after him jostled two women out of his way, then vaulted the railing before colliding with a luggage cart, but recovered quickly. The mishap put more distance between him and his quarry.

Schueller never even saw the man stumble. He hadn't looked back for fear of losing precious seconds and his lead. He spotted another down escalator and took it. The man almost missed his escape, but at the last second, caught Schueller's blur in his peripheral vision and doubled back.

One level below, everything looked different. Streams of people flowed rapidly in both directions, planes and cabs waiting. For a moment, Schueller was nowhere in sight. Frustration and panic flooded the man, until he caught a break. Schueller appeared, briefly hemmed in by a swelling crowd at a baggage claim carousel. The man tore down the corridor and pushed into the throng of passengers. Ten feet ahead, he saw Schueller work free of the mass and slip around a corner.

Certain he'd lost his pursuer, Schueller stole a glance and was stunned to witness the guy less than fifteen feet behind as he burst from the sea of people around the baggage area. Schueller's eyes searched wildly for somewhere to run. Despair overtook him as he realized he'd gone down a dead-end. Schueller kept running until he ran out of space. The only option left was a set of restrooms.

I'm not going to die like Zackers did, he thought, turning to charge back at the man.

Chapter Fifty-Six

The big man stood, catching his breath, unsure if he could block the much younger Schueller. He stared down his prey, at once trying to intimidate and perhaps convey an offer. The man hadn't risked bringing a weapon other than his fists, but they certainly counted. He needed that drive, but also had to avoid attracting attention.

"Schueller, wait!" the man shouted. "I'm a friend of your dad's!"

"Like hell!"

"I mean it," the man said, stepping a little closer. "The Wizard sent me."

"No way." Schueller continued looking for a way out, but at the same time he remembered his father giving him the name of the Wizard and wondered.

"Call your dad," the man said, looking over his shoulder as if waiting for someone.

"I would if he wasn't on live television right now."

The man checked his watch. "He's done. Call him."

Without taking his eyes off the man, Schueller pulled out his phone and speed dialed his father.

"Schueller, where are you?" Hudson asked in a frantic tone. "I just hung up with Agent Pearce. He said you weren't at the meeting spot."

"A guy came after me, says the Wizard sent him."

"Who?" Hudson barked.

Schueller threw the man his phone. "Convince him."

The man bobbled, but managed to make the catch. "Dawg, it's Gouge," he said into the phone. "Wizard said your security people, including the Secret Service, can't be trusted. They want something that Schueller has. He needs to give it to me."

"Give him the phone," Hudson said angrily.

"I'm throwing it back," Gouge said slowly, before giving it a gentle toss back to Schueller.

"Do you know him?" Schueller asked.

"Does he have the word 'TRUTH' tattooed across the fingers on his right hand?"

"Show me your fist!" Schueller yelled.

Gouge held it up.

"Yeah, I see it," Schueller told his dad.

"Then I know him."

"Do you trust him?"

"Tough question anymore. I only really trust three people on the planet," Hudson said.

Melissa, listening to someone on another phone, looked at her husband and relayed a message. "Hudson, tell Schueller they have the whole airport on alert. Everyone is looking for him."

"What do you have?" Hudson asked Schueller.

"A drive from Zackers. He told me it contained explosive information," he said, noticing several uniformed officers working through the crowd at the end of the corridor. "The police are coming."

Gouge turned around to see them approaching.

"What should I do, Dad?"

No response.

"Dad!?"

"Damn it! Give the drive to Gouge."

"Zackers died to get us this," Schueller said breathlessly. The police were getting closer, but their view of him was momentarily blocked by Gouge. Ten more feet, and they'd have the right angle to identify Schueller.

"I know, and I don't want you to die protecting it. Whoever killed him might go after you next." Hudson's voice cracked. "Whatever information is on that drive is our insurance."

Gouge looked over his shoulder again. "We're out of time," he said to Schueller, ready to take the drive by force if need be, but knowing the cops would have him in two seconds. As it was, facial recognition software in the airport's 3D surveillance system would ID him as the one who got the drive. The Wizard had warned him that whoever wanted the drive also had the power to access 3D.

"You have to give it to him *now*," Hudson said.

Schueller took one last look at the approaching officers, thought of Zackers' dead body slumped on the toilet, reached into his pocket, walked past Gouge, and made the handoff as if he were a professional spy behind the Iron Curtain during the Cold War.

The police spotted him a few seconds later. One called it in on his radio, the other jogged over to Schueller. He never looked back at Gouge, who had already slipped into a stream of people heading toward the departure gates. Three or four minutes later, Agent Croft of the US Secret

Service, accompanied by one of Vonner's private security men, met up with Schueller and the officers as they made their way back through the terminal. They escorted Schueller into a room used by customs officials and insisted on a full search.

"I'm sorry, but we received a tip that the man you were with may have planted an explosive device on you without your knowledge," the Secret Service agent said. "I'm sure you understand that for your safety, and that of everyone in this airport, and, of course, your father, we need to be sure."

There was no point in arguing. Schueller just hoped that the drive was safe, that Gouge had made it out of the building and was heading somewhere out of the reach of the REMies.

Is there even such a place? he wondered, then asked to call his father.

Schueller, driven by the Secret Service, reached Vonner's ocean-front mansion just after Hudson, Melissa, and Florence had arrived. They quickly headed to the beach for a moonlit walk, Secret Service trailing close behind. They spoke carefully and softly as Schueller gave them a full account of the tragic afternoon.

"Gouge is the man you met that day at Lake Hope?" Melissa asked.

"Yeah," Hudson said. "Childhood friend."

"Who went to prison?" Melissa noted.

"Yeah."

"And now he has this critical information that someone killed Florence's friend for?"

"Right," Hudson said.

"Prison?" Schueller echoed.

"Yeah," Hudson replied. "It's okay. He's a good guy."

"Where is he?" Schueller asked. "How do we get the drive back?"

"Do we even *want* it back?" Florence asked. "People want it badly enough to kill an innocent . . . " Her voice trailed off.

"No, we definitely need it," Melissa said. "Can you get in touch with Gouge?"

"I can try as soon as we get back. You all stay downstairs so it doesn't look suspicious, and I'll go up and see if I can locate him."

"The house is certainly bugged," Schueller said. "How are you going to talk to Gouge without tipping off Vonner?"

"Let me worry about that."

Upstairs in their suite, Hudson positioned himself on the floor, against a wall in the corner of the room where he believed there was no chance anyone could see his screen. He thrust the flash drive from the Wizard into the USB slot and waited for the matrix screen to clear.

Congratulations on winning another debate, the Wizard's words typed across the monitor.

Forget the debate. Where is Gouge?

I opened with a neutral statement because this time it's my turn to test your identity, the Wizard wrote. **Where was Wooley Swamp?**

At the confluence of the great creek and small stream just down from the sewer opening, Hudson replied, allowing himself only a brief moment of fond recollection of one of their childhood hangouts named in honor of a Charlie Daniels song. *Now where is Gouge? And how did you know about Zackers?*

I told you it's dangerous looking for the type of data he was after. To find that kind of fire means you're going to make a lot of smoke for others to see, and then you're going to get burned. The DarkNet is a minefield of cannibals and snakes, filled with horrors . . . brutally cold, distortedly wild. You leave footprints there, and a vengeful death comes looking for you in a digital blink.

Spare me your geek poetry. *If you knew, you should have warned us. Zackers went to school with Florence. He was just a kid, and he's dead only for trying to help us find truth.*

I'm sorry, I really am. Zackers found the Augusta30 post. The guy who wrote that is also dead. I've been trying to—

Just tell me where Gouge is.

I don't know.

What do you mean? You sent him.

I haven't heard from him since he got to the airport in Miami.

Is that the truth? Hudson wanted to reach through his laptop and grab the Wizard. *Gouge has the drive Zackers gave Schueller just before they killed him!*

Chapter Fifty-Seven

Crouched in the corner of an upstairs bedroom inside Vonner's mansion, Hudson felt as if the walls were closing in.

I sent Gouge to get Zackers' drive so the REMies wouldn't get it, came the Wizard's words across Hudson's laptop.

Then where is it? I want it! Hudson typed back, suddenly unsure about the Wizard's motives and loyalties.

Zackers found the truth, Hudson thought. *I need that information desperately. What is the truth?*

How is it that you're an expert on REMies and the CapStone conspiracy anyway? The same stuff that I'm right in the middle of? It's a pretty big damned coincidence, wouldn't you say?

Dawg, you don't get it? I thought we've been through this. I'm into CapWars and REMies exactly because you are in it. It's all connected, man, it's all out there. We've been on this collision course since we were kids. How do you think destiny works? Woodword and Bernstein were heading

toward Nixon forever. Edward R. Murrow and Joesph McCarthey, Bill Clinton and Monica Lewinsky . . .

Okay, maybe that last one was about something other than destiny.

Destiny, huh? Maybe you should get a job with Booker Lipton's UQP, or the Inner Movement. In fact, maybe we should call the Inner Movement and ask if they have a psychic who can locate Gouge! Hudson said sarcastically.

Maybe.

I'm serious. Aren't you worried? They already killed a guy for that drive. They searched Schueller for it. You know better than I do, especially now with 3D cameras everywhere, that they'll find Gouge.

I know, but I can't do anything about that right now, so I'm not going to give myself a heart attack. He'll either contact us soon, or we've lost this one.

Lost what? The data or Gouge?

At this moment, I'm afraid they are one in the same.

You seem awfully cold when talking about our old friend.

He knew the risks, Dawg. If he transcends this plain, he's . . .

Anyway, Gouge and I are putting it all on the line for you.

For me? *You guys are doing this for Rochelle!*

No, Dawg. I'll admit, it's a great bonus that Rochelle might go free after all this time, but we're doing this for you.

Why?

Because we love you, man. And because we believe you might be able to wrestle control of the world back from the REMies.

Hudson sat there for several moments, contemplating

the shadows on the far wall. *Am I smart enough to handle this? Is the Wizard smart enough to protect the data? Can I really trust him? Can we even trust this thing?* he wondered, looking down at the tiny device sticking out of the usb port in his laptop.

Is this little drive that enables us to communicate really safe even with all the hacking? Hudson typed, as the Wizard's last lines were automatically deleted.

Completely safe.

Where did you get it?

I invented it.

Really? And you live in a storage shed? You could get rich off this.

Rich? You mean in money? But don't you understand? Money isn't real.

Then what is?

Friends you can trust. I thought you knew that.

By the next day, Hudson and Florence were in Illinois, while Melissa and Schueller campaigned separately in Ohio. There was still no word from Gouge. Even though it wasn't discussed in the media, officials across the country were looking for him. After 3D tagged him at the airport, and instantly matched his criminal record, Hudson's old friend was an easy mark.

So far, though, he'd eluded arrest. Vonner, Booker, Bastendorff, NorthBridge, the FBI, CIA, and NSA all had people searching for Gouge. Even Interpol had been notified, although they didn't expect him to flee the country. Using the DarkNet and back doors, the Wizard picked up and tracked what he could about the race for Gouge and Zackers' data, but he couldn't do anything to help. Gouge was on his own.

At the same time his people were hunting Gouge, Vonner had another unit working on digiGOLD. Vonner, like many REMies, had his fingers in various cryptocurrencies, especially Bitcoin, which, after a rocky start, was already a threat to many pillars of the establishment-economy, particularly the central banks. While the REMies' dual efforts to control and thwart Bitcoin resulted in slow adoption, fueled by confusion and government interference, it had also given rise to alternatives. The REMies had made inroads to all of them, but digiGOLD, which had gone about things differently, not seeking mainstream acceptance, seemed to thrive on *not* being accepted.

Now, his team was after more than infiltrating digiGOLD; they wanted an answer to what Vonner termed the "critical mystery," the method NorthBridge used to convert micro-fractions—siphoned-off transactions conducted with legitimate currencies—into digiGOLD.

"Somehow, they are able to move digiGOLD in and out of dollars, euros, and yen without a trail. Who's helping them?" Vonner asked Rex over a communicator. The fixer had been in Hong Kong meeting with a financial hacker they'd hired to trace digiGOLD and solve the critical mystery.

"It can only be a government or a central bank," Rex said. "We've gotten that far."

"That makes no sense. DigiGOLD undermines governments and central banks. Why would one of them help establish it, help to crack the economy which gives them power?"

"Exactly," Rex said. "Who?"

"Someone opposed to the REMies' control. But, like I

said, the banks and governments powerful enough to assist and conceal digiGOLD have more than a vested interest in the status quo—they are part of it!"

"Maybe, maybe not," Rex said. "Perhaps someone is going rogue."

"Who? Why?" Vonner slammed his drink down hard, spilling it. Immediately, he pressed a button to alert someone to quickly bring him another.

"We don't know yet, but eventually we will find them. Digital footprints are impossible to erase. They may be able to hide for now, but not forever."

"I've put our task force on it," Vonner said, referring to his equivalent of the National Security Council, who worked every single day in his organization's "war room" looking for advantages in the CapWar.

"We don't have much time. Bastendorff, Booker, and several other REMies are moving on digiGOLD," Rex said. "If they crack it first, we're in a mess. Not to mention they could now beat us to Gouge, which opens up another can of trouble."

Hearing the name Gouge caused Vonner to grimace. The situation infuriated him. Hudson had put the presidency, and fate of the CapWar, in jeopardy with his "Zackers-Schueller-Gouge stunt," and therefore the fragile stability of the world was at extreme risk. Hudson, his own man, the guy *he'd* chosen, had set in motion events which could lead to complete worldwide anarchy.

"I've got a hundred and fifty people after this grunge, Gouge. He'll be dead by midnight!"

Chapter Fifty-Eight

Schueller walked into the all-night diner knowing that more than just his usual Secret Service detail was watching him. Yet they couldn't have known in advance that Schueller would stop for a late-night snack after the long day of campaigning at several colleges.

"Hi there, honey," the pretty waitress, probably his father's age, greeted him. "What can I get you?"

"Chocolate shake, fries, and a bacon, egg, and cheese biscuit." He looked up at her nametag, and smiled. "Kelly, do you sell cigarettes?'

"No, honey, we sure don't. Hope that doesn't ruin your healthy meal." She laughed. "But there's a mini-mart around the corner."

Schueller thanked her.

About ten minutes later, she brought out his order. "Enjoy," she said with a smile, and then disappeared.

He casually ate a few fries while the two Secret Service agents assigned to him had coffee at a booth by the door. Schueller stopped eating when he came to what appeared to be a single fry wrapped in foil. Carefully and quickly he palmed it, and then in one smooth motion, slipped it in his coat pocket. Fifteen minutes later, he took a last suck on the milkshake, left a five-dollar tip, and headed back out into the cold.

Schueller bought a pack of cigarettes at the mini-mart, lit one in the parking lot, then called Hudson. An hour later, he boarded a flight for St. Louis, and was asleep before the plane reached its cruising altitude. On arrival, he hung around the airport, surfing the net on his laptop until Hudson's plane came in.

"Did you look at it?" Hudson asked his son after they hugged hello.

He nodded. "Sorry, Dad, it seems encrypted."

Hudson looked as if he'd just been knifed. "Damn. We'll just have to wait until the Wizard can get into it."

"What if he can't?"

"He can. He's the Wizard." Hudson smiled at Schueller. "I have to keep moving."

"Okay."

"Good job, Schueller. How's Kelly?"

"Do you know her?"

"Not for years." Hudson thought of the younger version of Kelly, the waitress who had dated Gouge for a while and been friends with Rochelle, and then his brain short-circuited, as it often did whenever he recalled the days that led up to that night. "I've got to go. Do I have it?" he asked, referring to Zackers' drive.

"You do," Schueller said, feeling like a spy. He'd slipped it into his dad's coat pocket as they'd hugged.

"Good, I'll transfer it in a few hours," he said, looking deeply into Schueller's eyes.

"How?"

"The Wizard made me a special device, but don't worry about that. The less you know . . . "

"Okay, but don't lose it."

"Don't worry, Gouge has already made copies. Lots of them." He didn't look away from his son. "How are you?"

Schueller genuinely smiled.

Hudson smiled back. "Okay then."

A few hours later, from the back of an SUV, while claiming to be reviewing policy papers, Hudson followed the instructions and successfully zipped the contents of Zackers' drive across cyberspace to the Wizard.

Pound won Florida, Illinois, and his home state of Ohio. Thorne took North Carolina, and Cash won Missouri. Few political analysts gave Cash a chance now, declaring Pound a virtual lock for the Republican nomination. His popularity, like his delegate count, continued to grow.

The big shock was on the Democrats' side—Morningstar got Florida and Ohio, and Kelleher won Illinois. Newsman Dan pulled out a victory in Missouri and North Carolina, but managed to only finish second in the other contests.

"What do you make of that?" Rex asked his boss as they watched the results come in. "Bastendorff might not be as strong as we thought."

"Nonsense," Vonner said. "He just doesn't want his manipulations to seem too obvious." Secretly, Vonner hoped his nemesis was furious.

"Mistakes happen," Rex pushed. "Jimmy Carter, Trump . . ."

"This isn't a mistake," Vonner insisted while briskly walking up his custom treadmill, set on a steep incline.

"Can't control everything," Rex said, smiling as he walked out onto the patio overlooking the Pacific and lit a cigarette. He never once glanced at the ocean. Instead, he spread a series of seventeen miniature dice on the glass topped table and rolled them in a strange, systematic sequence that only he could understand. His expression changed from mild concern, to anger, to panic, and finally to amusement as the dice fell and he registered the numbers and combinations into his methodical mind, which had twisted into a painful precision from tens of thousands of hours spent inside the digital prisms of the DarkNet. He could find anything there. Thus far, Gouge had slipped through, by the only way anyone could anymore—he had vanquished his entire digital and cyber existence.

Back inside, Vonner was days past worrying about Gouge. He puzzled over the results of the Democratic primaries. Although Kelleher took his home state of New York, he hadn't won much else, and rumors abounded that he was about to pull out. Morningstar, however, was coming on strong, and had now won more states than Newsman Dan. The two rivals were nearly even in delegate counts. Both, expecting Kelleher to withdraw, were actively courting the Governor's endorsement. But with Morningstar favored in many of the remaining contests, including his home state of California, Kelleher's support was most critical for Newsman Dan.

Vonner studied all the maps and delegate counts, troubled, but not quite sure why. "Something isn't right," he said to Rex as the fixer returned from his smoke break. "We're missing a crucial piece . . . " Then the billionaire's face went white. "Wait, where is Hudson right now? Double security!"

Chapter Fifty-Nine

Hudson received regular updates from the Wizard. Gouge was safe, at least for now, but the encryption on Zackers' drive was proving extremely difficult to crack. The Wizard got in touch with Florence and Schueller, thoroughly questioning them on anything that Zackers might have said or done—*ever*—which might lead him to the key. Nothing.

However, Schueller did recall Zackers mentioning the word "digiGOLD," which the Wizard mistakenly thought might have been a clue to the way in, but soon discovered it was its own explosive topic. The Wizard pushed farther into investigating the world of digiGOLD. Soon, he realized that Zackers' death might have to do with something the hacker had uncovered about the virtual currency.

Maybe Vonner had nothing to do with killing Zackers, he told Hudson during one of their matrix-chats.

Any link between Vonner and digiGold? Hudson asked.

I haven't been able to find one yet.

Keep looking.

The thing is, Vonner would be one of the last people to want digiGOLD to succeed.

I thought it already was *succeeding,* Hudson said.

Only across the DarkNet, but if digiGOLD ever goes mainstream, it will bring down the banks and brokerage houses, which means the end of the global economy as we know it.

The Wizard sent Hudson a brief outline on digiGOLD. The report both terrified and fascinated him, and it left him even more uncertain about his course. An entity that created funds in a manner similar to the Federal Reserve and other central banks, but operated through some autonomous form of artificial intelligence, was incredible. Adding to the danger and wonder of it were other features, such as the source and destination of fund transfers being untraceable, accounts structured blind with no risk of being hacked. Governments couldn't seize digiGOLD assets, criminals could not steal digiGOLD, traders couldn't manipulate its value.

What would it be like to have a single global currency and no more cash? Hudson wondered.

The Wizard had discovered a reference to digiGOLD in a stray message he'd unlocked on the DarkNet. "*DigiGOLD is a chance to level the playing field. We can lock out the elites and leave them holding worthless currency from the old system. Stripped from wealth, they will become powerless.*"

It was a stunning idea. Income inequality had reached insane levels, with the richest eight people on earth controlling more wealth than the poorest four billion. But digiGOLD could change that in an instant.

Still, apparently not all NorthBridgers shared that view. In the same intercept, the Wizard found this response: "*We just want America back. They can do what they like in the rest of the world. People like Bastendorff who meddle will be targeted by the revolution. People who have legitimate business within the United States will be allowed, even welcome, but we will stop the others."*

The Wizard had shown Hudson that Bastendorff was backing Neuman and Cash. He'd also made clear his belief that elections are won and lost in the great glass towers of the money centers with no input from the voters, but Hudson couldn't buy that. Someone would know. Someone would talk. Someone would *stop* them.

"It's all about money and power, maneuvering and manipulating. Vonner has Hudson, Thorne, and one of the Democrats. He's making a move on the CapStone. Bastendorff has his candidates, and he wants the CapStone for himself."

Melissa didn't think it was that bad either. "Sure, Vonner might blur the line, cut corners, even be a totally corrupt, manipulative tyrant, but he's *our* tyrant. Win the election, and then you can make changes. Surely the president has *some* power?"

"But what if he doesn't?" Hudson said quietly.

Rex, walking up from the server room located in the lower level of Sun Wave, told Vonner that he'd picked up communications indicating Newsman Dan had already offered the VP slot to Kelleher, and that the New York governor was about to accept.

"That still may not be enough," the billionaire said, not sure why Bastendorff couldn't get his candidate across the finish line. "Morningstar has the momentum and the math on his side. Bastendorff might have bet on the wrong horse."

"Maybe not. Turn the TV on," Rex said, a trace of

urgency in his normally reserved demeanor. The fixer started clicking keys rapidly as windows on several large screens opened and closed in swift succession, with seemingly indecipherable data blurring in and out of view.

"Unbelievable!" Vonner shouted from his exercise bike. "I'll give Bastendorff credit, he sure has flair."

"What makes you so sure it was him?" Rex asked in a quiet monotone, as if he were far away. His fingers never stopped pounding the keys.

"Who else benefits so much from Morningstar's death?" Vonner asked, his eyes riveted to the TV screen's images of absolute mayhem. He brought up two other screens tuned to other stations with similar footage, but muted the audio. The announcer on the first station was giving a breathless account.

"I repeat, minutes ago, California Governor Morningstar was assassinated. The governor, a presidential candidate, had been speaking in Washington Park, in Portland, Oregon, to a large crowd, when what appeared to be a missile made a direct hit onto the stage. We have no confirmation of anything as yet, but as you can see in our live footage, the scene is one of utter carnage. I must stress again that we have no confirmation, but as you can see by this replay of the actual attack, dozens of others must also have been killed, and perhaps hundreds were wounded. First responders are just arriving, along with law enforcement, to this tragic event."

"New city, new victims," Rex muttered, "but same war."

The announcer continued. "We are waiting for word from the FBI and the Department of Homeland Security, but this certainly bears all the hallmarks of a NorthBridge attack."

"Bastendorff controls this network," Vonner said,

pushing a button on his bike which would alert an assistant to bring him a scotch.

"So?" Rex asked, somehow listening and typing frantically at the same time.

"There you go," Vonner said, pushing another button that would connect him to Fitz. "Bastendorff's pinning it on NorthBridge. Convenient."

"Is he?" Rex asked. "Or is it just supposed to *look* that way?"

Chapter Sixty

With Morningstar dead, Newsman Dan Neuman locked up the nomination. As expected, New York Governor Kelleher joined the ticket as his running mate. That, combined with a sympathy bounce from the loss of Morningstar, helped the Democrats jump to a double-digit lead in the polls over Pound.

Hudson still hadn't filled the VP slot, which created plenty of speculation. Vonner and Fitz were pushing for General Hightower. Schueller liked Professor Wiseman. But others inside his campaign, including Melissa, thought the bottom of the ticket needed to be someone with real governmental experience, similar to when the outsider Trump chose Pence. A shortlist of senators, congressmen, and governors quickly developed, but Hudson had long had someone else in mind, a person no one had considered.

Less than ten days before the Republican convention, while his staff was in the process of vetting the two finalists, Hudson shocked everyone, including Fitz and Vonner, by choosing Celia Brown, the African-American Republican senator from Illinois, known for her anti-war views. Fitz was dumbfounded. Brown hadn't been vetted, they had done no polling, and he didn't even know Hudson had said more than a few words to her since the early debates.

"I'm sure she'll work out," Hudson told his campaign manager and Vonner on a joint communicator call.

"She had *better*," Vonner said, so furious he was spitting his words. "You decide to bring on an anti-war fanatic—you do realize you're running as a Republican, don't you?"

"I'd hardly call her a fanatic."

"Really? She once introduced legislation to change the name of the Department of Defense to the Department of Peace. She has opposed every military action of the past two decades, and advocates bringing all of our troops home from around the world. *All*. Of. Them!"

"I like her," Hudson said.

"Oh, good," Vonner said sarcastically. "Let's just hope the voters share your feelings."

As it turned out, the polls showed it to be a brilliant move. The Republican base had no choice but to vote for Pound, regardless of who was on the bottom of the ticket, but Brown appealed to many liberal Republicans, independents, and even conservative Democrats who were fed up with the trillions spent on endless wars. Thorne, however, opened his radio show with the news, declaring, "'Pound-Brown' sounds like a cheap past-date cut of meat, or something that would wind up in your septic system."

Regardless of the shock-jock's constant barbs, between Brown's addition and a post-convention bounce, within a few weeks, Hudson had pulled back to within a couple of points from Newsman Dan.

Privately, Vonner remained outraged. "There are one hundred senators, ninety-eight of them belong to the

REMies, and he chooses one of the two that *don't*? He picks an *honest* senator? What was he thinking!?"

Hudson, in a hotel suite in Colorado, had just hung up from an equally exhausted Melissa, who was in New Mexico. It was as close as they'd come to being together since the convention. With the NorthBridge threat, the National Guard had been called out to protect both parties' conventions, and security had been extra tight at each subsequent event. The tension made each day more exhausting. He had some papers to review, and then a meeting with senior strategists and Fitz, before a day of stump speeches. Savoring the peace and quiet, he decided to resist the temptation to click on the morning news shows.

About to stretch out on the sofa, he suddenly realized he wasn't alone. Hudson jumped, then exhaled as if he'd just been punched. "How did you get in here?" His voice cracked in relief at the question, knowing he could have been killed if it had been someone else.

Linh motioned toward the door.

He shook his head. "The Secret Service would never have let you in unannounced."

She smiled. "Being the head of a large organization has some perks."

"The Inner Movement is not just some 'large organization.' I've checked. IM is on the FBI's watch list, and according to one of my sources, the Department of Homeland Security, the CIA, the NSA, and several other agencies have dedicated significant resources into tracking and infiltration efforts aimed at your movement."

She nodded, her eyes narrowing. "There are many who

do not understand us, who are confused, even threatened, by what the Movement is trying to accomplish."

"Enlighten me," Hudson said, unable to break her gaze, and not wanting to.

Linh laughed lightly, amused at his choice of words, knowing it was not an accident. "Perhaps we can help each other."

"I hope so," he said in an almost desperate tone.

"You *will* be the next President."

Hudson assented with his eyes, tired of being the only one who didn't believe this was a certainty, knowing that the leader of the Inner Movement was the last person with whom he should argue about the future.

"Humanity is at a very perilous point," she continued, "a crossroad that we may not survive."

Hudson almost interrupted to ask if she meant humanity might not make it, or Linh's Inner Movement, but her next sentence shattered his thoughts.

"If you live through your inauguration, we might have a chance to save the world."

He stared disbelievingly, not knowing which question to ask first. His throat closed, choking around words crumbling into fear and doubt.

"There are many threats, Hudson." This young woman with ancient eyes looked back at his troubled face and put him at ease by her mere presence.

Who is she really? he wondered. *And how in the world did she get in here?*

"My friend, the Wizard, told me I could trust you. Is he right?"

"Do you trust your friend?"

Hudson didn't know whom he could trust other than Melissa, Schueller, and Florence. Outside of those three people, everyone else seemed a possible enemy, and each day closer to the election it became even more difficult to discern friend from foe. He *wanted* to trust the Wizard, but there was so much going on that didn't make sense, and there were also too many unaccounted-for years. He knew he had to be extra careful, even with him. Sure, the Wizard had not revealed the secrets of that night from their past, but he could just be saving it, knowing that information would be far more valuable if Hudson won the presidency. The Wizard and Gouge would possess the power to destroy him, thereby giving them a way to control the leader of the free world.

"I don't know whom to trust," he finally whispered, but she had long since seen his answer in his eyes.

"Don't you?"

Talking to Linh was like climbing a mountain in a trance, and his frustration had reached its limits. "How *did* you get in here?"

"You have enquired about the Inner Movement?"

"Yes."

"Then you know we work with the metaphysical?" She looked at him with an expression that seemed to say, *Isn't it obvious?* and then, when he didn't respond, she continued, "You've no doubt heard of UQP—Booker Lipton's Universe Quantum Physics studies?"

"UQP is a rich man's folly," Hudson said. "I've checked it out, and I don't believe any of it."

"I know you don't."

"Then why are you here?" he asked, resisting the urge to ask again *how* she'd gotten in.

"Why did you come to see me in San Francisco?"

Her habit of answering questions with questions made him want to smoke a cigarette, something he hadn't done since his days in the army. "I don't know," he admitted, as much to himself as to her.

Linh nodded knowingly. "Our fates are intertwined, Hudson." She sounded so much older than him, even though she had to be twenty years younger.

"Our fates?" He laughed. "I'm talking about the fate of the country. *If* I become president."

"You say 'if' like it's a dangerous word."

"Isn't it?"

"Don't you want to be president?"

"I believe I can do a lot of good."

"*If* they let you."

"That's my point. The voters will make that decision."

"It's not up to the voters." She looked at him sympathetically. "It's never up to the voters."

"Tell that to Hillary Clinton."

Linh smiled. "I did."

"I'm sure you did." He laughed again.

"You never answered my question," she said gently, as if talking to a young student.

"Which one?" he asked, resisting the urge to add that she hadn't answered his. *Is she testing me for something? It feels like a damned test, the type where you never know the rules until it's over.*

"Do you want to be president?"

"Yes, I do, but even with all the influence and interference, it really will be the voters who will decide if I get to be president. Why else would we bother with all the speeches, promises, and damned political commercials?"

She shook her head. "What are you afraid of?"

"I'm not afraid."

"It's in your eyes."

"Then you tell me. You and your Inner Movement, New

Age ideas that most people find crazy or, at least, fantastical."

"It may be convenient for you not to believe in what we do, but what if I told you that at least fifteen presidents are known to have consulted with psychics?"

"I'm a history teacher, I know the stories, but that doesn't mean anything. Do you really think Reagan's astrologer changed history?"

"A psychic tried to stop Kennedy from going to Dallas. A seer warned Lincoln not to go to the theatre that night. McKinley—"

"A broken clock is right twice a day," Hudson said. "These psychics make a hundred predictions and three turn out to be true, and those are the ones they talk about. That doesn't mean—"

"It doesn't mean *you'll* be assassinated?"

"Exactly." But as he blurted the word, a nervous feeling overtook him. He could deny all the coincidences of history and lump the quacks together, even pretend nothing strange ever happened among the rulers of nations, and yet standing there, talking to this beautiful woman, a person who exuded such authenticity, next to her he felt himself a total fraud. "What do you want? Are you trying to warn me?"

"I'm telling you that in order to live, you will have to navigate the lies; more lies than you can imagine."

"Can you be specific?"

"Everything is a lie, and everyone is lying."

"That doesn't help me much."

"I can't be much clearer. Perhaps you will understand soon. But that's not really why I'm here." She stepped toward him. "May I?" she asked, extending her arms as if preparing to hug him.

"Uh, I don't think that . . . "

She met his eyes. Suddenly, all he could do was say yes. He felt her against him. Soft, like a breath, as if only light wrapped them together. Hudson's eyes closed. What seemed to be less than a second had passed, but when he opened his eyes, she was at the door.

Linh turned and smiled sadly. "I hope you survive, Hudson. I'll do everything I can."

"Will it be enough?" His question surprised him.

"I'm not sure." She turned the knob and left.

Two Secret Service agents came in immediately. "We didn't know you had company," one of them said questioningly.

"Neither did I," Hudson said, glad someone else had seen her. Otherwise, he might have feared he imagined the whole thing. So captivated by her mystique, it never occurred to him how risky it was to be alone in a hotel suite with a young woman on the campaign trail. A lecture would be in store from Fitz. It could not happen again.

Chapter Sixty-One

A nationwide heat wave dragged on through August. The notoriously slow news month proved to be no different this year—no new attacks from NorthBridge, no arrests or credible leads either. Polls still showed Newsman Dan ahead. Hudson continued campaigning, clinging to the notion that voters would still decide the race. The Wizard still hadn't gotten into Zackers' drive, but Gouge had managed to stay out of sight.

Fonda Raton threatened to shatter the news lull when she requested a meeting seeking comment before publishing a controversial post about Hudson's personal life and past. At first Fitz said no, but after seeing how upset Hudson was about what the piece might contain, he agreed on the condition that the campaign's press spokesperson could also be present. Hudson refused, and both men went to Vonner.

"No surprise you side with Fitz," Hudson said.

"We need to get out in front of whatever she has," Vonner said on speakerphone, while pointing to Rex and mouthing, *Get on this!*

"That's why I'm going," Hudson replied.

"What does she have?"

"I don't know."

"What do you *think* she has? Fonda Raton doesn't bluff. She has *something*. What could it be?"

"You tell me," Hudson said. "You know more about me than I do. What do *you* think she has?"

"More of this criminal affiliation garbage? Are there other unsavory characters we missed?"

"I can't think of anything."

"Then you won't mind if Fitz goes with you."

"I don't need a babysitter, Vonner. I'm going alone. I'll let you know what she says."

Vonner knew that Hudson had never gotten over the bugging of his house, and thought giving in to the candidate would be a good peace offering. The odds were good that Vonner would be able to get a recording of the meeting anyway. He also felt confident that, with a little over two months until the election—an eternity in political terms—whatever Fonda did, Rex could fix it.

"Fine, go alone, but ask yourself something. Why is this damned woman so fixated on you? She hasn't run a single negative piece about Newsman Dan."

"She told me it's because she hates you."

"Really? Maybe she isn't so bad after all," Vonner said, laughing.

Hudson's Secret Service detail was much larger now. They had swept the building hours before, and now, as the candidate entered through the hotel lobby, they were vigilant. It was an unannounced stop, but NorthBridge always seemed to know things no one else did.

Hudson entered the private conference room and was reminded of his first meeting with Vonner at the bank fifteen months earlier.

Could it have only been that long? he wondered. *I feel fifteen years older.*

"Hudson!" Fonda sang out. "Oh, how I've missed you."

"I'm sure."

"Don't be so stuffy," Fonda said, standing up with her arms open. "Give us a hug."

Before he could stop her, she embraced him, and as several agents moved closer, Fonda whispered in his ear.

"The room is wired. Let's go out for a walk." Fonda quickly pulled away and smiled at the closest agent. "Don't worry, words have always been my only weapons."

Hudson momentarily stared at her, not sure what to do. But, realizing she might have found out about that night with Rochelle, he decided to not take any chances on someone overhearing their conversation. He told the agents that he'd prefer to walk outside. There was much disagreement, but in the end, Hudson won, and soon Fonda and Hudson were walking side-by-side, trailed by ten agents. The exclusive hotel stood on a hill, its grounds lush in the way that only decades of attention and the southern California climate could provide.

"Why am I here, Fonda?"

"I want to do you a favor."

"Really? Last time we spoke, I recall you threatening to bury me."

"Are you familiar with a billionaire named Karl Bastendorff?"

"I might have heard of him."

Fonda smiled. "Then you know he's supporting Newsman Dan for president?"

"It's possible that I've heard a rumor to that effect."

"Do you also know the term R-E-M?"

Hudson resisted the urge to stop and look at her. Instead, he checked the distance to the closest Secret Service agent. He believed the conversation was about to go in the direction of Zackers. She had to have investigated his death, his life. Everyone knew Hudson's son had been there when he died, but the media seemed to have accepted that Schueller had just happened to find the body.

The media either bought the story or were bought off, Hudson figured. Either way, the heat had never materialized, and his son was safe. But Fonda wouldn't have believed it, even if it had been true. And she couldn't be paid off, not untouchable Fonda. She would have dug until she found that Florence and Zackers were at college together, and then she'd go further.

Fonda Raton is going to ambush my campaign with Zackers' suspicious death, and then expose the entire CapStone conspiracy! He took a deep breath, trying not to panic. *Vonner was right, I should have had Fitz here. But as soon as I tell them Fonda's plan, Vonner will find a way to silence her.*

Hudson suddenly realized that he was thinking Vonner would order Fonda killed, and that he was almost wishing for it so the problem could go away and he could still become president.

"Oh my god," he whispered to himself, spotting a bench nestled in flowering bushes and almost collapsing onto it.

"Are you okay?" Fonda asked, sounding genuinely worried.

"Yes," he said, making eye contact with the closest agent. The man also seemed concerned. Hudson waved and flashed a brief smile, wanting to quickly assure his security detail.

"Then you acknowledge knowing about the REMies," Fonda continued as she sat down next to him. "Therefore, you must also know of their involvement in the election."

"Is this your story, Fonda? Are you really going to write about the REMies?"

"No," she said in an uncharacteristically muted tone. "I don't have it yet."

"Then what?" he asked wearily.

"Your family. I'm going to post a piece on how you've neglected your family and can't be expected to run the country if you can't even take care of your loved ones."

"What are you talking about?" he asked, stiffening.

She handed him a copy of her story. As he started to skim it, Fonda fired off the main points.

"You have a chemically dependent brother, Dwayne, who lives on the streets half the time; a sister, Jenna, who was discharged from the Air Force under questionable circumstances; another sister, Trixie, the one running your hardware stores, and she's dating one of your ex-con employees; your son breaks the law every day with his pot smoking, not to mention the Miami Airport incident; and then there's the fact that Tommy Gouge, with his long rap sheet, is actually your cousin. His father, your uncle, testified at Rochelle Rogers' trial, a connection I'm still looking into, and—"

Hudson stood up and turned toward her angrily. "What does any of this have to do with the damned election?"

"It goes to competence," she said, as if it should have been obvious. "Also, you want to legalize marijuana, which is not a popular view among Republicans. Perhaps that's to help your son avoid landing in prison. What else can we expect you to do because of your propensity to be drawn to the lesser elements?"

"Lesser elements? Where do you get off, lady?"

"Don't take it personally, Hudson."

"You're attacking my *family*! How am I supposed to take it?"

"This is my job, Hudson. I'm sorry if it gets in the way of your ambitions, but the truth has to come out. This story is only the beginning." She looked at him pointedly, as if to emphasize the word "beginning."

Her expression sobered him. Gouge's father actually *was* his uncle, and the Rochelle connection was getting too close to the truth of that night. The rest of the media would take Fonda's lead and rip into the story until they found blood.

"You can't run it," he blurted.

Fonda smiled. "Do you realize this is the second time you've tried to suppress news?"

"I'm not trying to suppress anything. And this isn't news, it's a hatchet job!" he said, waving the papers.

"Why *shouldn't* I post it?"

"I wish I could tell you."

"Tell me right now," she said, taking out her phone and swiping the screen a few times. "Tell me the truth, Hudson. Tell me your secrets."

"There's nothing to tell," he said.

"Don't do that," she said, shaking her head. "The truth is the only thing that can save you."

"I don't need saving."

"Yes, you do."

"From whom?"

"The REMies." She stared at him for a long moment. "You know you do."

He shook his head.

"Come on, Hudson, I don't care about your family, and I know you've done a good job with your kids. All I want is Vonner, Booker, Bastendorff, and the rest of the REMies. Tell me what you know."

"I don't know anything." He so wanted to know what *she* knew.

"If I tap this button, the story about your family will instantly be forever on the internet, and also reach the inboxes of millions of my readers."

Hudson felt the sun on the back of his neck. He was sweating, and in spite of his hatred for the woman in front of him, he couldn't help but want to confess everything to her.

He inhaled deeply, closed his eyes, and exhaled. "I can't."

"You can," she said almost sweetly. "I know you have unlimited courage, Hudson. Do the right thing."

"Please don't post that story."

"You can stop it. Just tell me what I want to know."

"No," he said, slowly shaking his head.

"You sure?" she asked with a concerned expression.

"I can't," he repeated.

She stared into his eyes, squinting against the sun. She gave him one last questioning look, then tapped the button. "It's posted."

Chapter Sixty-Two

Fonda's piece on Hudson's family had the opposite effect on the voters than he expected. "Turns out not many people have a perfect family," one pollster said. "It's yet another reason for the electorate to identify with Hudson Pound, the everyman candidate."

The press didn't present a problem either. Vonner owned enough media outlets, and even Bastendorff's stations couldn't find anything to connect Hudson to Rochelle Rogers other than the fact that they were from the same town and went to the same high school. Still, it gave Newsman Dan plenty of ammunition with which to attack Hudson during the first general debate held in Philadelphia a few weeks after the story hit.

Security was lock-down-tight. There were more federal agents on hand than media or spectators. The event began with a moment of silence for the three candidates who had been assassinated. Hudson then asked that they take another moment to remember the six Secret Service agents who died in the Colorado attack. He meant it sincerely, but it was also a shrewd political move, reminding voters that Hudson had survived an assault from NorthBridge, and likewise showed his respect for law enforcement.

Hudson's debating skill, which had helped him defeat a large field of Republican challengers, was no guarantee against the polished Newsman Dan. As the evening unfolded, Hudson couldn't help but notice that he'd had almost every question during his mock debate prep. Not just the general topic, but almost the same wording. He suspected that Fitz had obtained the questions, and contemplating the unethical and possibly illegal act distracted him enough that by morning, most commentators were declaring the debate a draw.

Within days, polls reflected Hudson's poor showing, having him down another three points. However, it was more than the debate. Hudson began questioning all of the compromises he'd made along the way.

"Is this how someone gets elected?" he asked Schueller one morning over breakfast. "It feels a lot like cheating."

"That's because it is," Schueller responded.

Hudson felt ashamed. He'd always taught his children that playing fair was the only way to play.

Schueller saw the pain in his father's expression. "But, Dad, politics is a game where the only rules are that everyone cheats."

"A rather cynical view," Hudson said, knowing it was true.

"It's a rigged game. You gotta do what you gotta do in order to win. But you're different."

"How?"

"Because after you win, then you can *change* the rules. Change everything."

"Sounds like the ends justify the means."

"Not always a bad thing," Schueller said.

"No, but usually."

Schueller shrugged. There didn't seem to be a choice. "Anything from our friend?"

Hudson knew Schueller was referring to the Wizard and his efforts to crack into Zackers' drive.

"No luck yet," Hudson said. "I know the Wizard asked you, but can you think of anything else he said that could help us get in?"

"No."

Hudson ate another strip of bacon and glanced out the window of the hotel suite. He'd forgotten for a moment what city they were in until he recognized the Charlotte skyline. He could feel the pressure and stress physically. His chest and upper arms were always tight, and he couldn't recall the last time he didn't have at least a mild headache. Fonda would eventually get enough to go public with the CapStone conspiracy, and Hudson would appear to be just another REMie puppet.

Linh's warning also haunted him, made him paranoid, distracted him even more. He looked across the table at Schueller and wondered, *What if they assassinate me? What will become of my son?* Schueller was an adult, but Hudson didn't want him to have to live without a father just so he could try to change the world, a Quixotesque task at best, an impossible dream at worst.

Chapter Sixty-Three

Since Morningstar's assassination, virtually all open-air campaigning had been halted; no more speeches in parks, no more county fairs, picnics, or parades. Even indoor events had been substantially curtailed, which meant that with less than three weeks remaining until Election Day, this swing state rally inside a twenty-thousand-seat basketball court would be the largest event remaining. Organizers had hyped the speech and brought in far more people than the place could handle—a capacity crowd inside, another five to ten thousand out in the parking lots.

In line for hours, the faithful had been scrutinized by Secret Service agents as they passed through TSA-like screenings. The 3D cameras had also tracked their every move since each of them had left home that morning. Facial recognition, profiling, cross-indexing, databases, even dogs standing diligently beside cops. Vonner's private security firm had four hundred personnel on hand to supplement the federal agents, state, and local police, whose mission was to avoid losing a fourth presidential candidate.

Still, Vonner's head of security remained nervous. "Too many people," she argued. "NorthBridge has made it no secret they want Hudson Pound dead."

Hudson, for his part insisted, "You can't run. Live free or die." The candidate had become fond of quoting New Hampshire's official state motto, and often added the rest of the line from the state's Revolutionary War hero, General John Stark, "*Live free or die: Death is not the worst of evils.*" Even when NorthBridge posted a video of Hudson using the quote in one of his speeches over the caption, "*NorthBridge couldn't agree more with the gentleman from Ohio – death is not the worst of evils,*" he defiantly continued using it.

When many in the nation called for a halt of all campaigning, the current President gave a stirring speech about the price of freedom, and that: "We must resist all terrorists, foreign or domestic, who seek to steal our precious freedom." Polls showed that NorthBridge's reign of terror had stoked a rising patriotic fervor, which accounted for the rock star-like celebrity treatment which Hudson and Newsman Dan had increasingly seen on the trail.

"It's like a war zone," Melissa said on the phone with Hudson just before he took the stage in the stadium. "I'm in Missouri, and you'd think I was Elvis. I can't tell if they love us because they think we're so smart, so brave, or if they just want to see someone get shot!" she admitted.

"It's because we're brave. They know any moment could be our last," Hudson said, hoping he sounded braver than he felt, thinking back on the time Fitz had said this election was always going to be remembered for assassinations, as if it was the latest entertainment to distract the masses.

"Brave, stupid, I don't know. That's always the question we seem to be asking ourselves," Melissa said. "Maybe they just want to be able to say they saw us at our last speech."

"Crazy. Sorry to disappoint them, but my last speech will be in eight years."

"Really? You're down nine points in the latest national poll and *now* you're getting cocky?"

"The media may have given up on me, but I like being the underdog. It's the same way my hardware stores beat the big-box home centers. Underestimating me just gives me the room to maneuver. Sneak attack—I learned it in the army."

"Okay, soldier, I'm glad to hear you finally think you're going to win."

He really didn't think he would win, but he definitely wanted it now, and not just to save Rochelle, but to save the Republic itself, perhaps even the world. It was with that sentiment, that burning commitment in his heart, that Hudson Pound took the stage.

He stood behind the clear bulletproof shield and surveyed the sea of supporters. Chants of "WE. ARE. THE. CHANGE." repeated for more than five minutes before Hudson could get the crowd to let him speak.

He spoke for twenty minutes, with the eloquence of a Kennedy and a substance that only a former history teacher could bring. The crowd held in rapt attention, never doubting that Hudson could deliver not just victory, but deliver them from the long song of corruption that had been played in Washington for decades. Hudson Pound was their political savior.

"I know we're down in the polls," he said, wrapping up his speech. "I know they say I'm too much of an outsider, that I cannot tame Washington where others have failed; that my vision is naïve, my talk too plain, my support too thin. They say all kinds of things designed to discourage us. Well, are we discouraged?"

"NO!"

"Are we gonna prove them wrong?"

"YES!"

"Are we gonna win?"

"YES!"

"Are we the change?"

"WE. ARE. THE. CHANGE!"

He raised his right arm, pumping the air along with the chants. Shouting the words himself. Hudson *was* a rock star. Newsman Dan might be ahead in the polls, but the passion belonged to Hudson. He smiled broadly, his gaze sweeping the crowd of frenzied supporters.

Then, one face stopped him. A beautiful young woman, the only one not chanting, not even smiling. Her expression was torn in deep grief and something else. Frustration, maybe. It took a moment through her pained look to realize he knew her.

It was Linh, the leader of the Inner Movement.

What the hell is she doing here? Why does she look so upset?

Just then, the first bullet tore through him. Flesh exploded in a bloody, burning thrust. He hadn't heard the shot. His body went reeling, twisting to the floor. Splintering shards of wood burst from the podium. More shots! A split second after he hit the stage floor, a Secret Service agent landed on top of him. Another bullet ripped into his calf.

Above the now terror-filled screams of the crowd, he heard his security team shouting commands. More shots!

How many are there?

He tried to roll over, but the weight of the man on top of him was too much. A lot of blood.

This isn't all my blood!

He realized from the agent's groans that he'd also been hit.

He took a bullet for me. He may take more. He may die. I may die!

Pandemonium ensued. *Pop! Pop! Pop!* Shots rang louder, like fireworks, but he didn't know if they were "ours" or "theirs."

How did they hit me? They aren't magically bypassing the bulletproof shield.

Twenty thousand people were running every direction, screaming. Someone pulled him, and the pain in his arm caused him to clench his teeth. More shots!

It's an ambush.

He heard the word NorthBridge several times as agents shouted above the panicked crowd that had now become a rolling, moving hazard—a desperate mob. Hudson was wrenched to his feet.

"Teacher is hit. Teacher is down," he heard an agent say, using his familiar Secret Service code name. "Moving. Evac-op seventeen."

"We're still receiving fire," another nearby agent said. "From above, dammit, from *above*!"

Above, of course! Hudson realized that was the only place the shooter could be.

"Cherries waiting," Another agent said, appearing next to Hudson. Three men were supporting him, pulling, dragging, moving him to an exit somewhere.

"I'm okay, I'm okay," Hudson said, as they got safely into the backstage corridors.

"Yes, sir," one of the agents said. "We're trying to keep it that way."

Four agents, who'd been sent ahead to be sure the escape route was clear, ran toward them. "The back exits are blocked!" one of them shouted breathlessly.

"With what?"

"Flames! They've torched the whole area. We have to go out the front."

"Through the crowd? Twenty thousand scared civilians?" a stunned agent asked, already turning. "Through the shooters?"

Chapter Sixty-Four

It had been only four minutes since the shooting began. To Hudson it felt like hours, but he knew from combat that flying bullets have a way of twisting time.

The agents were arguing in clipped words. No way they'd make it through the crowd. People were already getting trampled. There was no protection from the shooters. Several agents were speaking into their radios.

Hudson questioned why they were supporting him and tried to put weight on his leg. A collapsing agony answered. A hand came from behind and wrapped something tight on his throbbing, blood-soaked arm. Hudson never saw who it was. The swarm around him ebbed and flowed, but even in the confusion, it seemed to be working as one giant organism.

Dozens of police and federal agents were filling the area. Hudson heard a radio report that said one shooter was dead, taken out of the rafters. "How many are there?" Hudson asked no one in particular, but he didn't get an answer. The irony of the chaotic scene was that in their desperate mission to protect the candidate, they hardly seemed to know he was there, or rather that he was a real person as opposed to a position to be defended.

"We've got a path!" an agent shouted as they turned again and advanced toward the back exits.

Hudson wondered about the fire, but he didn't have to wait long to see the flames leaping at them. "How the hell are we going through that?" he asked, looking at the wall of smoke and fire. Again, no one answered.

How awful the situation must be inside the stadium if we're going to try to push through that inferno, he thought, trying to ignore his increasing pain and mounting weakness.

Just as the heat began to feel as if it would melt his skin, a sudden, insatiable thirst overtook him. Lightheaded, he tried to turn back away from the raging fire, but the strong arms guiding him locked and continued marching forward.

Have I been betrayed? Are they sending me to cremation?

Seconds before he passed out, thousands of gallons of water, as if streaming from cannons, flooded in around them. Well-trained agents caught him before he hit the floor, somehow resisting the powerful water shooting at them.

How come it's not knocking them down?

Then everything went black.

When Hudson woke up, he instantly remembered everything, except how he ended up inside the ambulance. Two paramedics were working on him. They cut off his pant leg and shirt. An IV was in his arm. A Secret Service agent wearing a soaking wet suit was a couple of feet away.

Sirens were wailing all around as they raced toward the closest hospital.

"What's going on back there?" Hudson asked. "Injuries? Did everyone get out okay?"

"They're still clearing the place," the agent responded. "Three shooters are dead. Lots of injuries. I don't know how many—hundreds. Four or five agents among them, but I haven't heard any deaths yet. Seems they just wanted you, Mr. Pound. You got lucky."

"Luck had nothing to do with it," Hudson said. "The US Secret Service is the only reason I'm still here. How's the agent who jumped on me?"

"Terry Wright," the agent said. "He's alive. In another ambulance."

"He took a bullet for me," Hudson said solemnly.

"He took three."

Almost four hours later, Hudson was wheeled out of surgery.

"It was as if the bullets were defective," the doctor told him. "The one in your leg stopped just before the femoral artery, maybe because it passed through Agent Wright first, but the one that hit your left shoulder had the power and trajectory to continue on to your heart."

"What happened?" Hudson asked.

The doctor shrugged. "It just didn't. Sometimes these things are known only to God."

Hudson, not a religious man, nodded in agreement, thanked the doctor, closed his eyes, and gave another thank you to the heavens.

One of the many agents guarding his room came in with a phone. "Sir, it's your wife."

"Are you *really* all right?" Melissa's voice sounded as if she'd been crying.

"That's what they tell me," Hudson replied. "I guess NorthBridge must think I might stage a comeback and beat Newsman Dan after all, because they're sure going to a lot of trouble in trying to kill me."

"Do you want to quit?"

"Never."

"You're a brave man, Hudson Pound."

"Or stupid. I guess we'll find out which in a few weeks."

Both said "I love you" at the same time.

Florence and Schueller arrived at the hospital within an hour of each other. They were sitting and talking quietly by Hudson's bedside, waiting for him to wake, when two of their aunts and an uncle walked in. Hudson's brother, Ace, and his sisters Jenna, and Trixie. The three of them were devastated by the assassination attempt. They asked Florence and Schueller in hushed tones for the latest prognosis.

A little while later, just as a nurse came in to tell them there were too many visitors in the room, Melissa finally made it. As the patient's wife, she took charge and promised the nurse they would be respectful. A few more chairs were squeezed in, and they kept the conversations to a whisper. Melissa had heard from Fitz, Vonner, and about fifty friends and campaign staffers. Schueller and Florence had similar experiences, and they'd all been contacted by countless reporters. Trixie said the hardware stores had been inundated with flowers and well-wishers starting right after the news broke, and she'd just gotten a text from an assistant manager that said people from all over the country had been calling into the stores with prayers and offers of support.

Hudson opened his eyes and surveyed the "crowd" in his hospital room. "If you're all here, I must be dying," he said, a little alarmed.

"No, honey," Melissa said, taking his hand. "But let's make sure this is as close as you ever get."

Hudson looked past her to the flowers the Wizard had sent and recalled the message, a nurse had read him: *Dawg, you gotta live to win, gotta win to fix things.*

He thought of Rochelle. She had been his mission, but now it was more. NorthBridge might bring the country to civil war. He had to stop them. There was so much to fix.

He had to live.

Chapter Sixty-Five

NorthBridge posted a letter on its website signed by AKA Hancock claiming responsibility for the basketball stadium assassination attempt, which had injured three hundred and forty-eight people, but miraculously resulted in no deaths. In spite of an initial big jump in Hudson's poll numbers after the attack, by the day before the election, he'd slipped back. Newsman Dan Neuman would head into election day still ahead by six points.

Between security concerns and the slowly healing gunshot wounds to his arm and leg, Hudson was not able to maintain the same constant campaigning that his opponent could. A conservative pundit on cable news asked why NorthBridge had never tried to assassinate Newsman Dan. Instead of looking for an answer to the question, the pundit was fired, shamed, and visited by the Secret Service for allegedly suggesting that the terrorist organization should attack the Democratic nominee for President.

In those final weeks, Vonner's control of certain aspects of the media didn't seem enough. Newsman Dan was everywhere. The media bias toward the liberal Democrat who had once been one of their own could not be stronger. Going into the last debate held in Wisconsin, just five days before election day, Fitz seemed worried.

"There may be a question we didn't prep for tonight," Fitz said while nursing an extra-large Coke.

"What do you mean?" Hudson asked, remembering the odd feeling he'd had at the last debate when it seemed they'd prepped him for every question, even though they weren't supposed to know them in advance. "Did we get the questions?"

"Apparently not all of them," Fitz said, closing the door to the adjoining suite, which was filled with staffers.

"What the hell?"

"Look, Hudson, it's routine. The other side gets most of them, too. No one wants a president who can't answer a question." He paused to suck down his sugar and caffeine. "What's the capital of Uzbekistan?"

"Tashkent."

"Bless you."

"What?"

"All I'm saying is most people wouldn't know that Taznet is the capital of Uzbekistan."

"*Tashkent.*"

"See?"

"But I do."

"Yeah, you're smarter than the average bear on all that history and geography garbage. Point is, what if the moderator asks you something that you can't answer? I'll tell you what happens. You look like an idiot, you give all those undecided voters a reason to vote for Newsman Dan, and boom, you lose the election just because you didn't know where Shazmat is."

"*Tash-kent.*"

"Right."

Hudson nodded. It was yet another compromise, another lie he told himself, that the people would never know. But it would be okay, because if given the chance to be president, it wouldn't matter how he got there. He'd be a good president.

He walked slowly out on stage, a cane in one hand, his arm in a sling. Newsman Dan made a point of coming over and asked if he needed any help.

"Are you strong enough? We can wait a few more days, if you need more bed rest," Newsman Dan said. The debate had already been pushed back because of Hudson's recovery, and Hudson knew Dan was milking the situation to make himself look gracious and strong while Hudson seemed weak.

"No thanks, Governor. That's just what NorthBridge would want." Hudson never missed a chance to call Newsman Dan "Governor" since the two were campaigning as political outsiders, and yet Dan could not actually still claim that title.

The debate was uneventful for a while, but Fitz had been right; there was a surprise question, at least to Hudson.

"What would you do if you discover, as some evidence suggests, that NorthBridge is not a homegrown terror group as they claim, but are, in fact, sponsored by a foreign state? Would you take military action against that country, regardless of which country it is?"

The question was a minefield. Obviously, if a country was behind NorthBridge, it was a clear act of war. However, if the country was Russia, or China, then they'd be talking about World War III.

Hudson stumbled badly through a series of hypotheticals, stipulations, and conditional answers. Newsman Dan struck a sharp contrast, with facts, clear ideas, the appointment of secret commissions, intelligence issues, covert plans, special forces operations, and decisive answers about stopping NorthBridge and punishing their backers, but avoiding a nuclear standoff.

Hudson stood there looking weak, twice a victim of NorthBridge, a group who had so far escaped punishment. America's biggest fear, and it seemed clear that Hudson couldn't handle them, but Newsman Dan could.

With just days before the country voted, Hudson lost his first debate.

Chapter Sixty-Six

At seven p.m. on the night before election day, Hamilton found Hudson coming out of the restroom on the campaign bus as they headed to a late rally in the incredibly crucial state of Florida. Hudson still had a limp from the stadium attack, and although he had full use of his injured arm, there was constant pain. Hamilton noticed Hudson grimace as the bus jostled over a pot hole.

"You won't believe this," Hamilton said. "Fonda Raton wants an interview."

"Now?" Hudson laughed. At the same time, his stomach clenched. "You're joking."

"She probably wants to take one last shot at you."

Hudson nodded absently, thinking. "Set it up," he said.

"Funny."

"No." Hudson grabbed Hamilton's shoulder with his good arm. "Do it."

"Fitz would kill me."

"You don't work for Fitz. You work for me."

"Actually, I work for the campaign, and Fitz is the campaign *manager*, so technically I do work for Fitz."

"Well, after tomorrow the campaign is over. If I lose, you go back to Iowa. If I win, I'll have a job for you in the White House."

Hamilton smiled. "Consider it done."

Four hours later, Hudson, wearing a long, dark, wool coat, walked onto an outdoor observation deck at the Miami Airport. It was an unusually cold November night for southern Florida. The candidate had twenty minutes to spare. If all went well, he'd be sleeping in Ohio tonight with his wife, voting in his hometown in the morning, and then back to North Carolina to continue campaigning until the polls closed. There was still a chance that twenty-four hours from now, he could win the presidency, although the most recent polls had him slipping further—down ten points.

"You really do look battered," Fonda said as he walked out, limping. The area had been cleared and secured by Secret Service agents. Its elevated location and high walls on three sides made it relatively safe. Hudson liked it because between the jet noise and open air, it would not be an easy place to bug. "I'm so sorry you had to endure another attack."

"Are you?" Hudson asked, wondering if she meant the stadium, or her last anti-Pound post on the Raton Report.

"Of course I am."

He stared at her for a minute, searching for sincerity, and thought he might have seen a glimpse of genuine concern. "Why did you want to see me? Maybe a story about some assignment I didn't finish in elementary school, a past due library book, or the time I let my pet goldfish die?"

"Hudson, we don't really have time for this type of banter, do we?"

"What do you want?"

"Let me teach the history teacher some history," Fonda said. "Do you recall what happened in the 2016 election?"

"Of course."

"No, you don't. You only *think* you do." Fonda smiled, enjoying her set-up. "Your party, the Republicans, had finally fielded a decent slate of candidates. In fact, from a standpoint of those who actually had a chance to win, it was their best in decades. Hillary Clinton was terrified of all of them." Fonda looked back toward the building, as if expecting someone. "Hillary definitely hadn't been expecting Bernie to surge, but she never doubted she'd get the nomination. Only the Republican nominee could stop her final ascent to power."

"What about the missing emails, the FBI . . . ?"

Fonda waved a dismissive hand. "Please, are you kidding?"

After all he'd seen in this campaign, Hudson felt foolish for believing Hillary's nomination might not have been a foregone conclusion.

"The Republicans," Fonda continued, "had another Bush. Actually, the best Bush—a real governor of a big state, brains, fluent in Spanish, on and on. Then there was Rubio, a Hispanic Republican—young, energetic, good-looking. Kasich, the folksy, gentleman governor of Ohio—"

"He endorsed me," Hudson said.

"Nice for you." She patted his back mockingly. "But even before you, waaay back in 2016, the GOP had legitimate outsiders like Fiorina, a businesswoman, and Carson, an African-American surgeon, not to mention a solid pool of lesser-knowns. So how did they end up with Trump winning the Republican nomination?"

"Easy. The voters spoke. The electorate wanted a rebel. They were tired of the status quo," he said, still hoping that somehow history would repeat itself.

"Wrong."

"I watched it happen."

"You only think you did." Fonda shot another condescending smile. "You saw what they wanted you to see. Trump didn't win. They rigged it."

"Why would 'they' want Trump?"

"They didn't *want* him, they wanted him to *lose* to her. Trump was the *only* candidate in the Republican field who couldn't beat someone as polarizing as Hillary Clinton. She had the highest negatives of any nominee in history except for one other person . . . Trump."

"But if they can rig the primaries, they can rig the general, so why bother with the Republican primary? That seems like an awful lot of trouble. If what you're saying is true, with that kind of power, they could just hand the presidency to Hillary in the end anyway. And that didn't happen, so your point—"

"The voters wouldn't buy it. The people I'm talking about *can* make the outcome whatever they want, but they have to sell it to the masses. If Hillary won, and not nearly enough people had actually voted for her, the game would be up. We'd know—"

"What?"

"That none of it is real," she said, giving him a hard look. "During the 2016 election, even in those final weeks, you could go to any major news site online and not even see anything about Hillary. But there would be dozens of *anti-*

Trump stories. They *wanted* us to hate him more than her! And we did, because they found the most atrocious, egomaniacal, disaster of a human they could, to put against their atrocious, egomaniacal, disastrous candidate—and then they made him seem even worse. No one could stand the clown, even if they wanted to like him."

"I do recall hearing that Trump and Bill Clinton had a lengthy phone conversation about the election just weeks prior to Trump announcing."

"Coincidence?"

"So you're saying the voters are—"

"Irrelevant."

"If it's true, you should do something about it."

"Such as?"

"You're the most feared woman in political journalism, and I should know," Hudson said. "Why haven't you posted *this* story?"

"It's too big," Fonda said, suddenly sounding as if she were discussing a terminal illness. "Even if I had all the proof I needed . . . " She hesitated.

"What?"

"I wouldn't survive."

"You think they would just kill a journalist of your stature?"

Fonda laughed, but it trailed off into a weak, sad kind of chuckle. "They kill governors, they kill senators, political candidates . . . they even kill Presidents."

Chapter Sixty-Seven

Hudson stared at the journalist who had caused him so much trouble during the campaign, wondering what he should do. In a matter of hours, polls would begin opening around the nation, and the voters would decide if he or Dan Neuman should be the next president.

But would *they* really be the ones deciding? He didn't know anymore. Many of the things he'd believed before that day Arlin Vonner first entered his life, he now knew weren't true. They both knew they were talking about the REMies and the CapStone conspiracy, but what was the point? In a matter of hours, it would be decided by whatever means, and he couldn't do anything unless he won.

"Can I trust you, Fonda?"

"Oh, honey, don't you get it? You can't trust anyone."

He couldn't help but laugh, but it was a sad, ironic sound. She'd been as big an adversary through the campaign as any of the candidates he'd faced. It was a huge risk even talking to her this close to the voting. One post from her and tens of thousands of votes could sway—

maybe a lot more. But hadn't he already lost the campaign?

Unless she knows something.

"What did you come here for?"

"Not to ask you anything," she answered. "It's your turn to ask the questions."

"Are you setting me up?"

She laughed. "Someone set you up, but it's not me."

"If what you say is true, and the voters don't decide the outcome, who does?"

"You know it's the REMies."

He didn't want to talk about the REMies on the eve of the election. "Who specifically?"

They were standing less than two feet apart. She moved even closer to answer, and spoke softly. "There are many groups vying for control . . . Omnia, Mirage, the Aylantik, Techtrains, and others, but this time it's the REMies who are the biggest threat. They're the ones looking for the CapStone."

Hudson felt like he did when he found out Zackers had been killed and Schueller was still out there exposed. While relieved she still apparently didn't know the truth about Rochelle, this was much worse. Fonda Raton, probably the most feared, and certainly one of the last truly honest journalists in the country, was working a story about the CapStone conspiracy, and she knew a lot more than he did.

Who are these other groups?

Fonda had been watching him closely when she spoke. As an experienced interrogator, she saw the recognition in his eyes. She knew he knew. The tightening of his facial muscles, the quick grimace, it all told her what she suspected. He did know, but might not be part of it. That was a subtle, yet massive difference.

"Go on," he said, a little too urgently.

"These groups, and the different factions within them, have been slowly consolidating their power and control for generations. They think of it as building a pyramid."

She knows everything. Incredible! he thought. *She must know far more than I do. What if she thinks I'm in on it? That's why she's here. Dammit, this will be all over the internet in the morning!*

"Sometime in the past, they got to the CapStone, meaning each group had built upon the work of those who came before, and built it to a point where they could actually claim it all—total control. Whichever group or individual put the last piece in place—the CapStone—would win." As she spoke, she continued to read him, still certain he knew this much. "You can imagine that many people would want this power, so they began to fight for it. Not just against all of us in the unwitting masses, but *each other*!"

He nodded noncommittally.

"CapWars," she announced in a forceful whisper. "These are messy, brutal conflicts between titans wielding weapons we can't begin to understand—manipulations of economies, policy, and *thought*. Entire societies are used, controlled; epic struggles, and consequences be damned."

"Why are you telling me this?"

"You know why, Hudson."

"No, I'm not sure that I do."

"Because you're the final pawn."

He knew he should deny it. He wanted to laugh and pretend she was crazy. *It's a test. She wants to see if I know, and how deeply I'm involved.* He should have ended the meeting, he should have told her she was crazy, he should have done a lot of things. Instead, he just stared at her.

"It's hard to know how bad it will be this time, because of their Three-D system," she looked around until she spotted the closest camera. "Not the surveillance system, although that's definitely part of the escalation. But they have long used a different Three-D system: Deception, Distraction, and Division."

"How?" Hudson asked, trying to get information while only staying on the fringes of the conversation.

"Through the traditional media, and now social media, they manipulate and create events to distract us and, more importantly, divide us. Conservatives versus liberals, Democrats against Republicans, capitalism and communism, the US threatened by Russia, China, North Korea, Iraq, a constant rotating array of villains—Al Qaeda, Taliban, ISIS, whatever flavor of the week."

"Okay," Hudson said, unable to take it anymore. "You think I'm a pawn. I suppose you think Vonner is part of this —what did you call it?—'*CapStone*' conspiracy. And that he wants me in the White House to advance his agenda, to obtain the CapStone? Ridiculous."

She looked disappointed. "I understand you have to be this way. You want to trust me, but with the stakes, our history, the fact that voting is set to commence in mere hours, you can't. But it's more than that . . . isn't it?"

Test me? I can test, too.

"My point is, I'm somewhere between eight and eleven points down. I'm going to lose this election. So, what does that do to your theory? The all-powerful and dangerous REMies, these evil men building a pyramid, their pawn is lost, and they are defeated."

"I can tell you this much. If Neuman wins, then this is all just about another attempt at the CapStone." She stepped even closer to him now. "But if you win, then we're in a CapWar, and not just any CapWar, but the *finishing* CapWar."

"Finishing?"

"The pyramid will be complete, like it or not, whether the population knows it or not, and the winner of this CapWar will rule like an emperor with *total* control. That's what obtaining the CapStone is all about. Control."

"Control over the money?"

"Of course money, but control over even more important things . . . food, pharmaceuticals, and our minds."

Chapter Sixty-Eight

Hudson woke up in his own bed for the first time in months. The blue glow of the clock pierced the darkness. How many hours of sleep had he gotten? It couldn't have been more than four. His mind, already crowded with conspiracies, fear, and doubt, was further invaded by Fonda Raton's words and warnings. Everything she had said echoed like drumbeats, and his regret amplified at not pushing her to name the REMies. How far had she gotten? Why was she alive when they had killed Zackers?

He rolled over, his arm still aching from the gunshot—the doctor said it might always. Melissa lay next to him, still asleep. She had been a champion during the endless months of campaigning, complicated and worsened a hundred times by the danger, threats, and violence.

And all of it was for nothing, he thought. *She's not going to be first lady after all. Vonner, Bastendorff, Booker, REMies, they'll all go on without me. The world will keep spinning, but I'll just be selling hardware. Sure, there'll be a book deal, maybe even a decent advance, some speaking engagements, but the people will forget about me soon enough.*

Then he realized that the worst part wouldn't be missing out on all that power and the chance to push back against REMies; it would be letting down Rochelle yet again. She'd die in prison. Hudson would lose the election, but Rochelle would lose the most, her role as victim stuck infinitely on rewind and repeat. And, once more, it would be *his* fault.

"Is it time to vote yet?" Melissa said, without opening her eyes.

"Did I wake you?" Hudson asked, looking at the clock again—4:26 a.m. "Sorry, I've been restless."

"Any particular reason, or just the whole 'deciding if you get to be leader of the free world' thing?"

"I have a confession," Hudson said.

"If this is about a campaign trail affair, let me at least have coffee first," she said, her eyes still closed.

"Do you want to know the real reason I want to be president?"

"You mean it *isn't* because you've always wanted your picture on a postage stamp?"

"I grew up poor, you know that much, but you've probably noticed I never really talk about it."

"Of course I have, and every time I ask you why, you change the subject."

"There were three of us; inseparable best friends. Gouge, the Wizard, and me."

"The Wizard?"

"A nickname because he was so damned smart. He's the one trying to crack Zackers' encryption."

She nodded.

"We grew up together, hanging out at Gouge's dad's tire shop. As you know from the Raton Report, Gouge and I are actually cousins, but my dad didn't really get along with his brother, so I wasn't supposed to hang out with him. We did anyway, up in the parts loft of the tire shop. Our little secret club, complete with our 'Don't Tread on Me' flag."

"Cute."

"We'd drink, smoke cigarettes, get high, play cards, talk about girls, whatever."

"Why didn't your dad and Gouge's dad get along?"

"I don't know, happened before my time."

"Did they ever resolve their differences before your dad passed?"

"No," Hudson said, the single word dripping with regret, as if his father's feud had infected his life. "Anyway, one night, like a hundred others, we were up in the loft. I was seventeen, and we were stoned. Gouge's dad and a bunch of other guys were down below drinking and playing poker as usual. They had no idea we were in the building. We'd always listen to their jokes and stories."

"Sounds exciting," she said sarcastically.

"There wasn't much else to do. It was more fun than it sounds, especially when we were stoned."

"How'd you get in without them seeing you?"

"An outside window went to a lower roof and then down a stack of strategically placed pallets," Hudson said, seeing it all so clearly in his mind, wishing he could go back and change things. "So, that night, they get a call from a friend on the police force. Someone's car had broken down. It's a small town, and if the gas station is closed or whatever, then the call goes to the tire shop. They did basic engine service there, too. But by now they're all pretty lit, and it's raining, so they're pissed off about having to go out. Still, it's money, and business was slow. They've got to do it. Two of them take the wrecker, and when they come back, they got someone with them. A girl. A teenage girl. A black girl."

"Oh no." Melissa opened her eyes and sat up.

"Then it starts happening fast. I don't even know *how* it happened, but one of those guys started making a move on her, and she pushed back, but they were drunk. A bunch of fat, racist, drunk rednecks."

"They raped her?"

"Yeah." Hudson's hands were shaking. "I should have stopped them, but I was frozen. We all were. I think I started to move once when she first started screaming, but Gouge stopped me. We were scared. Then, suddenly, it seemed like it was too late. But, man . . . it was so horrible. She stopped fighting."

"She was afraid they'd kill her."

"Yeah! They passed her around. Once we'd seen it, I thought they'd—"

"Did they kill her?" Melissa grabbed his arm. "Please tell me you did not watch them kill that girl."

"No . . . well, you know, not physically. She was all quiet by then. Like . . . vacant."

"Repulsive."

"Then Gouge's dad started to change the tire on her car. He was pretty wasted, so it didn't go real smoothly, but he'd changed a million tires, so he finally got it. They were giving her the talk, you know. 'Don't tell no one or we'll hurt you,' kind of stuff. She just stood there stoic, church dress all torn."

"Church dress?"

"She'd been coming back from evening service."

Melissa shook her head. "Incredible. And she didn't tell?"

"Wait, this is when it turns into a nightmare."

"Oh, God. It gets *worse*?"

"Someone starts banging on the door. So they all kind of get scared for a minute, guilty as hell, and the girl's still there. But the guy banging isn't stopping. He starts yelling for them to open up." Hudson coughed and choked for a few seconds. "The guy calls the girl's name. They all look at her. One of them grabs her, wraps a hand around her mouth. He keeps pounding, yelling louder, so one of them goes to the door, and we start hearing all this shouting. Turns out it's her older brother. A big black man, a soldier, and he pushed past one of the rednecks, screaming for his sister."

"How did he know she was there?"

"I don't know. Maybe he called the police looking for her and they said they called the tire shop. Maybe someone saw. I don't know. Point is, he came in, and by then they had shoved her into a bathroom, but he sees her car. He looks around and sees these drunk rednecks zipping up their pants and whatever, and he starts yelling for his sister. They deny it, but her car's there, which blows their lies. Her brother picks up a tire iron and goes for one of them. That's when . . ."

"They killed *him*?"

"Yeah," Hudson said, tears in his eyes.

"My God."

"They killed him right in front of us."

Melissa gasped. "What about the girl?"

"They kept her tied up in the bathroom."

"For how long?" she asked, as if afraid herself.

"You have to understand this was southeastern Ohio in the mid-eighties. Appalachia. One of the guys there was a cop from the next town over. They all knew every man with influence in town. Twenty or thirty minutes later, they called the police. Said it was a break-in and self-defense."

"And that's how it went down?"

"Yeah. After the cops left and the body was removed, they brought out the girl. Gave her more of the talk about not telling anyone, only now it was 'they'd kill her and her whole family if she ever talked.' Then a couple of them drove her and her car down the road a ways and let her go."

"They really believed she wouldn't talk?"

"They *knew* she wouldn't."

"How?"

"Even if she did, no one would believe her story."

"Really?"

"That's just the way it was then." Hudson wiped his eyes. "These men were powerful in that small-town, rural kind of way. One of them owned a small parts factory where the girl's father worked. Another one had a brother who was mayor of Columbus. They *weren't* going to get caught."

"And they didn't?"

"No."

"But that's not the end of the story?" she asked hesitantly.

"Afraid not."

"Because the girl who got raped was Rochelle Rogers?" Melissa asked, already putting the pieces together.

"Yeah. The guy that kind of started it all, the one who brought her back to the shop, who first raped her, he was the one whose brother was the mayor of Columbus. And five years later . . . "

"The mayor of Columbus was elected governor of Ohio."

Hudson nodded.

"But why did Rochelle kill the governor? He wasn't even there that night."

"She wanted the guy to know what it was like to lose a brother. I've always assumed she was going to kill a family member of each man that had been there that night, but she wanted the governor first. Maybe because he was the authority, part of the system that allowed it all to happen."

"Probably just because the governor's brother was the ringleader. The first to violate her."

"Maybe."

Melissa just stared at him for a long time, letting it sink in.

"If I had won, I was going to pardon her."

"But, Hudson, she killed an innocent man. It's disgusting and tragic what happened to her, but the Governor wasn't there that night, probably never even knew about it. Two wrongs don't make a right."

"He *was* there, though. Maybe not in person, but he was a part of that culture, and it was that culture that gave rise to his power. I'm not saying he *deserved* to die. I'm not saying that at all, but he wasn't as innocent as it might seem."

"Wow," she said, climbing out of bed and standing with her hand on her hips. "Then am *I* guilty every time one of our country's drones accidentally kills a civilian?"

"Yes."

"Really? Then you are, too."

"Yes, and that's part of what my campaign is about. Taking responsibility for all the wrong things we've done and are doing."

"Then, I sure hope you win, Hudson, so you can test your theory and find out if it's possible to reconcile those views—guilt, and doing what is right. Sometimes right and wrong must coexist."

Hudson got out of bed too. "Anyway, it doesn't look like I'm going to win." He searched her face for disappointment. "Can you forgive me?"

"Hudson, don't you know? I love you no matter what." She hugged him. "You need to forgive yourself. You were a dumb, stoned kid."

"But—"

She put a finger on his lips. "And I believe in you. You're going to win today. And when you do, promise me you won't pardon Rochelle."

"Why not?"

"Don't you see? It won't change that night. As awful as that was, she made a choice, the *wrong* choice, and took justice into her own hands. She killed an innocent man. If you pardon her, people will want to know why. They *will* find out, and it *will* destroy your presidency. You won't be able to do any of the good; the *real* good that you want to do, that you *need* to do."

"She didn't deserve—"

"Of course not," Melissa interrupted. "But Hudson . . . I can forgive you for not turning those men in before Rochelle killed the governor, but I can't forgive you for throwing your life away by pardoning her."

Hudson wanted to argue with her. He needed to scream! How could she not understand the torment, the guilt, the grip that night had on every day of his life that came after? How could she say that Rochelle was wrong?

The rage of it all boiled just beneath the surface. A scream formed in his mouth, but the only words that came out were, "You really think I can still win?"

"You *are* going to win, Hudson. I predict that twenty-four hours from now, you'll be the President Elect of the United States of America."

Chapter Sixty-Nine

In spite of everything, Hudson couldn't stop campaigning. After he and Melissa cast their ballots in Ohio, she flew to Virginia for a full day of rallies and "get out the vote" efforts, while Hudson headed to North Carolina, then to Pennsylvania, and later up to Michigan. They would meet in Cleveland, along with Florence and Schueller, to await the returns once the east coast polls closed that evening. Vonner would be there as well. He'd taken the entire top floor of the Hilton Hotel.

Thousands were gathered in the adjoining Huntington Convention Center. Hudson and Melissa found a few minutes alone in their private suite.

"I've been thinking about Rochelle," Melissa said. "You chose Celia Brown as your running mate because of Rochelle, didn't you?"

"Not here," Hudson cautioned, but nodded silently.

"You're a complicated man, Hudson," she said with an impressed smile.

"Not really. It all gets down to guilt and shame, honor and duty, right and wrong. I'm actually quite simple."

In spite of his warnings to her, he brought up an altogether different sensitive topic. One that she could only assume he no longer cared if Vonner heard. "What I told you this morning, I've never told anyone before."

"Thanks for finally trusting me with that," Melissa said, touching his hand.

"Now there's something else I've been wanting to tell you."

"You're just full of confessions today, aren't you?"

"Unfortunately."

"Is this one the affair on the campaign trail?"

"No," he said, ignoring the joke again. "I was going to wait for Schueller and Florence to get here, but we probably only have a few minutes of privacy left."

"Fitz and everyone else are expecting us," she said. The senior staff of the campaign were in the "Election Center," on another floor, where they could monitor results from all the states and every major media outlet. They'd been expecting Hudson to join them thirty minutes earlier.

"They can wait," Hudson said. "Vonner's upstairs, and he can wait, too."

"Still don't think you're going to win?" she asked. "Polls have been wrong before, you know? Look at 2016."

"I'm not sure I care about winning or losing anymore."

Concern filled her face, but she remained silent as he walked to the window to gaze out over Lake Erie. The lights dancing on its dark waters seemed to capture his mood—somber, reflective, maybe a trace of hope.

"I have actual proof that this isn't the first election that Vonner has interfered with," he said, turning back to face her.

Melissa gave him a shocked look, one in which he detected a flash of anger. "What is it?"

He shook his head. "You know Vonner's a REMie, Melissa. He's one of the manipulators, and he's done everything possible to manipulate me into power."

"If that's true, then why do you think you'll lose?"

"Because Bastendorff is a better manipulator."

"If you do lose, that means Vonner also loses . . . then what happens?"

"Something. Something *has* to happen. Because whether I lose, or Newsman Dan loses, either way, the REMies win."

"You've got to confront Vonner, let him tell his side. Hudson, you know this man. He *put* you here. Have you even let that sink in, or have you been too busy chasing conspiracies? I know you think it's a long shot, but what if in a few hours you actually win, and suddenly you're the next president, and we're going to live in the White House? You, the leader of the free world?"

"Or Vonner's puppet."

"Talk to him," she said. "It seems to me that NorthBridge is a bigger threat to our country than a bunch of wealthy men."

They'd all been holding their breath for another NorthBridge attack. Everyone expected something to happen on Election Day, but the threat had actually helped bring a record turnout. Reports all day had suggested this would be the highest voter turnout in more than one hundred years.

"Don't you see? NorthBridge exists only because of what the REMies have done for decades."

"And don't *you* see? NorthBridge, the REMies . . . if you're the president, you have a chance." She moved close to him, put a hand on each shoulder, and looked into his eyes. "A chance to change everything you think needs changing, solve every problem, right every wrong."

He nodded. She was right.

"Just don't forget," she added. "Whatever you think of him, Vonner gave you this chance."

The early returns had the election too close to call, but by one a.m. Eastern time, the race was decided. As the Associated Press called Virginia and its thirteen electoral votes for Pound, Fitz grabbed Hudson and hugged him. "We did it! We did it! We elected a common man President of the United States!"

The final numbers:

Dan Neuman – 266 Electoral Votes

Hudson Pound – 271 Electoral Votes

Hudson looked over at Melissa, who had spent even more time in Virginia than he did. She smiled, but it was a bittersweet smile. He smiled back, a stunned, worried kind of smile. He mouthed the words *Now what?* to her across the jubilant room. The line from the 1972 Robert Redford film, *The Candidate*, made her laugh.

Melissa answered by pointing up. She wanted him to go see Vonner.

Hudson pointed to her and then to the bathroom. She nodded and headed toward that end of the room. It took Hudson almost three minutes to limp thirty feet, as everyone had to hug, shake, congratulate, and even kiss him. He made eye contact with Schueller and Florence, who were there with their partners, but it seemed impossible to reach them through the jubilant mob. Finally, Melissa and Hudson were locked in the bathroom.

He looked at the large, glass-enclosed shower with multiple showerheads and teak benches, and he wanted nothing more than to get in and try to rinse off the grime, the lies, the deaths, all the ugliness of the campaign, the false world he'd come to know. Instead, he grabbed Melissa and kissed her hard, desperate, his passion full of fear.

"Say something," he panted. "Tell me what the hell . . ."

"Congratulations, Mr. President . . . Are you ready?"

"*Yes!*" He laughed. Suddenly, it was real. It was his. *I can do anything!*

"Vonner is not some movie madman bent on taking over the world," Melissa began, still holding him. "There are many layers to power in the world. Vonner is obviously part of that, but the voters have spoken."

"Have they? We don't know that."

"You won. You'll be president. No matter what you think about the whole CapStone thing and the REMies, the president of the United States is certainly a huge, *huge* part of the world's power structure."

"But if the vote isn't real, I can't—"

"You must. No matter what!"

"I thought you'd be on my side." His resolve was crumbling. Hudson felt like he'd been hung on a pendulum—the noose tightening as he swung between right and wrong.

"Oh baby, I *am* on your side, but you're the president elect." She pushed her hand through his blond hair and smiled at their reflection in the mirror. "Can't you do more good in that job than on the local school board? You know so much more now. You know how the world *really* works. Fix it!"

"I don't know."

Someone was knocking on the door.

"Yes. You. Do. You fix things." Melissa stepped back and looked into his eyes. "Schueller once told you that the best chance the world had for change, for things to be right, was if you were president. I believe that. Your son believes in you. Florence believes in you. Who cares how? You know tens of millions of Americans want you to be president. You can do this!"

"If *they* let me."

The knocking, now continuous and louder, echoed.

He took one last look at Melissa and opened the door.

"What the hell were you doing in here? I was ready to pee off the damned balcony," the man said, barging his way inside. Then he realized who Hudson was. "Oh, my. Uh, sorry, Mr. Pound." He laughed nervously. "I mean, President Pound. Sorry."

Hudson pushed passed the man without a word. Melissa followed.

Florence and Schueller found their father as he made his way to the hotel suite's door.

"Congratulations, Dad!" Florence said, sounding elated, but he could see the conflict in her eyes. She looked at him, scared of what they knew.

Schueller leaned in and whispered in his ear.

"Okay," Hudson said, stopping to stare at his son for a moment, then reaching for the door.

Fitz had worked his way back across the crowded celebration. "Where are you going?" he asked. "We need to get you downstairs for your victory speech!"

"Upstairs first," Hudson said.

Fitz nodded. "Of course."

As Secret Service agents escorted him to the glass elevator, Hudson thought of the critical news Schueller had just given him.

Chapter Seventy

"He's coming up," Vonner said to Rex as he clicked the Communicator.

Rex nodded and checked the mini-syringe. It was ready. Death in minutes by "natural causes."

"I have no doubt I can convince him to do the right thing, but if I fail, he is never to make it down to those cameras."

"Understood."

"And his proof?"

"He has no proof. You know there's no proof. He just wants to get my attention."

"He still doesn't get it," Rex said.

"No," Vonner said, pouring himself a drink. "But the stupid bastard sure thinks he does."

"So how the hell did we beat Neuman?" Hudson shouted as

he charged into Vonner's palatial suite. "Bastendorff must be going crazy."

Vonner was only slightly caught off-guard at hearing his rival's name, but after a quick glance to Rex, who also seemed surprised, he recovered. "You should know by now that we can make polls say whatever we want."

"You can also apparently make the vote come out like you want."

"I always knew you were smart, Hudson. That's why I chose you."

"Chose me for what? To be your puppet? Well, I'm not interested."

"Okay, so what are you going to do?" Vonner asked coolly.

"I'm going to go downstairs and withdraw."

"And?"

"And what?" Hudson wasn't sure if he was bluffing, but could already feel things getting out of control.

"Then what are you planning to do?"

Hudson smiled. "Oh, don't worry about me, I'm not going to tell what I know. No one would believe it, and even if they did, I have a feeling I wouldn't live very long. There's probably one or two assassins down there waiting to take me out right now. Another moment in history, eh, Vonner?"

Vonner's face remained cheery, but otherwise revealed nothing. "Listen to me, Hudson. We've gone to a lot of trouble to make this possible." He pointed to the television, rolling state-by-state numbers of Hudson's electoral college victories. Scenes of the ballroom thirty-two stories below were filled with fanatical supporters waiting for the victory speech, waiting for the next President of the United States.

"Well I'm sorry I wasted your time, but I'm not interested in living this lie; in being part of your CapWar!"

Vonner raised an eyebrow at the way Hudson was throwing around dangerous words. They knew he had put a lot of it together, but Vonner considered Hudson challenging him to be quite bold. "My, you've been a busy boy, Hudson. But I have a hunch some of your facts got mixed up in the confusion of your run."

"I haven't mixed anything up."

"Yes, you have," Vonner said, standing up and walking toward Hudson. "And do you know how I'm so sure you have?" He didn't wait for a response. Instead, he stopped only inches from Hudson and stared hard into his eyes. "Because it's my business to mix things up and to make sure no one figures out what's *really* going on in the world. And you may be smart, and clever, and all the rest of it, but it's too big, and by that I mean unfathomable." He turned and retrieved a drink, took a swig, and set it down hard on a nearby table. "You haven't a clue as to the enormity . . . the CapWars have been going on for a hundred years before you were even born."

"Then educate me. I want the truth."

"You're not ready for the truth. Not nearly."

"Really? When do you think I'll be ready? I just got elected, or at least appointed, President of the United States. I think that qualifies me to be *ready*!"

Vonner nodded rapidly, rubbing his chin. "Okay, history teacher, let me give you some history. Reagan didn't find out the truth about how he got in the White House until six weeks *after* the election."

Hudson swallowed hard. *It is true. The system is rigged.* Hudson squinted at Vonner. The two locked in a visual game of chicken. *How long have Vonner and his kind been manipulating things? Decades? A century? More?*

"What did he say?"

"Who?" Vonner asked, breaking eye contact. "Oh, you mean Reagan? What do you think he said? He played the game, that's what he did. Now, Bush Senior and 'W,' of course, both knew how things were well before they even ran."

"They're REMies?" Hudson asked, his anger turning into a sick kind of regret.

Vonner nodded, seemingly enjoying himself. "Bill Clinton, on the other hand, he didn't learn the truth until several weeks after his inauguration. For a smart boy, he sure was confused. But ol' slick Willie didn't disappoint. He was a team player, that one."

"And Hillary?"

"Oh, poor Hillary. They'd made the deal even before the end of Bill's second term that she would eventually become the nation's first woman president. She thought it would be in '08, but—"

"The voters wanted Obama," Hudson finished.

Vonner laughed. "See? Even with what you know, you still forget. You still think the voters have something to do with it. No, the '08 Democratic primaries, like the 2000 general election, got caught up in the CapWars."

"Was Clinton yours or Bastendorff's?"

Vonner looked at Hudson carefully for a moment, as if deciding whether to answer; maybe wondering if the hardware store man would be brave enough or dumb enough to come in there wearing a wire. It didn't matter; the FBI Director was owned by the REMies. Finally, he answered, "Neither. The Clintons are run by another group."

"Geeze, how many of you are there?"

"Not that many."

Hudson stared at Vonner, his head swirling, but his resolve still strong. "So, Obama wasn't . . . ?"

"Obama was chosen like you were, except I understand they told him up front."

"He knew all along?" Hudson asked, startled. "Obama *knew*!?"

"Of course," Vonner said, as though it was a foolish question.

"Then what happened to Hillary? How come she didn't become the first woman president? How did Trump win?" he asked, thinking of what Fonda had told him.

"Trump was a mistake."

"How?" He couldn't imagine.

"We occasionally screw up."

"Who? REMies?" Hudson asked. "Judging by the state of the world, I'd say you screw up quite often. It's not just the presidency; it's wars, it's the economy, it's everything!"

"Yes." Vonner nodded soberly. "But, Hudson, we can end this. We can give it back to the people."

"Are you serious?" Hudson couldn't believe what he was hearing.

"Absolutely, but it must be done carefully."

"Wait, you're claiming to be . . . to be *good*? On the right side of this?" Hudson laughed. "Oh, please go on."

"It's true," Vonner said. "I'm not the enemy. I'm trying to stop all this, and I chose you to help me."

"Prove it."

"I'm not trying to beat Bastendorff because this is a game; because I want to rule the world like that lunatic."

"Then why?"

"I'll tell you," Vonner said, "but first you need to see something. Rex, could you please get me a zoomer?"

Rex, whom Hudson hadn't even noticed sitting back in a dark corner behind several computer screens, stood and walked to a nearby table stacked with gear. He grabbed a black aluminum briefcase and pulled out what looked to be a twenty-inch laptop, handing it to his boss. Vonner set it on a shelf between two of the floor-to-ceiling windows overlooking the city lights. Once he opened it, Hudson could see this was no ordinary laptop. The keyboard looked more like the controls one would see inside the control room of a TV station. Vonner quickly began manipulating the buttons, and soon images started flashing across the screen. Hudson couldn't believe what he was seeing.

Chapter Seventy-One

Hudson gazed into the monitor, trying to digest all the data. "That's my family tree?"

"Yes," Vonner said. "And see way up here? That's your three-times great grandfather, John Collins, a close acquaintance of both J.P. Morgan and John D. Rockefeller, helped orchestrate a victory in an early CapWar. Of course, they weren't called CapWars back then, but John Collins won it nonetheless. And make no mistake, the Panics of 1893-1896 were CapWars."

"I've never heard of John Collins."

"He was a very secretive man."

"No, I mean, even in my family, I've never heard anyone mention him as a relative."

"But he was. You can see the connection here," Vonner said, pointing to a dataset on the screen. "You can verify it yourself."

"I believe you. Collins is one of our family names, but I don't recall any relatives ever mentioning *his* name. Was John Collins wealthy?"

"Extraordinarily so."

"But as you know, I was raised poor."

"The money went down a different branch of your family tree. I can show you the breakdown, if you'd like."

"I'd be curious, but this obviously isn't the time," Hudson said, glancing up at the television monitors with wall-to-wall election coverage of his shocking victory. Neuman was just finishing a brief concession speech. "So, you're saying you chose me to be president because of some long-lost relative I didn't know existed?"

"I chose you because you met the criteria. Every point. Still, I must admit that the deciding factor was your connection to Collins. I thought it was a good sign that you're a descendent of a CapWar winner."

"You people are crazy."

"Who do you mean by 'you people'?"

"The one-percenters like you. Bloodlines, money, the elites . . . Or, do you prefer to be called a REMie?"

"I don't know exactly what you've discovered, or what you think you know," Vonner said, "but the world is not run by the *Illuminati*. There isn't some kind of long tradition where a secret society passes the keys of power down by way of a torch-lit, skull-adorned ceremony where cloaked men brand each other or drink blood from gold goblets. People like to imagine a grand conspiracy exists, but it doesn't."

"It's worse than that," Hudson said.

"Is it?" Vonner asked, his voice turning impatient. "That depends on your point of view."

"Then explain it to me."

"You mentioned the CapWar, so I assume you know something about it, but you have my part all wrong," Vonner said. "There isn't one conspiracy, there are many.

Everyone wants to rule the world, and there has been an invisible war going on for a hundred years to gain control—ultimate control."

"We're on the eighth stone of the CapWar."

"Very good," Vonner said, visibly impressed with Hudson's knowledge. "But don't be a fool, man. I'm not one of them. I'm the one who put you here."

"You put me here to use me."

"Hell yes, to use you in your position as president! But you and I, we're going to defeat the REMies once and for all!"

Hudson didn't know what to say. He desperately wanted to believe that Vonner was working for good.

"Hudson, I chose you out of hundreds."

"But the voters didn't."

"The voters never have." Vonner swept an arm toward the floor to ceiling windows and the city below. "You don't really think we would leave this to chance, do you? What, and let the masses decide what's right for them? Let *the people* choose the fate of the world? Ha! They don't know what the hell they're doing. These people can't even run their own lives."

"Maybe it would turn out better than you think. Better than it has."

"Imagine if we let someone get into the White House by chance. It's too important. It has to be orchestrated. The people electing the most powerful person on earth is a nice fairy tale. So is Santa Claus delivering presents to kids around the world. But neither one of them is remotely true."

"Didn't you say a few minutes ago that you want to give it back to the people? Yet, you're sounding a lot like a REMie."

"We'll give it back to them when they're ready. And we need *your* help to get them ready. First, we have to stop Bastendorff and the others from taking it all away. We're fighting on behalf of the people!"

Hudson glanced at Rex and walked to the window. He could see dozens of news trucks lined up in the parking area. The world was waiting for him to appear. They all believed it was real.

"Hudson, just because you don't like it, just because you didn't know, and just because I'm involved, doesn't mean it's wrong, or that I'm a horrible man," Vonner said, joining him at the window. "Bastendorff is trying to take over because of some delusional belief that he's divine royalty and needs to rule for the betterment of mankind. Seriously, that's where this guy's head is at. Bastendorff is the elite of the elite, the one-percent of the one-percenters."

"What about Booker Lipton?"

Vonner did a good job at not expressing his annoyance at Booker's name being brought up. "Booker Lipton thinks he's trying to save us from another 'evil' group of REMies—the Aylantik—who apparently claim to be trying to stop human extinction."

"And you're trying to save us from ourselves?" Hudson said, turning to face Vonner. "What is with you people? Is it that once you earn more than ten billion dollars, you suddenly believe you're a god? Incredible!"

"I wish you would trust me," Vonner said. "Give it a chance and you'll see I'm on the same side as you."

"What side am I on?"

"The right one. The one that gets to fairness, peace, prosperity, and justice."

Hudson heard the word justice and thought of Rochelle. His mind had been on her all night; first, when he was convinced he'd lose and thought he'd let her down again, and later, once he'd won and realized there was still a chance to help her.

"If I do this," Hudson began, "I have to know that no matter how I got here, *I'm* actually the president. The final decisions are *mine*."

"Of course," Vonner said, smiling, patting Hudson's shoulder.

"And I can do anything I want?" Hudson asked.

"Well, Congress might have some ideas of their own. And I'd prefer you don't start a nuclear war," Vonner said with a laugh.

"Nothing like that," Hudson replied, missing the joke.

Vonner looked at Hudson for a long moment, until Hudson, feeling the stare, met his eyes. "You cannot pardon Rochelle Rogers until the end of your second term."

Hudson coughed. Hearing Vonner utter Rochelle's name stunned him. *How did he know?* But he kept going. "That's too long. It has to be right away."

"Why do you want to do that? Were you dating her?" Vonner looked at Rex, still frustrated they had not found a connection.

Hudson ignored the question. "If I'm president, I'm going to pardon her in my first few weeks. My popularity can take the hit."

"Why don't we just transfer her to a minimum-security facility?"

"No."

"We could arrange an escape, give her a new identity."

"No."

"Come on, Hudson, be reasonable."

"She has to have complete freedom."

"*No one* has complete freedom."

Hudson nodded. "Maybe not." He couldn't argue that after all he'd learned. "But she has to at least have what the rest of us have. Why is that so hard?"

"She *assassinated* a popular governor, from your home state," Vonner said incredulously. "Are you out of your mind? We haven't caught NorthBridge yet. What do you think your precious masses are going to do when Hudson Pound's first act as president is to release a political assassin? There'll be hearings, people will call for your head—"

"You can fix all that."

"Do you think it's that easy to convince the public what to think?"

"Yes, I do." Hudson pointed to himself as proof.

"Let us take care of her," Vonner said, smiling placatively. "She'll be transferred, and along the way we'll just lose her. She'll wind up on a tropical island where she can drink margaritas and live out her days picking up shells on the beach."

"No. I'm going to pardon her so she can live in Ohio, or wherever she wants."

Vonner looked at Rex, and then back to Hudson. "Okay." Vonner took a deep breath. "I won't argue anymore as long as you'll take the office. Go down now and accept." He looked at Hudson warmly. "What about it? I'm asking you the same thing I asked that day at Titan Bank. How would you like to be the next President of the United States?"

"I need to do one more thing before I can answer."

"Damn it, Hudson, you'd think I was asking you to clean up a nuclear waste facility in your boxer shorts. We're talking about being *president*, a part of history, a chance to improve the world. We can stop the REMies once and for all, and you want to *think* about it?"

"Yes."

"Do you realize you won the election? That there are thousands of people downstairs waiting for you, a few hundred million more across the country wanting to see their new leader, and billions around the world who are going to hang on your every word?"

"I do."

"Ten minutes, Hudson," Vonner said. "You go talk to Melissa, or your kids, or the hardware gods, whoever the hell it is that will make you feel good about this, but do it in ten minutes."

Hudson thought of asking, "Or what?" but he didn't really want to know the answer right then.

Chapter Seventy-Two

Hudson, trailed by his Secret Service detail, went straight to Schueller's hotel room. His son was waiting.

"How'd it go with Vonner?"

"He claims he's on our team," Hudson said, pulling the Wizard's flash drive from his pocket.

"*Our* team?"

"Yeah." Hudson shoved the drive into his son's laptop and looked at his watch. "Says he's trying to stop Bastendorff."

"Of course he is, so he can be the emperor."

"No, Vonner told me it's so he can return control to the people."

"Do you believe him?"

"I've got about four minutes to decide."

The screen went matrix for twenty-some seconds, and then the Wizard's typing came across.

President Dawg! The stars have aligned!
Schueller just told me you cracked Zackers' encryption?
I wish you knew how impossible it was.

That's why we call you the Wizard, because you do the impossible. But I don't have time to bask in your glory at the moment.
Right, the victory speech.
Just tell me: Is Vonner good or bad?
It's not that simple.
Dammit, Wizard, make it that simple. I've got four minutes.
Vonner might be the best chance we have.
For what?
To beat the REMies. I mean, what do you do with all we've learned? It isn't like we just take something like this to the media, or even the Attorney General. REMies run everything, and they don't care how many people die.
There's a ton of data. Zackers traced a lot of it out. Amazing, he was. But we're short on time. I can give you the details later. Suffice it to say, we might be able to work with Vonner.
Yeah, but like you said, they kill people, they run everything, and I'm the one who has to risk it all to walk into that snake pit.
You're already in it, my friend.
How can I govern, knowing what I know, after all that has happened? That I won a rigged election?
It isn't just the election, everything is rigged . . . everything!

Hudson nodded slowly, and sat quietly staring out over the Cleveland's skyline reflecting off the cold, still waters of Lake Erie. Finally, he typed four words into his laptop, pulled out the flash drive before the Wizard could respond, and left the room. Schueller followed, but did not dare say a word. They were immediately greeted by Melissa, Florence, Fitz, Senator-Vice President-Elect Brown, Hamilton, and a mob of handlers.

A few minutes later, the Wizard's TV screen filled with a

triumphant Hudson Pound taking the stage, smiling like a bought-and-paid-for-politician, thanking his supporters and claiming victory. The speech was so convincing that if the Wizard didn't know better, he might have feared Hudson was going to be just like all the others, but the four words his old friend Dawg had sent moments ago remained above a blinking curser on his computer monitor, and left him with no doubt.

We are the change.

Next in the CapStone Conspiracy Series

vinci-books.com/capexperience

Hudson Pound's journey takes a dramatic turn.

Now in the Oval Office, he discovers the presidency is a gilded cage, and he's trapped inside with deadly predators.

Turn the page for a free preview…

CapWar EXPERIENCE: Chapter One

January 20th. The West Front of the US Capitol building was draped in American flags and packed with well-dressed dignitaries, including past presidents, members of Congress, governors, and wealthy business leaders—anybody with enough clout to get there was there. The typically rigid security for an inauguration had been ratcheted up to address the NorthBridge threat. NorthBridge, the domestic terror group which had promised a second American revolution, had already attacked establishment institutions and assassinated a number of political leaders.

The entire nation was on edge.

The country's law enforcement apparatus had saturated nearly a three-square-mile grid around the event with more than 30,000 personnel, including Secret Service, FBI, Capitol Police, and a dozen other federal, state, and local agencies. The US Military, expecting commando-like raids from the terror group, had added another 15,000 National Guard. The US Army was utilizing all protocols and alert levels for combat defense of the National Capital Region.

Arlin Vonner, the billionaire responsible for Hudson Pound's election to the highest office in the land, did not attend the inauguration. However, he was well represented by hundreds of his own Vonner Security agents aggressively scouring the town for NorthBridge assassins. Vonner had learned long ago that the bureaucrats were generally good at only two things—wasting time and money—and were certainly not good at preventing disasters. And that's exactly what it would be if Hudson Pound died before taking office.

Tarka Seebantz, one of Vonner's VS agents, led a team of four, but she'd rather work alone. The six-foot tall former CIA operative had been handling Vonner's problems for six years, but had only recently risen to the rank of team leader at the insistence of Vonner's chief lieutenant, Rex Lestat. He'd been impressed by her file and her skill sets; martial arts, weapons mastery, explosives, and, most important to Rex, computer tech and foreign languages. Rex, who normally didn't directly involve himself with operations such as these, had spent weeks tracking a specific and credible threat to the president-elect. As he continued to fight against the minutes that remained before the plot to kill Hudson was carried out, he fed real time data to Tarka.

The area was closed to vehicles, and Washington's normally rigid air traffic restrictions had been tightened to a military-enforced no-fly zone. More than one million attendees had entered through six public security checkpoints around the National Mall and Reflecting Pool. The weather had cooperated with a crisp, sunny day of fifty-two degrees —rare for Washington, DC, in January. Everything seemed perfect and perfectly safe. It was hard to imagine anyone getting near enough to harm the future president.

Hudson stood behind the bulletproof glass panels and smiled at his wife, Melissa. She had on a deep blue dress that matched his tie, and he wondered if that had been on purpose. He wondered a lot of things. First among those rapid thoughts was when would any of this actually start to feel real? That only led to a more frightening question—was *any* of it real?

The answer would have to wait, as the Chief Justice of the Supreme Court now stood in front of him, ready to administer the oath of office. Hudson took a deep breath and placed his left hand on the Bible held by Melissa. She smiled and met his gaze. They'd made it.

Nearly two miles away, well concealed in a rooftop ventilation system, a man known only as Kniike, also took a deep breath. He had been there for days—living, eating, sleeping; two containers in the corner held his waste. He couldn't wait to get back out into the fresh air, the light of day, the payday, once he killed Hudson Pound.

"Please raise your right hand and repeat after me," the Chief Justice said.

Kniike wrapped his right hand around his MacMillan TAC-50 long-range rifle.

Hudson didn't need the Chief Justice to utter the words. The oath was something Hudson had long ago memorized. It meant a great deal to him, but tradition dictated the order of things. Every moment of the day had been choreographed according to those long-ago established customs. Perhaps he could make some changes for his next swearing-in ceremony.

Tarka listened to Rex, Vonner's top lieutenant and "fixer," in her earpiece as she raced up the stairs. If his information was right, it might already be too late. If it was wrong, it was definitely too late.

"I do solemnly swear," Hudson repeated.

Kniike said a silent prayer as he sighted the president-elect in his crosshairs.

Tarka took the last twelve steps three at a time.

"That I will faithfully execute the office of president of the United States . . ."

The sniper had taken everything into consideration—wind speed, air temperature, humidity, even the rotation of the earth.

Tarka hit the door to the roof. Locked. Chained. Alarmed. Damn!

There would only be one chance at the shot. If Kniike missed, Hudson Pound would be inaugurated as president of the United States. Of course, that did not mean he'd live long enough to serve. There were contingency plans, but Kniike wouldn't get the big payment. He'd have to make do with the two-hundred and fifty thousand he'd already received. That wouldn't last as long as he needed, not long enough to disappear. But he'd make the shot, and collect the final million. Kniike had never missed a hit.

"And will to the best of my ability," Hudson repeated.

The key was the timing of the shot. They wanted Hudson dead before the oath was complete. The .50 caliber rifle cartridge would travel at approximately three thousand feet per second, meaning it would take almost three seconds to reach his target. At that distance, the level eight glass–clad polycarbonate panel could not be penetrated. Kniike knew this, but he also knew that the panel was supposed to have been replaced with an ordinary two-point-five-inch sheet of glass, which would shatter like cascading diamonds —a shower of glitter as the body fell. It had been arranged.

Tarka, out of time and options, fired three shots, blasting the chain, the lock, and the automatic alarm, then kicked the door open and darted onto the roof.

Kniike, finger on the trigger, heard the shots and blinked. Whoever it was, he would kill them in a few seconds, but first the president.

Kniike pulled the trigger.

"Preserve, protect, and defend . . . "

CapWar EXPERIENCE: Chapter Two

The explosion, visible from the Capitol, muffled by distance, came at the same moment that Hudson uttered the words, " ... the Constitution of the United States, so help me God."

"Congratulations, Mr. President," the Chief Justice said, shaking Hudson's hand as both men looked to the distant rooftop, where flames and smoke smoldered in what might have been a small building fire. Yet, in the age of North-Bridge, and on Inauguration Day, they knew more nefarious elements were at work. Neither noticed the sniper's bullet that had sailed forty feet above them and lodged into one of the massive columns which supported the capitol's dome.

Cheers and roaring applause had drowned out any sound the bullet's impact had made. The United States Marine Band, located on the tier below the president, played "Hail to the Chief." Hudson turned and kissed Melissa, then hugged his beaming daughter, Florence, and slightly dazed-looking son, Schueller. He knew his childhood friends, the Wizard and Gouge, were out there in the sea of onlookers celebrating, but he didn't know where.

A loud report of gunshots startled him, and everyone else—several people actually ducked for cover—but it was just the first round of the twenty-one-gun salute. Still, it reminded him that the tension and stress of the campaign had been magnified a thousand times by the oath he'd just taken. After several more minutes of excited good wishes from those gathered, Hudson stepped up to the podium.

"My fellow Americans, I stand before you today a humble, common man, one of you . . . and I came here to serve you. Our country is as divided as any time since the Civil War. More than one hundred fifty years ago, Abraham Lincoln stood here, having ascended to power on the eve of that bloody conflict, and implored, '*We are not enemies, but friends. We must not be enemies. Though passion may have strained it, it must not break our bonds of affection.*' Today, thankfully, we no longer argue over the cruelty of slavery, and yet we find ourselves nearly as intolerant of our neighbors' ideas and beliefs. Even before the scourge of terrorism burried its brutal fists into our daily peace, we were at each other's throats—right versus left, conservative versus liberals. We seem to have lost our way." He paused and made eye contact with some of the everyday-Americans watching. They were his people, he came from them.

"There was a place, throughout our history, where we always met, and got things done. That elusive common ground is still there, and we must return to it. Two hundred some years ago, Thomas Jefferson, at his first inauguration reminded us, and I paraphrase, '*Every difference of opinion is not a difference of principle. We have called by different names brethren of the same principle. We are all Republicans, we are all Democrats.*'"

The applause gave him a moment to reflect. There were four things he promised himself he would do as president: Free Rochelle; expose and stop the wealthy elites known as

REMies who controlled world events; defeat NorthBridge; and restore the federal government to what the Founders had envisioned. Only the latter two could he cite here, but between the lines, he silently pledged to do the others.

"We must change . . . " Hudson began, and then spent several minutes explaining how he believed that could be done before turning to the topic of NorthBridge. "This group of terrorists, who have been so destructive with their illegal and hideous tactics, enjoys far too much support from many of you out there. This speaks more to the failing of our system than the rightness of their so-called cause. Yet we cannot give in to the anger and frustration which overwhelm us. Instead, we must overcome it, and overcome it we shall.

"Franklin Roosevelt, taking this office in the midst of one of the darkest times in our history, said, '*This great Nation will endure as it has endured, will revive and will prosper. So, first of all, let me assert my firm belief that the only thing we have to fear is fear itself — nameless, unreasoning, unjustified terror which paralyzes needed efforts to convert retreat into advance.*' FDR showed us what could be done as we rose up from the depths of poverty to defeat the most evil regime the world has ever known: Nazi Germany, a country ruthlessly commanded by terrorists."

The president looked out over the sea of faces looking up at him and suddenly shivered, worried about a NorthBridge attack. He pushed his fear aside, paused only a second, and continued in a determined tone.

"The terrorists who infect our communities now have done more to defy our way of life, more to threaten our pursuit of life, liberty, and happiness, than all the challenges we have faced since the signing of the Declaration. And it cannot continue. It *will* not continue. We are better than this. We deserve more."

Applause.

"I pledge to you today that we will fix these things," the president continued. "We will find and defeat NorthBridge, and any others like them. We will do this together, standing on that common ground, basking in sunlight, working under the starlight, until it is right again. Because alone we might be lost, but together . . . we are the change."

Several blocks away, Vonner's fixer, Rex, watched the ceremony on television. Quite surprised that Hudson had lived through the event, he pushed the button on his communicator and waited for his boss to pick up.

"We got ourselves a president," Vonner said.

"Just barely," Rex responded, staring at an array of twenty-six dice in various colors arranged on the table in front of him. "Tarka made it there with less than a second to spare."

"Close call."

"No, I mean literally two tenths of a second later, and Hudson would have been history."

"She'll have a full-time job, shaving those fractions of seconds for the next few years," Vonner said, panting slightly on a stair climber. He was in Washington, but had chosen not to attend the inauguration. Although everyone knew he'd backed the rookie candidate, Vonner was sensitive to the appearance that Hudson would be a puppet. After all, the people had "elected" a man with no political baggage, beholden to no special interests, to change things.

President Pound was still reveling in the pomp and circumstance of the inaugural and readying himself for the parade in a popemobile-like car fitted with bulletproof glass, blast resistant armor plating, and sixty-six more of the latest security measures. He shook hands, waved, smiled, and acted as if everything was wonderful, but his mind was elsewhere. Hudson already felt like a zoo animal, trapped and on display. There was much to do, and he only had the vague outline of a plan.

DC was a pressure cooker capable of swallowing the biggest and most powerful. Many had come before him planning to make major change. He recalled Trump's call to "drain the swamp," but in the end, the brash billionaire found himself fighting through the muck and mire which had, in different ways, ensnared all who had come before.

President Pound's mission was different. The left and right were at war with each other, and the extremists on both sides had run out of patience, wanting nothing less than revolution. That climate had given rise to NorthBridge. Like Lincoln, Hudson faced the real prospect of a divided nation going to war with itself.

While trying to stop that from happening, Hudson's primary objective was to pry control away from the REMies. He believed that if he could do that, the reasons for NorthBridge would go away, and with it, the group's support. Without the REMies manipulating everything to their own selfish, greedy ends, the American people could win the final CapWar.

Riding down Pennsylvania Avenue with Melissa, both waving and smiling to the masses, Hudson wondered how he could possibly do what needed to be done with so few allies. If Vonner was truly on his side, it might be possible, but that "if" had kept him awake many nights since the election, and he was no closer to the truth. He didn't know how he was going to stop the REMies and stay alive. He wasn't even sure how to be president. The only thing he knew for sure was that he was in way over his head.

Grab your copy...
vinci-books.com/capexperience

About the Author

USA TODAY Bestselling Author Brandt Legg uses his unusual real life experiences to create page-turning novels. He's traveled with CIA agents, dined with senators and congressmen, mingled with astronauts, chatted with governors and presidential candidates, had a private conversation with a Secretary of Defense he still doesn't like to talk about, hung out with Oscar and Grammy winners, had drinks at the State Department, been pursued by tabloid reporters, and spent a birthday at the White House by invitation from the President of the United States.

At age eight, Legg's father died suddenly, plunging his family into poverty. Two years later, while suffering from crippling migraines, he started in business, and turned a hobby into a multi-million-dollar empire. National media dubbed him the "Teen Tycoon," and by the mid-eighties, Legg was one of the top young entrepreneurs in America, appearing as high as number twenty-four on the list (when Steve Jobs was #1, Bill Gates #4, and Michael Dell #6). Legg still jokes that he should have gone into computers.

By his twenties, after years of buying and selling businesses, leveraging, and risk-taking, the high-flying Legg became ensnarled in the financial whirlwind of the junk bond eighties. The stock market crashed and a firestorm of trouble came down. The Teen Tycoon racked up more than a million dollars in legal fees, was betrayed by those closest to him, lost his entire fortune, and ended up serving time for financial improprieties.

After a year, Legg emerged from federal prison, chastened and wiser, and began anew. More than twenty-five years later, he's now using all that hard-earned firsthand knowledge of conspiracies, corruption and high finance to weave his tales. Legg's books pulse with authenticity.

His series have excited nearly a million readers around the world. Although he refused an offer to make a television movie about his life as a teenage millionaire, his autobiography is in the works. There has also been interest from Hollywood to turn his thrillers into films. With any luck, one day you'll see your favorite characters on screen.

He lives in the Pacific Northwest, with his wife and son, writing full time in several genres, containing the common themes of adventure, conspiracy, and thrillers. Of all his pursuits, being an author and crafting plots for novels is his favorite.

Acknowledgments

This series took a little longer to write than my previous works. That's because 2017 was by far the most challenging year of my life. It was a real life and death period of time. In addition to the people who helped get this book and series out into the world, I have others to thank. Dr. Michael Yeh, Dr. Karen Sibert, Dr. Martha Cavazos, your skills, caring, and passion for what you do is extraordinary. There were also author friends—Michelle, William, Judith, Eric, and others—who stepped beyond our professional affiliations to make sure I knew they were there, that they were friends. A list of old friends who managed to say the right thing at the right time—Tony, Jennifer, Craig, Cathy, Lance, Eliz, Amy, Geoff, Maureen, Kate, Don, Carolyn, Mike, Germaine, Marc and so many more. There were also the prayers, healing energy, positive vibes, love, and good thoughts sent my way by thousands of people, many of whom are strangers. It all mattered. Thank you.

I dedicated this book to my brother, Blair Nelson Legg. He left this earthly plane on January 19, 2017. I was unable to attend his funeral, which was forty-eight hours after my first major surgery of the year. I'm sorry about that. I miss him. We talked a lot about this book, and he was looking forward to reading it—Blair was a big fan of my work. I mentioned in the Forward of this volume that I had two brothers who were Democrats, and two Republicans. Blair was one of the former, and was so liberal, in fact, that we joked that he died (after a long illness) on the eve of Donald Trump's Inauguration because he didn't want to live in a Trump world. Blair had a great sense of humor, clever and ironic. He's reading this series now somewhere by starlight, and I'm certain he already knows what I'm going to write next . . . and how it ends . . .

Getting this book done required the assistance of many.

My wife, Ro, lived this story and so much more. Her poetic mind and lyrical observations added dimensions to the characters that I might otherwise have missed. She also puts up with me writing everywhere we go—the beach, backpacking in the mountains, or driving down the interstate.

My mother, Barbara Blair, as always, claimed this as her favorite series. Her suggestions helped color key sections and, I must admit, getting to hear her reactions is great fun. I also owe her for my Washington DC/Northern Virginia upbringing.

My brother Baughan (the other liberal), who, in a sliver of time between San Francisco and Charlottesville, found enough hours to read and make some very useful political suggestions. Cathie Harrison, the chief beta reader of this series, discovered my first trilogy, The Inner Movement, in New Zealand, and wrote me her thoughts and appreciation. Since then, we've become friends. I'm glad for that. (Thanks Cathie, say hi to Buddha cat.) And the faithful final reader of all my books, Bonnie Brown Koeln, who continued fighting her own battles this year, and yet found time to root out the errors. I'm so happy you're in our family.

Speaking of family, thanks to Brae, Bryce, Baughan, Sally, Jim, Karen, Marty, Harriet, Mollie, Number Six, Julie, and all the other Leggs, Blairs, and Roemers, who helped. I'm also grateful to my copy editor, Jack Llartin, for the polish. And, finally, to Teakki, who patiently waited to play ninjas until I finished writing each day.

In the end, it's you, the readers, who make it possible for me to support my family by writing books. These stories are for you, and I owe you the biggest thanks of all. I appreciate you spending your time and money to go on these journeys with my characters and me. I look forward to going on many, many more with you.

www.ingramcontent.com/pod-product-compliance
Ingram Content Group UK Ltd.
Pitfield, Milton Keynes, MK11 3LW, UK
UKHW020332230226
468314UK00002B/24